Denise Robertson

REMEMBER THE MOMENT

PENGUIN BOOKS

PENGUIN BOOKS

Penguin Books Ltd, 27 Wrights Lane, London w8 5TZ, England
Viking Penguin, a division of Penguin Books USA Inc.
375 Hudson Street, New York, New York 10014, USA
Penguin Books Australia Ltd, Ringwood, Victoria, Australia
Penguin Books Canada Ltd, 2801 John Street, Markham, Ontario, Canada L3R 1B4
Penguin Books (NZ) Ltd, 182–190 Wairau Road, Auckland 10, New Zealand

Penguin Books Ltd, Registered Offices: Harmondsworth, Middlesex, England

Remember the Moment first published in Great Britain by Constable & Co. 1990
The Stars Burn On first published in Great Britain by Constable & Co. 1991
Remember the Moment, together with the Prologue and Chapter 1 of *The Stars Burn On*,
first published by Penguin Books 1991

1 3 5 7 9 10 8 6 4 2

The poem by C. H. Sisson on pages 290 and 317 is taken from
Collected Poems 1943–1983 (1984) by C. H. Sisson, and is reproduced by
permission of Carcanet Press Ltd.
The words of the song by Sting on page 343 are reproduced by
permission of Magnetic Publishing Company Limited.
Those by Gerry Goffin and Carole King, also on page 343,
are © 1960 Screen Gems–EMI Music Inc, USA, and are reproduced by
permission of Screen Gems–EMI Music Ltd, London WC2H 0BA

Printed in England by Clays Ltd, St Ives plc
Filmset in Monophoto Times

Contents

Remember the Moment

Tuesday 1 August 1989

It was strange to be seated at her desk without the sight of Keith's blond head on the other side of the glass partition. Emma shifted in her chair and tried to concentrate on the details of the Ryder contract flickering into place on her screen. Outside, the remnants of the Manchester morning rush-hour traffic churned towards the city centre. She would have closed the windows to cut down the noise, but the air was stifling even with them open. She had longed for the summer, but this unnatural heat was too much.

There was a rap on her door and Amy's pleasant, freckled face appeared. 'I've arranged cover for Keith on the Transio budget meeting. They can postpone till the 11th, and Ivor can do it then.'

'Good,' Emma said, switching off her terminal. 'And we're covered at weekends while I'm away?'

'Yes, Helen the first weekend, Malcolm the second and I'm doing the third myself.'

'Thank you.' Emma put her hands behind her head and stretched. 'It'll be nice to sit in the desert and think of you all flogging away here.'

'Sadist,' Amy said. 'You *are* lucky to be going to Egypt.' She advanced into the room and perched on the corner of Emma's desk. Her long legs were bare and tanned but a faint pattern of freckles showed through. 'The Sphinx by moonlight, the pyramids, the Nile . . .' She rolled her eyes in mock-ecstasy.

'The flies,' Emma said drily, 'and the tummy bugs. Not to mention sandstorms. You're better off here. Anyway, you'll be in Tenerife next month.'

'I thought that was fairly exotic until you came up with Egypt. And going alone . . . you're brave.'

'It's a package tour, Amy. I'm not going single-handed into virgin territory. Watch me get stuck with some withered Egyptologist.'

Again Amy's eyes rolled and Emma added, 'Female!'

'Teetotal?' Amy offered.

'And a born-again Christian into the bargain,' Emma said firmly.

'Perhaps I'm better off with Tenerife. All the same, the Nile by moonlight . . . and all the men looking like Omar Sharif!'

'He's not my type,' Emma said. 'Too pretty. Now go and get some work done. We're setting a bad example to the troops.'

Amy stood up. 'Heaven forfend we do that. Let me know if you're stuck with anything when it gets to the end of the week. You should try and get away Friday lunch-time.'

'Thanks,' Emma said. 'I'll see how it goes. Keith's being away makes a difference, but I ought to manage.' She should not be taking leave while Keith was absent, and they both knew it.

When Amy had returned to her desk Emma picked up her handbag and made for the loo. She turned on the cold tap and held both wrists under the flow in an attempt to cool herself. In the mirror her reflection looked guilty and abashed. It was horrible having to lie to Amy, shaming the way the untruths about the Sphinx and the Nile and the pyramids had rolled from her tongue.

She patted her flushed cheeks with cold water and ran a comb through her dark hair, trying to lift it from the back of her neck. Damn the heat. If it went on much longer she would have her hair cropped!

Back at her desk, she switched on the modem once more. In four days' time she would be up in the stratosphere, flying to the holiday of her dreams, but now she must concentrate on making sure she left everything at SyStems in apple-pie order.

She had opened the Manchester branch of the flourishing American parent company nine months earlier, designing the office lay-out herself and hiring her own staff. Keith was the first, to be her second-in-command. She had thought him a little young but his qualifications were excellent and he had told her he was a family man. She had approved of that.

Now there was a staff of twelve, if you included Keith. Two salesmen, two consultants to give the salesmen technical support, wonderful Amy in charge of admin., with two back-up staff and four programmers . . . though, as no one liked to be termed a programmer any more, they were now called analyst/programmers.

Emma tried again to concentrate on the screen and the client file on her desk. She liked Ben Ryder and wanted to do a better than excellent job of improving and streamlining his business. She had won the Ryder contract in competition with his accountants, an international firm who had branched out into Information Technology. Now she had to prove she could deliver the goods. The figures began to absorb her, and she forgot about anything else but the job in hand.

'I'm going home,' she told the upturned faces as she

walked through the main office two hours later. 'If anyone needs me they can reach me there.'

Amy was looking at her watch. 'Keith will have landed by now.'

Emma nodded, schooling her face to show just the right amount of interest. 'Yes, poor thing, he'll be jet-lagged.'

There were hoots of mock-sympathy from every direction. 'I'd swop him,' Amy said.

The office had one wall of glass and today it was like an oven. Emma shrugged into her grey cotton jacket as she pushed through the doors towards the lift. This week was going to be tricky. She'd have to be careful. Amy was not a fool; none of them was; she had appointed them for their brains. Foolish to disregard that now.

In the underground car-park her red Capri gleamed among sober blues and metallic greys. She smiled, remembering how Keith always teased her about the car, calling it her phallic symbol.

Once in the slanted leather seat she fastened her seat-belt. As soon as she got home she would shower and eat, and then sort out the clothes she was taking to America with her. And then she would open a bottle of good wine and grow maudlin until the phone call came and she could go to bed and wish away the days till Saturday.

Around her, Oxford Road seethed and slowed to a stop. She put the engine out of gear and relaxed her foot on the brake. Four days, 96 hours, 5760 minutes . . . she had always been good at maths. She was computing the seconds when the traffic started to move, and then she was out on to Anson Road and speeding towards her home.

6

The house looked good in the evening sunlight, the brick warm and weathered, the windows gleaming like tolerant, amused eyes. Except for Poppy's windows on the top floor with their silly ruched blinds. 'Straight from a French brothel, darling,' Poppy had said when she hung them. 'At my age, *ambience* is everything.'

Emma's lips curled at the thought of Poppy. Lively, outrageous, loving Poppy; twenty-five years her senior but more like a sister. If she was free tonight they could share the wine and talk. When Keith rang, Poppy would melt away. She always understood about love, even if she sometimes disapproved.

She ran the Capri into the drive and collected her briefcase from the back seat. The garden was bursting with colour, asters and cornflowers and nicotiana and one blood-red rose on a bush. For some reason it reminded her of the morning newspaper headlines: *Colonel Higgins killed in Beirut*. Somewhere in America a woman was grieving.

As she let herself into the cool of the hall she tried to banish such uncomfortable thoughts. She had grown up in this Manchester suburb, in this solid house with its high-ceilinged rooms and odd niches backed with the gleam of wood or 1920s stained glass. Closing the hall door behind her she saw that the door to Poppy's flat was a little ajar. Good! She was home. Emma pushed it further open and called up the stairs: 'Hallo ... I'm back.'

As she'd hoped, there followed an invitation to come up. 'Salad sandwiches and Piesporter,' Poppy said, wiping her already full mouth. 'Pull up a chair. I know it's far too early for alcohol but I was feeling deprived.' She looked shrewdly at Emma. 'So do you. He's gone, then?'

7

Emma nodded. 'Does it show?'

'Only to me, darling.' Poppy's sallow skin was lined, and her mouth had begun to droop, but the blue eyes were still lively. 'Anyone else will think you're fine, but I've been left behind too many times myself not to recognize the symptoms. Here, let me fill your glass.'

'He hasn't exactly left me behind. I'll be there myself in a week . . . less.' Emma hoped there wasn't a defensive note in her voice. They had argued the rights and wrongs of her affair with Keith before, and Poppy's disapproval was on record.

'Don't wind up like me, my love: that's all I have to say.' Poppy had said that several times, but tonight she chose to change the subject. 'The shop did well today. Nearly a thou. Not bad for a hot Tuesday.'

'Very good. When can I retire?'

The boutique had been Emma's mother's pride, specializing in the elegant and expensive, and Poppy had been her mother's assistant for as long as Emma could remember. Her mother had converted the upper half of the house into a flat so that Poppy could live there and stand in as her substitute at home as well as at work, when she herself was away on buying trips. So it had seemed to Emma sensible and fair to take Poppy into partnership when her mother died. Now Poppy ran the shop, and Emma handled the business side and reaped half of the profits.

'You can retire whenever you like, my love.' Poppy was looking smug. 'Of course, I can't promise you the exalted standard of living you enjoy at present, but you wouldn't starve.' The older woman was running scarlet-tipped fingers through her hair.

'That was gorgeous. Are you going out tonight?'

Emma asked, wiping her mouth and pushing away the plate.

'Yes. It's only Charlie. Still . . .'

'You'd like me to do your hair,' Emma finished for her. They sat by the littered table as she blow-waved the dark hair, thinning a little on top and tinged with grey but curling and vigorous just the same. Her mother would have tut-tutted and banished them to bedroom or bathroom, but Poppy liked to live in organized squalor.

'It's lasting with Charlie,' Emma said.

Poppy smiled. 'Four years. That's not bad going.'

'Why've you two never married? Mother was expecting it. She used to talk about being left alone when you married Charlie and I left home. She was going to sell this place then and move to Cornwall.'

'She'd never've done it. She'd never've given up the shop. It was her life.'

Emma concentrated on the head in front of her. No need to probe old wounds tonight; she had trouble enough. But Poppy was right, the shop *had* meant everything to her mother. It had been Poppy who had dried her tears in childhood and agonized with her throughout adolescence.

Emma had never known any other way of life, so she had not found it unusual that her mother spent long hours at the shop, travelled continually to buy exclusive stock and even at home pored over stock lists and forward projections. She had loved her daughter but ... 'I was never as interesting as a balance sheet,' Emma conceded and felt her eyes fill at the pity of it all. Where would she have been without Poppy? She switched off the dryer and flicked the hair into place.

'There now,' she said, 'you're beautiful. Go and thrill Charlie clean out of his socks.'

Downstairs in her own flat she opened windows into the warm, still August air. No movement fluttered the curtains, but the glass was cool to her fingers and she laid her forehead against it for a moment. Keith was thousands of miles away, too far for her to reach him if he had an accident. For a moment she was anguished, and then a new thought struck her: at least he would sleep alone tonight. The knowledge heartened her and she went to her room to change.

She still occupied the small flower-sprigged bedroom of girlhood. One day soon she must sort out her mother's room, have it decorated and make it her own, but as yet she hadn't found the heart to touch it.

She let her skirt slip to the floor and wriggled out of her tights. Her feet felt hot and cramped and she moved her toes gratefully. After Keith's call she would lie in the bath and soak for hours. It wouldn't be a waste of time if she used it to plan the week. She needed to get hair and nails done, choose her clothes, plug the gaps in her wardrobe that were bound to appear, and make sure everything at SyStems would run smoothly in her absence.

Ideally, she should not go away if Keith were not there to deputize, but the chance of a week together had been too great a temptation. Besides, half the companies in Britain were idling through this strangely hot summer, so business was not brisk – and Amy was an excellent administrator with five years' experience at Price Waterhouse. Emma folded herself into a towelling robe and padded barefoot in search of a cool drink.

Channel 4 News was preoccupied with Colonel Higgins. She switched channels but there was nothing to tempt her. It was half-seven: two-thirty New York time. Keith would be finishing his business lunch. If he was going to call, he would call soon. And he would call. She smiled, remembering how eager he always was, and stretched her arms above her head in exultation.

What had he said this morning? 'You'll have to lie like a trooper, Emma, if we're to get away with it.'

Manchester airport had been bleak and grey at six-fifteen. 'Got your specs ... book ... ear-plugs?' She had fussed over him, glorying in having him to herself for a little while, with no prying office eyes to see and disapprove.

'Love me?'

'You know I do.'

He said it, she said it, they repeated it, foolishly as though they were seventeen and need not feel guilty about a wife and children at home in bed.

'You'll be shattered tonight. Don't bother to ring.'

He had laughed aloud at the insincerity in her voice. 'You know I'll ring ... and you know you want me to.'

'I do, I do. Oh, God, I'm going to miss you, Keith.'

'Not for long.'

He had held her close then and Emma had felt peace seep through her, calming everything. In four days – an interval just long enough to allay suspicion – she would board the same flight and join him in New York ... She had arranged for him to spend two weeks at the parent office especially so that they could have one week together. The thought of being with him soon for seven days and seven nights had sustained her through the departure lounge. He was taller and smarter than any other passenger and she had lifted her hands to her mouth in delight that he belonged to her.

The phone shrilled suddenly, breaking her day-dream.

She expected to hear Keith, but the voice on the other end was the voice of a stranger and disappointment rendered her momentarily deaf. 'I'm sorry. Could you say that again?'

'Is that 17 Waverley Gardens?' The voice was male and, judging by the tremor in it, he was young.

'Yes. Who do you want to speak to?'

'Are you Emma Gaunt?' There was a note of defiance in the voice now and Emma's lips twitched.

'I am. And who are you?'

As if he sensed her amusement and was annoyed by it, his voice deepened and steadied. 'I'm Stephen Culrose.'

There was a pause, as though he was waiting for some reaction to his name.

'I'm sorry. But I'm afraid I don't see . . .'

'I want to know what you meant to my father?'

'*What I meant?* I don't even know your father, as far as I'm aware. Where are you speaking from?'

'Durham. And I'm afraid I know that you knew him. I want to know how well?'

If it was a prank or a con it was well done, but while he was blocking the line she couldn't hear from Keith. Emma was suddenly frantic to restore the phone to its rest.

'Look, I don't know whether you've made a mistake or you're up to some silly stunt. But I know no one called Culrose . . .'

'My father's name was David. David Culrose.'

'I've never heard the name Culrose before, as far as I remember. Not David, not Dennis, not anything! I'm expecting an important call, so I'll say good-night.'

Emma could hear his voice raised in argument as she lowered the receiver, and she half-expected it to ring again straight away. But it was silent, and she went back to her seat and the half-drunk Diet Coke.

Of all the crazy things! *'What you meant to my father.'* He must have the wrong number – and yet her name and address had been correct. She had an uneasy vision of a gang telephoning susceptible women. Perhaps she should ring the police? But to say what?

In the end she took her glass back to the kitchen and switched on the radio. John Ogdon, the pianist, was dead. She remembered the tormented genius as she had last seen him on television, looking bemused. Perhaps he was better off out of it. Still, it was a loss. She switched the radio off and went to the bedroom to look through her clothes.

She intended to travel light, taking uncrushable, inter- changeable items which she knew well and was comfort- able in. Now, as she took them down from the wardrobe and threw them on the bed, she saw that they would never do. The grey silk suit, perhaps, and the khaki dress ... but surely it would be even hotter in the States? She would have to raid the shop, and get Poppy to help.

From the dressing-table her mother's photograph re- garded her serenely. Dark eyes, grey streaked hair, bold face above a touch of white at the neck. What would she make of Emma's present situation? She who had found it so easy to stay aloof from men after the break- up of her marriage.

Emma needed to go to the loo, but the thought of isolating herself behind the bathroom door was unbear- able. Any moment now the phone would ring, on bed- side table or in the hall. She must be there, to stop it at the first shrill.

When at last the call came she seized the phone and

clamped it to her ear. She climbed on to the bed, sinking into the welter of silks and cottons, and then he was speaking, as clearly as though he were in the next room. 'Darling?'

'Yes. You're there, then.' What a bloody silly thing to say. He was talking about the flight and the hotel, and they were the last things she wanted to hear.

'I missed you today.'

'I'm glad. Love me?'

'You know I do. I can't wait for Saturday.'

'Me too. Do you think they suspect anything?'

'No. I wittered on about Egypt and my hols very effectively.'

'You're a devious woman! Perhaps that's why I love you.'

'How was Bernie?' Bernie was their American boss, at once the most beneficent and the most ruthless person she had met.

'*Very* friendly. Pleased with our figures, talking expansion. Full of praise for you, and talking of wooing you over here. "She went to Cambridge," he said and rolled his eyes. "So did I," I said, as nonchalantly as I could, and I swear . . . I swear he said, "Shucks".'

'You're making that up!'

'Yes – but he obviously *was* impressed with the way we were handling things. He says he appreciates that with all the big accountants opening IT departments we have an uphill struggle, but he's content with the number of middle-sized clients we have. One biggie would be nice, but he's patient.'

'Good.'

'Everything all right at your end? You will be able to get away, won't you?'

'Yes, I'm gearing up to leave Friday lunch-time. And

Amy will keep her finger on everything. I've told her to ring you if there's a crisis. I *didn't* tell her I'd be right there at your side – she thinks I'll be sitting on a camel contemplating the Sphinx. What are you doing now?'

'I'm in bed. I came straight here and flopped. It's a very wide bed, king-sized probably. I feel lonely in it.'

Oh God, if only she was there now. 'I love you, Keith. Will you be at Kennedy airport on Saturday?' Another bloody silly question: of course he would be there.

But a new and uneasy thought was growing inside her. Had he rung Lesley, his wife, yet? Had she come first, or was he saving the best for last? Would he whisper the very last goodnight of all to his wife, tucked up in the marital bed?

Emma felt tears prick her eyes. Everything was spoiled now that she had committed the one error a mistress should never make: she had thought about the wife. She tried to think of an acceptable way of asking if he had made the call, but there was no acceptable way. If she mentioned it at all it would spoil everything, destroy that fragile thread that bound them together across the miles.

'Sleep well, Keith. We'll be together soon.'

'You too, darling. I wish you were here . . . or I was there.'

They had spent a tiny handful of nights together – in her bedroom, in a London hotel, and once in a motel on the way back from Birmingham, when desire had overtaken them and he had phoned home with an excuse about the car. She felt desire catch her now, the urgent bearing down and then the contraction of muscles made for loving.

'Good-night. Sleep well. I love you . . .'

15

It took an age to lift the crushed clothes from the bed and hang them back in the wardrobe. Now that the call had been and gone, elation left her. What did it matter what clothes she took to America? It was the going that counted, not the trappings.

She moved into the bathroom once she had hung up the last garment and turned on the taps. A five-minute soak, a scrub, and then out and into bed, naked as God had made her. It was always the recipe for sleep. While she waited for the bath to fill she peered at herself through the steam that clouded the mirror. She was thirty-two years old. It was no great age, but five years older than Keith and nine years older than Lesley, his wife. Little blonde, brittle Lesley of the tinkling laugh, whom Emma had only seen at office parties.

'We'd gone around together for so long, Emma,' Keith had once said. 'I hadn't the heart to tell her I'd gone off the boil by the time it came to marriage. Both families were lined up to cheer . . . and I was the first with her. There's something about taking a girl's virginity . . .'

Emma had winced at his frankness but he was always honest: it was one of the things she loved about him. As she stepped into the warm water she realized the irony of her thoughts. He was honest with her, as honest as it was possible to be – but he was lying to Lesley, living a lie. The thought filled her with revulsion and then, strangely, with a longing for him so fierce that her wet fingers bit into the flesh of her abdomen. She seized the loofah and began to scrub until her skin stung from the assault and she could pull out the plug and leap for the bathmat.

Her face, when she cleared a porthole in the mirror, was flushed and anxious, her brown hair wet and strag-

gling. How much better she would look in New York.
She could lose five pounds in a week if she was firm
with herself. Deliberately she drove herself on. New
York would be an orgy, a welter of loving, an ecstatic,
endless fuck. She felt tears prick her eyes but would not
admit they might be tears of shame. Everyone had a
right to love, to sexual love. If you couldn't marry the
man of your choice you still had rights.

'I will not think of her.' She said it over and over
again like a mantra as she dried herself and used deodorant and powder.

She was slipping into bed when she heard a car draw
up outside, and then Poppy and her Charlie giggling
like conspirators as they mounted the stairs. They would
fall into one another's arms and love, and then sleep
contentedly in Poppy's ruffle-strewn bed. No matter
that they were old and should be past it: they were
lovers. Poppy would never grow truly old.

Emma banished Poppy to the limbo inhabited by
Lesley and tried to concentrate on New York. They
would be together for seven days, 168 hours, 1080
minutes . . . no, that was wrong . . . She struggled with
the figures but in the end they were overpowered by the
memory of a young voice on the end of a phone. *'I
know that you knew him. I want to know how well?'* She
had forgotten about the boy, but now he returned to
plague her. She had rudely almost cut him off. Still – if
he was a hoaxer . . .?

She turned on her side and summoned up a picture of
Keith smiling as she came through the Arrivals lounge,
taking her case and her arm. Then of Keith lying asleep
in a New York dawn while she kept watch. His face was
pale in the mornings, except where stubble darkened his
jawline. She smiled in the darkness. She had never

watched him shave or clean his teeth; there had never been the time. But a week would encompass everything – and then she would have a week alone at home to revel in the memory of it. She held on to that pleasant thought and it carried her into sleep.

2

Wednesday 2 August

The radio sprang to life at seven-thirty, still talking about death. Higgins the dead hostage and Ogdon the dead pianist; Ogdon and Higgins, with details of the London tube strike in between. Emma showered and stood naked on the scales at 9 stone 7. Not bad for 5′ 6″, but she would look better at 9 stone 2. She made brown toast and orange juice, and carried them through to the window-seat in the living-room.

Outside, the street was empty except for the paperboy making his way from door to door. As she munched her toast she heard the front door slam, and saw Charlie making his way to his battered Volvo, parked under a tree. He looked positively cheerful, and she smiled at the thought of Poppy above her, sated and happy. Perhaps they would marry in the end, and live happily ever after?

Poppy's real name was Mavis Hilda Beresford but she had discarded that in the War. 'It was a Yank, a GI, who said it first. "Come on, Poppy," he said and I knew it was the name I should've had from the start.' So Poppy she had become and flowered in the 1950s.

Now though, the bloom had faded. The blue eyes still sparkled but the skin around them was wrinkled. Her figure bulged comfortably everywhere, little foothills of flesh building up to a magnificent bosom; but the legs were still thin, brown and bare, on top of towering heels.

Perhaps she would turn out like Poppy, Emma thought, entertaining a Charlie in vented jacket and check cap? And, when she was no longer up to entertaining, sitting in an upstairs window to watch the world go by, as she was doing now? It was a chilling thought, and suddenly Emma was longing for the Capri and the traffic and the demands of a busy office.

Poppy was collecting milk and papers as she came into the hall. *'A good day for Capricorns,'* she read aloud. *'A day for all your plans to come to fruition. Want me to look up yours?'*

But Emma was half-way down the path. 'You make your own luck in this life. I've told you that before.'

Poppy grinned and blew her a kiss. 'I hate people who are sensible before nine in the morning.'

'Get my shop open, Miss Beresford,' Emma called back. 'I want results.'

Poppy responded with one finger waved aloft in a rude gesture, and Emma swung smiling behind the wheel of the Capri.

Down Wilmslow Road, right into Dickenson Road, left into Anson Road, then Upper Brook Street, past the university and into Oxford Road. Held up at the traffic lights before the BBC building, she watched the staff comings and goings. Some of the reporters must have been up all night writing bulletins about death in the Lebanon and tragic genius snuffed out at home. Perhaps hers was not such a bad job after all.

Amy was filling a vase with flowers when she entered Reception. 'Morning. Two messages on your desk. I've opened the post. Vital on the blotter, urgent in the tray, rest in the bin. And Harry Wattis wants you to lunch.'

'Does he want me to ring him?'

'No. He says the Excelsior at 1 o'clock. Ring if you can't make it.'

Harry Wattis had been Emma's first client and she had a special affection for him. Of course she would lunch with him.

She was almost into her own office when it came. 'Any word from Keith?'

'No.' Emma couldn't say he'd rung her at home – well, she could, but it wouldn't be wise. 'I expect he'll ring this afternoon.'

Emma was glad when she could close the door on Amy. It was awful having to weigh each word when really she would have liked to clasp Amy round the waist and say, 'He rang, he rang, he rang!'

Now she tried to marshal her work and put Keith out of her mind. Tonight she would tell him to ring the office, too. The others would expect a call. She sat down to work but it was difficult to stop her thoughts straying, and lingering over the events of the last few months.

She had worked for SyStems for nine years, ever since leaving Cambridge. First she had been a programmer, then an analyst, later a consultant in the London office. And then, last year, her mother had suddenly suffered a stroke. After visiting her in the Manchester Infirmary, Emma had returned to London to give in her notice.

'I've got to go to her. I'll hate leaving you, but I'm an only child.' Twenty-four hours later she was told she could open a Manchester branch if she chose to do so. Her mother had died before the Oxford Road premises were ready, but by then it was too late. She had already hired Keith and her stable, successful world had begun to tremble.

They had gone out for a drink that first day: she had told Keith the job was his and he had said they must celebrate. Champagne in the Excelsior bar, he triumphant and she feeling powerful and indulgent and not in the least attracted to him. And now? Now it was often difficult to remember whom she was lying to and what their particular lie should be. She had told the office staff she was going to Egypt because she had been there before and could lie convincingly about it when she got back from the States.

Only Poppy knew the truth, and Poppy thought she was a fool. Worse still, she disapproved. 'I don't like children coming into it, Em. Not kids. Men and women can take their chances but kids are different.'

Thinking of Poppy's strictures discomforted Emma. She reached for the vital letters and skimmed them through, making notes in the margin for Amy, putting moral dilemmas out of her mind.

The outer office was filling up, seven women, four men, all dependent on her for their livelihood, not lucky like her with money in the bank and a second string to her bow. She concentrated on her work, getting out the Wattis file so that she would be ready for Harry at lunch-time, ready to suggest innovations and economies, and behave like the intelligent, professional woman she was. She rang his office and asked them to fax her up-to-date details, and told Amy to bring it in as soon as it arrived.

She was still engrossed when Amy tapped and entered, the fax in her hand. 'We've got trouble,' she said in annoyance, coming to stand by Emma's desk.

Emma swung round in her chair. 'What?'

'The Semtec file isn't where it should be. Martin says Keith was working on it last week.'

'Have you checked his desk?'

'Yes . . . and his filing cabinets. Apparently he took it home to finish it before he went away. He must have left it behind there.'

'What about the disk?'

Amy frowned. 'The disk's missing, too.'

'And we need it? Of course we do . . . silly question. They're coming in this afternoon.'

Amy was nodding and pursing her lips, and Emma knew what she was thinking.

'We'd better send a messenger over to Keith's place for it.'

Again Amy nodded but her tone was doubtful. 'I thought of that – but Lesley's not going to know what we need, is she?'

It was Emma's turn to agree. No wife without specialist knowledge could be expected to locate one file among many.

'I could go and get it,' Amy said.

Suddenly curiosity filled Emma. This was a chance to see Lesley in her own home! It would be fascinating, and it made sense for her to go: she had the knowledge, the car, and this morning she had the time. Her desk diary, kept deliberately empty in readiness for her holiday, was proof of it. But how to put it to Amy? Fear prickled her skin, but she kept her voice calm.

'I'll go. It's only fifteen minutes away, isn't it? I'll have plenty of time to pick it up, get back here, and then go on to the Excelsior.' She was standing up, reaching for bag and jacket, and a wild excitement was growing in her at the thought of coming face to face with her rival.

'Are you sure?' Amy asked. 'I could get a cab . . .'

'No, I'll go. Ring his wife, will you, and tell her I'm

coming? I don't want to get there and find she's gone
out shopping.'

Emma went through to Keith's desk and checked the
drawers, half of her hoping the Semtec disk would be
there, the other half terrified she would find it. The desk
top was littered with the gifts she had given him – a
silver perpetual calendar, a malachite ashtray with silver
rests, an antique inkwell and pen-tray that had once
belonged to Ruskin ... all things to grace his office
because gifts from her could not be taken home. She
had longed to buy him a cashmere sweater, silk shirts
and socks – but how could they be explained? And now
she would be face to face with the woman from whom
so much must be concealed. Emma shut the last drawer
and went in search of her car.

'I've rung Lesley three times, but the line's engaged,'
Amy said as Emma passed her desk.

'Keep trying,' Emma answered and hurried on her
way. She had never seen Keith's house, although she
felt she knew how it would be, and the thought of
entering it, of seeing the setting in which he lived, was
becoming more attractive by the minute.

She was almost out of the city centre when she began
to wonder about the engaged telephone. Who could
Keith's wife be ringing now? One half of her brain, the
sensible side, listed butcher, baker, candlestick-maker.
The other tried to work out what time it was in New
York and whether he had rung her or she him.

As she waited to turn into Upper Brook Street she
acknowledged how foolish she was being. Of course
they would ring one another, just as they must have
slept together and loved together and, worst of all,
laughed together often in the last six months. Keith
would want to know about his children and his home.

He had another life . . . and it would not end because he crossed the Atlantic. That was something she must accept. She was his real love, that was the important thing. The traffic eased and she slipped into the flow.

The house was as she had imagined it, new and large and very 'young exec.', with a neat green lawn to the front and lavatera bushes placed precisely in round holes on either side of the door. There was a holder for milk bottles beside the step. You needed lots of milk when you had children. She rang the chiming bell, and put on her tolerant, employer face.

All the way there Emma had imagined the moment when the door would open and reveal Lesley of the office party, her fair hair drawn back into a flat black bow, high-necked black crêpe dipping at the back to reveal no underpinnings, good legs in high-cut black court shoes. But what she now saw in the open doorway was an adolescent, hair tucked behind her ears and obviously uncombed, a cotton voile wrapper over a matching shortie nightie, and bare legs ending in equally bare feet. In the background a baby was crying noisily, but the girl's eyes were fixed on Emma's face.

'It's not Keith, is it? There's nothing wrong?'

Emma smiled and shook her head. 'No, not a thing. Keith is fine. Hadn't you better pick up the baby?'

She was over the threshold and closing the door, and the girl was moving to the kitchen, putting a baby to her shoulder and turning back, still tense.

'We tried to ring you,' Emma said. 'We need a file, that's all. Keith is fine, honestly. We rang, but your phone was engaged.'

Lesley's face was clearing, and as her hand moved rhythmically over the baby's spine the infant ceased to cry. Now she tried to pull herself together – literally, tugging at the skimpy, not-too-clean housecoat and tidying back a strand of hair.

'I'm sorry. You must think I'm an idiot. It's just that with Keithie away ...' The foolish pet name struck home to Emma. *'Keithie', 'my Keithie'*: no greater sign of possession.

'Of course. I wish we could have got through to you on the phone first.'

'I was ringing Keith's mother in Winchester. She worries a lot. Look, can I get you some coffee?' Lesley's eyes were still agitated and her free hand plucked at the edges of the wrapper. There was nothing for it but to sit down over coffee and put her at her ease. But even as Emma sat down, the girl looked wary. 'She's not sure how to handle me,' Emma thought. 'I'm his boss, and she's in awe.' How much more frightened the girl would be if she knew the truth, appreciated the real threat!

Another child had appeared from nowhere and was peeping out from behind his mother's legs. That must be Tom. The baby was Zoë and the two-year-old was Tom. 'You'd better let me make the coffee,' Emma said and moved towards the kettle.

It was easy to assemble the things for coffee. Everything seemed to be on the worktop, some clean, some still unwashed. She spooned coffee from a jar and took mugs from the drainer. There was a flowered tin tray underneath the debris of a single supper, and she wiped it clean to reuse, trying not to be too critical of the clutter. It wouldn't be easy to be alone with two small children. And they were small: Emma had not bargained for how little they would be in the flesh, nor how young the wife. Behind her the baby started to cry again.

When she turned back to the table Lesley had slipped

into a chair, the crying baby in her arms. 'Is it wind?' Emma asked helpfully. Wind was the only thing she knew that made babies cry.

'I think she's hungry,' Lesley said apologetically. 'Do you mind?' Her hand was already slipping the breast from the flimsy nightie, the nipple, huge and bruised brown, moving into the baby's eager mouth. 'There now,' Lesley said, half to herself and half to Emma. 'Now we'll get some peace.'

'How old is she?' Emma asked politely, trying to repress distaste. Zoë was four months old, she knew her age precisely. She had cried bitter tears on the day of the baby's birth, until Keith had appeared at the door to tell her nothing had changed. She couldn't take her eyes off the engorged breast, the greedy motion of the baby's cheeks as it sucked, the girl's contented head down-bent over her child.

Now Lesley looked up and smiled. 'I hope we're not holding you up? Whatever you want will be in the study. I'll show you where it is when you've had your coffee.'

Emma nodded. 'There's no hurry.' She tried to think of conversation but they had only one thing in common and that was a dangerous topic. 'How long have you lived here? It's very spacious.'

'Yes. I ought to keep it tidier but sometimes things just gang up. We've been here since January.' Washing was piled on the floor beside the automatic washer and its porthole was already filled.

'It can't be easy when children are young. I don't have much experience – I was an only child, and none of my close friends have families yet. But I can imagine.'

'I miss Keith ... he's so good with Tom.' Lesley

stopped suddenly, remembering who Emma was. 'Of course I know he has to move around, it's part of the job. I'm not moaning . . . and usually I cope.'

I must put her out of her misery, Emma thought. Aloud she said, 'He says you're the perfect wife for a busy man so don't apologize.' She smiled as the girl's face cleared. *'I couldn't hurt her, Emma,'* that's what he had really said. *'She's not clueless, quite clever really, but she needs someone to back her up.'*

The baby screamed suddenly, lifting an angry fist to rub impotently at its ear and temple. 'There now,' the girl said, lifting it to her cheek. 'There now, darling. What's the matter?'

The little boy had left his toy cars and moved closer, reaching for the folds of his mother's nightdress. Ten o'clock and she was still in her nightclothes! A little spasm of distaste rose in Emma and as quickly disappeared. The children were clean and well fed, that was what mattered.

As she watched, the little boy began to rub the stuff of the nightdress rhythmically between finger and thumb. The other thumb went to his mouth and his eyes drooped. Lesley looked down at him, shifting the crying baby to her other shoulder. The bare breast, red now around the areola, still intruded into Emma's thoughts and she looked away as Lesley slipped it out of sight.

'He looks sleepy.'

'He's been up since half-past five,' Lesley said. 'I'll put him down in a minute and see if he'll have a snooze.'

They moved towards the study, the baby rubbing her head with two hands now, her face contorted with fury. 'There it is,' Lesley said, opening the door. 'Help yourself. I'll try and sort these two out. Just shout if you need me.' She had to raise her voice to be heard above the baby's roar.

The room was ordered and neat, a complete contrast to the cluttered kitchen. There were photos everywhere: a single baby . . . Tom probably; Lesley with a baby in her arms; boy and baby together; Keith smiling into sunlight, a baby in his arms. Emma stood there, transfixed by the snapshots, wanting to weep – until she remembered that what she and Keith had together was different. *Better!*

'I've never felt like this, Emma. Not like this. I love Lesley and the kids but what I have with you . . . it leaves me gutted. It's . . . unbelievable,' Emma put out a hand to his chair. She had known about the children all along, for Lesley had been seven months pregnant when the affair began. It didn't make any difference that she was seeing what she already knew existed.

She went through the drawers systematically, located the Semtec file, and straightened anything she might have disturbed. Then she went back into the hall. Upstairs she could hear the baby crying, louder than ever now, and she stood, uncertain, one foot on the bottom step, wondering whether or not to intrude upon the upper floor. But seeing where they slept together, the terrible closeness of the marital bed, would be the last straw. She waited until Lesley came out on to the landing, still apologizing, still pushing back the strands of fair hair, browning slightly at the roots.

'I'm so sorry. I've got Tom down, but Zoë seems quite distracted.'

'I expect it's wind,' Emma said comfortingly. 'And don't bother about me. I've found the file, and I'll let myself out. Don't worry about Keith . . .'

'Oh, I don't,' Lesley said, suddenly serene. 'He rings every night. He makes jokes and says it's so I'll know he's not out with a blonde, but he knows I trust him. I've always trusted him. He's a marvellous husband.' Behind her the baby's scream rose to a crescendo.

'You'd better go,' Emma said, her tongue feeling large in a suddenly dry mouth. 'Is there anything I can do?'

She was already moving towards the door.

'No, thank you very much, she'll be all right in a moment.'

'Well, if anything crops up while Keith's away, ring me. You don't have family in Manchester, do you? Keith said something once about you both being isolated.'

The girl was already retreating to her baby. 'I'll remember that. Thanks so much . . .' She laughed rue-fully. 'I'll try and have some clothes on next time you come.'

It was a relief to get into the car and let the tension ebb from her body. Emma felt physically sick, full of grief and anger and a kind of humiliation. She wanted to put her head down on the padded steering wheel and weep, but she was still in sight of Lesley's windows. She turned on the engine and depressed the clutch, but when she started up it was only to drive around the corner and park in the shade of a tree.

She had been a bloody fool to come – but it was over now. Emma tried to quieten her seething thoughts, but the images bubbled and boiled around her brain. Lesley's thin hand with the gleaming wedding band tucking back the straggly hair, offering the nipple, dropping to fondle the toddler's head. Reaching for Keith, stroking, fondling, rousing . . .

Emma put a hand to her mouth, feeling her stomach heave. She mustn't be sick in the car. Not here, in public. She reached into her handbag and felt for the round tube of dyspepsia tablets. Could you counter mental stress with antacid? Christ, that had been *awful*! Why, why, why had she ever consented to come? No, not consented . . . chosen. She had chosen to come face to face with Keith's wife.

In Emma's mouth the chalky tablet crumbled disgustingly, and she put up a finger to wipe the corners of her lips. Mustn't appear before Amy looking as though she had been frothing at the mouth. The thought of Amy and the ordered calm of the office soothed her. She turned on the engine, drove to the corner and waited patiently for a gap in the traffic.

She was glad of the lunch date ahead, of a man across the table to flatter and respect her for her brain. She had had enough of bodies for one day.

'Now,' Harry Wattis said when they were attacking their starter of mushrooms in garlic, 'I'm pleased with you. No point in beating about the bush. We're feeling the benefit of your input already . . . so much so that we expect to be in production by week 14.'

Emma made rapid calculations. 'Week 14 . . . then you ought to be finalizing your advertising and marketing campaigns now.' They fell to discussing details over coffee and brandy. Harry was profuse with his praise, his big, florid face screwed up with the intensity of his gratitude. 'If you need a favour, Emma, don't hesitate to ask,' he said earnestly, as he signed the bill.

'I won't,' she said fervently, and smiled.

They parted on the pavement with a handshake.

'That boss of yours is lucky to have you. I'll tell him as much when he comes to England again.' Emma stood smiling as the older man climbed into his chauffeured car, then she went in search of her own Capri.

It was four o'clock when she got back to the office, and by the time she'd dealt with messages and returned calls it was five. 'I'm calling it a day now, Amy. How did the Semtec run-through go?'

She listened to technicalities, resolutely shutting out thoughts of a small mouth closing on a nipple. Time enough later to brood about love.

Traffic was heavy on the way home and Emma drove well, glorying in the car and her own ability to handle it, nipping from lane to lane to get the best advantage, planning the evening ahead hedonistically. Poppy would not be home before six-thirty today but that was just as well. She wasn't in the mood for questions or good advice.

She let herself into her own apartment and pressed the button of her answering machine, which indicated that someone had left a message. It was the boy again, the boy from last night, whom she had entirely forgotten, his voice young and aggressive and with a definite northern lilt to it, filling the room. *'I rang you last night, now I'm ringing again. Please call me back on 091-7744322. I'll expect to speak to you today. It's getting to be urgent.'*

Emma didn't make a note of the number. It would still be there on the tape if she decided to ring back, but she didn't think she would need it. The anger and pain of the morning surfaced now, and she focused it on the boy. Damn cheek. Damn, damn cheek! Who the hell did he think he was, ringing total strangers and demanding a response? He could go to hell!

She scalded a cup-a-soup and sat at the kitchen table to drink it. Her kitchen was immaculate. No clutter, no washing, no dirty cups, no mountain in the drainer. It might be an operating theatre if it were not for the yellow tiles. But today she took no pride in its immaculateness. Nothing happened here, there was no thriving life to cause a stir, a mess. It was sterile, like the woman who owned it. She tipped the remains of the soup down the sink and opened a tin of chocolate biscuits. It was still only six o'clock and suddenly Emma needed and wanted Poppy. Even cross-examination and censure were preferable to being alone with her thoughts.

Tonight Keith would phone her and she didn't know how she would cope with his call. What would she say about her visit to his home? How could she explain it? The chocolate wafers melted in her mouth and she went on eating them, watching the box empty of everything except crinkled brown paper. She went on until she gagged, and then she went into the bathroom and put a finger down her throat, making the gooey mess reappear so that it could be washed away.

When she had rinsed her mouth and wiped her face she went back to the hall and played the boy's message again, before switching off the machine. He didn't sound like a hoaxer, he sounded like someone with a grievance – but she had never before heard his name or his father's. She ran through her past life. There had been men but not so many that she would not recognize their names. There had been no Culrose, nor anything like it. If she felt in the mood tomorrow she would ring him and sort it out, before he telephoned again! The last thing she needed at the moment was extra hassle.

She watched for Poppy at the window, hating the

empty house, the TV set behind her chattering gloom. It was a God-awful world, and hearing just how God-awful on the hour only made it worse. She watched the corner for Poppy coming from the bus stop, but it was Charlie's car which brought her home, drawing up at the door to disgorge Poppy and armfuls of parcels. They came up the path together laughing and talking, rubbing against one another like seventeen-year-olds while Poppy fumbled for her key.

Numb with misery, Emma waited, hoping Charlie would re-emerge and go. It was half an hour before he came out, but Poppy was on his arm, changed now into a black suit and clutching her Chanel bag. They were going on the town, or as much town as Manchester offered. Emma turned back into the room, resigned to her own company.

She lay in the bath until the water chilled, thinking again and again of her bizarre visit to Keith's family. *'I trust him completely,'* Lesley had said and Emma had taken the words at their face value. But had it been a simple statement of fact or was Lesley more complex than she seemed? Had it been a warning, a formula for saying: *'We are united, don't try to break us apart'*? Emma tried to summon up the pale little face but all that came was the sight of the baby straining for the breast.

She cupped her hands around her own breasts, seeing how foam dappled them and made them look even more insubstantial than they were. Lesley was a child, and yet she had given birth and could give nourishment. Emma felt threatened by the girl's so-obvious fecundity. Perhaps she herself was not capable of giving birth? She had had close shaves in the past, times when she shivered with fear at the non-appearance of a period, but all of them had come to nothing in the end. She had been glad about it at the time. Now, though ...

'I'm getting paranoid,' she said aloud and hoisted herself out of the water.

She went through to the kitchen when she was dry and brewed coffee, but the images persisted. Had Keith suggested Lesley was frigid? Never in so many words but it had been there in the air between them and she had welcomed it. Lesley might have given him children; she, Emma, had given him sexual fulfilment. That was how it had seemed. Today, though, Lesley had been tactile and loving, sensuous even. At the thought of the girl's nipples erect beneath the cotton voile, Emma shivered. He must reach out and touch her, trace the lines of that small, powerful body. 'Oh God,' she said aloud and put down the jug with a bang. She was imagining it all, investing everything with some terrible Freudian importance. She had been all right this morning, strong and happy. One twenty-minute confrontation couldn't have made such a difference.

When Keith rang she would tell him she had been to his home, collected the file and left. That was all. His wife had been pleasant, the baby had cried, full stop. The place had been in bloody chaos and his wife unwashed and undressed, but she would forbear to say so. 'You bitch,' she told herself and felt ashamed. 'I have to stop thinking like this,' she thought but her eyes were on the telephone. Any moment it would ring and she couldn't bear it. Not yet. She couldn't speak to Keith yet. She glanced at the window. It was still light outside. She could get dressed and go for a walk, but there would be a time when she must come back. It shouldn't have made a difference, seeing his family, but it had.

She moved to the desk and switched on the answering

machine, waiting while her own voice chanted its stilted message to prove it was in working order: *'There's no one here at the moment to take your call. Please leave a message after the tone and a telephone number where we can reach you.'*

She filled a glass with Glenfiddich and water and carried it through to the bedroom, leaving the door to the hall ajar. It was half an hour before Keith's call came, and when it did she let the machine do the answering. Then she listened as he left his message. 'Darling ... I'm sorry you're out, but I hope it's somewhere nice. I've had a good day, but I've missed you.'

She wanted to lift the receiver and confess her presence to him, but she couldn't. If she spoke to him, she would never find the courage to mention Lesley and once she lied by omission it would be too late.

'I have to think,' she said aloud as his voice continued.

'It's a huge city, noisy, cheerful. They seem to like our product. You are a clever girl! But it isn't your brain I want now. I love you, Emma, I can hardly wait for Saturday. Still, it's not long. Three more days and then we'll be together. You know how much I love you but it'll bear repeating. Keith loves Emma. Stop. Keith wants Emma. Stop. Love and kisses. Stop. That's your message, wish I could deliver it in ...'

Emma couldn't bear any more. She snatched up the receiver. 'Darling? It's me. I was in the loo.' Her voice echoed around the flat, amplified by the answering machine until it cut out, suddenly with a burr. 'That's better ... How are you?'

She listened as Keith repeated what he had said about New York and her imminent arrival. 'I've got so much planned. A week will never do ... not if we want

36

to spend time together.' His voice had softened and Emma felt all her fears melt.

'Not long now!'

She was elated when she replaced the receiver, but the feeling didn't last. She hadn't told him about her visit to Lesley but it was bound to come out eventually. When she climbed into bed she turned her head into the pillow and cried softly, only ceasing when the phone rang again and an indignant young voice echoed from room to room. 'I've left you one message and you've done nothing about it. It's Stephen Culrose, by the way. I spoke to you last night. Look, I need to know about you and Dad. If you won't get in touch, you'll leave me no option.'

His voice faltered then, obviously uncertain what *no option* could be. In the long pause she could hear his breathing. 'So you might as well ring me. Not tonight, it's too late. But tomorrow. You've got my number but I'll give it ag . . .'

His voice was interrupted by the guillotine as the machine cut him short, but his words went on in her head. 'I need to know about you and Dad.' There had been accusation in those words. Perhaps he was some Kafka-esque prosecutor come to confront her with a non-existent crime so that she might be punished for a real one? Perhaps it was all some Lesley-inspired plot to drive her mad? They needn't have bothered, she was doing quite a good job of going barmy on her own. She flung aside the duvet and padded into the kitchen to get another drink.

How could a man make the kind of love Keith made to two women? It would be impossible unless he was a complete cynic and if he was that, she would never trust her own judgement again. He was a nice man; she would not have succumbed to a cynic or a womanizer. Or would she? Was nature making a fool of her, driving her on to reproduce before it was too late? She put the cap back on the whisky and set down her glass. She had thought more about children in the last twelve hours than in the whole of the rest of her life.

Tomorrow – if she lasted through the night – she would sort it all out. She fetched a dressing-gown from the bedroom, switched off the lights and curled up on the window-seat with her drink, watching the clouds in the night sky changing shape, making lagoons and islands, reforming into continents, so that she realized at last how small and unimportant were her own affairs compared with the infinity of space.

3

Thursday 3 August

Emma tried hard to concentrate on her work but she
had lost her edge. Details swam across the computer
screen and where normally she would have devoured
them, this morning they overwhelmed her.

Amy came in at twelve-thirty, hefting her bag to her
shoulder. 'Going out for lunch?'

Emma shrugged. 'It's hot. I'm not sure I can be
bothered.'

Amy's legs were bare and brown, her feet encased in
thonged sandals, her toenails manicured and pink. 'I'm
coming to rely on her,' Emma thought, 'and I know
almost nothing about her.' She pushed back her chair.
'Oh, to hell with it. Let's go and eat.'

They sat at the back of the restaurant where it was
cool and dark. Above, in the glass-domed roof, a fan
whirred and Emma shivered suddenly, thinking of what
she had done. Here, face to face across a small table, it
would not be so easy to fence, to deflect Amy's questions, to lie convincingly about Egypt, about Keith,
about everything. 'I want to tell her,' Emma thought.
'Whatever the risks, I need to confide.' But even as she
thought it, she knew it could never happen. Amy worked
for her, and business and friendship didn't, or shouldn't,
mix. The irony of the thought struck her. Business and
friendship never; business and adultery as often as possible, please. She must stop thinking about Keith or
surely she would give away something.

They ordered spritzers and wafted the huge menus like fans. 'Pasta,' Amy said at last. 'If I don't, I'll spend the whole afternoon regretting it.' They opted for tagliatelle and sipped their drinks.

'This time next week you'll be in Egypt.'

'Here it comes,' Emma thought. Aloud she began to lament the difficulties of choosing holiday clothes.

'You've got a fashion business, haven't you?' Amy said at last. There was genuine curiosity in her tone and Emma relaxed. This was safe ground.

'It was my mother's. Her marriage broke up around the time I was born, and she came to Manchester. We belonged to Durham originally. It was just when fashion was becoming fun at the start of the '60s, and I suppose she had a good eye. Anyway, she built up a thriving business and gradually moved over to the top of the market.'

'Ooh, rich!' Amy said, pulling a face to show she was impressed.

'Fairly rich,' Emma said. 'Don't get carried away! When my mother died I went into partnership with her assistant – she was a family friend, really. So she gets paid, and two other assistants; we have someone in the workroom, there are massive overheads . . . I get half of what's left. And my pick of the merchandise, which can be nice.'

'So that's how you're so well dressed. We've wondered. You wear clothes well.'

The tagliatelle came then and they ate in silence till the edge was off their appetites.

'My mother and father separated too,' Amy said at last, sipping from her glass. 'Amicably. They just get on better if they live apart. When you think about it, marriage is an impossible concept. How can one person possibly fulfil all your needs, physical, emotional and intellectual. It's not on. They get together occasionally now and they really enjoy it. It's far better from my point of view.'

'It wasn't like that in my case.' Emma wondered how far she should go, but you couldn't hold back every dubious detail of your life. 'I never really knew the whole story – my mother wasn't a great talker. But I gather it was pretty horrendous. I never knew my father. They never made contact again – that was how she wanted it. Him too, I suppose.'

Amy's smile was sympathetic. 'Everyone's different.' She put down her fork and changed the subject. 'Do you think we'll hear from Keith this afternoon?'

'Sure to,' Emma said, fishing in her bag for her credit card. 'No, this is on me,' she said as Amy reached for the bill. 'We ought to work out what we need to say to him. There's something about long-distance calls that brings on brain-death.'

How would she tell Keith she had seen his wife suckling his child? She bit her lip hard to block out the memory.

Across the table Amy's face was pleasantly freckled, and guileless. 'He's really nice, isn't he? I mean, if I did contemplate marriage he'd be the type.'

'He's good at his job,' Emma said firmly. 'That's what matters to me.' But in bed he meant so much more.

They came out blinking into the sunlight and strolled companionably back towards their work-place.

'It's funny to walk in the sun like this, everyone licking lollies or grumbling about the heat, and think of that poor devil in Beirut ... the hostage, I mean ... wondering if he'll see another sunrise,' Amy said. Only then did Emma remember the other American hostage under sentence of death, his face on TV already like a death-mask. She mumbled something in agreement but she had suddenly remembered the boy on the telephone. *'You'll leave me no option.'* She would have to do something about him when she got back home.

Once upon a time she might have told Amy about the boy, knowing she had nothing to hide. Now, though, she was afraid to discuss anything because she had a guilty conscience.

Keith's call came at three o'clock. In America it was ten a.m. 'Miss you,' Keith said. She risked saying, 'So do I,' and then got down to business. When they had exchanged details and conferred she raised her free hand and waved for Amy.

'I'll pass you to Amy, then. We'll talk again.' *'I love you,'* she added, but only in her head. She still had not mentioned Lesley.

As she drove home at five p.m. the radio was droning on about the hostage. Life or death – it was strange to listen to the debate with a brilliant sun still high in the sky, with gardens either side of her spilling over with flowers, and children in shorts and underpants gambolling under garden sprays. It was proving a glorious summer, but underneath all this warmth and abundance there lay a hint of menace – of the greenhouse effect, a world heating up, eventually shrivelling because man had abused his own planet. Already there was a water shortage. What next?

It made for uncomfortable thinking, and Emma switched to her own world. If there was any further message from the boy she would have to respond. If she took time to reason with him, she could easily persuade him he was wasting his time. And her time! She negotiated the last corner and saw Poppy ahead of her.

'Good. You're back early.' Poppy's brow was faintly beaded with sweat and her sleeveless cotton frock, though stylish enough, did nothing for her figure. Older women should not bare their upper arms nor too much breast. Poppy's skin was patterned with a thousand tiny cracks and crêped at its folds. 'She's growing old,' Emma thought, and then, 'So am I. Life is running away, swirling down the plughole so that all that is left is a gurgle, and it's gone.'

'Come and eat,' she said. 'My turn.' Impossible to be alone just yet, transatlantic call or no transatlantic call. As Poppy followed her gratefully to the kitchen she checked the answering machine and saw the familiar circle that meant there was no message. Good! That took care of the boy.

They ate at the kitchen table, coronation chicken from Marks and Sparks, a salad tossed in vinaigrette, and a wholemeal baguette, all washed down with a good Liebfraumilch.

'I'm hoping to call in at the shop tomorrow,' Emma said when they had carried coffee through to the cool, north-facing dining-room. Poppy had pulled off her shoes, revealing feet puffed over the instep and scarred red where the shoe had rested and galled. Her toes were misshapen, her whole foot somehow foreshortened and pathetic. The sight of the naked, well-worn feet filled Emma with pity and with fear. It would come to her too, this down-grading of the flesh.

As Poppy rattled comfortably on about business and Charlie and the God-awful Arabs in Beirut who should all be strung up by their most private parts, Emma tried to imagine her as she had once been, black-haired and vigorous with her GI so that it would have come naturally to name her 'Poppy'.

'Penny for them,' Poppy said, suddenly subdued, and Emma blinked away the moisture that had almost betrayed her thoughts.

'Oh, it's nothing. I'm ready for a break, that's all.'

'You're still going, then?'

'Of course I'm going. Why ever should you think not?' Was there a note of uncertainty in her voice? 'That's why I'm coming in tomorrow. I need to buy quite a few things.'

They talked easily then, of silk and polyester crêpe de Chine and Swiss cotton – anodyne words to allay fears. They only took leave of one another and the subject of fashion when it was time for Poppy to prepare for Charlie's arrival.

'We're staying in tonight. It's too hot to do anything else. I longed for this summer, but the heat's too much.' Around the armholes her dress was darkened with sweat, and she picked uncomfortably at the straps with be-ringed fingers. 'See you at the shop, then, if we don't meet in the morning. I expect His Nibs will stay the night. He's nothing to go home for, so he says. Not "I can't bear to leave you, Poppy," you notice. Just, "I might as well stay".'

Poppy was pretending disenchantment but her face was already animated at the thought of his coming and staying with her. 'Does it never end,' Emma thought, 'this craving for another . . . *the* other . . . being next to yours?'

When Poppy had gone, still barefoot, to the stairs,

44

Emma cleared away the debris of the meal and then went to her bedroom to change. She was hoisting her dress over her head when she heard the doorbell. Poppy wouldn't ring; she would rap and call out, or try the handle and shake it. This was an almost formal ring, and as Emma struggled into a robe and slippers it came again.

When she opened the door a boy was standing there. Seventeen or eighteen by the look of him, bespectacled, a little spotty, the face deadly earnest above the inappropriate suit and tie. She knew who it was before he opened his mouth to betray his accent, and her weight was already against the door to deny him access.

'It's me.' The eyes behind the spectacles were hostile and afraid but also triumphant.

'I can see that,' Emma said. 'I don't know why you've come. You're making a terrible mistake . . . and if you've come all this way just to see me you're crazy. I don't know you or your father, or any other Culrose, or whatever it is you're called, so please go away.'

He was smiling now and she put up a hand to the neck of her robe. Any minute Charlie would come through the front door: no need to fear anything except a scene.

'You've never heard the name Culrose?'

'No. Never, ever, unless on the radio or something like that. Never in my private life.'

His hand was fumbling in his breast pocket. 'And I suppose this isn't you?'

He held out the photograph and Emma felt a sense of relief. It was mistaken identity after all, easily explained. She might even ask him in for a drink once it was settled. Except that the girl in the photograph, smiling up into the sun, *was* her!

'Where did you get that?' Emma took it from him, and turned it over – to see her own handwriting there: *'Portofino 1988'*.

'It was in my father's safe, along with this and this.' There were others, six in all.

'You'd better come in,' she said, her voice suddenly faltering, and stood aside to let him pass.

They settled on the settee and spread out the pictures on the coffee table.

'It's you,' he said accusingly.

Emma nodded. 'I'm not denying that. It's me, all right . . . last year in Italy. Greece the year before. That's on the day I graduated but I don't remember it being taken.' Her own face stared up at her, solemn under the borrowed mortar board.

'So now will you tell me?' The spotty face was truculent but vulnerable.

'Tell you what?' Emma asked, forcing herself to sound patient. 'Look, I admit these are photographs of me . . . my photographs. That's my writing on the back. But I don't know how or why you have them. You're asking for answers, but I'm the one with the question: What are you doing with these?' In spite of her efforts to keep calm, her voice rose.

His teeth bit into his lip in vexation. 'Oh God, I knew you'd be like this, even when I'd proved it. You'll change your tune, though, when you hear the rest.'

Any moment now Keith would ring but Emma abandoned all ideas of getting the boy out of her home before the call. 'I'm going to make coffee,' she said, 'and then we'll thrash this out. There's bound to be a logical explanation. I think you sincerely believe I'm lying to you. I know I'm not. If we talk reasonably we can work it out.'

She put on the percolator then went into her bedroom to change into something that would not keep gaping open at neck and knee. Once into jeans and a shirt she felt more in command, cheerful even. She put cups and biscuits on the tray and carried everything through to the sitting-room.

'Now,' she said, as she manipulated the cups, 'tell me where you got those photographs.' He had taken off the horn-rimmed spectacles. 'He's just a kid,' she thought and smiled encouragement as she handed him a cup.

'My father died last week,' he said. He was still watching her, expecting a reaction.

'I'm sorry,' Emma said, and waited for him to go on.

'He was buried on Monday and we had the will read. There's only me and April, my sister. She's still at school. We thought it would just be straightforward – two shares, and bits and pieces to the aunts and things. But it wasn't.'

Again he was expecting her to be moved – concerned or excited. 'Go on,' she said. Their glance met and she gave him eye for eye.

'You were named in the will.'

'*Me?*'

'It wasn't a two-way split, me and April. It was me and April and you. Not the house – the house is for me, and the cottage in Arkengarthdale for April. But the firm is split three ways.'

'The firm?'

'It's building supplies. We're one of the biggest family firms in the north.' In spite of himself pride was in his voice and on his face, until he remembered why he was there. 'So you can see why I have to know. What was between you and him? I'm not a child. Just tell me, and that'll be it. I won't argue or contest it or anything.'

Suddenly his chin came up. 'I won't let you into the firm: no way! But we'll buy you out, whatever it takes. I just want to know what's been going on.'

Emma heard Charlie cross the hall and clatter up the stairs. Had it really been only half an hour since she left Poppy? It felt like a lifetime. She looked down at the photographs and then back at the boy.

'Look, I know this must sound crazy but I honestly don't know what you're talking about. There's been some kind of mistake. I can't begin to imagine what it is ... but there never was *anything* between me and your father. I don't know him.'

A thought struck her. 'What about your mother?'

'My mother's dead. She died eight years ago.' Once more the eyes, curiously alert, boring into her.

'And you think he took up with me to fill the gap?'

'It could have been like that, or ...'

'Or I might also have been around while your mother was still alive? Sorry to disappoint you but I wasn't ... either of those things.'

Emma felt ill at ease suddenly, sitting there with the evidence on the coffee table in front of her and the pugnacious young face almost contemptuous in its disbelief. She took refuge in attack.

'How do I know this is not all some crazy stunt? After all, you ring me up bandying around names I've never even heard of, you force your way into my flat with a few photographs you might perhaps have filched from me, you talk glibly of a will and a ... for all I know ... mythical business. If I had any sense I'd ring the police!'

He wasn't shaken. 'Please yourself.'

It was checkmate but she wasn't going to be the one to back down.

'Have you some form of identification?' His hand slid to his pocket and she had a sudden crazy desire to shout 'Assume the position' as they did in every American cops-and-robbers movie when the villain reached for his gun. Instead she waited while he produced a driving licence, very new-looking, in a leather holder. *'Stephen Culrose,' The Wyndings, Gilesgate, Durham.'*

'Well, then, at least I know your name *is* Culrose.' What came next?

She was racking her brains for a clever ploy when the boy produced a slim silver pen. 'Have you a piece of paper . . . that newspaper will do.'

She handed him the *Independent* and he wrote something in the margin. 'There,' he said, returning pen and licence to his pocket and replacing his spectacles, 'ring that number in the morning. It's my father's . . . it's *my* solicitor. He'll confirm what I've told you.'

Suddenly, to her horror, she saw that his eyes were gleaming unnaturally behind the owlish spectacles. 'Oh God, he's going to cry,' she thought and was suddenly seized with a desire to comfort him.

'There's been a mistake,' she said. 'Honestly. Why should I lie to you now? And I don't want any part of your business or your money.'

He had wiped his nose with a folded handkerchief and regained some of his composure. She saw he was seeking words and put out a hand to his arm. 'I'll ring your solicitor tomorrow. We'll sort everything out. I want that now, as much as you do. I'm going to the States at the weekend so we must do something at once.'

He frowned and adjusted his spectacles on the bridge of his nose.

'He wants to trust me,' Emma thought. 'He wants to, but he can't quite bring himself to do it.'

Aloud she said: 'How old are you?' As soon as she said it she realized it was a mistake.

'I don't think that's revelant,' he said and she sensed a withdrawal.

'Relevant,' she said. 'It's relevant, not revelant.' She had meant to divert him but it didn't work.

'I didn't come here for a course in semantics,' he said scornfully. One up to him. He could use the right word when he chose.

'Sorry,' she said, 'that was rude of me. And I wasn't being nosy about your age – just sorry that you seemed to be having a difficult time at a fairly early stage.' He was mollified but she'd better tread carefully. 'Where are you staying?'

'I'm not. I drove here, and I'm driving back now.' That had pleased him. He was obviously proud of his driving.

'I see,' she said, trying to sound suitably impressed. 'It's a long drive.'

'I wouldn't have needed to come if you'd listened on the phone.'

He sounded so self-righteous that it stung her. 'Oh come on! Did you really expect me to jump, just because some boy rings me with a tale about my knowing his father?'

Oh God, that was the wrong way to handle him. He was reaching for the photographs. 'I'll keep these, if you don't mind, until everything's settled.' She did mind but a troop of the King's Own couldn't stop him now, as he stood up, bundling the photographs into his wallet and cramming it into his pocket. 'Thank you for seeing me . . . at last.'

'My pleasure,' she said as sarcastically as she could. To hell with him and his incipient acne! She had troubles of her own. 'I'll ring your solicitor tomorrow and tell him to sort you out . . . if such a thing is possible.' She flung the last few words after his retreating back and then slammed the door.

'Clever girl, Emma,' she said, helping herself to a generous Scotch and water. 'Beating up on teenies now. Very grown-up.'

In the kitchen she put on coffee and got out a mug. The impulse to run upstairs to Poppy was strong, but must be resisted, for a while at least. What the hell was going on?

She switched on the news to hear that the hostage had been reprieved. Thank God for that! But a terrorist had blown himself up in a London hotel. She would have to stop listening to the news if it was always going to be horrific.

She realized she had temporarily forgotten Keith in the same second that the phone rang.

'Darling?'

'Keith, it's you!'

'Of course it's me. How many other men ring you at night?'

She would have to tell him about yesterday. About Lesley. 'There's something . . .'

'Yes?' His voice was concerned.

'Oh, it's nothing . . .' It was there again, before her mind's eye, the eager little mouth, the engorged breast, his baby, his wife . . . fuck! She must say something. 'Well, it's odd, really. This boy turned up . . . he rang last night, and the night before. Anyway, tonight he turned up . . .'

'At the house?'

'Yes, of course. Here. Just now. He had photographs of me. Half a dozen.'

'What kind of photographs?'

'Nude photographs, of course – what other kind are there?' It was silly to squabble on a transatlantic phone line. 'I'm sorry, I'm a bit overwrought. They were snapshots, ordinary holiday photos. Some of them even had my writing on the back. One from last year – remember, I told you I went to Portofino? He had a snap of that, and one from my graduation day, and a clutch of others. That's not all. He says I've been left some money . . . well, a share in a business.'

'Left by who?'

'Well, that's the whole point. By someone I've never even heard of.'

'Look, Emma, I think you should call the police. It sounds like a stunt. He's not there now, is he?'

'No.' But she hadn't put the chain on the door. She would do it as soon as she put down the phone. She listened as he lectured her, enjoying the feeling of his being in charge. That had been part of his charm, in the beginning – that he who was subservient to her during working hours was so protective, even masterful, when they were alone together away from the office. If only he were here, now, in the flesh, it would be all right but there were several thousand miles between them, and it made for stilted conversation.

'I wish I was there, Emma, I'd soon sort it out. Are you worried?'

'No, not worried exactly, it's just bizarre. The boy wants to buy me out . . . can you imagine? Buy me out of something I don't own, that I've never even heard of? It's crazy.'

'Oh, God, I wish you were here, Emma.'

She should say it now, slip it in quite casually: *'I saw Lesley yesterday. We needed a file you'd left at home.'* But it wouldn't come. She couldn't acknowledge Lesley. If she did it would spoil everything.

'I'll be with you soon. At least . . .' The words surprised her even as they left her lips.

'What do you mean? You *are* coming?'

'Yes, of course. I only meant that with this thing blowing up . . . Still, I'm going to ring the boy's solicitor in the morning. That should settle it.' She was playing on the boy's visit in order to avoid talking about anything else — she knew it, and she couldn't help herself. 'All the same, it's a bit unnerving. Where did his father get these photographs?'

'I thought the boy had the photographs?'

'He did. He does, now. But they were his father's.'

'I see.' But he plainly didn't.

Suddenly Emma wanted to end the call. It was all spoiled now. 'How's it going, anyway? We ought to talk about that, it's what you're there for.'

'Things are going well, and I don't think there's anything else to report. Just get here as soon as you can.'

'Have you spoken to Lesley?' It was out!

'Yes. I rang a couple of hours ago and spoke to Tom. She said you'd called round yesterday. Sorry I forgot to return that file. I meant to say sorry straightaway, but you drove it out of my head, speaking about the boy.'

Of course! How could she have been so stupid? Of course Lesley would have told him — why should she conceal it? But if he knew she had been to his home, surely he understood how shaken she must be.

'Zoë was creating while I was on the phone. Lesley says it's her teeth.' Keith sounded complacent, almost

53

smug. He didn't realize at all how seeing his wife, his children had disturbed her!

Emma managed to get through the rounds of love and goodbye and put down the phone, but she didn't put the chain on the door as she had intended. Instead she mounted the unlit staircase to Poppy's door, hoping against hope that Charlie would have gone, but knowing his exit was always noisy and that if she had not heard him leave he would still be there.

She could hear them laughing through the door ... laughter and music and the occasional chink of bottle and glass. She sat down on the top stair, hugging her knees and wondering if she dared disturb them. She used to sit outside Poppy's door in the old days, hoping to be drawn in to warmth and comfort. But she was a big girl now. She got to her feet and went back downstairs.

In the living-room she picked up the newspaper and tore off the edge that held the solicitor's number. She would ring in the morning and tell him to unscramble whatever was in the will and deal with his client. He might know if there was some distant familial connection between the Gaunts and the Culroses ... and then she would finish getting ready for her trip and to hell with everything.

As she went about her bedtime chores she thought of last year when she had been preparing for Portofino. Her mother had been alive then, slim, elegant, those curious hooded eyes of hers dark and still, but loving. 'She did love me,' Emma thought and felt tears prick her own eyes. If only they had talked more often and more deeply. Had her mother known her daughter loved her? If you had not said it aloud, you could never be sure.

She put her rinsed milk bottle out on the step and looked at the night sky. It would be another hot day tomorrow, for the air was still and warm, even at ten p.m. A year ago her mother had been alive and Emma had not even known of Keith's existence. Now her mother was dead and Keith was the centre of her universe. She had been back from Portofino only one week when the call came to say her mother had had a cerebral thrombosis. She had lived for four weeks more. Emma had left London in September and opened the Manchester branch in October. So she had now known Keith for ten months. Ten months! She had only known him for three months when they became lovers, feverishly, in a Sutton Coldfield motel. There had been other men before him, plenty of them, but Emma had never known such complete abandonment.

Perhaps she had been particularly vulnerable in the aftermath of her mother's death? Would that explain the intense tenderness she felt for him, her need to cradle him against her, to be with him, body and spirit? She found she was pressing her hand against the door jamb until it hurt. Time for bed!

She slipped between the sheets and thought of how excitement had grown in her each day as they worked together – making excuses to consult him, exulting when he sought her advice on the flimsiest of pretexts. Both of them laughing a lot and complimenting one another's skills. Crazy, really: two whizz-kids at the mercy of their hormones, like any school-leavers. And then the loving.

She put out the light and remembered how they had loved one another. The memory soothed her and she was drifting into sleep when she remembered the boy and the phone number. Had she put it safe? In the end she got out of bed to make sure, and when she came back to bed it was to toss and turn until the early hours.

4

Friday 4 August

It was a relief to tell Amy about the boy. Poppy had
already gone off with Charlie when Emma woke from a
last-minute doze to find she had slept through her alarm.
Now she sat at her desk while Amy plied her with
coffee and sympathy. She made no mention of Keith or
Lesley or her sudden doubts about going away on
Saturday. It was enough to tell of the boy's disclosure
and watch Amy's eyes widen.

'What did you say?'

'What could I say? Just that I'd contact his solicitor . . .' She reached for the scrap of newsprint '. . . and
get to the bottom of it.' It was uncomfortably warm in
the office and the hair on her neck hung heavy and
damp against her skin.

'What will you do if the money *is* for you?'

'It's not money, exactly, it's a share in a business. A
family business.' She thought of the boy's determined face:
'I won't let you in to the firm, no way. But we'd buy you out.'

'I've never really thought about what I'd do with it
because I know it's not for me. And the sooner I ring
up and say that the better.'

As Amy left the room, closing the door behind her,
Emma dialled. 'Could I speak to Mr Eden, please? It's
in connection with the terms of a will.'

It seemed an age before he came on the line. 'Robert
Eden. Can I help you?' He sounded younger and more
human than she had expected.

57

'I hope so. My name is Gaunt, Emma Gaunt.'

She could sense the chill, even down the line. 'Of Manchester?'

'I see.' There was a pause and it exasperated her.

'Well, I'm glad somebody sees, because I don't.'

'I'm sorry?' He sounded anything but sorry.

'I don't see what you see. All I know is that a strange young man has pestered me with calls and finally forced his way into my home, gibbering about photographs and wills.'

'That would be Stephen Culrose?'

'That's who he said he was.' Suddenly it occurred to her that it was odd that this prickly individual immediately knew all about her. Solicitors must deal with dozens of wills, surely, and hundreds of bequests?

'I see.' He was at it again.

'Look, can we try and make some headway? I'm ringing because there's obviously been some kind of mix-up. Can you give me some facts?'

'The facts are that Stephen's father, David Culrose, died last week. He left an estate, value unknown. It's largely a building-supplies retailer. There were a few other bequests, the usual thing, but the business is divided three ways, between his surviving children, Stephen and April, and an Emma Gaunt of Waverley Gardens, Manchester.'

'But that's impossible!'

'I can assure you it's not. The will was properly drawn up, properly witnessed and registered. If you're that Emma Gaunt, you're a beneficiary.' The phrasing was judicial but the tone was cool to the point of hostility.

'But I never knew the man.'

'That may be true, but it doesn't affect the issue.'

'You don't believe me!'

'I neither believe nor disbelieve, Miss Gaunt. I'm here to execute a will, not indulge in speculation.'

'You are a pompous prig,' she thought. Aloud she said, 'I'd better come up and see this will for myself.'

'As you wish. You can probably see the next of kin then, and make some arrangement.'

This time Emma couldn't hold back. 'What do you mean by "some arrangement"? It sounds as though you expect them to buy me off.'

'That would be one alternative, certainly.'

She was suddenly choked with self-righteous indignation. 'I don't want their bloody business. I have a business of my own, if you're interested. I told the boy he could keep his precious family firm, but I do want to know what's behind all this.'

'Perhaps it would be better if you could come north and discuss it?'

'You'll have to leave it with me . . . I can't just drop everything here. And I'm going on holiday, which complicates things. I'll have to think it over and ring you tonight.'

When Emma put down the phone she sat for a moment, uncertain what to do next. She was conscious of Amy's eyes on her from the outer office. She couldn't just sit mooning into space.

She reached for the phone and dialled. 'Can I speak to Mr Wattis please? . . . Harry? It's Emma Gaunt. Yes, you too. Look, I need a quick favour . . . Yes, I did take you at your word! I want to check on a Durham firm, in the building trade. I could do it through the usual channels but that would take time. I thought that as it's your line you might know of them yourself, or could ask someone who did . . . You will? Thank you. The firm is called Culrose, at least I think it is ... Yes, it is sketchy. It's a family firm, probably of medium size ... Anything and everything. It's rather complicated but I'll tell you over our next lunch. My treat ... Thank you. Yes, I'd appreciate it ... Goodbye.'

She spent the next hour on the following month's work schedules, checking them with Amy before giving them to be processed. As she was clearing the last note from her memo pad, Harry Wattis rang back.

'Got a pen?'

'Yes. You're a pal, Harry. I won't forget it.'

'I won't let you. Now here it is – mostly gossip, but reliable. They're big. Well, they were big. Started out as timber importers round the turn of the century. Diversified in World War 2, and their stock shot up. They were going to float the company, when the old man died.'

'Was that David?'

'No, that was Edward Culrose. David was his son. He took over in 1960 and from then on it was downhill all the way, no one seems to know quite why. In the end it was drink that did for him, but that wouldn't explain the decline back in the '60s. Apparently he'd been a bit of a whizz-kid when his father was around – so perhaps he just overreached himself once he was boss. It's happened before. He sold the original site in Sunderland and set up in Durham in 1960, part wholesale, part DIY. Things came to a crunch in the late '70s, when he sold off most of the subsidiaries, for peanuts apparently. It's not a pretty picture now. Good site, good work-force, not much else. He died last week. Just got out in time, according to my source. If you're thinking of any sort of link with the firm, I'd watch it. It's bound to go down now.'

Emma thanked him and put down the phone. So

young Culrose had been left one third of a moribund business. Poor kid. And he'd said there was a sister. At least the two of them would have the lot when she herself pulled out. Except that the lot was worth zilch, according to Harry – and Harry was not the man to pass on duff information.

'Time you were leaving,' Amy said from the door, and Emma made an effort to drag herself back to her work.

'Will you be all right here?'

'Yes,' Amy said firmly. 'And if something crops up that's beyond me . . . which I have to tell you is doubtful . . . I'll ring Keith, just as you said.'

'Yes,' she said, 'that's right. Ring Keith if you're in trouble.'

'You don't look like someone who's off on holiday,' Amy said kindly. 'Loosen up. We'll be fine. And you'll only be away two weeks. What I'd give to see a sheikh at close quarters.' She rolled her eyes in ecstasy and it had the desired effect. Emma laughed and tension ebbed.

'OK, I'll go. If I sit here thinking about what could go wrong I'll never get away.'

She made her goodbyes round the office and went off in a welter of good wishes for a blissful holiday. Her face ached with the effort of smiling. If only they knew! She sat in the Capri for a few moments, trying to collect her thoughts. If she was going to New York tomorrow . . . even as she contemplated all that was still to be done, she knew that the significant word was *'if'*. Everything had changed. Not just seeing Lesley and the children, but the boy, the stupid boy with his spots and his horn-rims and his desperate need to know some-thing, anything. Her world had suddenly started to rock, and the only thing she wanted to do was go home and lock herself in her darkened bedroom.

Instead she started the engine and drove to the boutique. There, above the small, grey-lined window, was *'Esther Gaunt'*, her mother's name. Emma parked down the side alley and pushed open the door, sniffing the familiar smells of good cloth and lavender polish and Poppy's heady perfume, glad to get out of the sweltering heat of the day.

'Darling, just in time for a cuppa!' Poppy was coming up the stairs from the workshop, summoned by the doorbell. 'Tea for two please, Jenny. The boss's arrived.' They settled in the overstuffed chairs at the far end of the shop and sipped from outsize mugs.

'If I'm the boss, why don't I get porcelain?'

'Snob,' Poppy said. 'But if you've come to buy some holiday gear I'll run down for the silver plate. I'll even grovel.'

The summer clothes were on sales rails now, the main body of the shop given over to the autumn stock, rich colours and textures set off here and there by bowls of brown leaves and berried branches. 'They look almost real,' she said, nodding towards a floor-standing display.

'So they should,' Poppy said. 'You'll see why when you get the invoice. Still, anything to entice. Now, what can I do for you?' She reached to a rail and pulled out a dress chequered in pink and grey and white. 'Pure silk, flows like water. The Yanks have nothing like it and with your discount you'll get it for next to nothing.'

'I'm not sure I'm going at all, Poppy. Something's come up . . . well, more than one thing.'

'Come on, then,' Poppy said, easing her feet from her tight shoes and tucking one foot underneath her.

'I love her,' Emma thought and reached out to pat the older woman's arm. 'You are a comfort, Poppy.'

'Spill the beans, then. Better out than in.'

Poppy's eyes widened as she heard about the boy. 'Good God! What are you going to do?'

'Turn the bequest down, of course. But I want to know why, first.'

'It *could* be a family connection – your mother came from Durham, remember? She didn't talk about it much but there was family. Well, there always is, isn't there? And then your father had family as well. It could be his lot.'

'I don't think so,' Emma said. 'Mother never talked much, but there was no money in her background. Let's face it, Poppy, she'd have mentioned it if there had been. She was a bit like that.'

'A bit,' Poppy agreed. 'Still, she was a great girl, and she wasn't as hard as she seemed. Don't ever think that. I guess your father hurt her and she just closed up so that nothing would ever hurt her again. Some people do that. Me, I bleed a little and then I go on as before.'

'There's something else,' Emma said, knowing that it had to come out. 'I had to go to Keith's place yesterday. Well, that's not strictly true; I could have sent someone else. I chose to go.'

'To see his wife?' Poppy's eyes were like saucers.

'Yes. It was for work, we needed a file. And I wanted to see her face to face, just her and me.' She thought of Lesley opening the door, tucking her hair behind her ears, giving the baby her breast. Oh God!

'And it hurt?' Poppy said.

'Like hell. I'm shaken, Poppy, and not sure of anything any more. I felt . . . I can't say how I felt because it was all so jumbled up. It wasn't guilt: I've *never* felt guilty because I've never felt I was taking anything away from her.'

'Nothing?' Poppy's eyes were shrewd.

'No. It demeans a man to suggest he's half a pound of fudge, so if I take a slice there's less for her. It's not like that. What he has with me he wouldn't have at all if I wasn't around. What he has with her is separate. It exists, and I don't chip away at it. I couldn't even if I wanted to.'

'I see,' Poppy said. 'He is some sexual and intellectual athlete who has enough for all comers. If he takes up with someone in the States, I suppose he'll still have enough left over for you and his wife when he gets back? Send him round here: God knows I'd hate to see him stuck with a surplus! Emma, Emma ... you're fooling yourself. Or he's fooling you. Whichever it is, you're not using your brain.'

'I've got to get on,' Emma said, rising from her chair. 'I can't make you see. And I haven't got time to argue. I want the right that men have always had – to take love where I find it. Why should they always win out?'

'It isn't men that women have to conquer,' Poppy said. 'It's our hormones that defeat us in the end.'

Emma turned to the rails then, seeking the clothes she had come to buy. There was every shade, every texture, every cut. Sometimes she took a garment down and held it against her before replacing it on the rail.

'See anything?' Poppy said once or twice but Emma shook her head. She had lost interest in a holiday wardrobe. Not even the beautiful clothes she was handling could restore her appetite. She put back a silk dress and jacket in shades of cinnamon and turned to the door.

'See you tonight?' she said apologetically. 'I'm not in the mood for shopping.'

'Of course,' Poppy said, uncurling from her chair. She waddled down the shop on her misshapen feet and folded Emma in her arms. 'Take your time deciding, darling. He'll still be there when you've thought it through. If you still want him.'

Emma thought of Poppy's words as she drove home through the beginning of the evening rush. Of course she wanted Keith: the trouble was that deep down she wanted all of him, every little bit, however much she might protest to the contrary.

When she reached home she went into the kitchen and switched on the kettle and radio. The hostages had slipped from the news and the Hillsborough disaster inquiry was the hot item. It was all the fault of the police, according to the commentator: one particular policeman had fallen apart under pressure. Emma cast her mind back to the scenes of the football stadium disaster, the bodies pressed against the wire, gasping for air. Little wonder that someone would crack amid scenes like that. Suddenly she felt sympathy with the disgraced policeman. He must have gone out that day, smart in his uniform, secure in his record, confident in his ability to order and control. And then it had all fallen apart. Three days ago she had been secure and confident, and now her world, too, was falling apart.

She looked at the clock. Six-fifteen: it would be lunchtime in New York. Any time now Keith might ring, depending on how long he spent with Bernie. How would she tell him the truth, that her visit to his home still tormented her, that she was now unnerved by guilt, whatever she might have said to Poppy, and uncertain of his motives, of her own motives, of everything? How could she say she was looking forward to seeing him when she wasn't sure she was? She washed and changed into a cool cotton shift-dress and was brushing her hair on to the crown of her head when the phone rang. Would it be Keith, or the boy?

'Hallo.'

It was not a man's voice at the other end, it was a woman, speaking quickly, words tumbling over one another in her distress. 'Emma? Oh God, I'm sorry to bother you but I don't know who else to ask.' It was Lesley. 'Can you come now, quickly?' In the background the baby was still screaming but this time the toddler was crying too, a thin grizzly wail.

'What's the matter?'

'It's the baby . . . a mastoid infection, the doctor says. It's serious, Emma. Can you come? You said you would since Keith wasn't here. I've got to take her to the hospital. They're sending an ambulance, but I can't take Tom.'

'I'm coming,' Emma said. 'I'll come round now and we'll sort it out. Now attend to the children and wait. I'll be there in fifteen minutes.'

She picked up bag and car keys and looked around her. Everything was switched off; windows . . . well they could stay open till she got back. She turned on the answering machine and went into the hall. Poppy was coming through the front door, a string bag of groceries dangling from her wrist.

'I haven't time to explain, Poppy. Keith's wife rang. The baby's ill and she needs someone to help.'

'Is there no one but you?'

'No. They've only been living here a few months.

66

Anyway, I haven't time now. I'll see you when I get back.'

'You're a fool, Emma,' Poppy said and stood on the step to watch her down to her car.

She could have said 'no' to Lesley. There were emergency services for just this kind of situation. But she wanted to go – Emma acknowledged the truth as she sent the car speeding onwards. She was fascinated by her rival and her rival's kingdom and all it contained. But Poppy was right about one thing: she, Emma, was certainly a fool.

She saw the flashing blue light on top of the car as she rounded the corner and then the word 'Ambulance' on its side. Lesley was in the hall, the baby, quiet now, in her arms. Beside her a smart uniformed man held two overflowing travel bags. 'Right,' he said, 'can we get away now?'

'I've rung Keith and left a message,' Lesley said. She was dressed in jeans and denim shirt and looked almost boyish except for the breasts straining the shirt buttons. 'I've rung his mum, and mine. There's food in the fridge. Use our bed . . .'

She turned to her son as Emma tried to cope with the unwelcome news that she was expected to stay the night. 'Be good, darling. Be a good boy for Aunty Emma and I'll be back as soon as the doctor fixes Zoë's ear.'

The toddler had been silent, puzzled by all the goings-on. Now, as he realized his mother was leaving him, he opened his mouth to yell.

'Just go,' Emma said, seizing the struggling child as he clung desperately to his mother's legs. 'Just go! He'll be all right. I'll stay as long as you need me. But go now . . .'

She looked desperately at the ambulance man and he took Lesley's arm. 'Come on then, mother. Let's get you into the van.'

The child let out one scream of rage and fear as the door closed behind his mother, and then threw himself to the floor and started to weep.

'Come on,' Emma said, coaxingly. 'Would you like some sweets? Ice-cream? I'll play with you, if you like. Any game.' In the end she lay down on the floor beside him and put her arms around him. At first he stiffened and tried to throw off her embrace. In the end he accepted it and gradually his weeping turned to sniffling and the odd gulping sob.

'There now,' Emma said. 'Shall we go and make some drinks? I'm thirsty.' She wanted a rigid vodka and tonic, but she couldn't tell that to a two-year-old. 'Will you show me where mummy keeps the cups? Then when she comes back I'll tell her what a good boy you were.' Tom moved his head to look at her with a cautious eye. 'And your daddy. I'll tell him too.'

'I want a wee-wee.' He had suddenly decided to trust her but Emma was seized with terror. If only he had been a girl she could have coped. You lifted them on to the seat and it just happened. But boys . . . she thought of a small, limp penis and was even more afraid.

In the end he did it himself, lifting the seat, fishing inside his own trousers, even ending with a shake and pulling down the lever to flush. 'Good boy,' she said admiringly as he turned to the basin and held up his hands to be washed. So slovenly Lesley did train her children, after all!

She soaped and rinsed the tiny hands with the so-definite fingernails, patting them dry between the folds of the towel and then, suddenly, impulsively, lifting

them to her lips in a snatched kiss. 'All clean,' she said
and saw a ghost of a smile touch the small mouth.

She felt oddly elated as she followed him to the
kitchen. Perhaps there was no mystique about caring
for children? Perhaps it just came with the product? If
she had a child of her own . . .

It took a while to locate ice-cream in the overcrowded,
under-organized freezer. Several times she whooped with
triumph, only to discover that the boxes labelled 'Rasp-
berry Ripple' or *Tutti Frutti* really held cooked mince,
silvered with frost, or portions of gravy containing
carrot and potato and odd, obtrusive bones. At last she
found the real thing and spooned a generous helping
into a bowl.

'When's Mummy coming?' Tom said as he fed himself
quite efficiently.

'I'm not sure,' Emma said. 'Quite soon. As soon as
the baby's better.' She leaned forward to wipe his chin.

'When's Mummy coming?'

'I told you,' she said and then controlled herself. You
mustn't expect logic from a toddler. 'She'll be back as
soon as she can. If we play a game, and then you have a
little sleep . . .'

His mouth quivered dangerously and she saw she had
said the wrong thing. 'Well, we'll play a game and . . .'

In the living-room the phone rang and the child
slipped from his chair and made for the door. 'Wait a
moment,' Emma said, following him, but he had already
lifted the receiver. 'Who's that?' he said confidently.

Emma took it from him and held him off with one
hand as she lifted the receiver to her ear.

'Lesley?' It was Keith.

'No, Keith. It's me, Emma.'

'Emma? What's going on? I got a message .

69

'It's OK,' she interrupted. 'Everything's all right. The baby has something wrong with its ear but it's not life and death. I'm here with Tom, and Lesley's at the hospital. I expect she'll ring you when she has news.'

'You said Zoë's ear . . . has there been an accident?'

'No, I think it's an infection. It's painful and she's yelling a lot, poor little thing, but it just means antibiotics, I expect. And babies respond quickly.' She wasn't sure if that was true, but it sounded good. She had been holding off the little boy while he scrabbled for the phone. Now he ceased struggling and opened his mouth. *'Daddy!'* It was a wail and she heard Keith draw in his breath.

'Tom? Put him on, Emma. Tom? Is that you?'

'I want Mummy,' the child said when she held the phone to his ear. 'I want my Mummy.' Emma felt suddenly humiliated, and yet she couldn't just walk away from it.

'He's all right,' she said, taking the phone back. 'Just a bit upset.'

'Poor little devil,' Keith said and then, perhaps realizing he had been less than tactful, 'Are you all right?'

'I'm fine, Keith, but in all the circumstances I think I'd better put off my trip.'

'Yes. It's a shame . . . but I might need to come back quickly. I'll wait until I hear from Lesley, but if she needs me . . .'

'Of course,' Emma said. 'If you're needed here drop everything and come. Ring if you can't get a flight and I'll pull strings. Of course, it'll probably all be over by the morning. It wasn't that serious, you know. If you'd heard her yelling . . .' But the baby had been quiet when they carried it out of the house. If his baby died, she would lose Keith. He would never look at her again.

Appalled by her own selfishness, she tried to concentrate as Keith sketched in the day's events. 'It all sounds fine,' she said, 'but we'll talk about it tomorrow when the panic's over.'

'I love you, Emma.' It was as though he was reading her thoughts. 'I'm concerned about Lesley and the kids . . . my God, I'm concerned . . . but it doesn't affect *us*, you know that.'

Tom was crying quietly now, wearily, like a sad old man. 'I'll have to go Keith. Tom needs me. We'll talk tomorrow.' She put down the phone and gathered the child into her arms. 'Come on, you. Come beside me and get a cuddle.' She sank into the corner of the settee and drew him against her. 'I know you're sad, and I'm sorry, but Mummy will be back soon, and your Daddy too.'

'In an aeroplane?'

'Yes. In a big jumbo. Have you been in an aeroplane?'

He was struggling down from her knee and making for the toy box in the corner. 'Jumbo,' he said triumphantly. 'Brmm brmm!'

They were zooming planes into an imaginary hangar when the phone rang again.

'Lesley?' It was a woman's voice.

'I'm sorry,' Emma said. 'Lesley's been called away . . .'

'She's gone, then?' the woman interrupted. 'You'll be Miss Gaunt, my son's boss?'

So this was his mother. 'Yes. I'm holding the fort for a while, as Keith's away.'

'It's very good of you. I said to Lesley, there aren't many bosses you could rely on in an emergency. Still, your being a woman makes a difference, I expect. Women understand these things.'

There was a limit to how much gratitude Emma could take. 'I'm afraid I can't talk for long. Tom's a little upset. He's bound to wonder what's going on.'

'Of course. I won't keep you. I just wondered if there was any news?'

'No news is good news,' Emma said. Her brain seemed to have seized up, and clichés were all that would come. She made her goodbyes and put down the phone.

'That was your grandma,' she said. Tom was curled up on the floor and his eyes were drooping. He let her lead him towards the stairs.

'Which is your room?' she said, cunningly ignoring the plaque on the door that said 'Tom's Den'.

At the bedside she stripped off the tiny jeans and T-shirt, leaving vest and pants. The pants were easy but what about the vest? Did it come off for sleep?

'Do you keep your vest on?' she asked. There were blue pyjamas over the bed-head, so at least that was simple.

'Vest on,' he said, but when she tried to put the pyjama top over his head he squirmed and whimpered, 'vest off,' and then . . . 'Mummy? Mummy come!'

Emma pulled off the vest, guarding his ears with her other hand as she did so. He was so little! 'There now. If you get into bed . . . oh, do you want a wee-wee?'

He shook his head and cried a little as she folded him into the bed. 'Mummy come!'

'Yes,' she said, kneeling beside the bed. 'Mummy come soon.'

Once, long ago, someone had crooned to her at bedtime. *'Oh, lula, lula, lula, lula, bye-bye, do you want the moon to play with? Or the stars to run away with?*

*They'll come if you don't cry. Oh lula, lula, lula, lula bye-
bye, in your mammy's arms asleeping . . .'*

She was embarking on the fourth rendering when she
realized he was asleep, but she stayed there, motionless
and singing, until the eyelashes ceased to tremble on the
flushed cheeks and his breathing slowed until it was
almost undetectable. She left the light on in the bedroom
and on the landing in case he should wake and be
afraid. Poor little boy, he'd had enough to bear for one
day.

She rang the airline and cancelled her flight, then
went into the kitchen to brew tea, searching the
draining-board for cup and milk jug. Some of the things
she had moved on her last visit were still where she had
left them, but three clean baby bottles were standing
ready. Emma wondered briefly what Tom had for breakfast, and then decided to worry about it when the time
came. It was only nine o'clock, but she felt as though
the day had lasted for thirty-six hours.

She was washing face and hands in the bathroom
when she remembered her promise to ring Stephen
Culrose. They would think she had chickened out. Tomorrow she must ring him and his rude solicitor, and
explain the delay.

She went through to the bedroom and regarded the
double bed. King size. There was handcream and a
paper-back romance on one side table and a digital
clock-radio on the other. She could sleep on Lesley's side
or Keith's. Deciding on neither, she went in search of
alternative accommodation, but in the third bedroom
there was just a cot, and Tom was sprawled sideways
across his single bed. That only left the sofa or the bath.
Emma was about to collect pillows and duvet and go
downstairs, when she realized that she couldn't desert

the toddler. If he woke in the night he would need someone near, and she might not hear him from downstairs. She turned back to the master bedroom and gritted her teeth. They were uncleaned and felt vile when she ran her tongue over them. If only she'd packed a bag!

She didn't have a nightie, and she couldn't sleep naked in a strange bed, not even her lover's. Especially not the bed her lover shared with his wife. There might be semen on the sheets or the scent of his hair on the pillow. Lesley was an indifferent housekeeper: traces of him were bound to remain.

In the end she rifled a drawer, wincing at the sight of Tampax in a box and nipple shields in a plastic bubble. She found a cotton nightie and slipped it over her head. On her it was skimpy, but it would have to do. She had cleaned her teeth with her finger and was climbing on to the bed when she noticed the pillows – HIS and HERS in embroidered hearts. She was laughing as she put out the bedside lamp but her eyes were wet. Oh God, what was happening to her ordered life? 'I *am* a fool, Poppy,' she thought. 'I just didn't realize how big a fool!'

She had expected to toss and turn for hours, but sleep came almost before she had inhaled the odour of Keith from his pillow and seemed to last no longer before she was wakened by a wail. 'Mummy! Mummy!'

She picked Tom from his bed and carried him back to the king-sized divan. 'There now,' she said, 'there now.' He allowed her to curl around him, even briefly pinching at her arm before he put thumb to mouth. She heard the sucking, vigorous at first and then intermittent, and then silence. She was trying to sleep herself when he jumped suddenly in her arms and began to sob again. She cried then, until a line from a book came

74

into her head. It had been a book about the Vietnam war and in it a GI had felt this same complete despair. 'Don't cry, baby. God'll think of something.' That's what he had said.

She drew Keith's son closer to her and whispered against the downy head, 'Don't cry, baby. God'll think of something.' Except that He wouldn't. It would be up to her to care for this child and resolve her relationship with Keith and . . . the boy. In her last waking moment she wondered how she would manage it all but knew, with comforting certainty, that she would.

5

Saturday 5 August

She woke when it was still half-light, aware of the bed, warm and moist, around her. The little boy slept beside her, one arm half across his face, the other hand curled, thumb out, where it had fallen from his mouth. She lay for a moment, bringing the unfamiliar bedroom into focus.

Tom had wet the bed. It should have horrified her, causing her to leap for the shower. Instead it was a not-unpleasant sensation to lie there joined to the small warm body by a sensation of dampness that only grew uncomfortable when she moved away and the bed grew cold. She settled closer and thought about the day before.

It had been like a dream, all of it. Hearing of an inheritance – dying business or not, it was still a bequest. There would be all sorts of legal niceties before she could get out of it, and there was still the mystery of why she had figured in the will at all. And then the summons to this house. The room was becoming more distinct now as the light strengthened, and she looked around her lover's bedroom.

It had been nicely planned. One wall in something pale, probably magnolia. Two walls papered with small flowered sprigs and the third wall in the same pattern enlarged. Matching curtains, and an ottoman with a fitted cover to match the tub chair. Even the light shades toned or contrasted with what had been a tasteful plan. But somewhere along the line it had gone wrong. Clothes were everywhere, hanging from the front of the fitted wardrobes, piled on the chintzy chair, cascading from drawer tops, and even peeping coyly from half-open drawers. Shoes, high-heeled and keeling over, were standing outside the wardrobes as though waiting permission to enter. Jewellery, cheap and chunky, lay on every surface, curled around bottles and boxes and jars.

'She hasn't cleaned up in ages,' Emma thought and felt justifiably smug. It was easy to keep house if you had even a pinch of self-discipline. How did Keith, immaculate, organized, brilliant Keith, exist in such chaos? The thought of what he might do in this bedroom, activity that would blind him to its squalor, drove her out of bed, and as she met the air outside the damp nightdress struck chill.

She scuttled for the bathroom and turned on the taps. There was a sweet smell about her body, baby urine, pungent but not unpleasant. She put the damp nightdress into an overflowing linen basket and stepped into the cleansing water.

She looked at the shelf on the opposite wall. So he used a conventional razor! Two cans of shaving-foam and a packet of bright orange disposable razors stood alongside an aerosol container of a vaginal deodorant. Somehow this juxtaposition offended her more than the sight of them locked in one another's arms would have done. She couldn't resist heaving herself from the water to separate HIS and HERS and put a comfortable barrier of baby talc and cream between them, but as she sank back into the bath she saw that she had only made things worse, uniting them symbolically by the most important thing they shared: their children.

The towels on the rail looked grubby and she sniffed

until she found a neutral one to wind around her. Back in the bedroom she rescued her tights and pants from the radiator where she had hung them the night before. They were still damp but not too damp for use. She wriggled into them, one eye on the sleeping child in case he woke and saw her nakedness.

She felt better once she was back in her own clothes. Fetching her bag, she sat down at the dressing table to comb her damp hair and apply some morale-boosting lipstick and mascara. And then she saw, under the plate-glass cover of the dressing-table, photographs of Lesley and Keith and their lives together. Lesley radiant on her wedding day, Keith looking unbelievably callow at her side. Lesley, with an obviously new baby, squinting triumphantly into the camera. Lesley and Keith together, hand in hand, striding along a fairy-lamp-lit boulevard. Lesley stretched languorously on a beach, the camera with Keith behind it, caressing every inch of her body.

Emma moved the clutter so that she could see each snapshot. It was the second time in two days that photographs had had the power to shock her, but she could not stop looking at them, drinking in every nuance of expression and of body language. It was a terrible montage of happy family life, unbearable and irresistible. In the end she ran a comb through her hair and left her face untouched before going in search of coffee and comfort.

It was a warm day, but the sky was overcast. She opened the back door and went into the garden. White cast-iron chairs and table, a three-wheeled truck abandoned in a corner of the lawn: a family garden. She left the door open for fresh air and turned on the kettle and radio. Still Hillsborough – opinions for and against.

When the media got hold of a story, they wrestled it to death.

She located a brown loaf in the bread bin and made two slices of toast, carrying them through to the living-room in case the child cried and she didn't hear. When he woke she would have to strip the bed, even wash the sheets. She couldn't add to the chaos by leaving them.

She moved back to the kitchen and eyed the washing machine. It was already full, so she opened the door and dragged out the damp and tangled mass: shirts and socks and underpants jumbled up with baby clothes and Lesley's flimsy pants and blouses. No bras. She thought of the bulbous breast, oozing milk, defying containment. If she herself had a child, would she suckle or opt for a bottle, hygienic and perfectly balanced to nourish?

In the hall the phone rang out and Emma ran to answer before it disturbed the sleeping child.

'Did you manage? I forgot to tell you Tom wears a nappy at night . . . did he tell you?'

Emma considered telling a gigantic lie, saying she had thought of it on her own and all was well, but there might be a stain on the mattress to make a liar of her.

'I'm afraid he didn't. But don't worry, I'm coping pretty well. How's Zoë?'

Zoë was a little better and Mafeking was about to be relieved. 'Keith's mother is coming up. She says she can get here on Monday. Could you possibly hang on till then? I feel ashamed to ask, but I don't want to leave Zoë on her own and they say she might be here for a week.'

When Emma had reassured Lesley and put down the phone, she hung the damp washing on a white plastic drier, then went upstairs and contemplated the sleeping child. Did you wake them or let them surface of their own accord? And what did they have for breakfast at that age? Lesley seemed to think Tom capable of communicating his needs but it hadn't worked very well so far.

As if he had tuned in to her thoughts he opened his eyes and, seeing her, scowled. 'Mummy!' He struggled up in the bed, rubbing one eye with a fist. 'Mummy!'

'She's coming soon,' Emma said quickly, before the tears could start. 'She's helping the doctors make Zoë better and then she's coming home to you. Better hurry and get ready before she gets here.'

She was lying to him and she didn't like doing it, but if he started to cry where would it end? She held out her arms and was pleasantly surprised when he came into them and let her lift him from the bed. He was wet, soaking, so that she felt the sleeves of her shirt grow instantly moist where he rested.

'Let's get you nice and dry, and then we'll have brekky. Anything you want. Would you like egg and soldiers?'

He shook his head. 'Spiders,' he said with finality.

'Spiders?' She stood him down on the bathroom floor and decided not to pursue the breakfast thing. She had trouble enough stripping off the soaking clothes. As she turned on the bath taps he started to shrink from her and cry. 'No bath, no bath.' In the end he settled for a wipedown with a soapy flannel. It was only a lick and a promise, but he emerged from it glowing and rosy, peeping from the enveloping towel like a cherub.

She carried him to his bedroom and looked around. There were piles of clean clothes on the drawer tops, a load of washing not yet put away. She found vest and underpants, socks and matching shirt and trews. He lifted his arms and legs obligingly, and stood patiently while she fumbled with unbelievably tiny buttons and half-forced his feet into bunny-rabbit slippers. He was so small and so perfect. She smiled at him as she put finger and thumb around his upper arm and felt them touch, even overlap. 'There now,' she said, and kissed the brow that seemed too large for the baby face.

'Spiders' turned out to be cereal complete with plastic packet containing a rubber insect. He ate half his plateful and screamed with delight when she pretended to be terrified of the wiggly rubber creature. 'Again,' he said and held it out between chubby fingers. She cowered behind her hands, peeping between her fingers to see it advance and scream again. So far so good.

He took her hand when he was done and climbed the stairs beside her to the master bedroom. She wanted him to sit on the chair while she stripped the bed, but he wouldn't stay there and she found it difficult to do an efficient job on the soaking bed with one eye following his travel across the room and landing. There was a stain on the mattress but it was a small watermark inside other larger, dried-out stains. She settled for rubbing it with the face-cloth and scented soap, and left it to the air.

She was carrying the wet bedclothes down to the kitchen when she remembered the photograph of herself in Portofino. She had given that photograph to her mother, she was sure of it. Had there been two? As soon as she could get away from here, she would check her mother's album.

She fetched the nightie she had worn the night before, and Tom's vest and pyjamas, and added them to the washer, then she spent a happy ten minutes drinking coffee and watching them go round and round, the only price of peace being that she should scream at regular intervals when the rubber spider approached. If this was child-care, she could probably be quite good at it . . . if her laryngeal muscles could stand the strain.

As she rinsed her mug Emma caught a glimpse of herself in the mirror above the sink and was appalled at her dishevelled appearance. She had been so critical of Lesley, but now she had a little more sympathy. It was eleven o'clock, and apart from coping with Tom's breakfast and a wet bed she had little or nothing to show for it. She should have been on her way to Heathrow now, immaculate in easy-travelling clothes, expectation oozing out of every pore. Instead she was here, preparing to feed her lover's child.

A rake through cupboards and fridge proved worthwhile. There was a carton of raw mince in the fridge, and she cooked it gently with onion chopped small in case Tom didn't like it. She boiled potatoes and mashed them with sunflower margarine, and heated frozen peas to add colour.

She had intended to sit with him while he ate but in the event she found she was hungry too and matched him spoon for spoon. They finished off with fruit yo-ghurts and then he slipped down from the table and went in search of his coat. 'Park,' he said when he came back, holding up his anorak. So he could make his wishes known when he chose.

'You don't need a coat,' Emma said. 'It's a lovely day.'

She couldn't lock the front door because she had no key to get in again. She put down the latch so it would open at will but left the radio playing to discourage burglars. It was half-past one in the afternoon, so she wasn't really worried, but it was best to play safe, especially with someone else's house.

Tom led the way confidently enough, stopping to

look through fences whenever there was a sign of children or dogs. 'He's a happy little boy,' Emma thought and gave Lesley grudging credit for it. If she had a child, would it be like Tom? She tried to picture herself pregnant, chained to a pram, indulging a teenager ... but office memories kept intruding. Perhaps she was not cut out to be a mother?

She settled on a bench in the sun and let Tom roam free. Every now and again he came back to her as if to reassure himself she had not deserted him. He was like his father when he smiled. She hadn't thought of Keith all day, not properly. She closed her eyes, leaned against the warm wood of the seat and gave herself up to remembering.

She had only been aware of appreciating him at first. He was damned good at his job and it had been a relief, in the flurry of setting up, to be able to delegate. They had worked well together, partners. She had even sent apologies to Lesley when she kept him late. And then one night, when they had wrestled a particular problem to a solution, he had suggested a drink. They had sat in a booth of a spit-and-sawdust pub and felt the tension drain out of them, luxuriating in the fact that there was nothing to explain because each knew exactly how the other felt. That had been the start of it. There had not been a word, a glance, a touch but that had been where it began.

The following week they went to Birmingham to do a presentation, and coming back in the car the tension had mounted until she had felt herself actually itching with need of him.

'Shall we stop for a while?' he had said, his voice strangely thick as though his mouth were dry. She had said yes, and he had pulled into a layby and taken her in his arms. 'Not here,' she had said. That was all. No need to specify what must not happen in that public place. They had driven on to a motel, and the only disappointment had been that they could not make it last forever.

She had worried afterwards in case he took advantage of their relationship at work, but he had always behaved perfectly.

'Wee-wee!' Tom was pulling at her arm, his face anxious. Emma looked around for a public toilet but there was nothing in sight.

'It's all right,' she said, leading them across the grass to a clump of shrubs. He managed competently enough while she steadied him and then, when it was done, he looked up at her and smiled, a smile so intimate and ravishing that she felt her throat constrict. 'He likes me,' she thought and could have wept with pleasure. It was like a bad TV play, she realized, as they walked home: 'mistress cares for lover's child', a honey of a plot.

It was still overpoweringly warm and the air felt heavy, as though there was thunder about. She would have liked a bath and change of clothing, but Lesley's day clothes were unlikely to fit her and, besides, she wanted her own. Tomorrow, if she still had to stay, she would call a cab and ride to her home with Tom. She couldn't go in her own car because there was no way to make it safe for Tom. Little children could rattle about in a speeding car and wind up going through the windscreen.

Yes, tomorrow she would go home and pack a bag. She could bring her mother's album back with her and check on the holiday snaps. But supposing she found a blank in the album; how much further on would she be? Why would her mother have sent a snapshot of Emma to a stranger? Unless he was in some way related? She knew almost nothing about her mother's family, even less about her father's. When she got out of this present mess she would have to do some checking out. In childhood, she had missed having a father, but she had come to terms with it. Now, though, she wanted some roots, something to anchor her, as a husband and children might have done.

When Tom was settled in front of children's TV she rang the shop. 'Poppy? It's me.'

'Where are you? Not in New York?'

'I'm still at Keith's place, minding the two-year-old.'

There was a faint laugh from the other end. 'I'd give a week's pay to see you at it.'

'I'm doing very well!' Emma felt quite indignant. 'Anyway, I didn't ring up to amuse you, just to say I won't be home tonight but I'll definitely be back to-morrow. Maybe just to pack a bag, but I'll be there anyway.' She paused, seeking words. 'Poppy, have you remembered if Mother ever mentioned the name "Culrose" to you? "David Culrose"?'

'Not that I recall. I've been thinking about it all day. She wasn't a name-dropper, and it's the kind of name you'd remember.'

'It couldn't've been my father's family, could it? His sister's married name? He did have a sister, didn't he?'

'Yes. I think he had two, but one died. But I'm sure the other one's name wasn't Culrose. Your mother only mentioned her once. She was talking about marrying young ... well, I was and she joined in ... and she said something about her sister-in-law. The name was

85

something to do with ... it was ... Oh God, it's gone clean out of my mind. But it was something to do with pepper, spices ... something hot.'

'That's a big help, Poppy!'

'Why do you want to know?'

'I'm not sure, exactly. But I'm going north as soon as I can leave here, and I thought I might do a little checking up on my family tree.'

'Your mother would've hated that.'

'Why, Poppy?'

'I don't know why, darling. Just a gut feeling that she couldn't bear referring to the past, let alone digging it up.'

It was true, Emma thought, when she had put down the phone. She had never acknowledged it before but now she could see clearly that her mother had always shunned any mention of her Durham roots. There had been few mentions of the past, certainly no harking back to any cosy northern heritage. When they had gone on holiday, it had been to the south coast or the West Country. Emma had been twenty-one and at university before she saw Edinburgh or the beauty of the Border country. And when she had questioned her mother, there had been a stock answer: 'We were a small family. There's nothing left there now.'

Perhaps going north wasn't such a good idea after all? But she was coming to terms with the news about the will. It must either be mistaken identity or some ancestral quirk: whichever it was, she would be able to dine out on it eventually. It would make a good story. And she wanted to get out of Manchester for a while, as soon as she could. Anywhere would do, as long as it was a change of scene.

She scrambled eggs for tea, and served Tom's on a

bunny plate, encouraging him to eat to let the bunny rabbit out. It was easy enough to cope with him once you got the hang of it. He hadn't asked about his mother for ages now. Perhaps he'd forgotten all about her? She, Emma, could pick him up and take him off somewhere, like the woman in the Ruth Rendell story, and they could live happily ever after. She pictured it, the two of them together in a house by the sea, living for one another. You could live for your children – she had never had a child of her own, but even she knew that. But never to lunch out again and talk business, never to make a decision and know everything was riding on it, not just for you but for others: could she live without that kind of buzz?

It was easy to think that she could while they played with his cars, both of them sprawled on the floor mouthing 'Brmm, brmm' and indulging in wonderful crashes. But after a while the game began to get rough, the clashes more violent. Eventually Tom threw a car across the room, narrowly missing a pottery lamp. 'That's naughty,' Emma said, startled that she might have had to explain the breakage. He looked at her for a moment and then threw another car in the same direction.

'Now stop that!' Emma said, scrabbling the cars back into the toy box. When she looked at him again she saw that fat tears had gathered in his eyes and were teetering on his lower lashes. 'Come on,' she said soothingly and held out her arms. It was too late.

He cried while she ran his bath, and then sat sobbing in the warm water until his face grew red with distress. She felt her heart begin to pound and knew her own face was flushed. If anyone came in now they would think she was brutalizing him. 'Mummy!' he wailed between sobs and while she wrestled with the disposable nappy.

At first she fixed it too tightly and then, fearing injury, she made it too slack so that it gaped around the tops of his legs. She was trying for the third time when the phone rang in the bedroom. Nothing for it but to tuck him under one arm and lift the receiver with the other.

'Emma?' It was Lesley and she sighed with relief that it was not Keith ringing to discover how badly she was coping with his child. 'Everything all right?' Emma stood him down on the bed and slipped off her Rolex watch. Anything to buy a moment's silence. It did the trick. He flopped down on to the duvet and began to pull at the winder. It had cost the earth, but it was cheap at the price.

'Yes, everything's fine. We're just in the middle of bathtime.'

'Did you get out at all? I meant to tell you to take my Fiesta. It's in the garage, and the keys are in the drawer of the hall-table. It's got a car seat, so you'll be OK. I'm so sorry to put on you like this, Emma. Zoë's temperature's down but she's still poorly. I can't leave her, and Keith says I should stay here.'

So they had spoken: he had rung her at the hospital and they had conferred. He could have rung her, Emma, and got the news, but he had preferred to ring his wife. Emma felt a sense of outrage so great it threatened to choke her. She would make him pay. She would make them both pay.

'You're helping yourself to everything you need, I hope?' Lesley was getting ready to end the conversation, uttering platitudes about there being nothing in the fridge and the house being in a state.

'Everything's fine. Honestly. Did Keith say anything about cutting short his trip?' Emma's rage had turned sour and she felt flat.

'He said he'd fly back at once if I needed him, but I said I'd be OK. Now that we know what's wrong with Zoë, I don't feel so scared. I just want to keep her quiet and restful till the antibiotics work. You've been a God-send, taking over Tom at a moment's notice. I don't know how we'll repay you. Keith says he's not surprised but I'm amazed enough for both of us. There aren't many bosses . . .'

So they had discussed her, said how 'good' she was in a crisis. She had a sudden vicious desire to shake Lesley, to say something utterly basic and unequivocal and four-lettered. 'I've had your husband, Lesley. He's good. At least a nine and a half.' She tried to imagine Lesley, clinging to the phone in a hospital corridor, her world disintegrating around her. She couldn't bear to think of them discussing her, it felt akin to rape. She would never forgive him! When she put down the phone her fingers were white and they ached as the blood flooded back in.

She retrieved her watch and carried the toddler to his bed, suddenly overpoweringly weary. If she didn't sit down and put up her feet she would drop. She wondered if there was any booze in the house and decided to conduct a search as soon as she was free of Tom.

'Lie down like a good boy,' she said but he was already scrambling upright, his lower lip jutting alarmingly. 'I want my Daddy,' he said at last.

'You and me both,' she said and took him in her arms. She sang her lullaby and then a selection of Roger Whittaker interspersed with Lloyd Webber. She was starting on Johnny Todd when the vigorous sucking noises began and his body became heavier in her arms. There was satisfaction in laying him down, covering him up and smoothing the hair from his brow. She left the lamp on and put a soft toy on the duvet in case he woke, then made her way downstairs in search of a drink.

'I am shattered,' she said aloud as she scoured the kitchen cupboards. There was cooking sherry, and gin but no tonic. She thought of Keith's expertise with a wine list and began to hunt again. He must have a few bottles somewhere. There was nothing. She settled for gin and orange juice and grimaced with every life-giving sip. When she got back home she would open a bottle of St Emilion and drink it to the dregs.

She knew Keith would ring and she nursed her resentment as she waited for the call. Damn him and his vapid little wife. She would make him suffer for paying her mealy-mouthed compliments. So she was only doing what he would have expected! Perhaps he thought she had nothing better to do, that all she had to occupy her was him and his offspring? If so he was in for a surprise.

She wound herself up, fully aware of what she was doing, longing for a chance to put him down. But when at last he rang the sound of his voice sent the anger draining out of her.

'Darling, are you all right?'

'I'm fine ... and Tom is blooming. He's sound asleep.'

'I love you, Emma. I've been going spare here, thinking of what's happening. Are you sure you can bear it?'

'Of course I'm sure. I want to help. Don't be silly. He's a dear little boy.'

'He can be. Is he behaving himself?' They might have

been husband and wife, exchanging domestic inanities. 'It's very hot out here,' he went on to say.

'Same here. Hot and sticky. When are you coming home?'

'As soon as I can. I'll make it up to you, the spoiled holiday and everything. We'll get away together somehow. We could go up to Edinburgh for the Festival, you'd like that.'

Emma felt a tiny glow of pleasure blossom in her chest. Edinburgh in September would be wonderful. They would ride through the Scottish countryside together, exchanging glances when the road allowed, looking backwards sometimes to see the child in the back seat. She shook her head angrily to dislodge the image. They would never go anywhere together with Tom: Lesley would never allow it. Small powerful Lesley, who held all the strings.

'We'll talk about it when you come home,' she said and her tone was dismissive.

Emma looked in on the sleeping child when she put down the phone, and clicked off his lamp. If he woke in the night he would find his way to her bed. He knew her now. He trusted her. She was smiling as she turned out her own lamp until she remembered that this would have been her first night in New York, the first night they would have shared a bed with no thought of morning separation. She clenched her fists under the covers, trying to assuage the pain she was feeling, almost glad when she could not. She deserved this punishment . . . this was what you got for screwing a subordinate. It served her right. All the same, there was a limit to how much she could bear. She was almost glad when she heard the toddler's thin cry and knew that at least she would not have to sleep alone.

6

Sunday 6 August

Perhaps it was the sun chinking through the curtains that woke her. More likely it was the feel of small, determined, fingers pulling open her eyelids. 'Hallo, you,' she said, but now that Tom had achieved his objective he was turning away. She reached for him and felt his padded bottom. Dry except for slight traces of damp around the upper legs. A small glow of achievement blossomed as he wriggled from her grasp and went in search of excitement.

She was about to follow him, afraid of the stairs, when he reappeared. 'Brmm, brmm,' he said and climbed back on to the bed with his toy cars. 'Play garage,' he said. 'You play.' She took a car and made suitable swooping motions with it while she tried to gather strength for the day ahead.

Yesterday she had done almost nothing, and it had drained her. Today, with extra things to do, she would need to summon up her reserves, On the other hand, everything had been new and strange yesterday: today she would have a better idea of what was to be done. She was undergoing a crash-course in motherhood and it was not altogether unenjoyable.

She lay for a moment, marvelling at what had come out of a throw-away remark: '*If there's anything I can do* . . .' That's what she had said, or something like it. You said it every day in one situation or another . . . bereavement, moving house, influenza, burglary. You said it and it never occurred to you that anyone would take it seriously. Lesley had called her bluff with a vengeance. Had she simply panicked and reached for the first helping hand that occurred to her, or had she calculated her moves? 'Am I here as an angel of mercy, or to learn a lesson?' Emma wondered and could not find an answer. One thing she was sure of, though: she would weigh her words more carefully in future.

'Let's have breakfast?' she said to Tom, crashing her car with a gesture of finality.

'Sausages,' Tom said promptly. 'Five sausages.' There had been no sign of sausages in the fridge.

'What about eggs?' she said coaxingly and when he looked mutinous, 'Shall we have spiders again?'

'Sausages,' he said firmly and, seeing no look of assent, 'five sausages.' She deliberated whether to get a shower in the hope that he would forget. But what would he do while she was in the shower? What did Lesley do? Shower while he slept, probably, which was what she should have done. Now she settled for taking him into the bathroom with her and locking the door. She was one minute behind the curtain but he managed to create a fair amount of chaos even in sixty seconds. He was not in the least interested in her naked body, and she sighed with relief. Whatever she did for him today, she was not going to enter into a discussion about birds and bees.

When she was dressed she took off his nappy, relieved to find it was only damp. What did you do if it was the other? Sooner or later she'd have to cope.

She carried the soiled napkin downstairs and out to the bin. It was another lovely day.

'Sausages,' Tom said when she came back into the kitchen. She felt her jaws tighten with exasperation.

'There aren't any sausages, Tom. No sausages. None.'
He went over to the fridge-freezer and pulled at the
lower door. In the third drawer down she found frozen
sausages, plump and icy.

'Five sausages,' he said but she put only two into the
microwave to defrost. She must retain at least the semblance of authority.

He ate one sausage and toyed with the other. 'You're
a good boy,' she said. She stood up and took down a
red mug. 'Juice?' she asked but he was shaking his head.

'Daddy's mug.' She looked at the red mug. It had
Keith on the side in white letters. She turned back to the
shelf and they were all there. *Lesley, Tom* and one with
a feeding lip marked *Zoë*.

Emma poured him juice in his own mug and sat
down at the table. 'Does Daddy have juice?' It was said
half to make conversation and half to draw him out
about his father.

'Daddy has coffee, Mummy has tea, just Tom has
juice.' It was the longest sentence she had heard him
utter. So Lesley made coffee especially for Keith.

'Daddy has . . .' He was pondering the next word.

'Yes?' she prompted.

'Daddy has to go to work,' he said.

'Do you love Daddy?'

Tom was nodding but his mind was already on something else. 'Yes,' he said and then, as though it went
with talk of love, he held up his mouth to be kissed.

'You're a good boy,' she said, a sudden urge to cry
welling up in her.

'Go see Mummy,' he said, climbing down from his
chair. 'Go see Mummy then Daddy.'

'We will,' she said, gathering up the plates. 'We'll go
and see Mummy today.'

She washed and changed him, picking out matching everything in honour of the hospital visit. 'You have a lot of clothes,' she said admiringly. 'Can I borrow some?' He gave her a knowing look and she laughed out loud. Keith's son could see through flannel, even at two years old.

He played in the garden while she hoovered and dusted and cleared some of the kitchen clutter. It was a challenge, locating the proper home of cutlery and containers. Perhaps you could fill your time in a home: she had never considered it before, but perhaps it was possible. While she stood at the sink, looking out at the child in the garden, she thought about their conversation at the breakfast table, the confident way he had spoken of his mother and father.

She had never known her own father, since her parents had split up around the time of her birth. She had missed him in childhood, especially after she went to school. Everyone else had a father. She had wanted one too, and if she couldn't have that comforting presence in her life she wanted to know why he had abandoned her and deserted her mother. 'There was no one else,' Esther had told her when she asked. 'It was just that we were never suited.' Emma's father had never contacted her, and by the time she was old enough to think of looking for him, he was dead. 'I didn't tell you when it happened,' her mother had said. 'You were just starting at the High School. It didn't seem appropriate.'

So Emma's father had slipped out of her life without even a ripple. She had tried many times to raise the subject of the past, but her mother had always evaded her questions. 'It's water under the bridge, Emma,' or 'I don't want to talk about it now.' And then it was too late, altogether.

Emma shook her hands free of suds and tipped the bowl to drain it. Had she ever sat at a table with her father? Had he fed her sausage or juice, or screamed at rubber spiders to amuse her? It had never been really important before. Now it seemed crucial.

She dried her hands and looked through the fridge. If she'd had any sense, she'd have shopped yesterday. Tom would need a proper lunch. Her own appetite was non-existent.

In the end she peeled potato and carrot and opened a tin of corned beef, grilling a slice till it fell to pieces and adding it to the vegetables. She was eager to get to the hospital and then to go on to her own home. She needed to know about the photograph: was it the one she had given her mother, her enigmatic mother? She would pick up some clothes and some food there, too. Hopefully she would be relieved tomorrow, but whoever took over would need feeding.

Tom ate the corned beef hash obediently, letting her spoon it into his mouth. By the time he had had enough she had become adept at catching dribbles and not over-filling the spoon.

'I love you,' she said, when he was washed and had submitted to the hairbrush. His crown was yellow and smooth and when she stroked it single hairs clung to her hand, powered by static electricity.

'Love you,' Tom answered equably, and she knew then that Lesley too must play the loving game with him.

She thought of her own childhood, trying to remember if her mother had ever stroked her head or whispered words of love. There had been affection, certainly, and pride, and kindness sometimes amounting to indulgence. But had there ever been love-games between mother and daughter? Had her father ever swung her high in the air or dangled her from his knee? In adolescence, when she had tried desperately to conjure up his memory, there had been nothing at all, so that she had sometimes wondered if he had ever existed.

'Come on,' Tom said impatiently, tugging at her arm until she rose obediently and went to get the car.

It took her a few minutes to familiarize herself with the Fiesta controls. Tom sat patiently in his safety-seat behind her while she inched forward out of the garage and reversed, located horn and choke, and adjusted the seat to her longer legs. 'Right,' she said. 'Off we go.'

As she drove towards the hospital she wondered what she should say. What would she have said if the situation had been just what it appeared? She'd have talked about Keith quite naturally, the job, how long he would be away. A sudden unwelcome thought struck her: what if Keith had told Lesley about Egypt? It would have been quite natural for him to say his boss was going on holiday. But Lesley had never mentioned it, not even when she was asking Emma for help. That meant he hadn't told her, not exact details anyway, or she'd have expected Emma to be demanding to be relieved so she could get away. He'd probably kept quiet about the whole thing. It would have made sense, but the fact that he had not mentioned her was irritating. A battle raged inside her at times like this. Her head knew that certain things must be if she and Keith were to go on; her heart could not bear that it should be so. 'Come on, Tom,' she said as she pulled into a parking space. 'We're going to see Mum and Zoë.'

At a kiosk in the lobby she bought chocolates for Lesley and a bunny in cellophane for the baby. In the lift she held Tom's hand, glancing down now and then in case he needed reassurance. But his face was tranquil, his smile that of a friend. 'He likes me,' she thought. 'He really likes me.'

The illusion lasted as far as the ward door. As soon as he caught sight of his mother he pulled free of Emma's hand and hurtled down the ward. Lesley smiled at her briefly and then concentrated on her son. Had he been good? Eaten big dinners? Helped Aunty Emma? He ignored all these questions and explored the new situation, trying to climb into the cot beside Zoë, who lay on her back, still flushed but sleeping peacefully.

'She looks fine,' Emma said. 'I bought her this.' She slipped the toy into the cot. 'And these for you.'

Lesley was rising to her feet. 'Thank you, Emma.' She strained to reach Emma's cheek, her lips soft and childlike. 'You've been so good, I don't know *how* to thank you. But we'll make it up to you when Keithie gets back, you'll see. He feels, just like I do, that we couldn't have managed without you.'

'It's nothing.' All Emma wanted was for this girl to shut up. If she knew the truth, what would she say? If she knew the truth about her Keithie? 'I've quite enjoyed it, actually. Tom's good company.'

'Has he behaved himself?' Lesley was off then, chattering about nappies and feeding and how good the nurses had been and what she must do with herself before Keith arrived back. 'I look a terrible mess.'

In fact she looked remarkably pretty, her pale face drawn, with shadowed eyes, but bright with relief that it was over and her baby on the road to recovery.

In the end it was Tom who secured Emma's release, becoming too boisterous for the ward and allowing her to say: 'I think we'd better go now. I'll bring him back tomorrow, if you like, but you look as though you could do with a rest.' He cried briefly and had to be torn from his mother's skirts but by the time they reached the car-park he had cheered up.

'We'll go to my house now,' Emma said, as she reversed out of her space. 'You can play at my house for a while.'

With luck, Poppy would be at home and would take care of him while she packed and looked through her mother's things. There would probably be messages too, and she'd need to pick up eggs and bread and anything else that could be useful. Lesley's face kept intruding into her thoughts, animated and laughing because her world had ceased to rock. It must be frightening to be so tied up in a husband and children, to be reliant on another human being for your happiness. Most women did it . . . take Poppy and her Charlie . . . but she came from different stock. Her mother had never been dependent on anyone except herself. 'I'm like her,' Emma thought, 'a self-sufficient woman.' Esther Gaunt would have liked that title. It had made her a cold mother, though. Or perhaps cold was the wrong word: 'distant' was better. A distant mother, loving and caring, but always at a remove.

Emma carried Tom out of the car and up the steps to the hall. Poppy's door was ajar, and she called up the stairs: 'Poppy, it's me. I've brought someone to see you.'

Poppy came out on to the landing clad in a peacock-blue djellaba, rollers spiking from the top of her head like a crown.

'Who's this, then?' She smiled at Tom but when she turned to Emma her face clouded. 'You're not getting yourself involved, I hope? I've heard of some bizarre

situations, I've been in a few, come to that, but, God –
this takes the biscuit!'

All the same, she held out her arms to Tom and
looked pleased enough when he came.

'Can you keep him for a few minutes while I throw
some things in a bag?' asked Emma.

Poppy nodded. 'I suppose so . . . but do you have to
go back? Where's the family?'

Emma frowned and shook her head. 'Not now. I'll be
back tomorrow, when one of the grans is coming to
stay. I'll give you all the details later.'

'Do you mean to say the wife doesn't know? No, I
suppose she doesn't or else she'd never allow this.' She
was nodding at Tom as she spoke. 'You'll get attached,
you know. You're only human, however you may pretend.'

It was good to make her escape down to the peace of
her own rooms. Emma shut the door behind her and
looked around. All ordered, all familiar. There were
two messages on the answering machine, and she pressed
the switch and turned up the volume. The voices followed her as she moved round the kitchen and then
went into her bedroom.

*'This is Stella Ritchie. Are you free on the tenth of
next month? There's this man I want you to meet.'* She let
the message roll through; she could check it later and
put it in her diary if necessary.

The boy came next. *'You promised to get in touch.
You'll have to do it eventually. I don't know why you
keep putting it off.'*

Emma tried to tell herself he was whingeing but, in
reality, it was honest anger she heard in his voice. She
was seized with a sudden amazement. This business
with the boy was the weirdest, most bizarre thing that

had happened in her entire life! An inheritance from a stranger – it was the kind of thing that made the front pages of the tabloids. And yet there had been times, many times in the past few days, when she had forgotten all about it. At any other time she would have been obsessed by it, been thinking of it day and night, ringing friends for advice, perhaps even consulting her solicitor. Certainly she would have taken it seriously. As it was, she had hardly taken it in. It seemed not to matter, to be so far out on the periphery of her life that it could have been happening to someone else, a character in a play.

She went into her bedroom and began to pack an overnight bag. Tomorrow she would do something serious about the boy, not in response to his angry phone call but because, whether or not she liked it, she had become involved in a legal process and must treat it with some respect. Making the decision relieved her, allowing her to consign the boy and the will to the back-burners of her mind and get on with her packing.

She took three pairs of pants: that would surely be enough. A nightdress, a robe and slippers. Two clean shirts, two pairs of jeans, one of which she changed into to make room in the bag. Everything she put into the bag cheered her. Without your possessions you felt vulnerable; when you had a spare pair of clean knickers you could face up to anything.

She packed an insulated bag with stuff from the fridge and tipped her fruit bowl in as well. She carried the bags into the hall and pressed the button on the answering machine once more. It flashed E for empty and then, when she failed to clear it down, began to recite its messages again. *'You promised to get in touch.*

You'll have to do it eventually. I don't know why you keep putting it off.'

Emma suddenly wanted to ring him back, but she didn't have his number. Shit! She fished in her bag and found the piece of paper on which he had written the solicitor's name and phone number. It was probably a business number and this was Sunday evening: still, at least she could say she had tried. She dialled and then, as she heard the male voice at the other end, lowered herself to her knees beside the telephone table, a little taken aback.

'I'm sorry. I didn't expect anyone to be there.'

'Why ring then?' The tone was uncompromising and Emma felt her spirits revive.

'Who is this?'

'It's Robert Eden. Who are you?'

'It's Emma Gaunt. I'm ringing because . . .'

'You were going to ring on Friday,' he interrupted.

'Yes, I know.' She refused to apologize. He had the manners of a badly brought-up ticket tout. 'Something else cropped up.'

'Something so all-demanding that you couldn't pick up a phone?'

'Yes. As a matter of fact, yes.'

'We must excuse you then.' Robert Eden sounded far from forgiving. 'However, as this is Sunday, my day of rest, I'd appreciate it if you came to the point. There are two young people of whom, apart from representing them professionally, I am rather fond. They are understandably distressed by their father's premature death and bewildered by your inclusion in his will. The least you can do . . .'

It was her turn to interrupt. 'You said "Premature" death?'

There was a pause and she realized he was regretting what he had said. 'Yes, well, perhaps premature is the wrong word. I meant to say "early death". He was only fifty. You don't expect to lose your father at that age . . .' Again there was hesitation, as though he were picking his words carefully. 'Still, all that is beside the point. It was your suggestion to come here, but it could all be handled at a distance. I'd need proof of your identity, of course. Perhaps your solicitor . . .'

'I don't want it,' Emma said starkly. 'Whatever it is he's left me, I don't want it. I *am* interested in knowing if it's really me he meant it for, and if so, why – I'll admit that. But I neither want nor need the bequest. I have more than enough money of my own.' There was satisfaction in being able to say that and know it was true. Even greater satisfaction in the silence at the other end. Gaunt – one; pompous lawyer – nil. She had the whip-hand now and she used it.

'I'd have rung your client but I don't have his number. He's also a very aggressive young man. You might speak to him about that if you care so much for him. Tell him I'll come north when I'm ready, not one moment before. And all the calls in the world won't make me move any faster.'

Robert Eden had recovered now and he intervened before she could go on. 'I see. Well, you've made your position very clear. I'll tell my client to expect you in the next few days. Good evening.' Before Emma could reply she heard the click of his receiver.

Damn him! She should have had the satisfaction of ending the call. So it was evens now: one to her, one to him. She grinned at herself in the mirror. Forty-eight hours alone with a two-year-old had certainly revealed her true mental age. Tit for tat was for the schoolyard. She must make sure that by the time she went to Durham she had regained some maturity.

She went out into the hall, half expecting to hear whimpers from above, half hoping Tom had missed her. But there was only the sound of giggling which grew as she mounted the stairs to Poppy's door. Almost there, she remembered the photographs, put down her bags and ran back downstairs. What had a fifty-year-old man, a total stranger as far as she knew, been doing with her holiday snaps, not to mention her graduation-day photograph? She opened the door of her mother's room, expecting the old familiar scent of perfume and flowers. But there was only dust and the unmistakable odour of disuse.

Emma sat down on the bed and looked around her. It was only in fairy-tales that you could lock up a room and keep it enchanted. In real life, a neglected room sagged. Where once there had been crisp chintz and linen and shining surfaces there was only dust and decay. The African violet on the mantelpiece had shrivelled to a fossil and even the mirror of the dressing-table was clouded. It would probably strike an outsider as a room in need of a spring-clean. To her, who remembered it as it had been, it was a reproach. Tomorrow, or as soon as she was free, she would do something about it – perhaps restore it to its former state, perhaps blitz it out of existence and create a room of her own. She postponed a decision as to which and started to look for the photograph album.

She expected it to be in the dressing-table, but there was nothing but the usual jewellery: costume pieces in a Terry's chocolate box, better ones in velvet-lined cases. Her mother had loved her jewellery. There would be decisions to be made about that, too, and most of them with Poppy in mind.

Emma turned to the chest when the dressing-table yielded nothing, and hit lucky with the top drawer, where there were several yellow packets of holiday snaps, and then the album behind. She lifted it, carried it to the bed and turned to the first page. Emma at the seaside aged four or five, tummy protruding above spotted pants. Nothing before that, which seemed odd. And no photographs of her mother, unless with her. She riffled through the pages. There must be photographs of her as a baby somewhere, and of her mother and father before she was born? No time to search now, though. She turned the pages looking for gaps but found none. If the source of those pictures in Durham had been her mother, they had been given away before they got as far as her album. Emma closed it with a snap. No time to go through the packets today; she was trespassing on Poppy's good nature.

She carried the album back to the drawer and slipped it into its place. There was a small box at the back of the drawer, dark corded silk, the size of a cigarette packet. It looked like a jeweller's box, perhaps one to hold a watch. Emma pulled it out, intending to put it with the rest of the jewellery, and opened it up.

At first she thought it was an insignia, a mass of gold metal in an odd shape with four inset stones which might, or might not, be gems. Whatever it was, it was ugly. She picked it up, feeling the prick of a pin on the back. So it was a brooch! She carried it to the window and saw that it was indeed a brooch in the shape of a sheep, crouched to the ground. The carving of the fleece was really quite clever, but the sightless eye in the gold head was offputting. She put it back into the box and slipped it into the desk drawer. Odd that her mother had never mentioned it. The box looked almost new.

She took a last look round, repeating her vow to do something about the dereliction, and ran back upstairs.

Poppy's room was always dishevelled by normal standards, but now it looked like a bomb site, its frilly scattercushions and roly-poly arm-rests strewn around the floor. Poppy was spreadeagled on the carpet, a triumphant Tom astride her. 'Gee-up,' he said, seeing he had an audience.

'No more,' Poppy moaned. 'I'm dead!'

'What's going on?' Emma said, attempting to restore order.

'Only rape and pillage of an elderly spinster. What've you been feeding this one on, four star?'

Tom was stretching adoring arms to Poppy's still recumbent form. 'More horsey. Gee-up!' Poppy moaned and rolled on to her face, the tot bestriding her. Panting she raised herself on to her hands and knees, carrying him upwards on her back like a rodeo rider. Her backside, in the satin djellaba, loomed like a mountain range but the bare pink feet looked small and oddly appealing. She embarked on a vigorous bucking session while Tom clung limpet-like to her shoulders. She would have made a marvellous grandmother, Emma thought, as she bent to scoop him up in her arms.

'Come along, range-rider. Time you were going home.'

Poppy accompanied them to the door, wheezing with exertion, her large breasts heaving under peacock-blue satin. 'Don't think I approve of all this, Em, because I don't. All the same, he's a wee smasher.' She reached to kiss the little boy. 'Bye-bye, darling. Come and see Aunty Poppy again.'

Emma saw her face change suddenly, from doting grandmother to coquettish adolescent. Charlie was coming up the stairs towards them, clad for once in an open-necked shirt and slacks. 'Hallo, then, who's this young man?' His curling moustache had caught the toddler's eye and the older man pulled it out obligingly and let it fall back into place.

Tom laughed a little nervously, and Charlie turned his attention to Poppy. 'Got the joint in, old girl? Sun's nearly over the yard-arm. Time for the beef and three veg.'

'I don't like him,' Emma thought suddenly. 'For all the cheap and cheerful chatter, I wouldn't trust him an inch.' She made her goodbyes and carried Tom down to the car, all the while thinking of Poppy waiting hand and foot on such a sham. Women were fools.

She was half-way to Keith's before she could acknowledge that what she had felt just then was simple jealousy of the one person who could monopolize Poppy's attention to the exclusion of everything and everyone else.

Behind her, Tom was surprisingly silent and when Emma glanced in the mirror she saw that he had fallen asleep, sagging in the car-seat like a forlorn little parcel. As soon as they got home she would put him to bed, poor little thing. She realized she was smiling foolishly and it unnerved her. Tomorrow she would hand him over to his grandmother or some other proper person, and never see him again. No time to get sentimental about someone else's child. Not even Keith's.

A few drops of rain spattered her windscreen and she watched in amazement. It seemed so long since it had rained. If it kept up till she got back to the house, she would stand out in it and feel it on her face and neck.

Sunshine was all right for a while, but you couldn't beat an English rainfall.

She looked at the dashboard clock. Five p.m. and a long night to spend alone. She tried not to think about the phone-call from Keith that was sure to come. She couldn't respond to him as though they were mere acquaintances, but the thought of indulging in intimate chat with him from his wife's phone was more than she could bear. She reached for the radio button and as the news began she let the ills of everyday life drive her own troubles temporarily from her mind.

7

Monday 7 August

It was still hot and clammy but at least the forecast was promising rain. Emma could not remember such a long, hot summer. Perhaps during her childhood – but then every childhood summer was sunny and every winter a time of pristine snow.

She washed the breakfast dishes while Tom played in the garden, thinking of Keith's call the night before. His mother had rung with details of her imminent arrival to take charge, and Emma had just put down the phone when it rang again, almost immediately. She had picked it up, half-expecting to hear the grandmother's breathless tones with yet more detail of her journey and what she would expect to find when she got there. But it was the son, not the mother.

'Emma! You're still there, then?'

'Yes. Haven't you rung Lesley today?'

'I did. Zoë's improving by leaps and bounds, I hear.'

So he had known she was still here, trapped in his house by his child and its need of her.

'How has today gone?' she said, trying to sound executive.

'Well. Linkman likes our ideas on the new software.'

'Good.'

'I see Abrahamson tomorrow, so fingers crossed.'

'Yes.'

'I love you, Emma. You've been a brick.'

She wanted his gratitude, certainly expected it; but

once again it irritated her. 'It's OK. I don't mind really.'

'No, honestly, Emma, w – I'm really grateful.'

He had almost said, '*We're* really grateful.' So they had discussed her again, husband and wife. Dear, good, untypical-employer Emma, always at hand in a crisis! God's truth! She tried to think of something, anything, with which to wound him. 'It's so hot here. I wish I'd planned to go away somewhere cool.'

But he wouldn't take the bait. 'It is hot. I'll be glad to get out of New York, and get home soon. There's not much here for me without you.'

'Of course. Come back as soon as you can.'

'I'm longing to see you, Emma.' Here was her chance.

'Me too, but I may not be here. I must go to Durham and settle this business of the bequest . . . you know, I told you about it?'

Keith sounded crestfallen, and at once she was contrite.

'But that won't take long: a day, two at the most. I'll probably have it sorted by the time you get here. We planned your two-week stay thinking it'd give us time together. Now that's off . . .'

'You *could* still come to New York. Once Lesley's home . . . or as soon as mother's in charge?'

So he would rather spend time with her than fly home to his sick daughter. Emma felt at once elated and disappointed in him. Or was he playing a bluff, knowing she would not come? Was he confused lover or cynical deceiver? It was a relief when their goodbyes were said and she could go to her bed.

Now she leaned on the draining-board watching Tom at play and recalling every line of the conversation. Why had she been so mean? Perhaps she was less in

love than she had thought? Or was some terrible conventional streak she had never suspected surfacing?

The phone rang in the hall and she dried her hands
on a tea-towel as she ran to answer. It was Lesley.

'I just thought I'd check what time Mum was coming.'
So she called his mother 'Mum'. The cosiness of the
image was a further defeat. Lesley had it all tied up.

'She's arriving around one. I'll have some lunch ready
for her. After that I'll get away, if you think she'll be
OK.'

'Of course. We've imposed on you enough. I'll never
be able to thank you, Emma, but I'll try when I get
home. You must come to dinner when Keith gets back
. . . or we'll take you out somewhere really nice. Before
Mum goes, so we'll have a baby-sitter. Keith's going to
get home as soon as he can . . . he's desperate to see
Zoë.'

Oh, how easily she could puncture her rival's com-
placency: *He won't be home if I fly out to join him*!'
That's all it would take to bring the smug little bitch
down to earth. Except that she couldn't do it. Besides
if she had said 'yes' last night he might have back-
pedalled madly, and come home anyway.

When Lesley had gushed her gratitude once more and
said goodbye, Emma dialled her office number. 'Amy.
No, I'm not calling from Cairo, I'm still here.'

Amy was full of sympathy to hear of a holiday
cancelled to do a good turn for a colleague. 'Well, I
think you're a brick. You mean, there really wasn't
anyone else, not a soul?'

'Afraid not. Their families aren't in this area. Besides,
that business in Durham – you remember, the boy? –
I'll have to do something about that. I just wanted you
to know I'll be at home on and off if anything crops up.

And I'll ring in occasionally. But I'm sure you'll handle everything brilliantly.'

She did have confidence in Amy, she reflected when she had rung off. Not only that, she liked her. Perhaps Amy might become more than a colleague eventually? It would be nice to have a friend of her own age in Manchester. All her girlfriends from school and college seemed to have migrated to London, or married and moved to Cheshire, and she seldom saw them now.

She returned the tea-towel to its hook and looked at the kitchen. Not bad! At least you could see the working surfaces. But as she went to check on Tom in the garden she wondered how well she would have coped with a baby and a husband as well as a toddler. 'Don't get cocky, Emma,' she thought and the sight of her chipped nails on the edge of the door brought her further down to earth. Running a home was not a doddle, and if she ever had thought that, she was rapidly changing her mind. She had not really had a minute to herself since she got here, except after Tom's bedtime, and by then she was quite ready to sink into a torpor. She had tidied the kitchen and fed the washing-machine, but had never actually got down to any real housework. Guiltily she surveyed the kitchen floor and realized it needed a wash with mop and bucket before grandma arrived.

After that she dusted and hoovered the living-room, shaking out cushions and tidying the piled books and videos that seemed to be everywhere. She found some sewing behind a cushion, turquoise-blue cotton voile, a tiny dress with the bodice already smocked in white and lemon. For Zoë no doubt. So that was how Lesley spent her evenings! She felt a pang of remorse at the thought of the number of evenings Lesley had spent alone on her account, and then a sense of exultation. What she had with Keith was good – the best! She mustn't lose sight of that.

There was time to take Tom to the park before preparing lunch. He held her hand and chattered inconsequentially on the way, and she liked it immensely. He was good fun. If ever she and Keith did get together permanently, she would enjoy his children. You read such dreadful things about step-parenting, but Emma felt she would be rather good at it, better than at the seven-days-a-week drudgery of proper parenthood. All the same, a child of your own ... and your lover's ... each of you fused in one perfect other being. She could get through the baby stages somehow, and then it would be good to have a growing child, an intelligent human being to challenge and fence with and sometimes comfort. Someone to comfort you when you were past it.

Emma was saved from morbid thoughts by the sight of lady bowlers in action. Large-busted ladies, immaculate in white pleated skirts and clumpy white shoes. 'Ducks,' Tom said, for no apparent reason, and she laughed out loud at the appropriateness of his word.

They stayed too long at the bowling green and had to race home to prepare lunch. Ham and salad and hard-boiled eggs in paprika mayonnaise. Tom tasted everything as it was washed and chopped and garnished, and then ran out to play again, burping happily.

Keith's mother arrived in a taxi, perspiring slightly inside her grey worsted suit and high-necked blouse. 'Dear me, isn't this a carry-on?' She wasn't what Emma had expected – a small, insignificant woman with iron-grey hair and an incipient moustache on her upper lip. She had three cases and an overflowing plastic carrier.

'Well, you don't know how long this sort of thing will last, do you? I've told my neighbour not to expect me back till I arrive. Thank goodness for the Neighbourhood Watch. I've got some nice pieces ... I wouldn't like to see them go.'

They tried to sit Tom down at the table but he was disinclined. In the end Emma buttered him a piece of Ryvita and let him go.

'He's ever such a good little boy, usually. I expect he's overwrought,' his grandmother said. 'Of course he's bright, and they're never easy to handle. I should know, my Keith ... well, of course, you know the intellect! Reading at three, as true as I stand here. My friends wouldn't believe it, so I said, "Read this newspaper, Keithie ..." and off he went, just like Alvar Liddell. He's never been a bit of trouble. Married a lovely girl – not a great housekeeper, but a great one for her home, all the same. That's what matters.'

Emma sat on, letting the words flow over and around her.

'Nowadays, you hear such things! Broken homes, babies scattered here and there like so much confetti. It wouldn't've done in my day. But I never had to worry with his father, and I've never had to worry with my son. "He'll never let you down," I said to Lesley. "You won't find him with lipstick where it should not be."'

Emma couldn't take much more of it, this blind faith in a man who was not worthy of it. She had already had it from Lesley, now from his mother. How she would love to speak out – but the triumph would be short-lived, the fall-out never-ending.

She made coffee and then went upstairs to collect her things. There was not much of Keith in the bedroom, hardly anything at all. It was Lesley's room, Lesley's boudoir, the place into which he would creep to claim his conjugal rights. 'Oh shit!' she said out loud and then went downstairs to say goodbye. Briefly to Tom, who had other things on his mind. Interminably to his grandma, who went into raptures at the sight of the red Capri. 'You modern girls, you've no need to get married! You've got it all for yourselves.'

It was silly to cry, Emma thought as she blinked back tears on the way into town. She was tired, that was the trouble. Tired and confused, and she would have to do something about it if she were to sort out the Durham business and then snatch a few days away somewhere before going back to work.

She pulled into the car-park of a supermarket and grabbed a trolley. She had deliberately run down her cupboards because she was going to New York; now she would have to stock up again. She resisted the impulse to buy pleasure foods, chocolate and cream and goo. If she did she would binge on them, and then be filled with self-disgust. Instead she went for wholefoods and wound up feeling virtuous but deprived.

She decided to call on Poppy and cadge a cup of coffee, but the shop was full and she found herself displaying a cashmere skirt and shawl to an elegant lady who fingered the seams suspiciously and left empty-handed.

'Thank God,' Poppy said, when the last customer could be left to an assistant. 'Let's have a cuppa in peace.' They retreated to the darkness at the top end of the shop and settled with their mugs.

'You've got rid of Baby Bunting, then?' Poppy asked.

Emma nodded. 'He wasn't a scrap of trouble. I could have carried on really. It was . . . well, quite nice.'

'That's exactly why I'm glad it's over.' Poppy's mouth was pursed, a rare event. 'We don't want you going broody, not at this juncture. And don't tell me you're too level-headed – your kind are the worst when they kick over the traces. I've . . .'

'. . . seen it,' Emma finished for her, in a fair imitation of the older woman's tone.

'Yes, miss. I've not only seen it, I've lived through it. I know what it can do to you, that yen for a baby of your own. And the present set up's not right for you to have one.'

'If you mean Keith, he's very right. He's the only man who has ever satisfied me, Pops. I don't mean physically, although there's that too. But we think alike, we share the same ambitions, we have the same sense of humour, God dammit. And you say I should give this up – this match – because he happens to be married to someone else. I don't want to hurt anyone. She has her territory, let me have mine.' It was time to change the subject. 'How's Charlie?'

Poppy looked at her steadily for a moment, as though to say, 'I know what you're doing,' but the lure of talking about her man was too much for her. 'Now Charlie *is* getting broody. Very much pipe and slippers. He even voiced it the other day, not in so many words, but just something about it being a mug's game being on your own at our age.'

'I'll have turquoise-blue for my bridesmaid's dress,' Emma said reflectively. 'Pure silk, gunmetal shoes . . .'

'You'll have to mend your ways, miss, before you follow me down the aisle,' Poppy said, and then, leaning to pat Emma's arm, 'I couldn't bear to see you hurt, darling. I'm not going all goody-goody on you ... I'd have a nerve to do that, the way I've lived ... but I want the best for you.'

'I'll bear it in mind,' Emma said. 'Now pin back your ears: I need some help. I'm off to Durham tomorrow, to see the Culrose boy. I want to poke around a bit and see if I can trace any long-lost relatives, and you're my only link, Poppy. So put your brains to steep ...'

'I'll have to find them first, darling. I will try, but I'm not hopeful. What about your mother's papers and things? She wasn't one for confiding in people, you know that, but there must be something written down. Birth certificates, that sort of thing?'

'I'm going to go through them. I looked last night, just to see where those photographs might have come from, but it was a bit gruesome in that room. Still, I'll have to get down to it.' A thought struck her. 'I did find something, a brooch. Costume jewellery, a big gold thing in the shape of a sheep with some odd ornamentation. The outside of the box was a bit faded, but inside the lining was like new. I don't think she'd ever taken it out.'

Poppy shook her head. 'Can't say I ever saw it.'

Now that she had ruled out the possibility of its being a gift from Poppy, Emma felt free to criticize it. 'It was ugly in a striking kind of way. I just thought it was odd that Mother never wore it.'

'You'll find all sorts of things, once you start,' Poppy said gloomily. 'Esther was a bit of a magpie.'

'You can help me tonight?' Emma suggested. 'I'll cook ...'

But Poppy was shaking her head. 'Not tonight, Josephine. Charlie's picking me up here.'

Emma felt utterly cast down at the thought of a night

alone but it wouldn't do to show it. 'Going somewhere nice?'

'A meal and some jazz thing. You know him and his Fats Waller.' Privately Emma thought Charlie was stuck in a time-warp, somewhere around the end of the war, but Poppy was humming 'My Very Good Friend the Milkman Says', and the smile on her face was one of pure contentment.

They rifled through the new stock together, Poppy picking out an item now and then and holding it against her hip. 'Try this. Treat yourself!' In the end Emma bought a mohair jacket in a rich wine colour and wrote out a cheque.

'You could take our mark-up off?' Poppy said, and then, when Emma shook her head, 'What a little goody-goody you are. There ought to be perks for the joint proprietors.'

'There are,' Emma said drily. 'They're called dividends, and we collect them once a year. Now get cracking and sell something to outsiders.'

She kissed Poppy's cheek on the step and tried to look cheerful. 'Have a good evening. See you tomorrow.'

It was still unbearably hot out in the street, and she counted the days till the end of August. Surely the weather would break before September?

Emma listened to the news as she drove home. The dock strike was finally over, and Liverpool dockers were going back to work. She tried to feel pleased, disapproving of the strike-weapon as she did, but it had been such a non-event that she couldn't welcome its ending as a triumph of common sense. Perhaps they had a point, after all? Without all the facts you shouldn't judge, but all too frequently you did.

She made an omelette when she got home and carried it through to the window-seat. The garden looked parched, the grass a sickly grey-green, the leaves of the trees drooping. If *only* it would rain! She felt arid herself, in desperate need of refreshment. She needed Keith, needed his arms around her, his voice in her ear. But she didn't want to take his phone-call and she knew it would come. He would ring Lesley at the hospital, then his mother at home, and then, and only then, his mistress. She said the hated word again and again under her breath. *Mistress, whore, bit on the side*: was she any or all of those things? When she was with him it was so easy to believe all was right. Now, with the Atlantic Ocean between them, it was unbelievably difficult.

The egg stuck in her throat and eventually she pushed the plate aside. It was not the distance that was shaking her, it was the contact with Lesley, with Tom, with his mother ... those pillars that made up Keith's real life, and made what he had with her seem so insubstantial. It would be different when he came home and they could screw. *Screw, screw, mistress, mistress* ... face it, Emma, that's all you wanted, that's all you've got. No use whingeing now.

She had to do something to break this mood, so she carried her plate to the kitchen and then made her way purposefully up to her mother's room. But on the threshold she chickened out. Not tonight, she was not in the mood for nostalgia. She was not in the mood for anything. She went back downstairs and grasped the other nettle, Stephen Culrose's solicitor.

'Hallo, this is Emma Gaunt. Sorry to ring after hours, but I had no option. I promised to call when I was free to come north, and I'm leaving in the morning. Around noon probably. I'll eat on the way, and be with you about three-thirty ... No, I'm staying for a day or two, until we've worked things out ... No, thank you, I've booked into an hotel.'

She hadn't as yet, but she didn't need help from him. He was going through the motions of being polite but his innate boorishness showed through. She'd heard about north-eastern men. He probably had a down-trodden wife somewhere and belonged to a boozy rugger club.

When she put down the phone Emma looked through her AA book for an hotel, and booked herself in for three nights at the five-star St Nicholas. It was seven-thirty. If Keith was going to ring ... she reached out and flicked on the answering machine. When she felt up to it ... after she'd had a drink ... she'd return it to manual. But not just yet.

She was trying to come to terms with the change in her own attitude. She had always been anxious to demonstrate how grown-up she was about his commitment to wife and children, understanding about cancelled dates, about the frantic need to check body and clothing for tell-tale signs. How could she now retract that acceptance of his other life? Impossible to explain to him how the sight of Lesley, attractive even though unwashed and scantily dressed, had thrown her. How the sight of a baby, his baby, at its mother's breast had made the earth not only move for her but rock uncomfortably on its foundation.

It was ten o'clock when he rang, at the end of his working day, but the switch was still down and she made no move to lift the receiver.

'I wish you were there, Emma. We couldn't talk when you were at my place. Well, I felt you felt a bit constrained. I can understand that. But I wanted to talk to you tonight, to tell you how much I love you. I wish to God I had more to offer you. Sometime, maybe ... definitely ... one day, I'll be a free agent. But, oh Emma, I want you. I need you. You can stuff my damned job, if you think that's part of it. We'd have come together if we'd met in different circumstances, you must know that in your heart. Anyway, you're not there ... so I'll just say it again. I love you. I'll ring later on ...' His words were cut short as the tape ended. She got to her feet and played his call back again, and then again.

She lay for a long while after she went to bed, the room growing dark and shadowy around her, sometimes dozing, at other times thinking furiously – about Keith, about Poppy, about the Culroses and their uncharming legal adviser, about Lesley, sitting in a hospital now, the baby probably at her breast, her world secure around her like a shell. Did she owe Lesley anything? Was there such a thing as sisterhood? She felt it with Poppy, and lately with Amy. But surely Lesley was her opponent, her enemy?

She thought of Tom then, Tom of the silken hair and dimpled knuckles, the obstinate speech and the seducer's smile. 'I want him,' she whimpered and curled in the bed, arms around upbent knees. But who it was she wanted and what she would do if she had him was shadowy. 'I want,' she thought, straightening out at last and trying to compose herself for sleep, 'I want. There is a want in me. A lacuna, a void.' She surveyed her own incompleteness for a while, blaming it alternately on her upbringing and her lack of gumption. She tried very hard to think of the next day and the journey to Durham, concentrating on the logistics, on putting faces to those people she had not yet seen – the sister and the rude guy.

None of it worked and at last Emma got up and put on the new mohair jacket over her nightdress. It was light as thistledown, luxurious and all-embracing, and for a very little while it comforted her. In the end, though, it was not enough. She went downstairs, hovering over the phone until, when at last it rang again, she could snatch it up and say, 'Darling, I'm here!'

8

Tuesday 8 August

Emma listened for the sound of Poppy on the stairs, and hurried out to meet her. 'You won't see me tonight, remember? I'm going north. And do *think*, Pops, I'm depending on you. Here's the hotel where I'll be staying: I've put the Durham code on the number already, so you've no excuse. Ring me if you think of the least little thing. I'll let you know when I'm coming home.'

Poppy smelled delicious when she enfolded Emma in her arms. 'Take care, darling, they're savages up there, by all accounts. And for God's sake bring some rain back with you. I'll expire if this lasts much longer.'

It was hot and clammy, even in the semi-darkness of the hall. Poppy's face shimmered with sweat, and powder was caked around her eyes and nose. She looked old this morning and Emma was suddenly afraid.

'It's going to rain tomorrow. The forecast says so.'

'I'll really try to come up with something. I know it was a spice. Marjoram? Paprika? P'raps not. But it was something hot. Not that it's going to do you much good if I do remember, because I haven't a clue about the address.'

'I'll look it up in the phone book,' Emma said. 'There won't be too many Paprikas or Marjorams in the Durham directory. You think of the name, and leave the rest to me.'

'Why don't you look up Gaunt?' Poppy said as she went over the step. Emma had already thought of that, but her mother had always suggested that her own and her husband's families had dwindled to nothing. The elusive sister-in-law, whose name would no longer be Gaunt, seemed the only hope. All the same, it might be worth a try . . .

She waved Poppy off and then went back to her bedroom. The impulse to postpone the Durham trip was almost overwhelming but she was not going to give way. Her bedside clock said nine-fifteen: too early for a drink. She settled for coffee, sitting at the kitchen table and trying to organize her muddled thoughts.

'This is crazy,' she said at last, shaking her head to dislodge the picture of Lesley, naked and suckling her child. She rinsed her mug under the running tap, handling it so clumsily that it caught the edge of the tap and chipped. 'Shit!' she said and dropped it into the wastebin as she went back to her bedroom.

For the first time in her life she was emotionally stirred: that was all it was. She had grieved when her mother died, but had never allowed it to surface. Poppy had been the one who wept. And then Keith had come along and she had channelled everything into her feelings for him, almost glorying in the fact that she could never possess him completely *because* he was a married man with children. In a funny way it had made her feel safe, less vulnerable. A week ago she had felt so safe, so goddamn certain. Now, she felt like an amoeba, a lump of jelly with an uncertain nucleus, prey to almost anything that came along.

She blew out her breath, as though to expel negative thoughts, and began to pack methodically. Enough for three days and almost any eventuality. Track suit and sneakers for off-duty, and power-clothes for the demolition job she intended to do on the lawyer. She had softened towards the boy, recognizing what a shock it must have been to find a total stranger treated equally in his father's will. No wonder he had come on so strong at the beginning.

The lawyer – she couldn't remember his name – was another matter. He was not entitled to an attitude. It was unprofessional. And yet his dislike of her had been almost tangible, even over the phone. Well, sod him, he was about to get his come-uppance. It would do her good to let fly! It was quite a while since she had intellectually emasculated a man ... not since Cambridge ... but it was like bicycle-riding. You didn't forget the knack.

She felt almost cheerful as she loaded the car. It was not yet ten o'clock as she drove into the city and parked behind Portland Street. Getting her hair done was the first step in her master-plan.

She allowed her arms to be slipped into the pink gown and surrendered herself to soothing hands. She had a manicure while her hair was lamp-dried, and closed her eyes so that no one would feel the need to converse. A junior brought her a cup of coffee and Elton John sang softly and skilfully from outer space. *'It seems to me you lived your life like a candle in the wind, Never knowing who to cling to when the rain set in.'*

Poor Marilyn Monroe, never quite getting it right. She couldn't remember Monroe's death, but she had seen newspaper pictures of the sparsely furnished bedroom where the candle had finally flickered out. And yet the image lingered. Wonderful, wonderful Elton John. Though the image of the flickering candle was also disconcerting, somehow.

She opened her eyes as he moved on to the more optimistic 'Yellow Brick Road', and was humming along with the music when she saw the girl in the mirror, also clad in a pink gown, a sybaritic smile on her face, the child held on her knee against her breast. Mother with child! The gold band on the wedding finger was like a badge of authority.

Emma closed her eyes again but it was too late. Her jumbled thoughts had been re-activated: Lesley, Keith, Tom, the Culrose boy with the accusing eyes, Lesley, Lesley, Poppy getting old before her time, Lesley, Lesley, and the gaping mouth at the nipple. She squeezed her eyes shut, trying to think of the journey. Leeds, Wetherby, Scotch Corner . . . she had checked it on the map. But the map would not materialize in her mind's eye, only the girl in the pink gown who had Lesley's face, and the baby at the breast who was Zoë. And Keith, benign, watching his wife nourish his child. Oh God, damn men. Damn mothers. Damn hormones. Damn hormones most of all!

She was glad when she was done and could walk out of the salon, slipping her earrings back, catching sight of herself in a mirrored column but taking no pleasure in the sight. If she had a child, she would still be able to work. They could sell the shop, and Poppy would put her feet up a bit and rock the crib. It would work out. She would love Keith's child, but would he? What would her child mean to him and, above all, where would it rank?

She glanced at her watch when she had unlocked the car. Eleven-twenty. She wanted to go to Keith's place and see Tom again, but it wouldn't do. Instead she drove to the hospital and parked in a side street.

'I wouldn't ask, sister, not out of visiting hours, but I'm leaving Manchester and I just wanted to see Mrs Oliphant before I went.'

The sister was middle-aged and tolerant. 'I'll let you have five minutes. After that it's lunches so you'll have to go. I wouldn't do it for everyone, but Lesley's a little treasure.'

Emma smiled but even to herself it felt like a grimace. Trust Lesley to be *persona* very *grata*. She had the knack!

'Emma!' Lesley's greeting was almost a squeal of pleasure and Emma felt her own face soften in return.

'Lesley, I'm off for a few days and I just wanted to check that you and Zoë were OK before I went.' *Was* that why she had come?

'We're fine. Zoë's blooming – feeding and sleeping all the time.' The baby lay in the crib, sound asleep. 'And Tom's on form, too; I've just spoken to mother. You did such a good job of looking after him, that's why he's so settled.'

'And I cleaned up your chaotic house,' Emma thought but did not say it. Instead she said, 'He was an absolute darling. You're lucky to have him . . . and Zoë.' There was too much fervour in her tone. Surely Lesley would suspect?

But Lesley was beaming agreement. 'I know. I am lucky. Keith's so good . . . and I have the children.' Her eyes narrowed and her voice slowed, and Emma knew she was thinking how she could phrase a few words of encouragement to her husband's spinster boss without giving offence. If Lesley said, *'One day you'll be happy, too,'* she would strike her.

Instead she found herself leaning forward to kiss Lesley's soap-fragrant cheek. 'Well, take care. I'm staying at the St Nicholas Hotel in Durham. Ring me if anything goes wrong. And tell Keith to come home as soon as he can. I expect he rings you?'

'Every night,' Lesley said. 'Every night, without fail. I really am a lucky girl.'

'Yuck, yuck, yuck,' Emma told herself as she walked back to the car. 'Yuck, yuck, yuck, and smug, smug, smug, and *wouldn't* she get a shock if she knew.' Except that Lesley would almost certainly be wise and noble in the event and emerge with all-round admiration. 'I want to hate her,' Emma thought, 'I need to hate her. But I can't.'

It was soothing to concentrate on her driving. The M62 was crowded at this time of day. A sign flashed up: *Bury, Rochdale, Oldham, Leeds*. A beautiful old viaduct appeared, and mill chimneys, giving way to trees and dry, parched grass. There were pylons, Triffid-like, along the way, and the Pennines spreading, fold on fold, purple and mysterious in the far distance. *Rochdale, Oldham, Leeds*. So Bury had been left behind.

The road was rising now, and on the left she could see Saddleworth Moor. Impossible to hear those words or see that God-forsaken place without thinking of Brady and Hindley. The leader and the acolyte? Or vice versa? Certainly Hindley displayed none of the qualities of someone whose natural place was the back seat.

She was glad when the road began to descend, and houses appeared, and she was passing over the River Calder. She pulled into a service point then and drank coffee while she looked out over the distant hills, trying not to think of anything but the remainder of her journey. Leeds, Wetherby, Scotch Corner, Durham: names she knew at the back of her mind, but which didn't mean much.

The great sprawl of Leeds appeared almost as soon

as she was back on the road, two tower blocks standing sentinel. She negotiated a tangle of tunnels and narrow roads, and then she was out in the countryside again, and before too long the majestic towers of Durham were before her.

She found the St Nicholas Hotel without much difficulty. It was quiet and elegant, and her room looked over fields and woodland. She brewed tea and took milk from the tiny fridge: she hadn't eaten since breakfast, but she didn't feel like food. She took out the telephone directory, in which she looked up 'Gaunt' – half a page of them, but none inspired her. Smiling, she looked up Curry with a 'y' and Currie with 'ie'. Six of one and four of the other. Giggling, she turned to P for Paprika, to no effect. She didn't look at Coriander or Basil. Instead she looked up Culrose D. Only one. *Culrose, David, The Wyndings, Gilesgate, Durham.*

She dialled the number and heard a young female voice answer at the other end.

'Could I speak to Stephen Culrose, please?'

'He's not here, he's at the yard. I can give you that number.'

Emma wrote it down and murmured her thanks. So the boy was attending to the business! She dialled the new number and asked for the boy again. A moment later he was there, at the other end of the line.

'It's Emma Gaunt. I'm in Durham now, at the St Nicholas.'

'I see.' He cleared his throat and she knew he was playing for time. 'Well, then, we'd better arrange to meet.'

'That *is* what I came for.' She hoped she sounded dry and not acid. 'Will you come here, or shall I come to you? I'd suggest your solicitor's office, but it's probably too late for today. Of course we could leave it until . . .'

'No!' The word almost burst from him. 'No, no sense in wasting a day. The sooner it's cleared up, the better. Can you come to our house this evening?'

Emma arranged to be at his home at seven o'clock, and then got undressed for a bath. There was a sachet of bath oil in the bathroom and she squeezed it into the swirling water. What would she find tonight – baronial splendour or seedy middle-class? The boy had a good appearance, but his state of suppressed agitation had made it difficult to judge anything else about him.

Emma lay in the scented water and thought about the night ahead. Arguments, probably. The boy was determined to believe the worst of her, and there was the sister too, probably equally adolescent and disapproving. How did you convince two children that you were not their father's whore? She could tell them the truth: that two other children had the right to disapprove, but not them? Except that that would do nothing for her image.

When she confirmed that they could keep their precious business, they might change their attitude, even become grateful? Well, that was not to be encouraged: the last thing she needed was a pair of orphans leeching on to her. The boy had all the makings of an importuner. She stepped from the bath, checking her nails to make sure her manicure was still perfect, then set about her make-up. Whatever she encountered tonight, she meant to encounter it in style.

It was seven-fifteen when she drove through the gates of The Wyndings, a sprawling grey stone house with mullioned windows, glinting now in the evening sun, a high-peaked slate roof and a Virginia creeper winding its way up to trail along the heavy cast-iron gutters. It looked like a Victorian vicarage, but there was no church in sight, only a stable block on the left, converted now to garages.

She got out of the car and crunched across the gravel to the imposing front door. Behind her the city still shimmered in the heat but she felt cool in the apricot silk dress. Her arms and neck were bare, her legs free of tights or stockings. She had gold clips in her ears and her hair was swept back into a French pleat. She felt she looked the cool executive: now all she had to do was prove it.

As she lifted a hand to the bell she realized that she had not thought of Keith for at least an hour. More importantly, she had not thought of Lesley. She heard the bell ring inside the house and the sound of a woman's feet on a tiled floor.

Emma felt her composure falter when she saw the girl: fat, plain and sullen, unadorned except for the lipstick that made a scarlet gash in the solid whiteness of her face. 'I'm April Culrose,' she said, her mouth twisting slightly as though in appreciation of the irony of her name. '*Laugh*,' her eyes said, '*get it over!*' Aloud she said, 'You'd better come inside.'

'I'm Emma Gaunt,' Emma said, feeling she should identify herself.

'I know,' the girl said and there was a wealth of disapproval in her tone. The boy was coming down the stairs, buttoning his waistcoat. The heat was almost unbearable but he was wearing a three-piece suit, shirt and tie. The girl, too, was inappropriately dressed, with a cotton cardigan over a paisley dress more suited to a grandmother. And yet the house was tasteful, elegant even.

'We'll go into the study,' Stephen said. Emma inclined her head, trying not to show her amusement at his pomposity, and followed him into a wood-panelled room with a window looking out on to water.

'Is that the river?' she asked.

The boy went to the window. 'No, it's a beck.' She moved to his side and looked out on a formal garden, a little overgrown but full now of flowers and trees burdened with apples. 'My father did the garden. We have a man, but Dad was really the one who organized it. We'll have to get down to it soon.' He turned away and walked towards a roll-topped desk.

Emma turned towards the fireplace, where a watercolour of snow hung above a marble mantelshelf. 'Is that a Farquharson?'

The boy was coming towards her, a silver photograph frame in his hand. 'Yes. It belonged to Dad.' He held out the photograph. 'This is my mother and father.'

It was a challenge and they both knew it. She took the frame from him and gazed down at a more mature and slightly more elegant April gazing adoringly at a fair-haired man with the uneasy smile of the reluctant subject. She looked at them for a long moment, glad that theirs were the faces of strangers, then she handed it back.

'They're very nice,' she said, meeting and holding his eye, 'but I've never seen either of them in my life.' His pupils flickered as though with relief, but he didn't speak and his face retained its expression of mistrust, his misery all too plain. 'He wants to believe me,' Emma thought, 'but he doesn't know what else to think.' In the doorway the girl stood, watching her brother, waiting for decisive action.

'Look,' Emma said firmly, putting her bag on a side

table and moving to a chair. 'I've come here to find out what's going on. I'm prepared to tell you everything about myself and my family, and if you're equally frank we're bound to sort it out. Perhaps there's some family link? Perhaps your father owed my family a debt? The sooner we start, the sooner we'll succeed. And when we have the answer, I'll have all I want from you. I'm quite well off, actually, and the last thing I want is another commitment, so if you see me as a threat, forget it.'

Before Stephen could reply there was the sound of a car outside and the swish of wheels on gravel. 'That'll be Robert,' April said, suddenly animated.

Emma settled herself in the leather armchair, rested her hands on the arms and crossed her legs. 'Wheel him in,' she thought, relishing the thought of a clash.

She had bargained for a lot of things, but not that he should be handsome. Arrogant, certainly, and a bit too sure of himself, but undoubtedly handsome. He was through the door and advancing towards her when she realized that he walked with a limp. The upper part of his body was well developed, massive even, and his eye-level would be about the crown of her head. But he strode on one leg, bringing the other into line with a slight wrench of muscles not designed for the action. 'Damn him,' she thought, 'he's going to get the sympathy vote.'

He towered above her, holding out a hand. 'We have met, at least on the telephone. I'm Robert Eden. I was David Culrose's solicitor, and I now act for Stephen and April.'

He smiled at the girl as he spoke and her sullen face lightened. 'She's got a crush on him,' Emma thought and felt a shaft of sympathy. It vanished swiftly as she went into battle. Robert Eden's grip on her hand had been firmer than was necessary.

'Do sit down,' she said sweetly, as though giving regal permission.

He ignored the remark and went to stand with one arm resting on the mantelshelf. 'Well, now,' he said, 'where do we start?'

The boy had moved to a corner cupboard and was taking out glasses. He signalled with his eyes and his sister went to his side. 'We have whisky, gin or sherry,' he said. Emma opted for sherry and took the brimming glass from the girl's trembling hand. Her nails were bitten to the quick and the cuticles were untrimmed and sore.

'Thank you,' Emma smiled, but there was no answering glimmer, just stolid disapproval. She turned to the solicitor. 'Before you arrived I was saying that I'm prepared to be very frank. If Stephen and April are equally open, I'm sure we can find our way through this . . . mystery.'

His eyes were sceptical. 'Mystery? Surely not.'

'Mystery,' Emma said firmly. 'I have just seen a photograph of David Culrose, and he's a total stranger to me. No doubt I can prove this if I have to, but if you can summon up the intelligence to see that I'm telling the truth we can save a lot of time.' She made herself sound doubtful of his ability to exercise even common sense and saw his lips firm in annoyance.

'If I do take your word, Miss Gaunt, where do we go from here? You have been left a bequest. Given that my late client did not just open a Manchester telephone directory and stick a pin into the G section, how did he come to leave you a sizeable portion of his estate?'

'I've been wondering about that. At first I thought it

was just a simple error, a similarity of names, something like that. Now I think it's not. There must be a connection of some sort. Somewhere our families are linked. The sooner we get down to pooling our knowledge ...' They were all looking interested. When they found out how little she had to put into the pool they might change their minds. She drew in her breath and began.

'I live in Manchester, although I was born here. I don't know where ... just that it was Durham. I was born in 1957, which makes me thirty-two. My parents split up shortly after I was born and I have no recollection of my father. His name was John Gaunt, and he came from mining stock, as did my mother. She was a very ...' She hesitated for a moment, trying to choose the right adjective. 'She was a very clever, determined woman. It must have been difficult but she built up a business, an exclusive dress shop ... a boutique. It did well, she made it succeed. I had an excellent education – private schools, university. Now I'm an IT consultant.'

Stephen and April were looking blank. 'Information Technology. It means I understand computers and that sort of thing. I worked in London until last year, when my mother took ill. My firm were very helpful. They were already thinking of expanding, so they set up a Manchester branch and put me in to run it. My mother died last year. I inherited her business, and I still have it. I run it in partnership with a friend and colleague of my mother, and it does well. So you see, between what I earn myself and what I make from the shop, I have money enough. I've never seen the man or woman in that photograph. I've never heard the name Culrose in connection with my family, although I'm beginning to suspect that's where the tie-up is.'

She paused a moment, then went on, 'What puzzles

me is that my family were of good, solid Durham stock but very definitely not wealthy. This house . . .' she nodded around the room . . .'speaks money, old money. That's a Farquharson, the furniture is mostly Georgian or good Edwardian. So there was a social gulf between the Gaunts and the Culroses. But if the connection, the link, was master and servant, why give me an equal share with his children?'

She looked at the boy, sunk in his chair but appearing somehow relieved. 'Whatever the reason, whatever we find, I'm not accepting the bequest. If that doesn't convince you I'm not covering something up, it should.'

The lawyer was running a speculative tongue along the edge of his teeth. 'Your mother,' he said. 'She died last year. Was she elderly?'

Emma grinned at him. 'I'm way ahead of you, Mr Eden. My mother was sixty-six when she died. Mr Culrose was only fifty. I don't think I'm his love-child. Besides, if I don't know my father, I certainly know who he was.'

She felt her cheeks colour a little. 'Well, I promised to be truthful so I might as well admit I know next to nothing of him. But he did exist, I assure you, and he died some years ago. I intend to contact any relatives I may have up here while I'm staying in Durham. It's possible they may help, although we can't count on it.' She offered up a prayer that Poppy would come up with something and then went into the attack. 'Now, I've bared my soul. What about something in return?'

She was looking at the boy as she spoke but something made her glance at the solicitor. His brows were down as though he was doubtful about her request.

'Well?' she said, looking back at the boy again.

The girl got up from her seat and went to the drinks cabinet. 'Do you want another drink, Robert?'

He held out his glass and she refilled it. She was about to return to her seat when he touched her arm. 'Miss Gaunt, April.'

She looked at him and then turned dutifully to Emma.

'No, thank you,' Emma said.

'It's all quite simple,' the boy said suddenly. 'My family has been in business since 1840.' There was a touch of pride in his voice. 'Dad sold the original business in Sunderland in 1958, and set up here in Durham. He married my mother in 1968. Her father was in the church. I was born in 1970 and April three years later. The business is building supplies, as I told you. We have a big turnover.' Again there was pride in his voice, but Robert Eden was shifting uneasily. 'I went away to school,' Stephen continued. 'My mother died eight years ago. Dad hasn't been well for some time ... he – worked very hard.'

He was floundering and Emma took pity on him. 'I'm so sorry, I know how you feel. Losing my mother was very painful for me and I still haven't got completely over it. It takes time.'

They had all forgotten April, but now they saw she was crying openly, rubbing her nose with the back of her hand and biting at her lower lip. Emma wanted to go to her but it wouldn't help. They were strangers.

'Come on, Pud,' Stephen said, uneasily. It was Robert Eden who went to her and handed her his handkerchief.

'I think we've cleared the air a bit,' he said, turning back to Emma. 'Shall we call it a day and start again tomorrow? There are some papers in my office it might help you to see.'

Emma was about to refuse when she saw his brows knot and the almost imperceptible shake of his head. He had something to say that he didn't want the boy and girl to hear.

'Very well. If you think it will help.'

'Do you want me to come too?' Stephen's tone was eager.

'I don't think so,' Eden said, as though he were still considering it. 'You have such a lot to cope with, it's a pity to waste your time on paperwork. I suggest I see Miss Gaunt tomorrow morning, and then we all meet up later in the day and go on from there.'

'Perhaps you'd be my guests?' Emma said. 'I'm told the meals at the St Nicholas are good. Would you all join me for dinner?' Suddenly she realized how grand she sounded, and felt her lips twitch. Fencing with Mr Eden was making her behave like a soap queen. But no one was grabbing at her invitation, so perhaps she would be left with egg on her face.

'Well,' said Robert Eden, 'I suppose we could do that.' He really was boorish, Emma thought. He made dinner with her sound like a dental appointment!

'That's settled then.' She got to her feet. 'I do hope you'll come, April. I could do with some female support.' The girl's eyes were red-rimmed but at least she was nodding. 'What time tomorrow morning?' Emma asked Robert Eden, and then cut in before he could reply. 'Shall we say ten?' She had the upper hand now and she liked it. She reached for the door and turned the knob. Nothing happened. She tugged again.

'Allow me.' His hand was large and freckled and turned the knob with ease. His shirt cuff lacked a button and the cuff was slightly frayed. Emma sum-

moned up her dignity and said, 'Thank you,' with all
the sweetness she could muster.

'Are you all right for transport?' he asked as they
moved to the front door. She was barely conscious of
his limp as she fished in her bag for her car keys. 'Yes,
thank you,' she answered and walked down the steps to
her Capri. The boy and girl stood in the doorway, Eden
behind them.

'See you tomorrow,' Emma said, reserving her smile
for the young people. If the car failed to start at the
turn of the key, she would sell it for scrap. It responded
beautifully and she drove as well as she possibly could
till she was out of sight of the gates.

She ought to eat something before bedtime but she
didn't feel like food. She parked in the hotel car-park
and went up to her room. The restaurant had been full
and noisy, and the room-service menu failed to impress.
She opened the mini-bar and mixed a gin and tonic.

There was talk of the cricket tour on the box, and
when she switched channels Mr Hawke of Australia
was pontificating. Emma wondered, not for the first
time, why he didn't do something about the plight of
his own indigenous people before offering advice to the
rest of the world, and then she switched him off.

The elation she had felt in the Culrose house was
leaving her. She neither wanted nor needed this extra
hassle. Suddenly she wanted desperately to turn back
the clock, to make it a week ago, when she was preparing for America and seven days of love.

The images came now, tormenting her. The Lesley
she had seen in the skimpy négligé; the Lesley of the
well-scrubbed face in the hospital, everybody's favourite

mum; the Lesley of her imagination, always with Keith. But she did not imagine them together, naked and writhing, and that intrigued her. It was not their coupling that tormented her, it was their comradeship: that intimacy of shared problems, shared joys. He would know everything about his wife, every tiny personal detail, the things she herself hid so carefully from him as her lover, like the fact that she shaved her legs or used tampons when she menstruated or that one breast was larger than the other. He would know all these things about his wife, take them for granted almost. He would see her as she really was – sometimes unwashed, uncombed, smelling of milk or baby urine. They were flesh of one flesh in a way that she and Keith could never be, however savage their coition.

Emma let the tears come for a while, and then she got up and washed her face. She knew exactly what was wrong. It was the week before her period, which was half the problem, and too much had happened too quickly in the last seven days. Apart from that, she had drunk sherry and gin on an empty stomach. She patted her face dry and applied lipstick and mascara. A quick comb through her hair and she was ready to face the world. She picked up her bag and made her way down to the restaurant. Tomorrow she would find out what Robert Eden was concealing, and if she was to deal with him as she wished, she needed food, a bath and a good night's sleep. The first two she would attend to herself, the third was up to the gods.

9

Wednesday 9 August

It was dark and overcast as Emma drove into the city centre. By rights that should have made it cooler, but it continued to be hot and clammy. Emma had put on a suit for her meeting with Robert Eden and the skirt band sawed at her bare skin. As soon as she got home she must lose five pounds. Considering the number of meals she had skipped lately the suit should be hanging on her, but these things never did work out as they should.

She parked in the multi-storey car-park and made her way towards the cathedral. Durham was beautiful, its narrow streets thronged with people, chattering and talking. She could see the tower of the cathedral soaring into the grey sky and the bulk of the castle brooding above the houses: Robert Eden's office was almost in its shadow. The nameplate said 'Silver and Eden', so he was the junior partner.

He kept her waiting only a moment before she was ushered into his office. It was pleasantly decorated in off-white with an old but still pretty carpet on the floor and a cabinet in the corner stuffed with sporting trophies. There were chintz curtains at the window and leafy trees beyond. Her eye went back to the cabinet, and as Eden pulled out a chair for Emma he smiled ruefully. 'I ought to put them out of sight. They only serve to irritate me.'

'What were they for?'

'Most things ... most sports, that is. I was fairly good at everything, exceptional at nothing. And then this ...' He nodded at his gammy leg. 'A car crash – nothing glamorous like a sporting injury. Still, it could have been worse. Do sit down.'

He was making an effort to be pleasant and Emma tried to reciprocate. 'It's good of you to make time for me.'

'Not at all. It's my job to execute the will. Stephen and I are co-executors.'

There was a knock at the door and a girl entered with a tray of coffee. He thanked her and began to pour. 'Sugar?'

'No, thank you.' Emma took saccharin from her bag and dropped one into her cup. They were nice cups; new but nice nevertheless. Probably Doulton, if she recognized the design. Eden offered her a plate of shortbread and, when she refused, took a piece himself, chewing enthusiastically.

'Sorry, I didn't have time to make breakfast.' So he was unmarried, or else his wife worked, too. Or was too lazy to make her husband a meal. Both his cuffs had buttons today, though. No clues there.

'These papers you wanted to show me?' she said, when pleasantries had been exchanged.

'There are no papers. Well, I suppose I could rustle up a few but they'd be irrelevant. I asked you to come here because, now that we've buried the hatchet ...' Eden was grinning, but Emma was not yet ready to unbend. He raised his brows and nodded slightly, acknowledging the rebuff. 'Well, I thought I ought to put you in the picture about David Culrose. It's not too pretty. Nothing horrific, but things I'd rather not discuss in front of a man's children.'

It was her turn to nod. 'I see. Thank you.'

She let him top up her cup and settled back. He bit into another piece of shortbread, laid it in his saucer and began.

'You heard Stephen say it was a long-established business. From 1840, I think. That was a Nathaniel Culrose. He started a timber business out of the port of Sunderland, Swedish timber mostly. He married a Swedish girl and they prospered. I know all this because they're a bit of a northern legend – or they were. The firm grew between the wars, and Edward Culrose, David's father, left him a prosperous business. Unfortunately Edward made the mistake of dying comparatively young: I think it was in 1957, somewhere around then. David was still not much more than a boy at that time, rather like Stephen today. He'd've been about eighteen too. Very attractive young man, by all accounts, but he was a wreck when I took over his affairs five years ago. Booze. That's what killed him.'

He saw Emma's frown of puzzlement. 'Did Stephen suggest it was his heart? Well, he died of an internal haemorrhage caused by cirrhosis of the liver. But there was something about him, right up to the last – charm, I suppose. It's not a quality I've ever possessed but I recognize it in others.' Something bitter sounded in his tone, something beyond sarcasm.

'You said the business originated in Sunderland?' asked Emma. Eden nodded.

'Yes, that was what David inherited: a thriving builders' supply business in Sunderland, with offshoots in some of the outlying districts. But he sold out almost immediately, and set up again here in Durham. At first it went well; that was the beginnings of the DIY boom.

But he'd lost his early enthusiasm for the work, by all accounts.

'I grew up in Belgate. It's a colliery village,' Eden went on.

At the back of Emma's mind something stirred. Belgate: she had heard that name before, once, a long time ago.

'My father was an unpaid official in the miners' union. We moved to Durham city when he became a full-time officer. I went to school here, studied law, and joined Saul Silver when qualified. By that time the Culrose business was in trouble. David Culrose just didn't seem to care. He'd married in the late '60s. She was the local vicar's daughter, a plain, awkward woman. He was courteous to her but he never loved her, any fool could see that. They had the children. She kept house, he drank.'

'Didn't the children make a difference?'

'He loved them after a fashion, and they certainly loved him. You've seen April: my God, I'm sorry for that kid. Stephen has a dying business on his hands. There are competitors, now, thriving, thrusting organizations that are wiping the floor with Culrose and Co. You've inherited a third of nothing much.'

'What about the assets? There must be some. What kind of site do they have?'

Eden looked startled and for the first time Emma grinned. 'I'm sorry, but I'm a business-woman, remember? My mind automatically clicks into gear when you present me with a problem. I'm not looking to asset-strip to get my share. I'm thinking of the boy and girl, what they'll have if the business goes. You don't seem to think much of its viability?'

'There's a good site. Equipment. Stock. A loyal if

inept work-force, although they'll be a liability if the firm goes down and they have to be paid off. But the consequences of selling out would be disastrous for the boy. He's bright – he turned down an Oxbridge offer to join his father. I advised against it, but you should've seen the fervour. If the business goes now, however well he comes out of it he'll see it as a defeat.'

'For a while. But if he bales out now he'll at least have a stake. He can build something new of his own.'

Eden's tone was sharp: 'You do have a business brain, Miss Gaunt. I envy you your incisive way of looking at things.'

It was a reproach and Emma's old resentment stirred. 'I don't think there's any point in our discussing the future of the Culrose business empire, Mr Eden: that will be up to you and your clients. I came here to work out why I've been drawn into all this, and nothing you've told me helps.'

'You have no Sunderland connections?'

'Not as far as I know. Unfortunately, as I said last night, I know very little. How long do we have before you have to execute the will?'

He threw up his hands. 'As long as it takes, within reason. I'm certainly not going to do anything in a hurry. My only worry is whether or not the boy can hold the business together *pro tem*. If he's forced to sell eventually, a lot will depend on his current trading figures.'

'If he sells out as a going concern, you mean?'

'Yes. I think that's a possibility we should at least keep in contention. For the time being, anyway.'

Eden held out his hand as Emma left his office. 'Truce?'

'Truce,' she said. 'At least till we've shared our meal to-night.'

She walked in the ancient city up narrow streets to the Palace green. The cathedral lay ahead, not grey as she had expected, but beige and beautiful. She went inside and kneeled in the mystic darkness. She had almost forgotten how to pray. 'Our Father, which art in Heaven, hallowed be thy name. Please make sense of all this, God. If you exist, that is. Someone, something give me a quiet mind.' She put her head on her hands and for a few moments there was nothing, no images to torment her. Refreshed, she got to her feet and walked into the open air and back to her car.

As she crossed the St Nicholas foyer and asked for her key, the hall porter looked up and smiled. 'There's a message, Miss Gaunt. From a Miss Beresford.'

Pleased, Emma tore it open. '*Good news, ring me,*' it said. Too impatient to go up to her room first, she made the call at the reception desk.

'Poppy? It's me. I got your message.'

'Darling, it's lovely to hear you. I remembered, poppet. I thought and thought, just like you said . . . and it came to me. Mustard!'

'That's my aunt's name?'

'No, darling. Colman's. Colman's mustard. She was called Colman. I told you it was something hot.'

Emma was still laughing as she ran up to her room. Colman. Not uncommon, but at least it wasn't Brown or Smith. She opened the directory and ran her finger down the columns. Plenty of Colmans, but a manage-able number, even if she had to ring all of them.

She struck lucky on the eighth call. 'Forgive me for

bothering you. I'm trying to trace a Mrs Colman whose maiden name was Gaunt?'

'That's my mother-in-law. She was Peggy Gaunt before she married Dad.' The girl at the other end sounded pleased, even excited to volunteer the information.

'Is she . . . is she still . . .' Emma was trying to find a nice way of asking if Peggy Colman *née* Gaunt was still alive, but the girl misinterpreted her intentions.

'Oh yes, they're still in Sunderland. Do you want their address?'

'Sunderland?'

'Yes. They've lived there for as long as I can . . . well, since before I met Billy. She came from Belgate originally, if that's what you mean?'

So it *was* the right one. She had heard her mother mention Belgate once, she was sure of that now. 'I see. Yes, if you could give me her address . . .'

Emma bought an A-Z of Sunderland in the hotel papershop and looked up St Peter's Walk. It was near to the river, according to the map, so it should be easy to find. She had bought a Mars bar along with the A-Z and ate it in the car as she drove out of Durham.

In the Sunderland town centre she negotiated a one-way system until she found herself going over the bridge. It was one o'clock. Lunch-time. She wouldn't like to interrupt a meal. On the other hand, she didn't have any time to stooge around. She pulled up for a moment, located St Peter's Walk on the map exactly, and drove up to her aunt's door.

It had been warm in the car, and it was even warmer out on the pavement. She ran a finger around her skirt band and eased the neck of her jacket. The house in front of her was modern and neat. Behind her she could

see the yellow cranes of the shipyards, and tower-blocks
on the far side of the Wear. She looked at her watch,
wondering again whether or not to knock. It would be
breakfast time in New York. Would Keith be sitting
down to hash browns, or was he even now on a plane
coming home? Home to Lesley. But Emma was not
going down that road again, not now. She lifted a hand
and rang the doorbell, while her stomach suddenly
churned at the prospect of facing an aunt she had never
seen.

It was a man who answered the door. Thin hair
carefully combed across a bald pate; a face seamed and
creased with lines of good humour above a short-sleeved
shirt with a panther motif on the breast pocket.

'Mr Colman?'

'Yes, pet. What can I do for you?'

'Well, actually, I think I've come to see your wife.' '*I
think I've come*': what an idiotic thing to say. 'I mean, I
have come to see a Mrs Peggy Colman who was Gaunt
before she was married. I'm Emma Gaunt, so we're
probably related.'

'Well, you better come in for a start, lass.' He was
reaching out to almost lift her over the threshold.
'Peggy!' His voice echoed up the stairs and round the
small front room into which he ushered Emma. There
was a sideboard groaning with cut-glass, each item set
on a crocheted ecru doily and one or two holding
artificial flowers.

'I expect she's out the back,' the man said. 'Take a
seat and I'll fetch her.' Emma sat down on a dralon
settee and looked around her. Photographs stood on
the mantelpiece, a laughing baby prominent, and a
bookcase was packed with fairly sombre tomes. Emma
leaned forward to look at the tiny paperback section.

The *New English Bible, Fragments of Faith, The Christian Way* ... either Aunty Peggy or the smiling uncle was into religion!

The woman came in at last, smoothing her hair and walking with her body at a forward angle, as though to hide her bare legs in their fluffy carpet slippers.

'I was just out the back. Eddy says you're called Gaunt. That was my maiden name.' Her tone was suspicious and Emma tried to sound calm and matter-of-fact.

'Yes, I'm Emma Gaunt. I live in Manchester and I'm just up here on a visit.'

'Oh yes?' The woman had subsided into an armchair, pulling down her skirt and looking quickly towards her husband for comfort.

'My mother's name was Esther.' Emma went on speaking although she could sense the sudden hostility in the room. 'She died last year, of the after-effects of a stroke. Anyway, I came up here ...' Better not mention the Culroses. Not yet. 'I came up for a few days, and while I was here I thought I'd look up some family, if I could find any.'

'How *did* you find us?' The woman's voice had hardened and she no longer looked at her husband. 'She's angry,' Emma thought and was surprised.

'My mother's friend, Poppy Beresford, remembered having heard your surname. I rang all the Colmans in the directory – as many of them as it took to reach your daughter-in-law, anyway.'

'Our Liz?'

'I'm not sure of her name but she was very helpful.'

'So Esther's dead,' the man said suddenly. And then, 'I expect you'd like a cup of tea?' He was off without waiting for an answer.

'Why have you come, then?' The woman's voice still held hostility. 'I mean, why – after all this time? Leave it a bit longer and you needn't have bothered at all.'

Emma could hardly say that the idea would never have occurred to her but for the death of a total stranger. 'I came . . . because I wanted to fill some gaps in what I know about my family. My mother never said much, except that she and my father couldn't get on and parted by mutual consent.'

'Hah!' The grim face opposite was lit by a kind of humour. 'I like that. That's typical Esther. "Mutual consent".'

Emma fought the desire to defend her mother. If she antagonized this woman now, she'd get nothing. 'Well, that's one of the reasons why I'm here. So far I've only heard one side. I loved my mother – I still do – but I'm old enough, and I hope sensible enough, to know there'd be two sides.'

'Oh, there were. There were two sides!' The woman was almost jumping in her chair with suppressed anger.

'She's my aunt,' Emma thought. 'She's my father's sister, not just a stranger. I must try and remember that.'

'They were married twelve years. Twelve years! Esther couldn't've had a better man. We were well brought up: my father was Chapel and he taught us right from wrong. I knew Esther wasn't right for our John, but you couldn't tell him that. He worshipped her, pandered to all her airs and graces, waited on her hand and foot. The one thing he wanted was a bairn. A bairn of his own. And she waited until she was having a bairn, and then she left him. Upped and went, just like that!'

'But why?'

'She said . . . I remember her exact words . . . she

said: "I've got to go. If I stay now I'll be trapped." And John still didn't see her for what she was. He sold the house and gave her the lot. £500. It may not sound much now, but it was a fortune then. It finished him. A living death, that's what he's had, poor lad. Deprived of his only child.'

'Tea's up.' Eddy was coming through the door with a tray bearing cups and a tea-pot. 'Get it while it's nice and hot, now. Sing out if it's too strong. I like a good brew meself.'

Emma took the cup with its pattern of silver leaves and red dots. 'Thank you.' She must have misheard but she had to know. The woman had said 'he's had': present tense.

'When exactly did my father die?'

'Die?' They spoke in unison, each face equally startled. 'Die?' the woman said again. 'He hasn't died, although he's not far short.' And then, as comprehension dawned: 'So that's what Esther told you. I might have known!'

Emma felt her senses slip away for a second and then steady. 'So he's alive?' In spite of herself, her voice went up on the last syllable as though someone had punched her. Opposite, the woman's face darkened and her lips moved as though she was too full to speak.

'He's in a hospital, lass.' It was the man who spoke. 'Now drink your tea and then she'll tell you. You'll have to give her a chance, for John's her only family now. Apart from the bairns, that is.'

'What did Esther tell you?' the woman said woodenly.

'Well, nothing really. When I was little, she used to say my father had gone away. Then, when I was old enough to understand, she said they hadn't got on together, so they'd decided on separate lives. She said my father loved me but he wanted to live on his own. When I was . . . oh, coming up to O-levels . . . I got this urge to find him, and that's when she told me . . .' Emma's words dwindled as she understood. Once she had been old enough to look for her father, her mother had deliberately obscured the trail.

'Warm my cup, Eddy.' He moved obediently, and, as the tea was poured, the woman seemed to gather herself together.

'Our John worked for Culrose's then . . .'

There it was, the connection! Emma raised her cup to her mouth to stifle the urge to speak, and let her aunt continue.

'He went there as a boy and old man Culrose thought a lot of him. Treated him like a son. He was foreman by the time he was twenty-eight. He was a good lad, a good Godfearing man. He married your mother, and she seemed nice enough – always stylish, and she kept a nice home, I'll give you that. They had a house in Dovedale Street: everything nice, and no tick. They had everything they ever wanted – except a bairn. And then she fell pregnant. He was like a dog with two tails. "This is the Lord's doing, Peggy," – that's what he said. And then Esther upped and left him. Went off! To London, we thought. I could go on and on, but where's the point? It broke him, that's all. He packed in his job, sold the house, and gave her all the money: that's what narked me. After what she'd done to him!'

'What did he do then?'

'He never amounted to much after that. Old man Culrose would've come seeking him, but he died around then and the young one was too taken up with himself and his fancy car. Our John went into one room in

Foyle Street, him that had been a house-owner. He did odd jobs, drew the social . . .'

'Where is he now? And why didn't he ever contact me?'

'I don't know. She probably told him not to, and what she said was gospel to him. As to where he is, he's in the Geriatric Unit. He's been there for four years, since he was sixty-three. He's two years younger than me, and from his looks he could be my grand-dad.'

The man was looking at Emma sympathetically. 'All this has come as a shock, I suppose? We thought you would know, all these years. I did think of trying to find you when John went into hospital but . . . well, we . . .'

'I stopped him.' Peggy Colman's tone was final. 'I couldn't see you had a right to know, not after thirty years.' Her eyes had filled with tears and the cup trembled in her hand.

'I think we should leave it for now,' the man said coaxingly. 'We've all had a bit of an upset. Let it rest for a day or so, and then we can thrash it all out.'

'May I come back and see you?' Emma asked as she stood up to go. The woman nodded and Emma reached out to touch her cardiganed arm.

'She gets a bit full when she thinks about John,' the man confided as he let her out of the door. Behind them the woman was sobbing quietly in the front room. 'Don't take her too seriously. She's a good woman. She must be, the years she's put up with me.'

'Where is my father?'

'He's in Ward 12 at the Bishopwearmouth. It's on the road into town. But don't go rushing in to see him. It's not easy. He's well down.'

Emma walked back to the car, her legs trembling, her teeth chattering in spite of the heat. She had a father.

She had always had a father! In the doorway the man stood, hands in pockets, until he lifted one in farewell. She smiled at him and started the engine, but once more it was just to drive around the corner, out of sight. This was getting to be a habit. She laid her head on the wheel and let waves of nausea overtake her. Where was it going to end, the labyrinth of deceit and revelation?

Against her closed eyes Lesley rose up, Lesley smiling, Lesley legal and in her proper place. Perhaps she was being punished for what she had done to Lesley? Except that the seeds of her present misery had been sown long before Lesley was born. She started the car again and this time she carried on back to the hotel.

She found the Bishopwearmouth Hospital in the telephone directory, and asked the hospital switchboard for Ward 12. 'I'm ringing about a Mr Gaunt. John Gaunt.'

'Are you a relative?'

'I'm his – daughter.' To her own ears it sounded false, but whoever was at the other end seemed to accept it.

'I see. Well, I'm afraid Mr Gaunt is rather poorly just now.'

'Can I see him?'

'I think I'd leave it for today. He's just fallen asleep. Come in if you like, but I doubt you'll find him awake. Tomorrow might be better.'

Emma felt a sense of relief as she put down the phone. By tomorrow she would have collected herself. What did you say to a father you had never seen: 'Long time no see'? She was laughing and it wasn't pleasant laughter: she felt a sense of outrage at her own behaviour. What was funny? And then, as her guffaws became stronger and the tears fell, she realized she was having hysterics. She wanted to sit down but some inner strength carried her into the bathroom to sluice her face with cold water.

It worked, but even as the laughter ceased she felt her legs grow weak and had to sit down on the closed loo, holding on to the handbasin for support.

Suddenly she wanted and needed Keith. If only he were here now, to comfort her, to tell her what to do! Even to speak to him on the phone would help, but where would she find him? She stood up and rinsed her face again, and then she went back to her bedside and dialled his home number. His mother would know his movements, and she could pretend to be checking on Tom and Zoë.

It was not Keith's mother who answered. 'It's me, Lesley. I'm home. Yes, Zoë's fine. She was doing so well, and since they needed the bed they offered me the chance. I nearly took their hand off! Where are you?'

Emma couldn't explain to Lesley, nor could she ask outright where Keith was. 'I'm in Durham. I wanted to get away for a few days. I have family up here.'

'Oh, that's nice for you. But don't stay away too long. Tom's been asking about you.' Her voice faded as she turned away from the receiver. 'Hasn't he, Mum?'

So Keith's mother was still there! 'Is . . . everyone all right?'

'Yes. Zoë's her old self and Tom's making such a fuss of her. And Mum's being a brick.' Why didn't the silly bitch mention the one person who mattered?

'That's nice,' Emma said, feeling foolish tears clog her throat.

'Are you all right, Emma? I haven't asked that so far. What about you? I'm expecting Keith home tomorrow – Friday at the latest, he says. He'll want to see you and say thank you for everything.'

I need him now, right now, this minute, Emma thought, but she kept her thoughts to herself. He would be home soon: twenty-four or forty-eight hours. She must get back to Manchester as soon as she could, since he wouldn't be able to come to her. That was how it must always be: he must place wife and family first. And by the time the children were grown and his tie with Lesley weakened, it would probably be too late. 'I'm wasting the best years of my life,' she thought.

When Emma put down the phone she lay down on the bed and closed her eyes. The digital alarm said four-fifteen. Only four-fifteen, and she felt as though this day had lasted for at least a hundred hours. Robert Eden and the Culrose pair would be arriving at eight. She turned on her side, drew up one knee in the foetal position and tried to sleep, fighting images of her irate aunt, of Lesley, queen of her home once more, of Keith, striding across some airport somewhere, of her mother who had been such an easy liar and, just before she slept, a picture of her father, wan on a hospital pillow but alive somewhere, waiting for his only daughter to reach out for him.

Emma woke with only ten minutes to spare, just time to wash face and hands and change into a dark silk shift with pearls at her ears. 'I look awful,' she thought, taking one last look in the mirror. There were rings round her eyes and pink rims to her eyelids. She sprayed herself with Opium and went downstairs in a cloud of Yves St Laurent.

They were coming through the swing doors as she

emerged from the lift, the lawyer in a dark suit and blue tie, the boy covered in three-piece charcoal and the girl in a mustard suit that emphasized her bulk.

'Hallo,' Emma said and reserved her smile for April and then the boy. 'Shall we have a drink before we go in?' The girl carried a small black grosgrain bag on a long gold chain – her mother's probably, and out of place with the suit. She was holding it in front of her with both hands, and Emma saw that the knuckles were white, so fierce was her grip. She let Robert Eden get the drinks . . . time enough to demonstrate her grasp of wine when they were at the table . . . and concentrated on putting April at ease.

'Robert says you had a good meeting this morning?' Stephen said, when at last they were all seated.

Emma nodded. 'Yes. He put me in the picture.' She said it easily and, catching Robert Eden's glance, saw approval there. And suddenly it was easy to tell them about her day.

'I told you I wanted to find out about my family. I knew I had an aunt – just had her name and a vague idea that she was in this area. Well, I found her today.' She had their attention now: the boy's eyes were hopeful, the man's wary, the girl's oddly trusting and sympathetic. 'She's a nice kid,' Emma thought and held April's eye as she went on. 'She gave me a shock. I told you last night that my father and mother were dead, and that was true, as far as I knew then. But I've discovered I have a father . . .' She felt her chin come up almost defiantly and this time she was looking at Robert Eden, expecting him to be seeking ulterior motives in her explanation. 'Don't ask me why I wasn't ever told he was still living. Presumably I'll find out eventually, but at the moment it's a complete mystery. My mother chose to lie to me. I thought he was dead, but he's alive. He's very ill, apparently. I'm seeing him tomorrow.'

Suddenly April's hand was on hers, rather warm and damp but comforting just the same. Too comforting . . .

'It's all right,' Stephen said awkwardly. 'We understand . . .'

Emma tried to make conversation, telling them about her day, leading up to the facts that might interest them, but it was difficult to speak naturally. She twisted the glass around in her fingers, for once at a loss for words and despising herself for it. At last she said, 'I think I may have discovered something. My father worked for your grandfather. Your father too, probably. I think he left at about the time your grandfather died.'

'1957?' Stephen said.

'Yes.'

Before she could go on the waiter loomed. 'Your table is ready, sir,' he said. Damn him, he was assuming Robert Eden to be the host.

'Thank you,' Emma said firmly, rising to her feet, intending to sweep into the dining-room. But the combination of wine on an empty stomach was too much for her. The room tilted and steadied, and then Robert Eden's hand was on her elbow. 'I can manage,' she said, trying to wrench away. She felt his fingers tighten until it hurt.

'Obviously,' he said and piloted her towards the table.

As the youngsters went ahead of them he bent to Emma's ear. 'I'm all for a war, Miss Gaunt. No quarter on either side. But I never employ my lance on a dead opponent, and you are looking distinctly moribund at the moment. So eat up and shut up for tonight. Tomorrow you can be as domineering as you please.'

Emma had sat out too many business crises not to know when to adopt a low profile. She would have her day with Mr Eden. Unfortunately, though, tonight was definitely his, and her only moment of triumph would be when she signed the bill.

10

Thursday 10 August

The promised rain had fallen in the night and the morning stayed cloudy with occasional showers. Emma was due at the Culrose yard at ten o'clock for a courtesy visit, arranged with Stephen last night. She had promised to visit the yard in the morning and take April out for tea at four. In between, she would visit her father in hospital. At night they would meet again, this time at Robert Eden's, to compare notes. She didn't want to take part in that get-together, but she didn't want to stay in Durham indefinitely, either. The sooner the mystery was solved the better.

In the end, dinner the night before had been bearable. The world had ceased to rock once she started eating and began to relax, and she had cultivated the boy and girl, at first in an effort to snub the solicitor, and then because their response was an incentive. As they hung on her every word they were like those tiny Japanese paper flowers that opened in water. Emma found it oddly moving.

Now she dressed in her hotel room, trying to work out what was suitable for the weather and the day's activities. She would have to go back to Manchester soon, perhaps tomorrow, to get some more clothes and to go through her mother's effects. She wished, now, that she had gone through them before. There must be something there, some clue as to what had gone on. And if she went back to Manchester there was always the possibility of Keith's arriving. He would come to her as soon as he decently could, she knew that. But if she was far away in Durham . . .?

She stood, irresolute, in front of the dressing-table mirror. Perhaps it was a good idea to stay here, inaccessible? Perhaps she should end the affair now? Except that she wanted and needed him. Not a man, not anyone: Keith! She felt an actual, physical withdrawal. It was nearly two weeks since they had made love, and last night, although her brain had whirled ceaselessly around the revelations of the day, her body had itched and ached for relief. She clamped large gold rings on her ears to lighten the plain grey dress, picked up her bag and went to collect her car.

The Culrose car-park, as she drove in, was three-quarters empty at this time of day. In the children's activity centre over by the entrance a solitary child was going up and down on a swing, and an elderly couple were combining to push a trolley towards their car. Business was hardly brisk, even for a Thursday morning. Perhaps it came alive at weekends, and was thronged with couples all intent on extensions or stripped-pine kitchens?

Emma had never had the pleasure of creating a home of her own. Soon she must clear out the house and impose her own personality upon her mother's room. She had a sudden mental image of taking her father there, creating a room for him, nursing him back to health and strength. First, though, she must find out whether or not they could even like one another, let alone live together. It had been surprisingly easy to accept the fact of his existence; what was difficult to come to terms with was her mother's deceit.

Stephen Culrose was waiting inside a glass-fronted

office, city-suited and bespectacled. Did he have any leisure clothes? Had he ever played with toys or run whooping through a forest? Emma's own childhood had been constricted by the demands of her mother's business, but there had been some fun – weekends in London with her mother, weeks away with Poppy in seaside boarding-houses or French pensions, hearing about 'the war' when everyone had been young and gay and full of *joie de vivre*. This boy looked as though he had been born sober-suited. All around him was evidence of a business gone to the bad: gossiping staff, unfilled shelves, a customer wandering vaguely, begging to know the price of the item in her hand.

'We'll have a look round outside,' Stephen said importantly. 'And then the sales floor. Then I thought we'd have coffee and I'll show you our office systems.' He smiled suddenly and ruefully. 'They might not be up to your standards.'

He went ahead of her, across the huge building. It was certainly a big site. There would be money in that if he sold – and on the evidence of what she had seen today, he would be well advised to sell.

'Dad always liked this section.' They were looking at piles of timber, paper bands fluttering forlornly between the stands, the wood yellowing in the damp and contrasting with neat bundles of red bricks, ready to be fork-lifted when sold. There was a scaffolding section, and, under cover, all the elements necessary for plumbing. 'Impressive,' Emma said, as they went back into the retail section, and saw the boy's chin tighten with pride.

She toured the racks of utensils, fingered the carpet samples, oohed and aahed at the kitchen displays and the patio furniture, stroked lampshades and towelling, and patted the head of a huge pottery leopard. 'I

wouldn't want to live with that, but there's no accounting for taste,' she said.

If he had been a client, she would have enjoyed
making the tour. As it was, she felt depressed. A fortune
was tied up in stock here, and in a forced sale it would
fetch peanuts.

They chatted over coffee and biscuits, brought in by
a sloppy but pleasant junior who called her boss 'Mr
Culrose' but treated him with the casual friendliness of
a schoolmate.

'Do you want to carry on the business?' Emma asked
and then, when Stephen bristled: 'I'm only asking out
of curiosity. I have no personal interest in what you do
with all this, but I'm intrigued professionally. You're
young, young enough to change direction. You could
go to university ... take up beach-combing ... anything. There's no rule that says you have to follow in
the family footsteps. And what about April? You have
to consider her interests, too.'

'Pud wants what I want,' Stephen said stubbornly.
He was probably right, Emma thought: poor April
would be unlikely to advance an opinion contrary to
her brother's ... about anything. This afternoon, if she
got the chance, she would sound the girl out about her
future. Now, though, she went into the attack.

'How do you know? Have you ever asked her what
she wanted, for herself? I'll bet you haven't. *If* you've
asked, you'll have said, "You do want to help the
business on, don't you, April?" What do you expect her
to reply to that: "Sod the business"?'

Stephen's eyes widened with shock at the oath – or
perhaps at the implication of her words. 'I know you
mean well, Stephen,' Emma went on. 'I admire your
loyalty to your father and the family name. But you

have no right to assume that April feels the same . . . or to make her feel guilty if she says anything other than, "Yes, Stephen, no, Stephen, three bags full, Stephen." And now let's get on with my visit.'

She saw words trembling on his lips. 'You're wrong about April,' he said at last. 'She makes her own decisions.'

They went through the stock records, personnel files, accounting systems. All worthy, but plodding. 'I only have to ask for a file and they can lay their hands on it straight away,' Stephen said proudly. Emma itched to point out that she could do the same thing unaided in her own business, merely by tapping a couple of keys. She contented herself with saying, 'Very good,' and smiling a lot, although the sight of staff lounging at their desks failed to amuse her.

When Stephen issued orders they were obeyed, but whoever obliged him immediately lapsed back into lethargy. 'Over-manned and under-motivated,' Emma thought. All the more reason for selling up. It was always hard to motivate an ailing work-force; for a nineteen-year-old with little or no experience it would be impossible.

He waved her off from the impressive glass portico, saying, 'See you tonight.' He sounded almost enthusiastic about it and Emma smiled and waved in return. It was one o'clock and she drove to the multi-storey car-park and went in search of a sandwich bar.

She found one overlooking the Market Square, which had an old grey church, and a guildhall, and a covered market beyond a gloomy stone entrance. She had a ham sandwich and coffee, and checked her watch at two-minute intervals. She wanted to see her father, could hardly wait to find out whether he fitted any of her yearning childhood images. And she wanted some answers. Once she could sort out the complications of her past, she might just be able to deal with the problems of her present and the dilemma of her future. 'It'll be all right,' she promised herself as she walked back to the car. 'It'll be all right because I'll make it so.' The damp turned into drizzle and she dived for the car-park and the safety of her Capri.

The visitors were waiting patiently outside Ward 12 when she arrived. They spoke little and shifted their feet a lot, obviously used to the wait. At last a young nurse, unsmiling, latched back the swing doors, turned on her heel and disappeared, leaving the waiting visitors to shuffle along in her wake. Emma walked down the corridor until she found a door marked '*Sister. Please knock and wait.*' She knocked and then, for the first time, realized that she would have to explain why she was visiting her father who was a total stranger to her.

In the event she had to knock again before she gained admittance, and in the mean time she had decided not to explain anything unless she was forced to it. The Sister was sitting at her desk and a young male doctor lounged against a filing cabinet.

'I'm Emma Gaunt. I spoke to you yesterday.'

'Oh yes,' the Sister said, swinging her chair round to face a trolley full of files. She pulled one out, opened it and turned back to Emma. 'So you're next of kin, then?'

'I suppose I am,' Emma said. 'Yes, I am. I'm his only child and my mother is dead. I certainly want to assume responsibility for him.' She was already thinking of private care. She could afford it, and it might be that he deserved it.

The Sister wrote down her details, crossing out another name, presumably that of her aunt. 'You'll find him on the right of the ward. He's awake, but not very communicative this morning, I'm afraid.' She smiled briefly and turned back to the doctor, and Emma went in search of her father's bed.

She walked the length of the ward without seeing anyone who remotely fitted her mental picture. She was tall and dark-haired, like her mother, but their features were very different. She had always believed that facially she must resemble her father. Several of the beds had a clutch of visitors around them, so they were ruled out; the visitorless beds all contained frail old men who could not possibly be her father.

In the end Emma went from one bed to another, glancing at the chart on each bed-rail. Simpson, Blackett, Johnson, Everleigh . . . *Gaunt*!

He lay on his back, eyes closed, his face emaciated and waxen pale. She checked the chart again: '*John Gaunt. Date of Birth 9.6.22.*' It fitted. She moved back to his side and touched one of the arms laid rigidly on top of the coverlet. Impossible to call him 'Dad' or 'Father'. She said, 'Mr Gaunt.'

There was no response and she touched him again.

Behind her a nurse appeared with an upright chair. 'Sit down, pet. He'll only speak if he wants to, so you might be there a while.' Seeing Emma's consternation, the nurse went round to the other side of the bed and leaned over her patient. 'John! You've got visitors, John. It's your . . .?' She looked at Emma, expecting a title, but Emma was in turmoil. Impossible to say 'daughter'. She couldn't shock him like that, and if he repudiated her, as he well might do, the humiliation would be searing. But if she said 'friend', she would be contradicting what she had already told the Sister.

'It's all right,' she said, regaining control of the situation. 'I'll just sit here till he's ready to talk.'

The nurse smiled and went off, and Emma sat down and edged her chair nearer to the bed. 'My name is Emma Gaunt.' Was it imagination or did his eyelids flicker? 'I'm your daughter. I would have come before now, but I didn't know you were here.' She couldn't say she hadn't known he was alive: that would be too cruel.

There was a faint blue stubble over his square jawline but the flesh of his neck fell away so that it looked as though head and torso were connected by nothing but a fold of skin. Emma tried again. 'I'm so glad I've found you at last. Your sister . . . my Aunt Peggy . . . she told me you were here.'

Suddenly the eyes flew open, pale blue with a curious yellow ring around the iris. Pale blue and cold. Emma smiled, trying to seem confident in a disorienting situation. 'Is there anything I can get you?' She had brought fruit and barley water, but perhaps there was something else. 'I saw a shop in the entrance. Is there anything you want?'

The blue eyes glittered, as though with amusement, and the mouth twitched. No words came but one hand started to pluck at the coverlet. Emma touched the other arm and stroked the striped pyjama fabric. Underneath there was only a hank of bone. 'I won't talk if you're tired. Unless you'd like to hear something about me? There's so much to catch up on.'

There was no mistaking the gesture that followed: his eyes closed and he turned his head away. Emma felt her eyes sting with hurt tears, but she went on stroking the arm. He was very ill and she had been a long time in coming, after all.

She sat on, her hand moving slowly up and down the arm, remembering her childhood. She had not felt the lack of a father until she went to school. Her mother and Poppy had surrounded her with love and fun, but they could not accompany her into the world of children. '*What does your father do?*' She had never been able to tell the truth in answer to that: that she knew nothing about her father except the fact of his existence. Instead, she had invented for him a tragic and early death. It had always been swallowed without resistance, just as she had later swallowed her mother's story.

She looked now at the bony head on the pillow, skull-like, with blue-veined eyelids, and tried to imagine it beside her mother's, but it was impossible. How had they ever come together? And once together, why had they separated? More important, why had daughter and father been resolutely kept apart?

'Dad ... it seems odd to say that, odd but nice. I wish you'd say something. Not much, I know you're not well. Do you want me to go away now? Just say something!'

The hand ceased to pluck at the cover as the head turned towards her. The eyes opened wide, meeting and holding her gaze. And then, quite deliberately, they snapped shut and the head turned away once more. It was a message and there could be no doubting its meaning.

Emma got to her feet, moving the chair carefully back to its place in the centre of the ward, and then she went back to the bed. 'I'll come back, Dad. I don't want to lose you now that I've found you again.'

*

The chief difficulty about it all was that it defied belief. As Emma walked the long corridor to the hospital entrance, she kept thinking about the day she had interviewed Keith. Everything had been normal, easy; she had been in charge of her life. Now, suddenly, there was no area of her existence that could be regarded as secure. Past and future, emotional life and professional standing – they were all in the melting pot, for she had jeopardized herself and SyStems the moment she took a subordinate into her bed.

That was what you never bargained for – the presence of an inner self that could crave nourishment, no matter how far you ascended outwardly. She had thought she had everything when they gave her the Manchester office, but what little it had in fact amounted to, she had blown. There was no way she could go back to work the week after next as though nothing had happened, discuss her aborted holiday with Amy, drink coffee and talk about forward projections.

She was unlocking the door of the Capri when she realized she was being too hard on herself. She was not here in Durham, unearthing family skeletons, because she had taken a lover: she was up here paying for someone else's mistakes. The only question was, 'Whose?'

She tried to banish thoughts of the hospital from her mind before collecting April Culrose from her home. It was still drizzling and the sky was grey and oppressive. She wanted to give the kid a treat, not add to her depression.

April came out on to the front-door step as soon as the Capri crunched across the gravel.

'Hallo,' Emma called. 'Get in out of the rain.' April had yet another lumpy suit on, this time with ecru stockings that made her plump legs look positively fat, ending as they did in laced-up clumpy shoes that were the height of fashion but not meant for April's ilk.

They drove, at April's direction, to a country mansion in wooded grounds, and went through the lobby, with its reception desk and tourist information, to a lounge where there were chintz-covered chairs and low tables, and an elderly waitress in black and white carrying trays of tea and cake-stands full of tiny sandwiches and cream-filled scones.

'I'm glad you could come,' Emma said, when they had been served. She *was* glad. It was nice to sit in this quiet room with someone who did not want to strike sparks. April was the perfect passive companion. She smiled briefly in appreciation of the compliment and bit nervously into a smoked salmon sandwich.

'What are you going to do now?' Emma asked. 'I imagine you did GCSEs this year?'

April nodded. 'I got three Bs and four Cs. And I failed Geography,' she finished, with a blush.

'Not bad!' Emma said admiringly. 'What are you planning next . . . take your As?'

April frowned slightly and put down her sandwich. 'That's what everyone wants me to do.'

'Everyone?'

'Stephen and Robert. Robert's a sort of guardian under Dad's will, and anyway, he's a friend. He says I should stay on at school and Stephen says I must. Then he says I can do Business Studies and join him at Culrose's.'

'But what do *you* want to do?'

'I don't know.' April looked as though no one had ever asked her that, and she had failed to consider it herself.

'I'd quite like to do something with children, I think a nanny. I like children. There's not much else I could do. I'm not really that good at anything.'

'You could do an NNEB: that's a qualification in nursery nursing. Or you could train as a nanny, there are one or two good schools. I could have done with your help a few days ago, seeing you like children.'

It was easy to talk about Tom, then, about her problems with the nappies and the early, early mornings. 'His father is a colleague of mine. He's in America just now, so I had to wade in and help.'

'Have you been to America?'

'Yes, several times. Have you?'

April had been almost nowhere. 'We used to go to Granny and Grandpa in Bath, but Granny died last year and Grandpa can't really do with us now. And we have a cottage in Arkengarthdale. I loved it there, but we haven't been for ages.'

There was a kind of resignation in her voice that at once aroused pity and anger in Emma. Why didn't the girl show some gumption?

'How long is it since your mother died?' She said it almost brutally, and immediately regretted her tone. April seemed not to notice. 'She's used to people being brusque with her,' Emma thought.

'She's been dead for eight years. I was eight when she died.'

'I was lucky,' Emma said, 'my mother died last year when I was thirty-one. But it still hurt a lot. It's a funny feeling when you lose your parents, as though your shell has been removed and left you exposed.'

April nodded solemnly. 'Yes, it is like that. It was awful when Dad died . . . and then there was the will. We didn't understand it . . .'

'I still don't understand it,' Emma said. 'But I'm going to. I think I begin to see a glimmer. At least we know now that your father knew mine. They worked together.' If only her father had spoken today – perhaps he could have made it all plain.

'Robert's been such a help,' April said suddenly. 'I don't think I could have borne it all without Robert.' There was something about the way she said 'borne it all' that meant she was talking about more than death.

'Has it been tough?' Emma asked.

'Pretty tough,' April said and looked as though she might have said more but thought better of it. Emma remembered what Robert Eden had told her about David Culrose's drinking habits, and reached out to squeeze April's stubby-fingered hand. 'What are you wearing tonight? I'm quite looking forward to seeing the lion's den.'

April's face lit up with amusement. 'Do you mean Robert? He's not a lion, he's a pussy-cat.'

'Grrrral,' Emma said in a good imitation of a lion in pursuit of prey.

'He is nice, really. I mean, he's not all lovey-dovey with everyone, but that's because he's been so unhappy. But he's really good when you're down. He'll do any-thing to help people. Not just us – anyone.'

'Why do you say he's been unhappy?'

April leaned forward, eyes gleaming behind her round glasses. 'He had the most awful wife. She was someone quite posh, and her name was actually Deborah, but Daddy always called her Debrett. Robert worked really hard to give her lots of things, a nice house and every-thing. But she left him and went off with someone really rotten. And she took Robert's son. He's three – well, he was when he went, so he'll be nearly five now. Dad said there should be a law against it.'

'Does Mr Eden see his son?'

'Sometimes. But I think she does mean things like taking him on holiday when it's Robert's turn, and things like that. And he really loves him a lot. People think fathers don't love their children, but they do.'

They were silent for a moment, each thinking how true April's statement was, but for a different reason. April reached for a cream scone and cut it in two. 'I've tried to diet, you know. I've tried a lot of times but it never works.'

Emma nodded her sympathy. 'I know, I have trouble too.'

The girl shook her head, admiration shining from her eyes. 'You've got a lovely figure. And you wear such nice clothes.'

'You haven't told me what you are wearing tonight?'

April shrugged. 'Well, there's the Calvin Klein or the Bruce Oldfield ...' It was the first joke Emma had heard her make, and it was a good sign. 'Actually, I've got a yellow dress, well, mustard really. It's got short sleeves and I like the skirt. I think I'll wear that.'

'I've got my amber beads with me,' Emma said. 'One long rope. You can borrow them if you like, they look good with mustard. And ...' She leaned forward and lifted the girl's lank hair. 'Your ears aren't pierced – that's a pity. You could have borrowed the ear-rings too. Still, I'll bring the beads with me and you can slip them on as we go in. I'm calling at your place first so that Stephen can show me the way.'

They talked about fashion then, and music, the girl's face losing its stolidity as apathy departed. 'See you tonight,' Emma said as she dropped April at the door.

'Yes, see you,' April said and positively skipped up the steps to her door.

'If I had a year's sabbatical I could make something of that girl,' Emma thought as she drove back to the St Nicholas.

It was six o'clock and they were due at Eden's at eight. She hung up her grey dress and stepped into a tepid bath, running in more cold at the end until she was relaxing in cool, almost cold, water. It had rained nearly all day and yet the air was still warm, seeming to lack oxygen.

She allowed herself to think of the afternoon. Had her father deliberately tried to repel her? Had he even been aware that she was his daughter? If she was no more successful tomorrow she would ask to speak to one of the doctors and inquire about his mental state. She could ask about moving him, then, too. There seemed to be little or no stimulation in that ward: perhaps that was what her father needed.

The phone rang as she stepped from the bath. Fastening a towel around her, she scampered to answer it. 'Emma Gaunt.'

'Darling?' It was Keith. She moved the receiver to her other ear and secured the knot of the towel.

'Keith? You're back!'

'I got in this lunch-time. I'm in the pub now . . . said I was dying for an English beer. I couldn't wait until tomorrow to speak to you. How are you?'

'You mean you've left Lesley? You've just walked in the door after two weeks, and you've left her?' Water was running down her left calf and she rubbed it with her right instep.

'I'll be going back there in a second. Don't let's waste the few minutes we have. When are you coming home?

And how has it gone, up there? I've been thinking about you a lot.'

Once they had walked in the rain, laughing deliriously as it seeped through the shoulders of their macs to run neatly down shoulder-blade and spine. Emma mopped at herself, half-remembering how much she loved him, half-wanting him to ring off and leave her in peace.

'It's been weird, Keith, really weird.' She had wanted him so much last night, had even tried to contact him. Now he was here, on the other end of the phone, and she felt flat. Why was reality always so different from expectation?

'What do you mean by weird?'

She was starting to explain about the day's many events when she sensed that he was becoming uneasy. 'Are you worrying about getting back?'

'No. No, it's not that. It's just that this is a coin-box . . .'

'Don't let me detain you then!' He didn't give a shit, that was it. He wanted to rush back to his wife and kids. He had been away two weeks, and tonight they would make love, make up for all the missed opportunities. She saw Lesley in her mind's eye, abandoned, bestriding him, taking her dues, the huge breasts hanging above him, his mouth opening greedily to take the nipple.

'Emma?' She heard Keith feeding coins into the box, but it was too late.

'Go to hell, Keith. Go home! Fuck off! Go home and fuck off.' The towel had come loose and dropped at her feet but she didn't care. She took her free hand and smacked it against the wall, feeling the textured plaster biting into her palm and slapping the hand down again and again. She wanted the conversation to end but she

175

couldn't be the one to put down the phone. 'Go on then, go! Get to hell off this line! See if I care, see if I fucking care!'

Emma was suddenly filled with such shame that the receiver shook in her hand. 'I'm sorry, Keith, I'm sorry. It's been a rotten day. Go home now. We'll talk tomorrow.'

'Are you all right? Oh darling, I wish I was with you. I'll come up if you want me to? To hell with everything. Zoë is fine now, and I can leave. I'll catch a train in the morning.'

'No.' Emma's voice was sharp. 'No, I don't want you to do that.' Reason was reasserting itself. 'One of us should go in to the office, Keith, and it can't be me, not at the moment. You go. We'll talk some time tomorrow. If I need help, I'll ask for it, I promise you.'

When she had put down the phone weariness overpowered her. She couldn't go out tonight, no matter what. And then she thought of April, waiting for her amber beads. She would have to go. She picked up the towel and rubbed the back of her head, where the hair was wet, then she climbed into bed, reaching to set the alarm's half-hour snooze button.

She closed her eyes, trying not to let unpleasant images intrude. Tonight she would go to Robert Eden's house and eat and drink, give comfort to April and enjoy a little verbal fencing with a man. A man who could not hurt her because she cared nothing at all for him. That was enough to open the door. She cried then for a man who had the power to crucify her because she cared for him too much – and sat up in bed suddenly, shocked by her own confession. She had always told herself that what she felt for Keith was purely physical, that when it was over she would walk away untouched. So much for non-commitment.

In the end, she got out of bed before the half-hour was up and dressed with care, putting pearls around her own neck and slipping the amber beads into her bag. It was still drizzling when she reached the pavement and crossed the hotel car-park. If she had been at home she would have dressed appropriately and walked in the rain, holding up her face for heaven's beneficence before running back home where it was warm and dry. She slipped into her car and inserted a cassette of Vivaldi into the tape-deck. That would put her in the mood for a fencing match.

When she drew up at the Culroses', the boy and girl appeared before she could sound her horn. April must spend a large part of her life watching for something to happen. 'Come in my car,' Emma called. The boy hesitated, then turned and made for her passenger side. As April climbed into the back, Emma held the beads over the seat.

'You remembered!' The genuine surprise in the girl's voice made Emma sad. How awful to expect so little from life.

Robert Eden's house was old and small but unusual. 'He bought it after Debrett went,' April whispered, as they walked to the door. 'She cleaned him out. Dad said Robert got this by the skin of his teeth.'

Inside, the low-ceilinged rooms were white-walled and cosy. A log fire burned in the hearth, and there were good prints on the walls and applewood shavings in a bowl on a side-table. It didn't fit her image of the macho Mr Eden. Neither did the meal, which was well cooked and served on odd but beautiful porcelain plates. He cooked like a master-chef, and his table, decorated with purple asters, would have done credit to anyone. There was a centrepiece in the shape of a sailing ship.

'How beautiful that is,' she said.

'It's a nef,' Robert Eden replied. 'They can go back to ancient times and be hugely expensive. That one's Dutch. Late nineteenth-century.'

'Is it silver?'

'I hope so,' he grinned. 'That's what I paid for. It's appreciated in value in the last few years, and I couldn't afford to buy it now. I'm very fond of it.'

Emma looked up suddenly and caught his eye. It was full of amusement, even derision. 'He knows he's surprised me,' she thought. 'He bloody well planned it to be like this.' Aloud she said, 'You're obviously very good at taking care of yourself, Mr Eden.'

'Yes,' he said. Just 'yes' and nothing more. She longed to compliment him on his modesty, but if they played the sarcasm game she had a nasty feeling he would win. She was damning him quietly under her breath when she realized that whenever they locked horns she ceased to grieve or worry or fear for the future. There was only the lance to think about, the joust. Perhaps he was good for something, after all.

She smiled her sweetest smile and entered into the fray. Soon she would have to tell him about her father, perhaps hear other unpleasant things from him, argue points or make decisions. Now, for just a little while, she meant to enjoy.

The evening did not disappoint her. The conversation sparked and bristled occasionally but was never tedious. When they left the table they ushered her into the small, comfortable sitting-room while they all went off to make coffee. She could hear them chattering in the kitchen. 'They get on well together,' she thought.

On a side-table was a large book, not a glossy volume there for display but a volume of poetry: *Collected Poems* by C. H. Sisson. She picked it up and it fell open at page 92 as though by use. Poetry? Somehow she could not imagine Robert Eden reading poetry, but the book had the feel of a much-loved tome. She closed the book guiltily and replaced it as she heard them returning, thinking as she did so that there was a lot more to the character of Robert Eden than she had hitherto realized.

11

Friday 11 August

There were two messages on the machine when Emma got back to Manchester, an invitation to a cocktail party and one from April, a pathetic little message about nothing in particular. 'She wants me to come back to Durham,' Emma thought and was surprised at how pleased this made her.

She unpacked her bags and put her used linen in the wash box. Sun streamed through the windows, showing up dust on every polished surface. She had only been away three days but it showed.

Three days! Long enough to discover a father – a father she didn't like. She felt better for admitting it, even to herself, and went into the bathroom to take two paracetamol tablets. Her face in the mirror was strained and her skin felt taut and dry. She cleaned it with cleansing milk and applied moisturizer, but however supple she made her skin the tension was still there, in the bones of her face.

She went through to her mother's room and looked around her. It was more than a bedroom: it had been her mother's fortress, her private place. Emma had known better than to enter without knocking, but she had spent many happy times curled in the centre of the wide bed, watching her mother's triple reflection as she cleansed her face or brushed her hair.

Suddenly she remembered one night, a cameo distinct in every detail. Her mother dressed for an evening out, black silk crêpe falling to fragile, strappy, high-heeled sandals, lifting her arms to coil her hair, the slashed sleeves of the black dress falling back to reveal a turquoise silk lining. And suddenly she could see Esther, long pink-tipped fingers coiling the hair back from her face, the arms white and rounded, a gleaming bracelet falling from wrist to forearm. Graceful. That had been the word for her mother.

The sun filtered through the half-drawn curtains, casting shadows, making even solid mahogany seem insubstantial. Emma resisted the impulse to stand there, absorbing the shadows, remembering the ghosts. Instead she walked to the window and jerked back the curtains, seeing the dust spin in the sunlight as she stirred the draperies. She must do something now, make a move. If she did not, the room would turn her to stone. There was a small Victorian writing-cabinet on a side table, and the usual drawers and chests a bedroom contained. To go through them all would take ages.

She lifted the lid of the writing-cabinet. Neat drawer-fronts faced her, a plastic box of elastic bands, some headed stationery, a wallet of stamps. And an address book. She began to go through the pages ... *Adams, Anderson, Arden, Atkins, Baum, Beresford* ... Poppy with another address long since crossed out. She finished the Bs and turned to the Cs. A row of names, but Culrose was not among them. No Culrose but there, at the very bottom of the page, an address: *The Wyndings, Gilesgate, Durham*. So her mother *had* known the Culrose family, and known them in more recent years, for they had only been at the Durham address since the '60s.

She riffled through the rest of the pages and put the book aside. The first drawer yielded guarantees for electric appliances, her mother's BUPA membership card, her own birth certificate and her mother's marriage certificate. *'Esther Marian Evans, spinster and clerk married to John Gaunt, bachelor and sawmill operative.'* Witnesses M. A. Colman – Aunty Peggy – and E. C. Evans – unknown.

Emma picked up the birth certificate. He was there, under 'Name and Surname of Father'. John Gaunt. Gaunt John now, shrinking in a hospital bed. She closed the cabinet and began to go through her mother's drawers.

Family photographs, some of them dated and named, others blank, the smiling faces unfamiliar to her. One of her mother, as a girl, arms clasped around a young man. Was that her father? Papers, letters in torn envelopes, souvenirs. She put them all on one side for later perusal and carried on with her search. The box she had found in the other chest was there, when she came to the jewellery, its velvet lining brilliant as though never exposed to the light of day.

She lifted out the brooch. It was a sheep, definitely – the curling fleece chased into the gold, the head turned forward. Stones were set into the fleece, four of them. She peered closer, trying to identify them. One was bright blue with faint whitish streaks in it; one, pale green, might be an indifferent emerald; a red stone might be a ruby and a colourless stone was probably a poor quality diamond. They looked odd, none of them matching or complementing the others. And why was there no stone for the creature's eye? It stared at her, meek and sightless like a lamb ready for the slaughter. She put it back in the box and slipped it into her pocket. Poppy had disclaimed knowledge of it, but seeing it might jog her memory. The back was marked

9ct, so it had a value. A string of numbers was engraved there too, probably a jeweller's mark. Odd that her mother had never shown the brooch to her, not even to remark on its ugliness.

Emma went on with her search, putting some things aside, occasionally consigning other things to the waste bin, until she heard Poppy at the front door.

'Emma, I didn't expect to see you!' Poppy looked tired and overheated.

'I'm just passing through. Come on in and I'll make you an omelette.' She cracked eggs into a basin as Poppy poured white wine from the fridge.

'God, I could do with this, Em. We haven't had clients today, we have had the Gadarene swine passing through that showroom. I was straight with one. I said, "We cater for normality here, madam." Well, she drove me to it. Came in for a black dinner frock, tried on everything in the place including a plaid cape and deer-stalker, and then said we didn't have the range she was used to. So I said, "Obviously not, madam. We cater for normality here."'

'You didn't!'

'I did. Well, I almost did. I rolled my eyes and did my Quasimodo impression. That got rid of her.' Poppy tolled an imaginary bell and called loudly for Esmeralda!

'Shut up,' Emma said at last. 'I've heaps to tell you and no doubt you'll be off to get ready for Charlie in a moment.'

'Not tonight,' Poppy said, a faint note of relief in her voice. 'He's got some chaps' thing on. I'm glad of the chance to put myself in for a refit. It's cucumber on the droopy bits and bed with Barbara Cartland for little Poppy tonight. Still, let's hear your news.'

Emma told her story, leaving out no single detail watching Poppy's eyes widen in astonishment. 'You're kidding.'

'I'm not. He's there, in Ward 12. John Gaunt. My father, Esther's husband.'

'And can't speak?'

'Can't or won't. The nurses seem to expect him to speak sometimes, but he didn't say anything to me.'

Poppy was shaking her head in wonderment, and any lingering doubt Emma might have had about Poppy holding information back from her was dissipated.

'Look!' She fished the jeweller's box out of her pocket. 'This is the brooch I told you about. It wasn't with the rest of Mother's jewellery, it was in the bow-fronted drawers, right at the back.'

'It's an insignia,' Poppy said. 'Masonic or something. It's a ram, and those stones are a crest.'

'It's not a ram, it's a female, whatever female sheep are called. No horns. What do you think the stones are?'

Poppy looked at it for a moment. 'Gallstones?' she suggested helpfully. She looked more than ever like an elderly and mischievous pug and Emma leaned forward to kiss the fleshy cheek.

'Not gallstones, Poppy. Not even close. Now, think! Is there anything else you can tell me? Use your brain. You know – thought processes. Little grey cells. You came up with Colman, which was brilliant, but you and Mother were closeted together six days a week for years, and she must have said something else.'

'She did . . . but it was all flip. You know, "After all I've had to put up with," or "I married once. I wouldn't make that mistake again." She did once say her in-laws were religious maniacs, if that's any help.'

'Not a lot.'

'Sorry. I could invent something, if that's what you want. Otherwise, the cupboard is bare. I mean, you know me, I told her everything, every orgasm practically. She just never indulged in all that, herself. She'd spend hours talking shop or about how she would decorate this place. But there was a marked absence of the nitty-gritty.'

'When exactly did you first get to know her?'

The omelettes were ready now and they sat opposite one another at the kitchen table.

'When she had the Duke Street shop. You were two, so it would be . . .'

'1959,' Emma said.

'Yes, 1959. I came to Manchester to get married, believe it or not. Stars in the eyes, shakes in the knees, the lot. He was manager of a string of wine and spirit stores. "Captain Melchett", he liked to be called. I threw up a good job to come here on the strength of his proposal, and the second night I was here he told me he was going back to the wife and kids in Brighton. So much for the gallant captain.'

'What did you do?'

'Well, I'd burned my boats, hadn't I? My life has been one long Armada, darling, I tell you – singeing scuppers, the lot. Your mother was looking for a part-time assistant, and I got the job. I had the figure for it then. We clicked. I wouldn't say I ever loved your mother, but I respected her. If she said something you could rely on it like Holy Writ. Come to think of it, she was the one constant in a sea of inconstancy in my life. I'll always honour her for that.'

'But she didn't confide . . . no, don't apologize. I was her daughter, I lived with her right up till I went to

Cambridge, and what do I know? And I've been thinking about it, Poppy: why didn't I ask? Because she
made it clear that the past was forbidden territory. She
never said, "Don't ask" – I just knew it wouldn't be
well received, that's all. Were there any men in her life?
I don't remember any, but then I was a child most of
the time and after that I was away in Cambridge.'

'Nary a one, darling. Plenty of offers, but she could
freeze a man at a hundred yards. I took it she'd had
enough with your father . . . that it had been that bad!'

'Oh God,' Emma said, 'if that's true, it's awful.'

'Let me give you a refill,' Poppy said, wielding the
wine bottle. 'There are times when cirrhosis is infinitely
preferable to contemplation.'

They sat on until the bottle was empty and then fell
on one another's necks before parting. 'Do you want
any help with Esther's things?' Poppy asked.

'No, thank you. I think I've done for tonight, anyway.
I'll follow your example and go to bed. I want to be off
in the morning – I kept on my room at the hotel so the
sooner I'm back the better.'

She stood in the hall until Poppy ascended out of
sight. 'Good-night. Sleep well. If I don't see you in the
morning I'll ring you from Durham. I expect to be back
here early next week.'

She went into the kitchen, hearing welcome rain
pound the windows, and cleared away the debris of the
meal, leaving the dishes to drain and wiping down the
work-tops. She didn't care much for housework but she
loved restoring order. In a way, it would be good to get
back to the office. She was good at her job, and knowing
she was good at it gave her confidence. She was out of
her depth away from it, an astronaut loose in space,
nothing without his ship.

She put the brooch back in her mother's drawer and carried the certificates and other fragments of family history through to her own room. She might as well take them to Durham, just in case they could be useful. She would have to have a go at Peggy Colman, too. Aunt Peggy Colman. Aunt Peggy. She tried it all ways, but it didn't fit. She couldn't feel any kinship with her aunt, though, oddly, she did feel a bond of a sort with her aunt's husband. He might bear cultivating.

She had washed her hair, bathed and was blowing her hair dry when the phone went.

'Emma?' It was Lesley.

'Lesley! Is anything wrong?'

'No. Oh, God . . . it is late, isn't it? Quarter to ten – I didn't realize. You weren't in bed, were you?'

'No. No, I was just pottering about. How's Zoë? And Tom?'

'They're fine. Actually, Tom's the reason I'm ringing. It's his birthday a week on Tuesday and he's adamant that he wants Em-em there. So come if you can. I can do with all the help I can get – there'll be ten two-year-olds plus the odd mum.'

It was unlikely that Tom had asked for her by name, unlikely that he even knew her name. Lesley was just being kind. All the same, if he had remembered her . . .

She was standing there, pleasure-filled, when she heard a key in her front door. Only two people had keys: Poppy, who was safe upstairs and never remembered her key anyway . . . and Keith!

He came through the doorway, shaking raindrops from his hair and the upturned collar of his jacket. She put a finger to anguished lips and mouthed 'Lesley'. He nodded, but did not look chastened. He went on flicking water from his forehead and pulling at damp cuffs while she pretended to his wife that all was well.

'I'd love to come. Is there anything you can suggest for a prezzie?'

'You can't go wrong with a car, not where Tom's concerned. But don't spend too much ... he loves Dinkys. The important thing's to come.'

'Oh, I'll be there, I wouldn't miss it.' Thank God that Lesley couldn't see her face, her flushed, deceitful, lying face. She stared at Keith, forcing him to meet her eye. How could he stand there as though she were chatting with a stranger? She made her goodbyes and put down the phone.

'God, that was awful!' He nodded. 'Where does she think you are, Keith?'

'I've been out with some of the golf-club guys. Poker at someone's house. I made my excuses.' He hesitated. 'I can't stay long. Lesley would never check up on me but ...'

She didn't let him finish. 'Of course you can't stay, you should be on your way now.' She moved towards him, seeing he was beginning to shrug out of his jacket. 'Don't, Keith, there's no point. I can't stand this ... this hole-and-corner business. That was your wife on the phone.' He looked hang-dog, but Emma couldn't stop. She kept thinking of Lesley, framed in the doorway, a child at her skirts. 'Did you hear me, *your wife*? Jesus Christ, I don't believe you!'

He was looking at her now, not saying anything because there was nothing he could say. But she wanted some reaction, some denial, some affirmation, something, anything to ease her pain.

'Do you hear me? For God's sake, give me a fucking answer.' His eyes widened in disapproval of her language and she found it to be the last straw. It was all there – the pain of coming face to face with Lesley, with her father, with poor ugly April whom hardly anyone loved, with the little boy who had slept against her belly, damp and warm. 'I can't bear any more,' Emma said. 'I can't. . . bear . . . any more.'

It was over. Keith held out his arms and she went into them, feeling the ripple of flesh over muscle, the sensation of hair beneath the silky fabric of his shirt, the comfort of his chin above her head. It felt so right. She pushed him gently to one side and walked ahead of him into the bedroom.

They made love slowly, anxious to omit nothing, using sensation to blot out pain. 'It's good,' he said, his lips drawn back over his teeth in an effort to prolong what they had.

'Good,' she said. 'Good, good, good,' and then it was on them like a rolling tide, lifting them high and casting them crashing on to the beach to lie like stranded whales, gasping for breath.

Emma moved first, turning on to her face, wriggling closer. 'I wanted you.'

'I know.'

'I wanted you so much.'

'Me too.'

'Nothing else matters.'

'No.'

She couldn't, after all, blame Keith. It was her fault, too. She could have stopped him with one word, one lifted finger, but she had wanted him so much it frightened her, frightened her because the wanting had been purely physical. She had not wanted him with her head. Not in the least.

'I'll make some tea,' she said, swinging her legs to the floor. 'And then I want you to go.'

He hesitated in the doorway, when the moment of parting came. 'Will I see you tomorrow?'

'I'm going back to Durham.' Emma hadn't told him about her father: there had not been time. Now she didn't want to. She wanted him out of her house, that was all.

'Did you sort things out up there?'

'I'd hardly be going back if I'd sorted it out, would I? As a matter of fact, it gets worse, not better.'

Keith was coming back inside the room. She would have to tell him now. 'I've found my father.'

'Your father? But he's . . .'

'No, he's not. He's very much alive. At least . . .' Impossible to explain it all. 'He's alive, Keith, but in hospital. I'm going back to see if I can talk to him. Now, please, I've got to get some sleep.'

'I love you, Emma.' He said it quite simply, quietly.

'I know,' she said, aad closed the door behind him.

She put away the hairdrier and cleared the paraphernalia of her bath. It was midnight. Keith would be almost home by now. She pictured him garaging the car, going into the house, taking off his damp jacket, reaching for slippers. And Lesley, barefoot and sleepy, holding up her face to be kissed, twining those thin brown arms with the faint fuzz of hair on them up and around his neck, locking them tight to bring his mouth down on hers.

Emma got into bed, but the images persisted. He would come from the bathroom, smelling of peppermint and soap. 'All right?' he would say and when she said 'Yes,' he would put out the light. Or perhaps he would be too eager for such niceties, coming to her already tumescent, eager, demanding, the thin brown limbs, arms and legs, twining around him, holding him, urging him on, riding him to the inevitable end.

She couldn't bear it. She got out of bed, reminding herself that he had lain there with her less than an hour before. There would be no love-making with Lesley, not tonight. Her face softened, remembering tongue and fingers boring into her. He loved her. It was better with her.

But in the kitchen waiting for the kettle to boil, she took stock. Where had he learned to make love so well – if not with Lesley? She, Emma, had taught him nothing, for all her experience. He had come to her tutored by a loving wife: they had learned together, taught one another. He knew how to pleasure Emma because he had learned by pleasuring another, and the other was Lesley. She knew it instinctively, had known it from the day she and Lesley came face to face and she saw for herself a woman fulfilled. Fool that she was, she had thought sex to be her province; now she realized there was no quarter of his life in which Lesley did not hold sway. Except the world of work – that was the only ground left to her, Emma.

'But that's not what I want,' she thought. It was a short step from this to wondering what she did want, and what he wanted from her. She could not answer the second but she wrestled with the first. What had she wanted from this affair? Sexual gratification, certainly. Shared intimacy. A meeting of minds. 'And I want a child,' she thought. 'Now, before I am too old. I want a child, someone who will love me unconditionally.'

She went into her mother's room and opened the wardrobe, smelling the familiar odours that had been Esther Gaunt. In the end she took down a grey crêpe dress and held it against her face, crying for a maternal closeness she had always wanted but never had. She turned to the dressing-table and unstoppered her mother's perfume. Madame Rochas, still pungent, the most evocative thing of all.

She cried for a long time, weeping freely, until she heard Poppy come in at the door. She had brought her key this time and that, in itself, was a departure.

'Did I wake you?' Emma said anxiously. Poppy looked tired and drawn but above all concerned, and Emma's conscience pricked.

'I couldn't sleep. Tossing and turning . . . I was glad of the excuse to get up.' Poppy's candlewick dressing gown was soft, her arms inviting. 'There now, what's the matter?'

'I love him, Poppy.'

'I know, darling. I know.' That was all Poppy said, but each knew what the other was thinking – that going to Keith's home, embracing his wife and children, had been bound to lead to tears in the end.

12

Saturday 12 August

Sometimes her father's eyes opened and held Emma's own, but whether it was venom in his gaze or just disinterest she could not say. 'He's poorly,' the sister said, when she passed by, and then pursed her lips as though she didn't like the look of things.

'Don't die,' Emma thought. 'Don't die now, when I've just found you.' But her longing for him to linger stemmed from curiosity more than filial love. There was so much she wanted to ask him, so much she needed to know.

'Please,' she said once, when his eyes met hers, 'please talk to me. I want to ask you about the past. I know so little.' There was a momentary gleam that might have been pleasure or triumph at her frustration, and then he turned his head away.

Emma, hearing footsteps nearing the bed, looked up to see her aunt.

'You're here then,' Peggy said, sliding a chair alongside Emma's and sitting down.

'I came back today . . . this morning.'

'From Manchester?' Her aunt made it sound like Australasia and Emma smiled.

'Yes. It's only a couple of hours.'

Peggy shook her head in amazement and leaned towards the bed. 'How are you then, lad?'

The pale eyes stayed immobile but Peggy prattled on. 'Eddy sends love . . . our Billy and our Vera as well.

Eddy'll be in on Monday, after his bowls. Did you eat your dinner? Get your nourishment, that's the first step. Our Vera's Christine's started school. Only four. They push them nowadays.'

The blue-veined eyelids dropped under the onslaught of words, and Peggy sat back.

'He was such a bonny little lad,' she whispered to Emma. 'Bright as a button. He could've gone far. But there weren't the chances then, not for our sort. He was bucked when he got into Culrose's. Pleased as punch. They let him down in the end, though.'

There was so much Emma wanted to ask but the figure in the bed stilled her tongue. They shared the rest of the vigil, not speaking much and never above a whisper, until the bell rang to signal the end of visiting.

'It still doesn't seem quite real,' Emma said when they came out on to the hospital steps. It was drizzling, though radio and newspapers were still talking drought.

'It's real enough,' her aunt said. 'I should know: I've been coming here twice a week for four years.'

'Let me run you home,' Emma said, steering the older woman in the direction of the red car. Her aunt hummed and hahed but looked pleased all the same as Emma folded her into the passenger seat. They threaded their way through the town centre, Peggy pointing out landmarks as they went.

'But you don't belong to Sunderland, really,' Emma said as her aunt lamented the passing of the old Town Hall.

'No. I was born in Belgate, and so was your Dad. It's a pit village.'

'So how did you come to live in Sunderland?'

'Your Dad came here first. He never fancied the pit. A lot of lads didn't, but there was nothing else in

194

Belgate. John got himself an apprenticeship at Culrose's, when it was a proper sawmill, not a glorified shop. Oh, if you'd seen your Dad when he was a lad. He had a bit about him then . . .'

Peggy was going to lapse into bitterness again: it was already there in her voice. Emma steered her hastily back to the subject.

'So Dad came to work for Culrose . . .?'

'Aye, he did. And that's how I met Eddy. He worked for Culrose, too.' Emma glanced sideways and saw that Peggy's face had softened at the memory. As soon as she realized that Emma was looking at her, though, the lips firmed and the chin came up. 'She's a fraud,' Emma thought and smiled to herself.

It had started to rain heavily and the wipers were straining to clear the windows. They were on the bridge now, ready to turn down towards the sea.

'I married Eddy in 1947,' said Peggy. 'Your Dad had been wed to Esther two years then. They had a house, nothing but the best for her. We had two rooms in Devonshire Street, and were still there when we had our Billy. We got a house off the council when Vera was born. Then we moved to where we are now in 1984. Eddy likes it there. He can haunt the old places, you see. He started at the shipyards in '56 – you don't give thirty years of your life to a place and not get attached. He's off most days, mooching around there, happy as a butterlowie.' Again the softening of the mouth.

'You seem very happy together,' Emma said.

'We've been happy enough. I only wish our poor John'd had the same. To see him lying there now and to think of all the wasted years . . .'

'What happened exactly? I have to ask you, because my mother told me nothing – just that they couldn't get on, and she had packed up and left. I've never even been sure whether or not it was before I was born. Once I was reading a book about Byron: his wife took their baby and left him when it was a week old. I asked my mother, then, if that was how it had been for her, but she just brushed it off . . . said, "That's only in story-books," or something like that. But it was true about Byron.'

'I don't know anything about Byron. I do know our John yearned for a child – I saw his face when we had a family. It wasn't right.'

'No,' Emma said as the car came to a halt, 'no. If that's how it was, it wasn't right. Still, I'm here now, and I want to make it up to him if I can.'

Her aunt didn't answer. She was fishing in her bag for her key and when she spoke it was of her husband. 'He'll be out, likely. You're coming in, aren't you? I'll sharp have the kettle on.'

There was a lightening of the atmosphere between them now. They sat either side of the table, taking turns to pour tea or pass biscuits.

'I've often wondered what you'd turn out like,' her aunt said. She sounded not displeased with the result.

'Did he . . . did my father talk about me?'

Peggy Colman shook her head. 'I'd like to say he did. I expect that's what you'd like to hear, but the truth is he didn't. I never even knew you were a girl till I heard in a roundabout way once from someone who'd known your mother's mother.'

She sighed heavily as though coming to a decision. 'You might as well know it all. Not that there's much, but I suppose you have a right. They got married, like I told you, and they had a real nice home. Only a terrace but they had fitted carpets, the lot. Your Dad worked for Culrose's, and old man Culrose put your father on to watch the lad, David. He'd just come back from boarding-school and the old man wanted him to learn the job. It shows how well your father was thought of. Young Culrose was all flash – you should have seen his clothes. He had this sports car, a two-seater, you could hear it a mile off, and if you couldn't hear the engine he had a horn like a symphony orchestra! The whole town was talking about him and that sister of his. Birds of a feather, those two. Caroline, they called her. She went away to school, and came back full of airs and graces. She used to walk around with this dog . . . well, more like a Shetland pony, it was. Everybody knew them.'

She pushed forward her cup for a refill and then continued. 'Like I said, your father was set on to show young David the ropes. It was David this and David that and John the other: they were regular buddies. Presents for your father, and your mother asked up to the Culroses' house . . . And then old man Culrose died. There was a big funeral, with the whole work-force there, practically, and the yard closed for two days. What a firm that was . . . everybody knew somebody that worked for Culrose's. Or had worked for them. By then Eddy had gone to the shipyards, but he still stood outside the church, out of respect.'

'What happened after that?' Emma asked. 'To the firm, I mean.'

'I don't know that much, not the details. Your father and mother split up about that time, and your father left Culrose's, so after that I only knew what other people said . . . and what I saw in the papers. It was all in there when young David Culrose sold out.'

'I know I was born up here,' Emma said. 'My mother

told me that, and I've seen it on my birth certificate. But my parents had already parted by then?'

'Yes, she was just beginning to show when she left him. She went to her mother for the birth, and then she went off, south. I never saw her again. Her mother was a widow and she lived near me but we weren't close and, anyway, she died soon after. Esther was an only one so that was the whole family gone. Your Dad, well, he was always religious, we were brought up that way. Perhaps he went a bit far. He sold the house to the first person that offered. £500, he got, which was less than he'd paid for it. She got the money, your mother. I heard she set herself up in business and did very well out of it.' Peggy paused then and probed her cheek with her tongue till she had controlled her feelings.

'All water under the bridge, of course. Esther went up in the world, but John lived in two rooms and never worked again. Not proper jobs, anyway, nothing permanent. He was a craftsman, but in the end he was no better than a dogsbody. It changed him, turned him in on himself. He never smiled again, I'll tell you that. His nose in the Bible or the newspaper, you couldn't get two words out of him.'

'Didn't anyone try to help him?'

'We all tried. Eddy went out of his way, time after time, but it was useless. All he got was a mouthful of scripture. Like I said, our John turned very religious. Anyway, that's about it. You've got no family but us, not on your father's side. There's only me and Eddy left, and you've got two cousins, our Billy and our Vera.'

Emma listened to the details of her cousins' marriages and occupations, but her mind was elsewhere. 'I'll go in and see Dad again tomorrow,' she said at last. 'Show him that I'm still here. Do you think he realizes who I am?'

Her aunt shrugged. 'I don't know. Sometimes I think he scarcely knows who I am, never mind a daughter he's never seen.'

There was the sound of a door opening and Eddy appeared.

'You can't drink this, Eddy, it's stewed. Make a fresh pot.'

When her husband had gone off to obey orders Peggy leaned towards Emma and patted her hand. 'They don't come much better than your Uncle Eddy. Not that I let him know that!'

It was four o'clock by the time the tea was drunk and reminiscence over. Eddy had talked of the old days at the Culrose yard, and now, when Emma got up to go, he offered to show it to her. 'It won't take more than five minutes, and then I'll put you back on the road for Durham.'

'Listen to him,' her aunt said indulgently. 'Any excuse to get back to his old haunts! Don't keep the girl there all night, Eddy Colman, mind. And you tell him when you've seen enough . . .' There was a slight hesitation and then, a trifle self-consciously, Peggy added, 'pet'.

'You're well in now,' Eddy said as he strapped himself into Emma's passenger seat. 'That's your aunt all over. You're either in or you're out, with Peggy!'

'Does "pet" mean I'm in?'

'It does. You have to understand my missus. A kind heart and a caustic tongue, that's Peggy Colman. Mind you, they're all a bit funny, mining folk. Me, I'm a townee. There's a difference.'

Emma smiled as she followed his directions towards the riverside.

'This town's built around the river,' Eddy said. 'That's St Peter's church . . . old as the hills. They say Bede was there once, the Venerable Bede.'

'I must explore it one day,' Emma said. 'I never knew there was such an ancient church here.' The sign said, 'AD 674'.

'You wouldn't,' Eddy said, as they pulled up beside the river, 'not if you go by the media. All they'll tell you about Sunderland is its bad points. Cobbles and unemployment, that's all you get from them. But this is a canny town, a skilled town. We've got know-how here. One day it'll come out.'

Across the river Emma could see a sign: 'North-East Shipbuilders Ltd, North Sands' and behind that houses and tower blocks. 'Are the shipyards all closed now?'

'All gone,' he said, raising a hand to point to a huge brick building, its windows blanked out with corrugated iron sheeting. A name was written on the gable end, faded now but still visible: 'N. Culrose and Son'.

'That's where it all began,' Eddy said. 'Your father came to work there, and him and me palled up. That's how I met your Aunty Peg. Love at first sight – well, that's what I tell her. It keeps her happy.' He was chuckling and Emma tried to keep curiosity out of her voice.

'So that's the business David Culrose sold?'

'Yes. The old man must've turned in his grave. Young David didn't so much sell it as give it away. Overnight, he was gone off to Durham to start out on a limb. I've always said that it was losing his father turned him funny.'

'Why did Dad leave the firm? Surely he could've gone with it to Durham if he'd wanted to?'

Eddy shook his head. 'I never could quite get the ins

and outs of that part. John went very religious, always breathing hellfire and damnation. The whole family were inclined that way, but in John's case it turned sour. He wasn't so much religious as resentful. And bitter, very bitter. Thank God my Peg's not like that, but she's tarred with the same brush, all the same. I tell her she should've taken the veil ... one of the silent orders.' He chuckled. 'It's never too late, I tell her, but she keeps on yakking! Your Dad seemed as though he tired of a working life. You'd find him in his chair any hour of the day or night, Bible propped open. He must've learned it from end to end before he was done.'

Emma let it go then, and listened as Eddy pointed out his beloved shipyards, closed and silent now.

'Who do you blame for the closure?' she said as they drove on.

'Fate, bonny lass, that's the real culprit. Fate and evolution. I've read up on the subject. At the end of the Great War British shipyards had the capacity to supply the whole of world demand – think of that! But we couldn't hope to keep on elbowing the rest of the world out. Of course, things picked up in the Second World War but then the rot set in again. And this government didn't help. The old Conservatives weren't a bad bunch, give or take a few, but this lot are cold fish. They'd cut your lifeline without a qualm to save the cost of a stamp. I'll tell you one thing though: the Sunderland yards were doomed the moment they were nationalized. Till then, we had a dozen yards on the Wear: Shorts, J. L. Thompson, Bartrams, Doxfords, Greenwells, Austin and Pickersgill, the North Eastern Marine ... but all of a sudden we were one big happy ship. And when the axe fell, we all went. If there'd still been independent yards on this river, one of them would've survived. One would've scraped by till the upturn came. Now, they're done for – sacrificed so Belfast and Scotland can hang on a little bit longer. Tell that to future generations of Sunderland youngsters.'

Emma dropped him off at the bridge and threaded her way back on to the Durham Road. She watched for the towers of Durham, picking out the cathedral from a few miles off, thinking all the while of the night before. Had that really been her? Was that really Keith? Did he care? She had still not reached an answer when she arrived back at the hotel and stripped for a shower.

Tonight she was meeting the Culroses and Robert Eden again. She felt her spirits rise at the prospect of some verbal sparring. Of course, now that she knew of Eden's sad past, she ought to go easy on him. 'Fat chance!' she said out loud and tore the sachet of shower foam apart with her teeth.

She wore her black cotton shift with a tan belt and sandals and her favourite gold hoops in her ears. Her hair was swept up on to the top of her head and the feeling of air on the nape of her neck was pleasant. She would be glad when August was out. Even when it rained, the atmosphere was humid and enervating. She sprayed herself with Opium, put some essentials into a black clutch bag, and was ready for anything. Robert Eden had arranged to drive her to the restaurant, although 'arranged' was probably the wrong word. 'I'll pick you up at seven-thirty,' he had said in lordly fashion and, before she could protest, 'It's stupid and wasteful to take three cars. You're on my way, so it won't put me out.'

She had looked at Stephen and April and seen their

'green' expressions. 'Yes, that makes sense,' she'd said meekly. At least she could deprive him of the satisfaction of victory.

His greeting, when she came down to the lobby, was an inclination of the head. 'Watch what you say to-night,' he said as they went to the door. 'Bearing in mind what I told you, I mean. I don't want the kids to dwell on their father's ... weakness, for want of a better word.'

'So Papa Bear worries about the Baby Bears?' She hadn't meant to sound so cynical.

'If you like. Just watch your tongue, that's all I ask.'

'You ask too much!' She was really mad now, wonderfully, gloriously angry, which made a pleasant change from feeling guilty and neurotic. 'I, Mr Eden, am very used to exercising discretion. Unlike you, I can not only "watch my tongue", as you so charmingly put it, I can also conduct my clients' affairs without becoming emotionally involved. An achievement which seems to be beyond your grasp.'

She thought he would apologize once they got out to the car but Eden contented himself with seeing her into her seat and going round to his own door. 'We're eating Italian,' he said, as he fastened his seat-belt. 'I hope that's OK?'

She would have loved to lay claim to a pasta-allergy, but the call of spaghetti carbonara was too strong. 'That's fine,' she said. 'I'm ravenous. Let's go.'

The restaurant was small and dark and smoky from candles glittering in Chianti bottles on every table. Emma and April sat in corner seats in the booth, the men on the outside. 'This is nice,' Emma said as April gave a little shiver of pleasure. Tonight the girl looked less podgy, her hair shone from washing, and her blue linen dress was at least appropriate to the occasion.

'How's your father?' Robert Eden said, as they chewed on breadsticks.

'Poorly, I'm afraid. I haven't been able to talk to him yet. I have talked to my aunt, though – my father's sister.'

There was a pause as their starters were placed before them.

'She says that my father worked for the Culroses, in their Sunderland yard. When your father, Stephen, came into the business as a very young man, my Dad became some sort of PA to him, someone to show him the ropes. And then your grandfather died, at just about the time my parents decided to split up. So there was a connection between my father and yours ... a working one. That doesn't seem enough to lead to a bequest to another generation more than a quarter of a century later! Apparently my father has lived a rather hand-to-mouth existence for the last twenty years. If your father had cared for him, surely he'd have done something then? Or written my father into his will: that would have made sense of a kind.'

They were all regarding her solemnly. 'Come on, eat up. It's really my problem not yours. I've told you, all I want is the truth. You can have the rest.'

Stephen Culrose frowned. 'We might be curious too. It's all right to say you'll just opt out, but that doesn't really satisfy anything, does it? We all want the truth.'

If she hadn't known better, Emma would have sworn Robert Eden administered a quick kick to his client's shin. The boy grimaced slightly and his eyes went down to his plate. April looked nervously from one to another and then started eating as though her life depended on it.

'I've applied for probate,' Robert Eden said. 'That doesn't commit any of us to anything, it simply starts the ball rolling.'

'What happens if we never find out?' April said, her eyes round behind her spectacles.

'Oh, we'll find out, April,' Emma said firmly. 'I don't intend to give up until I do find out.'

'You seem able to get unlimited leave,' Robert Eden said.

Emma gritted her teeth. 'I'm my own boss, Mr Eden . . .'

'Do call me Robert,' he interrupted in silky tones.

'I'm my own boss,' she repeated, 'and apart from that, I'm on holiday at the moment. My annual leave. I should have been . . . in Egypt now.'

'Why didn't you go?' April asked.

'Was it because of all this?' Stephen said, sounding slightly shocked.

'No.' Emma shook her head. 'No, there were several reasons why I called the trip off, and this played a part. I might have gone off somewhere nearer home . . . but then you appeared, Stephen, and I got intrigued, and here I am. And here's my pasta, so no more talking.'

They ate and drank then, swopping feeble jokes and laughing a trifle self-consciously. 'We all need this,' Emma thought. 'Each of us is under stress. Me, because for once in my life I'm at a loss. Stephen and April, because they're orphaned and confused. And Robert . . . silly to go on using his surname . . . Robert is stressed because he convinced himself that I was a scheming harpy, and now he sees I'm not, he doesn't know what to do with me. And he cares for the kids.' However boorish he might be, he genuinely cared for his clients, these particular clients anyway.

'Will you come to lunch tomorrow?' April said, when they were out on the pavement.

Emma put an arm round the girl's shoulders and squeezed. 'Not lunch, I'm afraid. I want to visit my father and visiting hour is 1.45 to 2.45: too early for your lunch, I bet. I'd love to come to tea, though, if you'll have me?'

'I could do you sandwiches,' April said, 'if you haven't had lunch? Or something warmed up?'

'Sandwiches would be super.' Emma put out a hand and moved a lock of hair from April's brow. The teenager's skin was shiny and pimpled. 'See you tomorrow,' she said, resisting the impulse to lean and kiss the child's cheek.

'I'll give you your beads back then. I meant to bring them tonight.'

'Don't bother,' Emma said. 'I want you to have them and we'll look for some ear-rings too.' April smiled and Emma patted her hand. 'Sleep well.'

'She likes you,' Robert Eden said when they were in the car.

'I like her.'

'Yes, probably. But you'll be able to cope with your feelings. I'm not sure April can.'

'What do you think I'm going to do? Drop the kid as soon as I get what I'm after? I don't know where you got your views on the modern woman, Robert, but aren't they a trifle extreme?' That was hitting below the belt: Emma knew about his ex-wife and now he would know that she knew. 'Look, can't we stop the verbal fisticuffs?' she said, more gently. 'I really have neither the inclination nor the energy for it at the moment. My plate is full, I assure you.'

'OK.' Robert lifted his hands from the wheel momentarily, as though in surrender. 'OK. I admit I went over the top in the beginning – but look at it from my point of view. Those two kids have had, let me tell you, one hell of a life. Their father never really loved their mother, he just tolerated her and well they knew it. He drinks till he dies, leaving them with a business on the point of collapse – and along comes a strange woman with the key to the safe. What was I to think? I freely own I was less than professional: I wanted to throttle you, if you must know. I was wrong. I totally accept that you are what you say you are . . .'

Emma laughed. 'A nice girl? Is that how you were going to put it? If you only knew!' They were at her hotel now and the car was slowing. 'Look, come in and see if we can get a drink. Then we can not only bury the hatchet, we can see it off in style.'

They settled in the lounge with brandy and coffee. 'I'm glad we cried "pax",' Robert said, 'if only because it saves me from going home too early. I loathe that last hour between eleven and twelve. You can't go to bed before midnight on a Saturday night, can you? It's indecent somehow, once you're turned thirteen.'

Emma nodded, uncertain what she should say. He sensed her discomfiture and smiled. 'It's OK, I don't mind you knowing I'm the victim of a broken home.' He was joking but she could sense the pain beneath.

'April told me,' she said. 'Not in any gossipy way. She's fond of you . . .'

'And she pities me. I know. Her father told me to get out of my marriage three years ago. I expect she picked it up from him.'

'Was it bad?'

'Fairly. What about you? You're not married?'

'No.'

'But there's someone?'

'Yes, but it's complicated. Not easy, not easy at all, so I know how you feel.'

'Let's drown our sorrows. What shall we talk about?' Robert asked.

'Something neutral,' Emma said fervently.

'Politics?' He was being provocative, but only for fun. They talked about music, finding they shared a liking for the jazz guitar of Pat Metheny and the bass of Jaco Pastorius.

'Pastorius was with Weather Report in the '70s, then he got his own band, Word of Mouth. I have their albums. You can borrow any you haven't got.'

'His death was tragic, wasn't it?' Emma said.

'Yes,' Robert said. 'Something screwed him up musically, and then he was murdered . . . outside a jazz club, I think.'

Emma shuddered. 'And we think we have problems. Still, he's left wonderful music. I adore Weather Report. And Metheny's coming to Britain soon: I saw it in one of the papers.'

They sat on till the coffee-pot was empty and the glasses had been refilled more than once. 'I shall leave the car here tonight,' Robert said. 'The walk home will do me good. I'll pick it up in the morning. It wouldn't do to lose my licence.'

Emma nodded. 'You're right. Tell me something, my aunt mentioned a sister of David Culrose. She'd be Stephen and April's aunt?'

'Caroline. Or Caro, as everyone called her. She was, is, a character. Very good-looking, very posh, very confident. She used to come up to Durham quite often, but lately I think the whole situation got beyond her. She lives in London. Her husband is an MP – Tory, of course. With a constituency in the Home Counties. They came up for the funeral, and she's anxious for Stephen and April to go down and stay with her for a while.'

'Will they?'

'I doubt it. She intimidates them, especially April. April is . . . well, you know.'

'Gauche? Not any more than any other average sixteen-year-old. It's a bloody awful age. If you want to boost her morale, stop Stephen from calling her "Pud". I know he means it affectionately, but can you think of a more demoralizing sobriquet? What frightens me more, though, is that she doesn't seem to have any idea of what she's going to do with her life. She likes children but that's her only thought on the subject. Why isn't she going in for some training, aiming to get somewhere, taking an NNEB course?'

'We can't all be thrusting career women, can we?' The old taunting note was back in Robert's voice.

'Oh, I don't know. You sound quite bitchy enough.'

'*Touché,*' he said, rising to his feet. 'Good-night, Emma Gaunt. Sleep well.'

He stood in the foyer in mock salute until the lift doors closed on her. Emma winced then, thinking of him limping home to his lonely bed. Poor sod, alone with his jazz records. Just like her!

She saw the red message-light winking from her telephone before she put on the room light, and she picked up the receiver at once. 'Hallo. This is Room 404. You have a message for me?'

'Just a moment, madam.'

Was it Poppy . . . or Keith? She was pondering possibilities when the night porter came back to the phone.

'A Mr Keith Oliphant called, madam. He wanted you

to know he'd called twice. He'll phone again tomorrow. And he said he hoped you'd have a good night.'

When she put down the phone Emma sat down on the bed, feeling the pasta and wine heavy on her stomach, the brandy and coffee lying uneasily above them. Nothing for it but to make for the bathroom and retch until she could rid herself of the burden. She was not bulimic, she told herself as she got ready for bed; it was not that at all. It was simply that sometimes you couldn't cope.

Sunday 13 August

They were still talking drought on the radio as Emma drove towards the hospital. Apparently the situation was worst in the West Country, and was caused, so the commentator said, by holiday-makers flocking there instead of abroad because of last year's airport strikes. So she was not the only one holidaying at home. Emma smiled wryly and eased into a car-park space.

The bed her father had occupied the day before was occupied by someone else now, a thick-set man looking remarkably healthy and surrounded by a bevy of adoring female relatives. Emma walked the length of the ward, looking left and right, but there was no trace of her father. She began to retrace her steps, sure she had missed him, when the junior nurse approached her.

'Are you Miss Gaunt?'

'Yes.' Fingers of alarm first tickled and then squeezed her chest.

'Sister would like a word with you.'

Emma knew before she entered the room or saw the Sister's look of ritual sorrow. 'I'm afraid he went in the night, Miss Gaunt. Night Sister was with him. She says it was very peaceful. Now, can we get you a cup of tea?'

Emma drank the tea, sitting in the easy chair in Sister's office, the bustle of the ward ebbing and flowing through the door.

'Do you want to see him?'

Her initial reaction was to shake her head, but then

she thought better of it. She had done little enough for him in life: at least she could pay her respects in death.

He lay in the little chapel, a handful of flowers in a beaker beside him, a cross on the wall above his head. 'He looks peaceful, doesn't he?' the accompanying nurse said, almost admiringly.

'Yes,' Emma said, and it was true. The agony had left her father's face with the closing of his restless, penetrative eyes. He looked relaxed, even pleasant, only the awful pallor of his skin signalling that all was far from well.

'I hate to ask you,' the Sister had said as she left the ward. 'But if you could just sign this and take his things? We're so short of space. There's only a change of clothes, and his wallet, and £1.42p.'

Now Emma changed the plastic carrier bag that held these to her other hand, and walked out into the sunlight. In the car she took out the red leatherette wallet and opened it up, half-expecting to see a photograph of her mother or one of herself, cute in childhood. There were no photographs. Only two or three Biblical texts printed on card or cut from newspapers, yellowing now with time and air. A few receipts. A couple of newspaper cuttings so fragile they threatened to disintegrate at touch. Emma put the wallet into the glove-compartment of the Capri and drove out of the car-park. She must go and find her aunt, who deserved to know as soon as possible.

'He's gone, hasn't he?' Peggy Gaunt, now Colman, said when Emma came face to face with her. Perhaps it was the whispered conversation with Eddy in the hall, or perhaps some odd family telepathy.

'I'll put the kettle on,' Eddy said, and vanished.

'I'm not going to cry,' Peggy said, when Emma

squeezed her hand in sympathy. 'John's better off out of it. I've cried many a tear for him in life, and I've got none left for him now.'

'What should I do?' Emma thought as they waited for Eddy to fill their hands and minds with the welcome tea. Not for the first time in the last week, she was completely at a loss. She had lost her father, a cataclysmic event for most people, and yet she felt only the thrice-removed sadness one feels at the death of a stranger. And, if she was honest, a tiny frisson of relief that she would not again have to meet those tortured eyes.

'There'll be a lot to fix,' Eddy said when he had filled a cup for himself and taken a seat. 'You can leave it all to me and Peggy.'

'I want to pay,' Emma said fiercely. 'Please? It's really the only thing I can do: put up money. Let me at least do that.'

They demurred, but Emma could tell they were relieved. 'It'll be Chapel,' her aunt said. 'John might have fallen away in the last few years, but he was still a Christian.'

'Do whatever you think best,' Emma said. 'Don't spare any expense and leave the bills to me.'

'What about flowers?' her uncle asked.

'I'll get my own, I think,' Emma said. 'There'll be a florist in town.'

'And what about the paper?'

'There'll need to be an announcement in the paper. We'll have to say he belonged to someone . . . I mean, is he a dearly beloved father or what?'

They settled on: 'John Gaunt, dear father of Emma and well-loved brother of Margaret Ann.' Her aunt cried then. 'No matter what he was, what he turned into

213

in the end, he mattered to me.' And when Emma took her in her arms, 'You came back. At least you were here at the end.'

Emma cried too, then, partly out of sympathy, partly from confusion, but not at all from a sense of loss. She would have to think later about where she stood. At the moment she was neither bereaved daughter nor disinterested observer.

Suddenly she remembered about April, waiting with sandwiches. 'Can I use the phone?' she asked and went to tell April she wouldn't be coming to tea.

It was unbearably hot when she came out to the car – hot and sticky, with a sense of thunder in the air. Emma longed suddenly to be home with Poppy, in her own pad with the doors shut against the world. Or back in the SyStems office, Amy twirling in her chair as she talked on the telephone, Keith intent on his terminal, each of them separated from her by glass so that she was alone in a clean bubble where everything obeyed her command and no one entered except with her permission. Instead she was here, in a street above an alien river, preparing for a stranger's funeral, a host of unanswered questions gathering like spectres around her.

She glanced at her watch: it was ten past five. She got into the car with a backward wave towards the watching couple at the window, and sent the car speeding towards Durham and the comparative normality of the St Nicholas Hotel.

She changed into shirt and slacks and went to her bag to get her father's wallet. He must have kept the things in it for some reason, and they would bear closer examination. She hunted through her bag before remembering she had left the wallet in the glove-compartment of the Capri. She had retrieved it and was making her way back into the hotel when she felt the first drop of rain. Thank God, now it would cool down.

She had almost reached the stairs when she heard a voice behind her and turned to see Robert Eden, followed by the Culroses.

'We're so sorry about your father,' April said, genuine regret in her young voice and her eyes brimming with tears as she remembered her own father.

'Thank you,' Emma said. 'I am sad, but remember that I didn't really know him so I don't have the same sense of loss you two knew. What I do feel is a sense of frustration. If I'd looked for him sooner, who knows what I might have discovered?'

'We won't keep you,' Robert Eden said. 'But we didn't like the idea of you being here on your own, not tonight.'

She desperately wanted to be alone, but it was kind of them to bother. 'Let's go and have a drink,' she said.

They sat in the cocktail bar and talked of Emma's plans. 'I'm going back to Manchester again tomorrow, but I'll be coming back for the funeral. They think that'll be on Tuesday or Wednesday.'

'If there's anything we can do?' Stephen said and Emma smiled her thanks. She was grateful to them all, but it was a relief when Robert rose to his feet, moving nimbly round to pull back her chair. She admired the way he overcame his disability, turning it almost into an advantage.

'Sure you won't have another drink?' She tried to sound inviting but in fact she was itching to be rid of him and get on with the wallet and its contents.

As if he read her mind he shook his head. 'Thank you but I'll take a raincheck if I may. I'm in court in the morning and I have some homework to do. And you want an early start if you're going south.'

They walked out to the entrance and stood there as Stephen and April climbed into Stephen's car.

'See you,' April called, and Emma waved goodbye.

A wind was blowing up, the hint of more rain in it, and her hair whipped into her eyes. She was opening her mouth to wish Robert good-night when he bent his head suddenly and brought his lips into contact with the side of her mouth. It was only a touch but it startled her.

'Oh dear,' he said, before she could speak, 'that was definitely not a good idea.' The rain came then, squalling from nowhere, sending him running to the driving side of his car, forcing Emma into the hotel portico before she was drenched. When she reached safety and turned he was already driving out of the car-park, his wipers swishing angrily as though to wipe away the memory of an indiscretion.

As she went up in the lift Emma fingered her face where his lips had landed. How odd! But he was an odd man – harsh, and yet comforting to anyone he thought at a disadvantage. She had seemed an underdog tonight, confused and bereaved: that had been his motive, to express his sympathy.

When she got to her room she put it from her mind, changed into robe and slippers, and sat down by the phone to dial.

'Poppy?'

'It's you, darling. I was just thinking about you.'

'Are you alone?'

'Yes, quite alone. His lordship is wining with the

216

boyos tonight, so you can fire away. I'm glad to hear from you actually. I've been watching the box, and Steve Ovett's crying like a baby because he lost a race. I wish that was all I had to cry about.'

'Well, you can cheer up, I'm coming home tomorrow. That's the good news. The bad news is that my father died today . . . well, during last night.'

'Oh, Emma . . . I'm sorry. I know the circumstances are unusual, but a father is a father. And you've just found him . . . oh, God, that's awful.'

'I know. I feel . . . well, odd. It's as though the whole world's gone crazy, and nothing is as I thought it was. Touch something and it crumbles; rely on something and it fades away; find something, and hey presto, it's gone. When is it all going to stop, Poppy?'

'Well, come home to me, darling, I'm still good old reliable Poppy. What you see is what you get, I promise you. And it'll be lovely to have you back. Are you home to stay tomorrow?'

'No. I'm coming to collect something to wear at the funeral, primarily. That will probably be on Wednesday. But we'll have time to talk. I've so much to tell you.'

'You have? Oh God, I could do with a good gossip. Tell me you've met some northern mill-owner with a ton of brass and a weekend place in the Dordogne.'

'There aren't any mills up here, Pops. There used to be coal-owners but they got nationalized. Now it's trade-union leaders and Japanese industrialists, and they don't go in for little places in the Dordogne.'

'No, but think of the sushi and the electricals, darling. And they do say Tokyo has a nice climate.'

'Well, there is no man, Poppy, Japanese or any other nationality. I did get kissed tonight, but it was far from romantic, believe me.'

'If you tell me about it I might. Believe you, that is.'

'It'll have to wait till tomorrow. I'm coming early, and we'll talk and talk. Give Charlie the night off.'

Emma boiled the kettle when the call was over and carried coffee to the bedside table. The contents of John Gaunt's wallet fluttered on to the bedspread, and she moved them into place. There were seven Biblical texts or allusions. She put them in a neat pile, and looked at the newspaper cuttings.

One was dated 1957 and told of the closure of the old Culrose yard and the transfer of the business to the new owner's premises. Another, about changes in social security regulations, had been marked with a ballpoint, as though her father had been noting those details that concerned him.

Emma read the Culrose cutting again and again. It interested her, but it told her nothing new, nothing relevant. She turned to the receipts, hope deserting her. It would have been too easy to find her answer like this. All the same, she had hoped.

One receipt was for a transistor radio, bought in 1976. The other, creased and fingered almost to transparency, was from a jeweller: *'T. J. Winston and Son.'* Emma had heard that name somewhere, and she was still racking her brain over it when she saw what the receipt was for. *'To making and supplying a 9 ct gold brooch in the shape of a ewe-lamb, according to buyer's own specifications. £480.'*

She sat back on her pillows, trying to think. *'Winston and Son'*: the name on the box in her mother's drawer. *'Winston and Son, 5, High Street, Sunderland.'* She had seen the name when she found the box, but it hadn't registered then. She looked at the date of the receipt: *'25th October, 1957'*. 1957! That year that threaded its way through everything. £480. She tried to do sums to work out its value in today's terms. Several thousand pounds, certainly.

So in 1957, her father, out of work and estranged from her mother, had commissioned a wildly expensive and bizarre piece of jewellery and given it to the wife who had so mistreated him. It didn't make any kind of sense. Suddenly Emma wanted to tell someone, anyone about her discovery, but it was nearly half-past ten. Too late to ring anyone, except in dire emergency.

She was putting the contents back into the wallet, keeping the receipt on one side, when the phone rang.

'Emma? It's me.'

'Keith, where are you?'

'I'm at home. Lesley's in bed, asleep. The kids have both been playing up, and she's taken them into our bed. I'll go into Tom's bed when I go up.'

Emma couldn't think of anything to say and for some strange reason she now didn't want to begin about the wallet and the receipt. Above all, she didn't want sympathy for her father's death: she felt an impostor when people sympathized with her. It was her aunt who deserved their concern.

'When are you coming back, Emma? I miss you.'

Again, she felt reluctant to tell him her plans. Her hair hung heavy against her neck and when she put up a hand to lift it away her head was moist with sweat. The hotel room was far too hot, in spite of the rain.

'Oh God, it's warm, isn't it?' She couldn't shirk, she must tell him. 'Actually, I'm coming home tomorrow.'

'You are! Oh, I'm glad. What time?'

She wanted to fudge things. 'I don't know exactly. It could be late. There's a lot happening up here.'

'Well, it doesn't matter. I can get away any time.'

Suddenly Emma felt motivated. 'You can? You have a very obliging wife, Keith.'

There was a small intake of breath at the other end of the line. 'Darling, I know you get upset, and I understand. If I could only be there ... I do care about you so much. I love you, Emma. And Lesley's fond of you too – I wish you could hear her talk about the way you mucked in when Zoë was ill.'

Emma waited for a long moment before she replied. 'In the whole history of inept remarks, Keith, that one must be a winner. I am not heartened ... *not* heartened ... to hear that my lover's wife thinks I'm a good egg. Only a cretin would think I might be. It's late, and I've had a lousy day.' If she didn't wind up this conversation, she would cry. 'I've got to go now. We'll talk tomorrow.'

'I'm sorry, darling, I was only trying to explain. I'm no good at this kind of thing on the phone. I want you here, now, face to face, so I can show you how I really feel.'

From behind him, somewhere in the house, a baby cried.

'Sounds as though it's going to be a bumpy night,' he said, sounding embarrassed and wretched.

Emma felt her heart melt. 'Get to bed now, darling. We'll talk tomorrow. I'll ring you at the office and tell you when I'll be back.'

When she put down the phone she went to the mini-bar and got herself a gin and tonic. She was physically exhausted, and yet she had never felt less like sleep in her life. But the really strange thing was how the memory of Lesley obsessed her. Tonight, when she had heard the baby crying, she had wanted to be there – not with Keith, but upstairs with Lesley, holding out her arms for the baby, sharing the load.

Outside there was a sudden rumble of thunder. Emma switched off the lights and crossed to the window, pulling back curtain and sliding frame to look out on the night. As she watched, lightning flickered and danced across the sky, throwing the world beneath into relief, turning buildings and roadways a strange blue, the shadows blacker than ink, like the treetops that waved from side to side as though overcome with grief.

She stood there, trying to analyse her own feelings, until the rain began, fierce and steady, bouncing off the rail outside her window so that her face and torso received a fine, cooling spray. She stood on for a while until the rain increased in intensity and she was driven back inside in search of another drink.

When at last she climbed into bed the rain was still beating a tattoo on anything that got in its way, and she was thinking of how it would be to comfort a child, still its sobs, and carry it, hiccuping quietly, back to its bed. Only this time the child she imagined herself succouring was a child of her own.

14

Monday 14 August

Emma left the hotel car-park at seven-fifteen, two hours after she had left her bed, glad to be up and about in the early morning light. She had paid her bill and booked a room for the next day. Behind her, in the car, her bags were packed, soiled linen neatly on one side, the plastic wallet sandwiched between her toilet bag and her hairdrier.

She was going home to collect decent mourning clothes for the funeral and to see if the brooch did tally with the receipt, as she suspected. But she wanted, needed, to see Lesley again. All night she had tossed and turned, dreaming sometimes of being at a disadvantage, afraid, and helpless to help herself. In the dawn greyness she had listened to the birds' first brave cheepings and had given way to her overpowering urge to confront Lesley once more. 'To see if she is real,' she thought, not comprehending why she should say something so foolish.

And now she was heading for Manchester and that executive des. res. with the untidy kitchen and immaculate study. She switched on the radio, hoping for diversion, but the news was of the runner Steve Ovett and his tearful outburst of yesterday. P. W. Botha, the South African premier, was to resign. She tried to welcome the good news but it seemed not to matter on this dull, suffocating English day.

Emma checked the dashboard clock. If she wanted to

catch Lesley *en déshabillé* she would have to be early, but not so early that she arrived before Keith left for SyStems. She eased her foot on the accelerator and settled in her seat for a leisurely 120 miles to Manchester.

While the signs slipped by ... *Scotch Corner, Wetherby, Leeds* ... she thought about the brooch. £480: a fortune to a man with no job back in 1957. She tried to summon up the brooch, to remember what had made it so special. It had to be the same one ... how many sheep-shaped brooches could there be? And the stones, stuck on the sheep's back like a saddle? She had thought them paste, but if they were gems that would go some way to explaining the price. She might be sitting on a valuable item. It had cost John Gaunt the price of his house, that was certain.

The golden sheep – what had the receipt said? A ewe-lamb – was beginning to take on intriguing proportions. Her father had commissioned it: that in itself was unusual. It wasn't something you did every day, if ever ... unless you were the Duke of Windsor or Richard Burton. Had it been a bribe to bring her mother back to the fold? Was that the significance of the lamb? If so, he must have loved her very much. And her mother had kept it. She had never used it but she had kept it safe. Emma felt her eyes prick suddenly. How awful if they had really loved one another but been too proud to admit they were wrong and reunite.

By the time she reached the city outskirts she was feeling decidedly sentimental. Perhaps she should stay away from Lesley today? But in her heart of hearts she knew that if she did so she would regret it later on. Better to do it now and get it over. Then, when she had picked at her wound, she would treat herself to a hairdo and a good lunch to raise her morale before she saw Poppy and took out the sad clothes of mourning for another airing.

When she was almost there she stopped at a corner newsagent to buy gifts: a glossy monthly for Lesley, a brightly coloured picture book for Tom, and a glass globe full of swirling snow for Zoë.

Keith's house looked the same, neat raw brick and everything utterly symmetrical. It looked as though Mr Wet or Mrs Dry would pop out any moment to say the weather had changed. If only it would! When she released her seat-belt her dress clung wetly to the small of her back and her thighs burned from contact with the seat.

She was sure that Lesley would be dressed this time, on top form and still euphoric about the return of her husband. But it was the same waif-like figure that greeted her, this time with a whoop of joy and two skinny arms right around the visitor's neck.

'Come in, come in. Tom, look who's here ... Aunty Emma!' Lesley's hair was caught back this time, fastened into a fuzzy turquoise holder, but the cotton nightie and wrapper were the same, the bare legs and feet with the chipped pink nails identical.

Tom appeared in Batman pyjamas, uncertain at first, looking to his mother to dictate the mood. She nodded and smiled, pushing him forward to hold up his face for a kiss. 'There now, you were wondering when Aunty Emma was coming back.' He turned suddenly and ran, to reappear a moment later with a bright yellow racing car. 'Brmm, brmm,' he said, making swooping motions to simulate fast travel.

'You go into the lounge, it's sunnier there. I'll bring

coffee. Take Aunty Emma to see your garage, Tom, there's a good boy.'

There were cars strewn on the shag-pile carpet and the baby sat in a yellow high-chair, a soiled bib around her neck and traces of breakfast around her mouth. A half-filled mug of coffee stood in the hearth, beside an opened paperback, laid face down to keep the reader's place. Margaret Drabble's *The Radiant Way* – so that was what Lesley read! But drinking coffee and reading in an undusted room, children and mother still in their nightclothes, the breakfast dishes undoubtedly un-washed in the sink if not still on the table – it was . . . Emma sought for a civilized word . . . sloppy.

'There now . . . this is nice. Keith went ages ago. He's going in early while you're away, and working all hours. I hardly see him, except at weekends.' Lesley talked with animation, the restraint of their first meeting all gone. 'She thinks we're friends,' Emma said to herself, and felt ashamed.

'Zoë seems fine,' she said aloud. As if she'd heard, the baby started to whimper.

Lesley raised her eyes to heaven. 'She's probably hungry. Let's get our coffee while we can. She never stops feeding . . . still, I suppose it's better than being picky.'

So she was going to feed the baby. Emma felt a quiver of excitement, of terror almost, the feeling you might get from probing delicately at a stitched wound, wondering if the sutures would hold or the flesh would gape suddenly, allowing the innards to spill forth in an endless, bloody stream.

The baby's whimperings gathered strength and volume, and Lesley took a huge gulp of her coffee. 'Better get it over. She had egg and bacon breakfast and

225

it seemed enough, but she wants some milk.' She stood up and began to extricate the baby from the chair. 'You don't mind, do you?' She was slipping breast from cotton covering. 'Only some people are so funny if you do it outside, and sometimes you can't help it. Keith says I shouldn't take any notice, he says they're only jealous . . .'

Emma nodded, trying to take her eyes off the baby's cheeks. In, out, in, out. Her ears sang with the pain of it. Clever Keith, finger right on the spot as usual. Jealousy, that was what consumed her now. She gripped her cup and saucer, resisting the urge to raise her hand to her own breasts, to feel them swell and engorge, to take the baby from the usurper and clamp the questing mouth to her own nipple.

'You like children, don't you?' Lesley said, smiling and pouring salt into the wound.

'I don't know much about them really,' Emma said. 'I'm an only child, so I had no young brothers or sisters. And we're a small family, so no cousins either.' Suddenly she could hear her aunt's voice: '*You've got two cousins, our Billy and our Vera.*' What a mess she was in, what a labyrinth of lies and half-truths was closing around her, her own and those of a generation gone.

'Poor thing,' Lesley said sympathetically. 'I've got heaps of relations. Too far away at the moment, but at least I know they're there. Most of them came for Zoë's christening. I know Keith asked you, but you couldn't make it. The Doulton nursery set was lovely, though. Too good to use. It's in the cabinet for when she grows up.'

'I was in London that weekend,' Emma said, 'or I'd have been here.' She lied easily this time. In fact she had

226

spent the day between bed and bath, weeping into her gin while Poppy alternated between offering comfort and prophesying doom.

The baby was falling asleep, its mouth going slack in concert with its drooping lids, then jumping into pump action again as the eyes snapped open. Emma watched, fascinated, her coffee growing cold in her hand, until at last Lesley took her nipple between first and second fingers and removed it gently from the baby's mouth. 'There now,' she said, slipping the breast into hiding, rising smoothly to lay the baby down on the dralon settee and put a cushion alongside it as a prop.

'She is dralon and shag-pile,' Emma thought exultantly – her triumph turning to ashes as the girl's face looked towards her, alight with friendship.

'I'm so glad we got to know each other, Emma. It's a pity poor little Zoë had to suffer to bring it about, but it's an ill wind, isn't it?'

Emma nodded and smiled as Lesley returned to her chair, curling her legs up and holding the toes of one foot in tiny, determined fingers. Had they fucked last night . . . or this morning? Did he wait until the baby was sated and then reach out . . .?

'You must be glad to have Keith back?'

'Oh yes.' Lesley pulled a little face. 'It's been like a second honeymoon . . . and he's been wonderful with Zoë.'

'She means to hurt me,' Emma thought. 'She must know it goes through me like a knife.' Aloud, she said: 'I don't know what it's like to be husband-less but I can imagine.'

Lesley tucked her hair behind her ear again. 'Forgive me for asking . . . tell me if I'm nosy and I'll shut up . . . but is there someone? You're so attractive . . .'

'There is someone,' Emma said, keeping her voice as steady as she could.

'Serious?' Lesley asked.

'Yes,' Emma said, 'it's serious. He's important to me, but how it will end I don't know. It's too early to say.'

'Is he nice?'

'Yes, he's nice. Very like Keith in many ways.' This was dangerous but she couldn't help it.

'Oh ho,' Lesley said. 'Hold on to him, then. He's worth having.'

'I mean to hold on to him,' Emma said, and then, 'I have to go, I'm afraid,' she said abruptly, and got to her feet.

In the car, Lesley's quick kiss burning into her cheek, Emma let the tears come. They were tears of fury, not at Keith for his duplicity or Lesley for her prior claim, but that she, Emma Gaunt, who had won a well-deserved reputation for competence, should allow herself to be swept, rudderless, towards the rapids that were surely waiting round the bend. And should even paddle furiously to bring calamity nearer!

In the beauty parlour she waited while they flicked through lists. Yes, she could have her hair done at one by Michelle while Gina did her nails, and before that Velody could give her a cleanse and facial massage. She submitted to a pink gown and was laid on a paper-covered couch like a virgin prepared for ritual sacrifice.

'You've got one or two pores,' Velody said, bringing down the inspection light.

'Yes,' said Emma in a penitential manner, and closed her eyes while her hair was bound back by a tissue band.

228

'There now.' Butterfly fingers were patting and teasing her tired face, delicious smells were circulating as cool lotions followed one another, each more soothing than the one before. She tried not to think about the morning's events, but when her thoughts turned to the day before, at the hospital, that too was painful. She was casting around for anodyne images when fingertips touched the corner of her mouth, like the butterfly kiss she had received the night before. Her lips curved, until she remembered the business in hand and surrendered her expression to the masseuse.

It was strange how a kiss from a man you liked ... because now she did like Robert Eden ... could leave you cold, and the glance of a man you almost despised ... the shock of her train of thought brought her head up from the pillow.

'I'm so sorry. My leg went into the cramp. I jumped.' She lay back and tried to relax, thinking how your own intellect could betray you. A part of her, somewhere, blamed Keith for a situation that the rest of her, the overwhelming majority of her, was doing everything it could to foster.

After that she thought about mundane matters like lunch and packing and what she could cook tonight to tempt Poppy to share her meal, and after a while the upward movement of skilful fingers lulled her to peace.

'There,' Velody said, 'almost done.' This time the lotion was bracing, ice-cold and invigorating. Emma opened her eyes and consented to look in the mirror at a skin ten years younger than the one she had brought with her.

After that she was shampooed, asked about holidays and where she was going tonight, and set under lamps for her hair to be dried. Gina filed her nails, complimented her on her cuticles and painted above her half-moons with a fetching shade of coral-pink.

Emma was regretful when it was time to slip out of her pink nylon shroud and face the world outside. It was dull outside, but even the pavement gave off heat. Emma paused outside the Save the Children shop and gazed at artefacts from the Third World mingling with the secondhand bric-à-brac the West no longer wanted.

A black velvet display board was studded with brooches and ear-rings and the occasional pearl-headed stick-pin. She went inside and handed over a ten-pound note in exchange for a silver four-leaf clover on a box-link chain. 'Keep the change,' she said, and went back outside into the humid afternoon air.

It was three-fifteen when she got back to the flat. She carried her bags inside and put on the kettle. There were three messages on her machine, but none of them needed immediate attention. When she had brewed tea she carried it through to her mother's room and then went back to collect her handbag. Inside was the wallet and the jeweller's receipt. She straightened it out: *T. J. Winston and Son.* Was that the name on the box that held the brooch? She lifted it from the drawer and saw that it was.

She took out the brooch and turned it around in her hand. '*Made in the shape of a ewe-lamb*'. Now that it was pointed out she could see the delicate lamb-like quality of the creature's face and body, the close curl of the fleece – even the sightless eye looked gentle now. Why had the jeweller not used one of the gems for the eye? And why were they grouped like that in the centre of the carcase, four stones in a line, neither matching nor toning?

She looked at them closely. Now that she knew the

brooch had come from her father it had assumed enormous importance. The first stone was an opaque deep blue with white veins, and a cast of violet. Not a gem, then, but a stone of some kind. The second one was clear and green: not the green of an emerald, more like an aquamarine perhaps? No, greener than that, so probably an emerald after all. The third was a ruby, a clear brilliant red, each facet sparkling. The fourth stone was clear, too, and colourless but she didn't think it was a diamond. If it was, it was of poor quality. So – blue, unspecified; then green, could be an emerald; then a ruby; and then an inferior diamond or piece of paste.

Rubies had gone up in value lately: she had read that somewhere. Something to do with Burma becoming inaccessible. And the brooch itself was heavy – the gold alone must be worth a packet. She cupped her hand around it and raised it to her eye. Her mother had told her once that you could always tell a diamond by the way it would shine in the dark. But all of the stones gave off a glint of some sort, so perhaps it was nothing more than an old wives' tale.

She took the brooch and its box back to her room and slipped it into the front pocket of her travel bag. The jeweller had a Sunderland address. If he was still there, she would pay him a visit. The brooch was unusual, and if he remembered supplying it, he might remember the occasion of the gift. She emptied her bag and put it ready to refill, then she went through to the kitchen to see what her freezer would yield.

When she had found something to cook she checked her watch: five-fifteen. She might catch Amy, if she was lucky. She should really have checked that all was well sooner than this. Nothing could be seriously wrong or Keith would have mentioned it, but Amy wouldn't know that. Since Emma was still in England, Amy would expect a call and if it didn't come she might wonder why.

While she waited for the number to ring out she thought of Keith. He would be gathering his papers together, putting them in briefcase or drawer, reaching for his jacket, going down to his Audi, turning out on to Oxford Road, negotiating the traffic, eager, impatient to get back home.

She felt her nails dig into the palm of her hand at the same moment that she heard the voice at the other end: 'SyStems.'

'It's me, Emma. Is Amy still there?'

Amy was there and happy to hear from her. 'Everything's under control. That is not to say that you haven't been missed. I have a strand of pure white hair that wasn't there a week ago. Seriously, though, we're fine – especially since Keith got back. Pity about his little girl . . . well, of course you know. I forgot about your Mary Poppins act. That raised some eyebrows, I can tell you.'

Emma felt her skin suddenly prickle. 'Really?' Her voice sounded arch and hostile to her own ear.

'Well, you're hardly the nanny type, are you? Glamorous exec, got her own branch at thirty, half the girls here using you as their role-model. You with a mouthful of nappy pins was a whole new concept.'

'That's what you're paid for, accepting new concepts. As a matter of fact, I was rather good at it.'

'That figures. Nice kid?'

Emma thought of Tom in the morning, warm and damp and loving. 'Very nice. Now, tell me what happened at the Transio meeting. Did Ivor cope?' She nodded approval as Amy reported success, and promised to ring again. It would be good to get back to the office, to feel the pull of a demanding job. Good to see Keith again in a civilized atmosphere. But she would have to be careful what she said to Amy. In retrospect, perhaps it had been a mistake to tell her about Stephen's initial call? Still, too late now. She would just have to be more careful in future.

By the time she heard Poppy's key in the door she had chicken joints in bechamel sauce, potatoes and green beans keeping warm in the top oven. 'Hi! I've got food here if you're interested.'

'Darling,' Poppy looked torn two ways, 'I could eat a horse but . . .'

'But you're expecting Charlie? I did enough for three, so if he comes he's welcome.'

'*When* he comes . . . he'll definitely be round later. He's been tied up with that franchise thing of his, but he promised he'd finish early tonight.'

They ate with one ear cocked for Charlie's arrival and a bottle of Chablis passing backwards and forwards across the table.

'So you're taking the brooch back with you?' Poppy asked when Emma had told her tale.

'Yes. Oh, it's thirty years ago, so I'm probably flogging a dead horse, but at this moment I'd try anything.'

'What about this solicitor guy, this Eden? Your tone, when you speak of him, has mellowed somewhat.'

'It has. You're not detecting anything, Poppy, I freely admit it. He's a bit macho for my taste, and he had a fair go at bullying me in the beginning. But I have put him right on that score, and, to be honest, I think he was genuinely sympathetic when I told him about my father. You've got to see it from his point of view: there

I was in the will, a thirty-year-old bimbo for all he knew. What else could he think?'

'Does he believe you now?'

'I think so. And more importantly the kids believe me. When this is all over I'm going to invite April here for a week. Bring her to you for some freebies.'

'Freebies? I'd do it like a shot, but I have this grasping proprietor . . .'

'Seriously, though, Poppy, you'd like her. Stephen too, although he's less vulnerable. I feel drawn to the girl: she has no one, and she's so . . . so accepting.'

'You, my dear, are getting broody. You'd better see it for what it is before it's too late. Come to think of it, April could fill a gap. Otherwise . . .' Poppy's jowls quivered with foreboding.

'You're joking,' Emma said easily. 'It's 1989, darling. We have ways and means. Remind me to tell you about them sometime.'

'Ta,' Poppy said. 'In my case the stable door is firmly shut. But you, my love, are a walking time-bomb. You have ten, maybe twelve, fertile years left. What you're feeling now . . . and I know you are, so don't dissemble . . . what you're feeling now will get more intense. There'll be times when you'll wonder if you can hold out any longer. I know. That's the way it was for me.'

'Did you want a child?'

'No, darling, I never do things by halves. I wanted a brood of children, steps and stairs, boys, girls, a houseful.'

'But you didn't do anything about it?'

'I played Russian roulette a few times. You know – if it happens it's Fate, that sort of thing. In the end, though, I saw sense. I could hardly keep myself in those days, let alone a kid. And there was another reason.'

'I know what's coming,' Emma thought. 'I know and I don't want to hear it.'

'It's selfish, Em, to bring a child into the world without a father. If it happens, it happens and you have to make the best of it. But to do it in cold blood, that's something else. Mr Right never came along for me, but you've still got time.'

'What if Mr Right's already come along but someone else got there before me?'

'Tough,' Poppy said and this time her face and voice were resolute. It was a relief to hear footsteps in the hall and let the argument vanish in a flurry of welcome for Charlie.

They sat him at the table, each of them fussing over him for their own reasons. 'This is the life,' he said, tucking his napkin into the top of his yellow waistcoat. 'Chicken. Yum, yum. And a good wine. I could get used to this.'

Emma looked at Poppy, at her glowing maternal expression. 'Oh Poppy,' she thought, 'if you imagine you're out of the parent trap you're sadly mistaken.'

Poppy and Charlie went off eventually, so that Poppy could change for a trip to the pub. 'A thousand thank-yous,' Charlie said with a flourish, bending to kiss Emma's resistant hand.

'Why don't I like him?' Emma thought. She had no basis for her feeling except the pricking of her thumbs, but pricking there certainly was. And besides, he wasn't good enough for Poppy. Who was?

When she had cleared the table and washed the dishes she pinned her hair under a cap and showered. She would have liked to spend the evening with Poppy, jogging her into recollections of life with Esther Gaunt. Poppy might know all sorts of things, if her rag-bag of a memory could be satisfactorily trawled.

She glanced at her bedside telephone as she put on her nightdress. She ought to ring Keith; she should have done it earlier in the day, but it was as though seeing Lesley had satisfied her. She had never even considered ringing him, and yet he had never been far from her thoughts. If only Poppy had been free tonight. She started to assemble the clothes she was taking back to Durham. Dark grey for the funeral, two Swiss cotton shifts . . . she was rooting for matching shoes when the phone rang.

'Emma. It's me, Keith. I'm round the corner in the Ivy House. Is it all clear? I'm coming up.'

'No.' She didn't want him in her home, not tonight, not yet. 'No, don't do that. I'll come down. I could do with a drink. How did you know I was back?'

'Lesley told me you called round. She was over the moon. It makes me feel so guilty sometimes, Emma.'

'Well, keep it to yourself, Keith. I can't take much more at the moment, and certainly not your angst.' She sounded short-tempered and hard and she made a deliberate effort to soften her approach. 'Look, I'll be with you in a few minutes. Get me a spritzer. I'll be there before it's poured.'

She applied make-up and perfume before she let herself out of the house, dressed in track-suit and sneakers. There was a pain low down in her groin, a sign of a period not far away. Normally, at this time, she could feel her breasts thrusting against blouse or sweater, turgid and vaguely uncomfortable. Tonight, though, they felt somehow diminished. 'I could never sustain a child,' she thought. Poppy had said she was getting broody but that was not exactly true ... or so she thought. Could you ever be sure of your own intentions? She turned out of the gate and made for the pub, vowing to get back to the safety of Durham as soon as she could.

Keith was quiet and sympathetic when she told him about her father. 'Poor Emma,' he said, tracing her metacarpal bones with a single fingertip. It was usually calculated to relieve her tension, but tonight was different. She looked him in the eye and admitted it.

'I feel strange tonight, Keith. It's not just my father, it's everything.' She wanted to tell him how large his wife loomed in her condition but this was not the time or place. 'I don't want you to come back with me tonight. Well, I do want you to ... you know that ... but it can't be, not tonight.'

Keith nodded with understanding. 'It's OK. I knew it was around that time. I just wanted to see you.'

He thought she was menstruating! Emma was at once outraged at this familiarity and then relieved. He was looking at her with concern and she felt a glow of pleasure. He did care. Whatever the rights and wrongs of it all, he cared for her as deeply as he cared for Lesley. And for now, at least, that must be all that mattered.

15

Tuesday 15 August

Emma had vacuumed and dusted, put a load of washing through the machine and thrown out most of the contents of the fridge by nine-thirty, and a glow of virtue was beginning to suffuse her.

She was scalding an instant coffee when the phone rang.

'Emma?'

'Amy! Is everything all right?'

'Everything here's fine, don't worry. Running like clockwork. I don't know whether I should've bothered you . . . I wasn't even sure you'd be there . . .'

'Get to it, Amy,' Emma thought.

'But she did seem flustered, and there's no point in my contacting Keith, even if I could manage it,' Amy continued.

'Do you mean Lesley?'

'Yes, sorry . . . I'm making a dog's breakfast of this. She rang five minutes ago, hoping to catch Keith. She has to take the baby to hospital today for an outpatient appointment, only her Fiesta's conked out. She was hoping Keith would let her have his Audi, but he's gone off in it to Sutton Coldfield. I've tried his carphone but he doesn't answer. She says she'll get a cab, but with two kids . . .'

'I'm glad you rang me,' Emma said firmly. 'We can't let her go by cab. She might wait hours to get home again and Tom's such a handful. Leave it to me.'

'Will you try and raise Keith at Transio? He's there till twelve. I can ring him if . . .'

'No,' Emma interrupted, 'leave it to me. I'll take her myself.'

'I thought you might,' Amy said. 'It's awfully good of you,' but Emma was already depressing the rest and dialling Lesley's number, consumed with fear that she might be too late. A fever to see Lesley again, to carry Tom down the neat front path, to shepherd them all in and out of the hospital, was consuming her.

'Lesley? Oh, good. Look, they phoned me from the office . . .'

'Emma!' Lesley sounded aghast. 'I didn't mean to make waves . . .'

'I know, but they did the right thing. I'd've been upset if I'd found out later. Now, have you phoned for a cab?'

'I've tried two places but they've nothing for another half-hour. I was going to ring another number . . . I've got Yellow pages . . .'

'I'm on my way. What time have you got to be there? Eleven? We'll have heaps of time. I'll be with you in ten minutes.'

She changed from her catsuit into a red seersucker dress and slipped her feet into red pumps. The leather thonging bit into her flesh and she cursed the shoemaker and the warm weather fluently while she searched for a substitute. She couldn't drive in floppy sandals, not with two kids in the car.

In the end she wore navy canvas deck shoes with a red trim and decanted her black bag of yesterday into a navy raffia shoulder-bag. She would need her hands free to deal adequately with Tom . . . or perhaps even Zoë. If Lesley was chicken about the consulting room,

239

she might take her place, put her cheek against the other tiny cheek to show solidarity, murmur 'There, there' and rock Zoë gently if she cried. Listen intelligently to the doctor and see his appreciation of her mothering. She thought of Keith then, his eyes on her, full of tenderness because she was caring for his child.

Suddenly the ridiculousness of her thoughts flooded in. Lesley would never chicken out, not where her children were concerned. She would walk in proudly, carrying Zoë, and Emma would be left behind to catch the crumbs. She clipped in her best Dior gold hoops and went out to the car.

The traffic had abated and she made good time to Keith's house, gliding neatly into the gutter alongside the ramp.

'Coo-ee!' Lesley was waiting in the doorway, baby in arms, Tom hanging on her skirt. 'Could you take Zoë? I just want to check the back door.'

The baby was unbelievably light and fragile in Emma's arms, her face at close quarters cherubic and wise.

'Hello, Zoë.'

The blue eyes regarded Emma solemnly for a while before the grin came, making her so like her father that Emma's breath caught in her throat.

'Right ... everything's OK.' Lesley looked almost smart in a denim skirt and matching T-shirt banded denim and white. 'Shall I take baby? Don't pull my skirt, Tom, darling. Look at Aunty Emma's lovely car. What colour is it? R –' She held the R until Tom obliged with the rest of the word. 'Yes, it's red. Like Aunty Emma's dress.'

Nothing for it but to surrender the baby, and when it smiled with pleasure at the reunion nothing for it but to say, 'There now, you're with your mum again.' She lifted Tom in her arms and carried him round the Capri, pointing out its special features while he brmm-brmmed to his heart's content.

'It's a lovely car,' Lesley said wistfully. 'Sometimes I think what I could've done if we hadn't started a family ... Not that I'd ever have been a super career woman like you – but I can dream, can't I?' She reached to ruffle her son's hair. 'Still, you can't have everything.'

'Smug bitch,' Emma thought, wrestling with the gears and her temper at one and the same time. 'Smug, smug bitch! Cow, cow, cow! Silly mistaken cow, because you *could* have everything if you had even a semblance of a brain.'

Remorse was suddenly bitter in her mouth and she forced herself to chatter with Lesley all the way to the hospital car-park.

'It gives me the shivers, this place,' Lesley said. 'Ever since Cleveland.' Her arms tightened around the baby. 'I heard a mother on the TV say how they just came and told her they were taking her children away. It frightens you. And then when it was proved they'd got it wrong part of the time, they went on insisting they were right.'

'I know,' Emma said. 'I was shocked at the support those two doctors got from other paediatricians.' She was about to say that a diagnostic success rate of 75 per cent didn't say much for standards within the specialty when she realized that would not bring much comfort to a mother about to enter the lion's den. 'Still, it's all over now,' she said airily.

'No, it's not,' Lesley said stoutly, starting to clamber out of the back seat with Zoë in her arms. 'Some of the parents are suing, and I hope they win.' She straightened up and glanced apprehensively towards the Out-patients Entrance.

'Don't worry,' Emma said fiercely. 'If they try anything on with you I'll be in there like a shot to threaten them with my solicitor.'

'Just threaten them with Keithie,' Lesley said, smiling. 'He'd go berserk if they tried to touch his precious children.'

'Keithie, Keithie,' Emma thought as she followed Lesley into the waiting-room, holding Tom's hand in hers. He would die for his children: for Lesley too, if need be. It was only constancy that was beyond him. And then, as always when she thought badly of him, she was consumed with guilt. If he was unfaithful, she was his willing accomplice.

The waiting-room was full of children and mothers with more than a sprinkling of fathers too. 'Keith would've been here if he could,' Lesley confided and then, remembering Emma's status, 'Of course, work has to come first.'

'Not always,' Emma said. 'Sometimes life must come first.' She said it with such fervour that she had to look sideways at Lesley to see if she had noticed, but Lesley was as perky as ever.

'Oh I know. I mean, if it was really urgent . . . but you're here and that's such a help.' She reached to touch Emma's hand. 'I don't know how we'll ever repay you.'

'Oliphant.' A nurse was reading out names from a list.

'Here,' Lesley called, rising to her feet. She moved towards the nurse, Zoë in her arms, Tom fastened leechlike to her skirt.

'Stay with Aunty Emma, darling. Mummy won't be long.'

Tom cried and struggled as Emma restrained him and Lesley disappeared through the doors of the consulting-room.

'Look,' Emma said, desperately, aware of critical eyes all around. She pulled off one of her Dior ear-clips and held it in front of him. He looked at it for a moment, still weeping, and then curiosity overcame him. He held it in his hands and began to pull the clip up and down, then held it out to her. 'Tom put in.' Emma bent her head and he tried to fix it on her lobe.

'You try it.' She attached it to his ear and he looked around in triumph. If only someone would laugh at him or applaud, but they were all hunched over their own children and oblivious of what a delight Tom was.

'I love you,' she said into his hair. It was silky against her lips and smelled of soap.

'Go down,' he said, wriggling. 'Tom go walk.' She left her bag on the seat as a sign for Lesley in case she came back early, and let him lead her out into the corridor. It bustled with signs, this way 'E.N.T.', that way 'Cardiology'. The floor was polished rubber and made obliging squeaks as they walked. Tom pulled a gleeful face and began to drag his footsteps.

'Eeek eek,' he said.

'Eeek eek,' she responded, feeling elated with her success. She was keeping him happy. She could do it.

An old woman was coming towards them, trudging slowly up the corridor. She paused for breath and eyed them. 'He's a bonny little lad. Three is he?'

'Only two,' Emma said proudly, sweeping Tom into her arms.

'The only one, I'll bet,' the old woman said knowingly. 'Mammy's pet!'

'She thinks he's mine,' Emma thought, and was at first disconcerted and then jubilant.

'He is a bit,' she said, looking suitably abashed as the old woman moved on. Tom's eye was on her, quizzical, as though he knew she had lied.

'Time to go back,' Emma said and set him down on the ground.

They had only a moment or two to wait until Lesley emerged, beaming. 'He doesn't want to see her again for a month, unless I'm worried.' She sounded self-important and Emma felt a sudden shaft of anger at the thought of Lesley and the paediatrician together in a cabal.

'That's nice,' she said shortly and moved towards the door.

'Has Tom been good?' Lesley asked, and Emma nodded. 'He's always good with me.' Two could play at competence.

'Have you got time to have lunch?' Lesley asked when they reached the car-park. 'I promised to take them to McDonald's. Tom wants a hat.'

Emma wavered and then Tom said, 'Em-em come for burgers,' and the die was cast.

'Burgers it is,' she said and turned on the engine.

They settled either side of the plastic-topped table, food appearing as if by magic.

'Keith brings Tom usually,' Lesley said. 'He calls it the boys' night out . . . except it's lunch-time.'

'Has Keith always been good with the children?' Emma couldn't bear to hear Lesley talk of Keith, but something inside kept egging her on.

'Oh yes, right from the beginning. I know some men

don't take to it at first, but Keith couldn't wait. He used to talk to my bump . . .' She looked coyly at Emma as though it was not to be believed. 'He used to tell it all the things they would do together . . . all men's things. Lucky it was a boy. But he was just the same with Zoë, and then when she was a girl he was over the moon.'

'*It doesn't make any difference*': that's what he had said on the day Zoë was born, holding Emma tightly in his arms.

'Over the moon,' she said aloud. 'I should think so too.' There was sibilance in her ears, as though all the words in all the world were rushing through her head. 'You must be pleased about being discharged from the hospital. Wait till you tell Keith. I expect you'll be able to get him at the office this afternoon.' It was a struggle for Emma to speak normally but she managed it.

'No,' Lesley said confidently, 'he won't be back till this evening. He's coming straight home, about half-six he thinks, and I'm making steak and kidney pie. Don't ask me why, on a day like this, but that's what he wants.'

They talked of food then, and cholesterol, and low-fat spreads. 'Do you cook for yourself?' Lesley asked. 'I never did when I was at college. If I didn't eat with someone I just pigged it on crisps.'

'College?' Emma said, surprised.

'I did a B.Ed.,' Lesley said. 'I only taught for two terms, though. We got married in October at half-term, and I started with Tom straightaway. A honeymoon baby.' She leaned to touch her son's cheek.

'So he wasn't planned?' It went against the grain to pry but Emma couldn't resist it, even though the price was pain.

'No, not a bit. It was disastersville for a while, and then Keithie got promoted and we all settled to the idea. I'm glad now. I mean, if we have one more ... two at the most ... I'll still be in my thirties when they're all safely at school. I might go back to teaching then, or I might retrain. Keith says I should retrain.'

What had he said about her to Emma? *'She's not dumb ... quite clever, really ... but she needs to be pushed.'*

'As what? Retrain as what?' Emma heard herself saying it but all she could think of was: *'one more ... two at the most ...'*

'I don't know. There are lots of options. Not with your fingers, Tom.'

'One more ... two at the most,' sang in Emma's head as they paid the bill, Lesley spurning Emma's American Express in favour of her own Access.

'I must dash,' Emma said when they reached the neat red brick. 'It's been lovely, but I must get back.'

'Oh, must you? There's plenty of dinner for three ... still, steak and kidney in a heat wave, I don't blame you.' She was pulling a deprecating face but there was pride in her voice, pride of ownership.

'Take care,' Emma said when they were all decanted on to the pavement, and waved until she reached the corner. 'Don't cry, baby. God'll think of something,' she told herself over and over till the pain subsided.

She had one more task to perform before she could make for home, something she had intended to do that morning. She drove to the florist's and collected the wreath she had ordered yesterday by phone. She had asked for a small wreath, roses and freesia, without green. It lay on her back seat like a bridal bouquet, the blank card with its grey border sticking upwards like a flag. She carried it into the house and unpegged the card. '*In fond remembrance*'? No, there was nothing she could remember fondly about her father. '*Deepest sympathy*'? That too was inappropriate. But what was appropriate? In all the history of recorded time, had there been anyone who found and lost a father all in the space of four days?

In the end she tucked back the card uncompleted and put the wreath in the fridge under polythene. She would think of the right words by tomorrow. She would have to.

She showered and changed into a caftan, carrying Diet Coke to the window-seat. It was four o'clock. Somewhere Keith would be checking his watch, licking his lips at the thought of steak and kidney pie. The burger and chips shifted uneasily on her stomach and she wondered if it was too late to get rid of it. In the end, she drank her Coke and burped happily until the feeling of fullness subsided.

The street outside had a sprinkling of home-goers now, sixth-formers with haversacks over a hunched shoulder, office workers on flexi-time scurrying home to enjoy the last of the sunshine. She might implement flexi-time in the office if things continued to go well.

Behind her the house was a silent cavern. Poppy, Poppy ... hurry home, Poppy. They could eat in the garden except that if Poppy got as far as the hall, she would want to flop in the cool, not roast outside.

On an impulse Emma crossed to the phone and dialled the shop.

'Poppy? No, I'm fine ... I just wondered if you were seeing El-Andrews tonight? No? Good. How about I come over and pick you up and we eat out? . . . Oh, you choose . . . Chinese it is. About half an hour, OK?'

She moved around the bedroom, picking out cool, comfy clothes, tying her hair off her neck with a scarf, putting tiny gold studs in her ears. Comfy, comfy, comfy. Once she had got to Poppy she would be all right. Inside her head a thousand outrages were clamouring for attention: death and despair and envy, envy above all. But not now. Not yet. She was taking Poppy to dinner, and grief would have to wait its turn.

She parked behind the shop and walked round to the front, passing the Save the Children charity shop. Inside, the enthusiastic voluntary helpers were tidying up – nice women with hopeful faces. In a little while they would go home, content with the knowledge of a job well done.

Emma pushed open the door of the boutique and stepped inside. Usually she was interested, even excited, by the rails of beautiful garments. Today she couldn't have cared less. At the end of the shop Poppy was dealing with a solitary customer, a plump woman in her late forties with beringed fingers and a discontented face. Poppy smiled at Emma and winked slowly to indicate rich pickings. The woman was pulling out a fistful of credit cards, selecting one and passing it over.

'And you'll send it all by Friday?'

'Of course.' Poppy was reaching for the phone to obtain authorization from the credit-card company for what looked like a big sale, and Jenny, the alteration hand, was coming through the workroom door, her pincushion on her arm.

Emma turned away, pretending to be a browsing customer, while Poppy spoke quietly into the phone and the woman sat with the serene air of one who knows her credit is good.

'Thank you,' Poppy said and put down the receiver. 'That's fine. Now if Jenny can just do her twiddly bits ...' Sometimes the credit-card companies refused to sanction a sale and the atmosphere would become electric as the rejected customer displayed outrage and disbelief in equal proportions. Today, though, all was well and Poppy sidled up to Emma.

'A thousand quid. She's worn me out, but it was worth it. I'll just see her over the step, and we'll be off.'

'OK. No hurry.'

It was comforting to stand, fingering silk and wool and chiffon. When she was a child she had had a tiny silk-covered eiderdown, made for a doll's cot, which she had called her 'silkies' and carried to bed every night, fingering it with thumb and forefinger, the other thumb in her mouth. Her mother had shuddered as the eiderdown grew tatty and threadbare with washing, but she had never taken it away. 'She did love me,' Emma thought and felt her eyes fill.

Tomorrow she would attend her father's funeral. Would Esther Gaunt's shade be there, ready to make amends for the wasted years?

'Goodbye. Thank you so much.' Poppy was arming the customer over the step in a wave of expensive perfume. 'Right,' she said, immediately. 'Let's go.'

They settled in the Lotus Garden, in a seat at the back where it was cool and dim. 'This is nice,' Poppy said as a fragrant tea-pot was set in front of them and they sipped the scented tea.

'Why did we ever put milk in tea?' Emma wondered, as the China tea freed her palate.

'To save cows from being redundant,' Poppy

answered. 'Now let's order.' Around them the Dim Sum waitresses plied their trade, but they ordered from the huge gold-tooled menu. 'Crispy sea-weed ... crispy aromatic duck ... mushrooms on the side ... and wine.' Poppy looked up defiantly. 'And if you mention calories ...'

'Would I ever?' Emma replied, and ordered seaweed and quick-fried prawns with seasonal vegetables.

'Now,' Poppy said, 'we must talk. You've buzzed in and out so much lately I can scarcely keep up. What've you been doing today?'

To lie or not to lie? Emma held the unhandled cup to her lips to gain time.

'Nothing much.' But she couldn't meet Poppy's eye and the damage was done.

'You haven't been round there again, have you? Oh God, you have. Emma Gaunt, have you no shame? You're hanging round that girl like her best chum, and you're laying her husband behind her back. You've got nerve, I'll tell you that!'

'I went to give her a lift to the hospital, that's all. What did you want me to do? Let them walk?'

'If they couldn't afford a taxi, yes. If I were her ... whatever her name is ... I'd much rather walk than ride with my feller's mistress.' Poppy's jowls were quivering with disapproval. 'Can't you see, Em? It's not nice. I've had affairs with married men ... who hasn't? ... but I can honestly say I never smarmed up to the wife. It's *infra dig*, Emma, and you know it!'

'You don't understand. It's far more complicated than that ...' Emma was desperately seeking excuses, but they wouldn't come and she couldn't find words to explain the truth: that she yearned to see her lover's wife and children, was excited by them, came alive at the pain of knowing them. 'Let's talk about something else. I've so much to tell and ask about.'

Poppy gave her a jaundiced look but she let the argument go and Emma breathed out with relief as Poppy spoke.

'Is everything fixed for tomorrow ... the funeral is tomorrow, isn't it?'

'Yes, tomorrow morning. They're taking care of it at the other end. I've got a wreath to take with me. I can't think of what to put on the card, that's the snag.'

'Hmm.' Poppy pursed her lips. 'It is tricky. I mean, anything effusive would be over the top but you don't want to seem cold.'

'I don't ... not just because he was my father, but because there's Peggy to consider. She sees it all so clearly: loving daughter tracks down wronged father in the nick of time, weeps at the graveside, the works. But I don't feel like weeping, Poppy. I wish I did, in a way, but how can you weep for someone you never knew? I don't know what the man was like, so how can I mourn him?'

'She never talked about him ... Esther, I mean. She never said a word against him, though.'

'You must have got an impression, Poppy. You're very intuitive. I'm sure you could come up with something if you tried.'

Poppy was grinning. 'Intuitive! Next time you tell me I'm a nosy old cow I'll remind you of that. Still, to be serious – I always imagined it was a clash of wills, if you want the truth. Your mother was a gutsy lady, who could never have been a stay-at-home wife. I thought he was probably a typical northerner ... "put my dinner on the table, woman," ... and that she wouldn't wear it.' She paused, considering. 'And to be honest, I thought there was probably a snob factor. We hear a lot of wives who don't keep up with upwardly mobile husbands, but it can be the other way around.'

'You haven't really told me anything about *him*,' Emma said despairingly.

'Yes, I have. I've said he was a "Northern Man". Andy Capp.'

'No.' Emma was remembering the emaciated figure in the hospital bed, whose face had been more like that of a tortured saint in a Renaissance oil than a blunt, uncomplicated northerner.

'Anyway, enough of me. What about you and Charlie? He seems to be leading a busy life lately?'

Poppy looked at her shrewdly. 'If you're thinking what I think you're thinking, forget it. There's no other woman. Charles and I are at the stage where one man/woman at a time is enough.' She was suddenly serious.

'There comes a time when all you really fear in life is being alone. You cease being picky over relationships. There are lots of things about Charlie I don't particularly care for ... details. But you make allowances, because what matters in the end is that other presence, there when you need it. Charlie'll always be there for me. You can't say that of your Keith, because he has other commitments, greater priorities. And that's why I'm so set against it. You're my blue-eyed girl, Emma Gaunt, and I want the best for you. I don't want you to wind up like me, pretending that what you have is what you want.' She reached to pat Emma's hand. 'Don't look so tragic.'

'I'm OK. It's just that I can't bear to hear you talk like that, as though you were giving in.'

'I've already given, honey child. I have surrendered,

capitulated, put down my musket, raised my hands in the air and called out "*Kamerad*" . . . but on the whole, I've no grumbles.'

'*No* regrets?'

'Oodles, but where do they get you? I had a good time while it lasted. God, the '40s and '50s! Say what you like about the war, people really lived then. You squeezed every little drop out of every little minute. There was this pub in Bloomsbury, they called it the Polish corridor . . . we had such fun. They all had these little gold fillings in their teeth . . . I can still see them winking away when they opened their mouths. And the manners . . . sweep you off your feet with the manners. But they expected to be paid for it. Insatiable, that's what the Poles were.'

'I thought that was the GIs?'

'Don't you believe it. American men are pussy-cats. They let you tie bells on their necks.'

The waiter was approaching, ready to shred the crispy duck.

'I want more of this later,' Emma said, as her quick-fried prawns appeared. 'It's a lot more exciting than the official war history.'

They talked lightly then, relishing the food, until it was time to go.

'You need an early night,' Poppy said, 'what with a long drive and a funeral in front of you.'

They parted in the hall. 'If I don't see you in the morning I'll think of you. Take care.' Poppy kissed her fondly on the forehead and turned for the stairs.

Emma let herself into her own flat and checked the machine. No messages. Good!

She was getting ready for a bath when the phone rang, and she hesitated. What if it was Keith? But when she picked up the receiver it was Eddy Colman, ringing to confirm the final arrangements for the funeral.

'And you fixed up your flowers?' he said, when he had checked that she knew time and place.

'Yes, I'm bringing them with me.'

'There's one more thing, pet.' Emma knew from the tone of his voice he was embarrassed but when he spoke again he sounded earnest and convincing. 'You're to walk in front, pet. Chief mourner. It's what she wants.'

'I can't do it, Eddy.' She couldn't call him uncle, not yet. 'If things had been different, yes. But as it is, I'd feel a fraud.'

'But it's what Peggy wants, pet. I'll grant you she has the right, but if this makes her happy ... I know you mean well, wanting to give her pride of place. But according to her, you're his daughter, and it's only fitting you lead in.'

'All right, if you're sure it's what Aunt Peggy wants.' The name tripped off her tongue, taking her by surprise.

'See you tomorrow, then. I'll have the kettle on.'

'You do,' she said, smiling, and put down the phone.

It rang again, almost immediately. Eddy again or Keith? She let it ring out until the answerphone came into play.

'Darling? I don't know where you are. Perhaps you've already gone back to Durham. I just wanted you to know I'll be thinking of you tomorrow, the fondest thoughts. Take care, darling, and if you get this in time, sleep tight. I love you.'

Emma wanted to reach for the receiver but she had had enough emotion for one day. Instead, with Keith's words echoing in her head, she went to the fridge for the wreath. '*Fondest thoughts, Emma,*' she wrote on the card and put it carefully back in place.

16

Wednesday 16 August

It was sunny today but a wind had blown up, flattening the roadside grass and sending plastic bags hurtling across the motorway like guided missiles. On the radio they were reviewing the day's papers: the Kenneth Branagh and Emma Thompson wedding-plans *ad nauseam*, and, according to the commentator, a picture of Mrs Thatcher wheeling her grandchild in a pushchair.

'This we must see,' Emma thought.

Now that the day of the funeral was actually here, she felt more able to cope. Her period had started the day before, and the terrible premenstrual blues were leaving her. She felt sadness at her father's death, but not grief. If she had known of his existence she would have sought him out sooner; Esther Gaunt had made sure that did not happen, but Emma did not feel bitter about her mother's deceit. That might come later when she uncovered the reasons behind it. At the moment she felt only an overwhelming curiosity.

She reached the St Nicholas at eight-thirty and checked into her room. The girl at the reception desk greeted her like an old friend and it was comforting to be so welcome.

She stood at the window for a moment, looking out on the beautiful Durham landscape, trying to come to terms with all that must be accomplished in the next few hours, then she changed into her grey suit, checked that the brooch was in her handbag, and went down again to the Capri. There was an hour and a half before she must ride in the cortège, and before that she had an errand to accomplish.

The jeweller's bell jangled as she entered the shop.

'Can I help you?' The girl behind the counter was blonde and supercilious.

'Can I see Mr Winston ... if there still is a Mr Winston?' The girl eyed her up and down for a moment. 'He's very busy.'

'I'm sure he is,' Emma said firmly. 'And if anyone else could help, I wouldn't dream of bothering him. Unfortunately, that's not so, so if you would get him for me, please?' She left no loophole and held the girl's eye as she finished speaking.

'I'll see if he's free,' the assistant said grudgingly, and vanished behind a screened door, leaving Emma to gaze around at the well-stocked shelves of Doulton and Spode, the plated-silver wedding gifts, the cases and cases of rings, all seeming to be a gem surrounded by minuscule diamonds. There was nothing unusual, nothing exotic, nothing that did not come in rows, and Emma felt her spirits sink. It looked as though she had come on a wild-goose chase.

She turned back to the inner doorway as a man of about thirty-five appeared, the assistant in tow. 'Oh dear,' Emma said, smiling.

The man smiled back. 'Well, I know I'm not God's gift but I don't usually get as bad a reaction as that.'

Emma shook her head. 'I'm sorry. It's not you, it's just that the Mr Winston I hoped to see would have worked here thirty years ago.'

'My father ... or my grandfather. He hung on till he was well over seventy. Dad retired last year, to the Lake District. Are you sure I can't help?'

Emma took out the box and pushed it across the counter. 'I wanted to ask about this. It was in my mother's effects, left to me in her will. It intrigues me.'

The man had picked out the brooch and was examining it. 'Interesting.' He turned it over and screwed an eye-glass into place. 'It's my grandfather's work, all right. He loved tricky jobs ... priced them down if he fancied doing them. He was a goldsmith, a working jeweller, not a glorified salesman like me. I regret it, not apprenticing myself to him when I had the chance, but you know what it's like ... I couldn't see the point at the time.'

'What can you tell me about it?' Emma pressed him. 'There's a number on the back – is it your record number?'

'No, it's nothing to do with us. Looks more like a date, or something like that. It's grandfather's work, though, that W with a J superimposed. And then there's the carat mark.' He weighed the brooch in his hand. 'It'll be worth a bit. I can't say I fancy it much, though.'

'That's one reason why it intrigues me. It *is* ugly. The stones look cheap, and as though they were put in at random. And why stones at all? If they'd used one for the eye ... but stuck in the middle like that!'

He was examining it closely. 'That's lapis lazuli, that first one. No mistake about that. The second one could be a tourmaline. I'm not an expert like Grandad, but I know a bit.'

'I thought it might be a poor-quality emerald?'

'No. I can do some tests but I think it'll turn out to be a tourmaline or a garnet of sorts. The red stone is a spinel.'

'Not a ruby?'

'No, sorry to disappoint you. Nor is the end one a

257

diamond. It's a gemstone of some sort, but there's no quality there. As a matter of fact, you've got me intrigued now. Why take this quantity of gold, which was never cheap, and stud it with inferior stones? If you care to leave it, I'll check them out exactly. And if I can find the old man's record book – for when, did you say? Thirty years ago? – there might be some of his original notes.'

'I've got the receipt,' Emma said proudly. 'It's got the exact date on it.'

'Good show. It'll make a change to handle something unusual. It's all carbon-copy stuff now. First sapphires and diamonds like Lady Di, and then everybody wants a ruby like Fergie. If the next Royal wants a slab of concrete set in pearls, I'll have a window full of it. But this . . . you could spot this a mile off, couldn't you?'

'Yes,' Emma said, 'it's individual. That's why I want to find out about it. It must have been given to mark something special, and it'd be nice to know what.'

'Give me twenty-four hours,' he said as she left. 'No promises, I'm not an expert, as I said, but I'll have a shot.'

'Very nice,' Aunty Peggy said, nodding towards to where the wreath lay on the stairs.

The house was strangely quiet and half-dark because of the curtains drawn across the windows in respect. 'Come into the front room,' her aunt said and ushered Emma in among strangers. They were mostly middle-aged and dressed in winter clothes of grey and navy and black. The men steamed slightly, the women dabbed furtively at their matted make-up.

'This is Emma,' Peggy said. 'Our John's daughter.'

There was satisfaction in her voice that the prodigal had returned, even at the eleventh hour. Emma couldn't take in all the names, but she smiled at them sweetly and took whatever hand was proffered.

'There now,' the last of them said. 'You sit here by me. Have you come far?'

As Emma subsided on to the chair arm she felt her aunt's fingers tighten on her arm. 'Three wise monkeys,' Peggy hissed and then moved on.

Emma was trying to work out this cryptic aside when the interrogation began.

'You didn't see much of your father, then?' The woman's eyes were bright with interest.

'No,' Emma said, attempting to look sad and uncommunicative. It didn't work.

'I thought you didn't, because he never talked about you – and we were his neighbours for years.'

Emma was trying to think of an evasive answer when the cavalry appeared in the shape of Uncle Eddy. 'I'm sorry to drag you away, Emma, but your aunt's hit a snag.'

Her aunt was waiting in the kitchen with a brow like thunder. 'You didn't say anything, did you? Good. News of the World, that one: she'd ask the Pope about his wooden leg. You stop here along of me. They can't be much longer – it's ten to eleven already.'

Two girls entered the kitchen, dressed in funereal colours and trying to control what appeared to be normally jolly facial expressions.

'This is our Vera,' said Peggy Colman proudly. 'Your cousin, Vera.'

Emma held out a hand to the taller of the two.

'Hallo, Vera. I'm very glad to meet you at last.'

'Me too. You could've knocked me down with a

259

feather . . .' She got no further, for her mother's frown dried the words on her lips. The other girl held out a hand.

'I'm Liz . . . Billy's wife. He couldn't be here today. He's a charge-hand so he can't just stop off. We spoke on the phone, remember?'

'Of course,' Emma said. Liz had a freckled, friendly face and reminded her of Amy, sitting quietly at this moment in that other, ordered world. 'I wish I was there now,' Emma thought, but she shook the girl's hand warmly and asked them both about their families, trying to make all the moves a dutiful, if newly discovered, cousin should make.

The cavalcade of cars arrived at five to the hour and the funeral director greeted Emma as though hers was the first bereavement in recorded time.

'Bear up, my dear. Bear up,' he said. There was a greenish tinge to his bowler and dandruff on his velvet-collared coat. It was August, an August of record temperatures and drought, and they were all dressed for Siberia. Emma felt a bubble of hysteria rise up in her and quelled it instantly. There was nothing funny about her present situation, nothing at all.

It was easier once they had been ushered out to the cars and she was sandwiched between her aunt and uncle and another couple who spoke of her father as though they had been close friends. If her aunt was to be believed, John Gaunt had been almost a recluse – and yet so many people were ready to proclaim friendship, even dabbing their eyes occasionally and wearing expressions of extreme despair.

Emma followed the coffin into the chapel, watching it jiggle alarmingly as one of the bearers got out of step, and then followed the funeral director's instruction to sit in the front pew. She bent her head and prayed fervently to a God she did not believe in: 'Please God, let it be all right. I'll promise you anything if you'll let it be all right.'

They sang 'The king of love my shepherd is' while the minister regarded them benignly from above his book and frequently forgot the words. He was good at making them up, though, and Emma felt a crazy desire to applaud some of his better efforts.

'They are burying my father,' she thought as they sat down, 'and it feels like a Whitehall farce.' She was at once appalled and relieved that it should be so. She felt disoriented enough without having to take part in a meaningful service. But when she glanced sideways at her aunt and uncle she saw that it certainly held meaning for them.

The minister spoke movingly of 'John'. He had been a quiet man, an uncomplaining man. To some people he might have appeared cold, but those gathered there today knew better. Emma felt her head move in a small involuntary denial, but then they were singing again: 'When mothers of Salem their children brought to Jesus, the stern disciples held them back and bade them depart.'

'He always liked this one,' Peggy whispered in between verses. 'Right from being a little lad at Sunday school.'

The procession re-formed and Emma took her place. 'Not long now,' Eddy whispered and she smiled agreement.

She was moving from darkness towards the light of the doorway when she saw them: Robert Eden with Stephen and April, standing respectfully in the last pew. It was so unexpected that her composure cracked. Tears came, and then Uncle Eddy was guiding her through the sunlight and into the waiting limousine. Her aunt looked at her tear-stained face approvingly as they drove to the crematorium. 'Let it out,' she said, patting Emma's arm. 'At least you feel for him.'

After that it was easy. Emma filled cups and showered sausage-rolls and cream cakes on to importunate plates.

'It went off very nice,' her aunt said, when the tide had receded, leaving them beached on either side of the fireplace. 'Put the kettle on, Eddy. I haven't had a proper cup all day. Our Vera and our Liz would've stayed, but they've both got bairns to see to.'

'Yes, it went off well,' Eddy repeated, when they were all supplied with tea.

'You will be sure to let me have the bill, won't you?' Emma said. She saw them exchange looks.

'He's left a few bob,' Eddy said at last. 'Not a fortune, but enough to pay for this lot and a little bit over. We'll let you know how much when it's all done-up.'

'Please,' Emma said, trying to speak forcefully without appearing to hector, 'please try to understand that paying that bill myself is desperately important to me. It's the one thing I can do for him. I neither want nor need anything my father has left – surely you can see that I have no right whatsoever to it. It's yours. We'll talk about it tomorrow, because we're all a bit overwrought now, but I won't change my mind. Do believe that.'

As she drove back to Durham she wryly acknowledged that she was becoming quite good at refusing bequests. Except that her father had not left her anything, she was quite sure of that. It was Aunt Peggy who was trying to do what she thought to be right. Emma wasn't sure whether or not her father had recognized her in the hospital, but if he had there had been no paternal affection in his glance nor anything resembling it.

When at last she reached her room at the St Nicholas she kicked off her shoes, slipped out of her grey suit and lay down on the bed. Her cheeks burned from wind and sun and salt tears, and there was an uncomfortable feeling in the pit of her stomach which usually accompanied her period but which this time felt ten times worse.

'It has to end soon,' she told herself. 'Like everything else in life this chaos must come to a conclusion.' She tried to remember if there had been other confusing times in her life. Going to university, perhaps? No, that had been exciting, not frightening. And last year, when her mother had died and she had had the new branch to set up, she had felt under pressure but not in the least overcome by it. She was better when she had something to do. Part of the trouble now, almost the whole of it in fact, was that she didn't know what to do next. There *was* one thing she could do, though. She got to her feet and retrieved the papers and photographs she had brought with her from her mother's room.

It was strange to sift through the mementoes of her mother's early life. She read each letter, scoured each document, hoping all the time to come across something important. There was nothing. The photographs were equally unproductive – an older couple who might well be her grandparents; her mother on what looked like an office outing; one or two snaps of young men in the unmistakable apparel of the late 1940s.

She was almost to the bottom of the pile when she found the folded tissue paper. She opened it carefully, anxious to see what had been so carefully preserved, but it was only the torn half of a theatre programme –

Brigadoon performed at the Sunderland Empire from June 6 to June 12 in 1957. Emma looked carefully down the cast and turned it over and over in her hands but could find nothing of any significance. Except for the fact that it had been so carefully preserved! That was odd. And it was dated 1957; the crucial year. She folded it carefully back into the tissue and returned the papers to their container.

Tonight they were all meeting at the Culrose house to look over some of David Culrose's papers. Perhaps she would have better luck there? She had had to lie to her aunt about that evening, and it grieved her. She had said she was visiting an old school-friend, and when her aunt had wanted more she had embroidered it. She had wanted to tell the truth, but she wasn't sure it was the right time to say she was in touch with the Culroses, much less a beneficiary under David Culrose's will. She would have to know much more before she confessed to that. Perhaps there would be an answer of sorts tonight? In the end, though, if there was no answer, she would have to accept it. In a year or so, if life treated her well, she would have forgotten the Culroses, or almost forgotten them.

An image of April came into her mind, fat, plain April whose face would alter so if you coaxed a smile out of it. Perhaps she might keep in touch with April . . . birthdays and Christmas. Nothing too tying.

She had spent all day in formal clothes, and now she showered and pulled on cotton slacks and boat-necked T-shirt in blue. It was going to be a working evening, anyway. Soup and sandwiches, April had promised. If someone didn't do something soon, April would become a drudge. It wasn't that Stephen looked down on her or lacked affection for his sister, it was just that they were

both being pushed into roles. His was tycoon, hers was
handmaiden. She would have to have another word
with Robert Eden before she went home for good For
all his faults he seemed genuinely fond of April, but
whether or not he was fond enough to overcome his
own in-built chauvinism was another matter.

Emma had insisted on going in her own car tonight
and Robert Eden had not argued. Since the incident of
the kissed cheek he had returned to the old, distant
Robert of first acquaintance. Perhaps he regretted his
impulsive gesture, or feared she might make too much
of it? Well, if that was his problem, he would learn his
mistake.

Emma parked her car in the drive behind Robert
Eden's Volvo, but April was at the open door before
she ascended the steps.

'You've come, then!'

'Of course I've come,' Emma said, and April nodded
and smiled. 'She's pleased to see me,' Emma thought
and felt a sudden transient lump in the throat.

April led her into a small, oak-panelled room lit by
lamps placed here and there. Robert Eden was standing
by the fireplace, and Stephen kneeling on the floor, an
open drawer lifted from its chest before him.

'This was Dad's room,' April said. 'He used to call it
his den. All his things are in here.' The room was
shabby but comfortable and Emma looked around it
with curiosity. A bowl on a side table was filled with
brightly coloured pebbles and April saw Emma's eyes
light on them. 'We used to bring them back from the
beach. Boody, Dad called it, and if we found a special
bit we got an ice-cream.' They moved towards it.

'Which were the special bits?' Emma said and April
picked out a red piece.

'It's all glass,' Stephen said from the floor. 'It's bits of old bottles washed smooth by the sea. Most bottles were blue or green, so those bits are common. Red's quite rare, and a purple bit is really special.'

'I see,' Emma said. 'I'll have to remember that.' She moved to a chair. 'I haven't seen the Durham coastline. Is that what you meant when you said "the beach"?'

April nodded. 'There are super beaches here. Miles and miles of them. Dad used to say if we had the weather we'd be the greatest holiday resort in the world.'

'In Britain, Pud,' Stephen reproved her.

'In the world,' April said defiantly and Robert Eden echoed his support.

'She's right. This is the greatest country, ergo the greatest holiday resort.'

'You two always stick together,' Stephen grumbled, but he was not displeased. Emma looked from one to another, thinking that whether or not they knew it they were becoming a family.

'This was Dad's private drawer,' Stephen said, when they were all seated. 'I want to look at things first, and then we can pass them round. Well, there may be some things . . .'

'. . . you want to keep private,' Emma finished for him. 'I understand that. I think it's very good of you to let me see anything.'

They passed items around: photographs, press cuttings about the Culrose firm and the Culrose family.

'They were a big part of Sunderland, weren't they?' Emma said. It seemed that the Culrose name had been attached to everything in the old days, a seal of approval on the doings of a town.

They were almost at the bottom of the drawer now
and had found nothing of any significance to Emma.
And then Stephen held up a theatre programme. '*Brigadoon*, Sunderland Empire, June 6–12 1957,' he read
aloud, and then, 'This can go out. There's only half of
it, anyway.'

'Let me see,' Emma said. Her heart was thumping
uncomfortably as she took it. She held it in her hand,
regarding the torn edge. 'I know where the other half of
this is,' she said. 'It was in my mother's drawer. I found
it there last week. It's in my hotel room now, along with
some other papers.'

'So that's it, then,' the boy said. 'They knew one
another!' He accented the 'knew' so that Emma looked
at him sharply, thinking he was using it in the biblical
sense.

'It's only a theatre programme,' April said uneasily.
'That doesn't mean much.'

'Not "just" a programme, April,' Robert said gently.
'A programme torn in half because two people wanted
to remember an evening together. Your father kept it
here in his special drawer.'

'My mother had wrapped her half in tissue paper,'
Emma said. 'It obviously meant a lot to her.' She
hesitated. 'I think it means they . . . they . . .'

'Had a great affection for one another,' Robert Eden
finished for her.

'But how did your mother and my father know one
another?' Stephen was still looking for a way out.

'They did know one another,' Emma said. 'My aunt
told me that. When my father worked for your father,
my mother was sometimes asked to the house, to your
grandfather's house I suppose.'

'Perhaps they were all friends?' April said. 'Perhaps

Dad really cared for them both ... your mother *and* your father?'

Emma knew what April was trying so desperately to discount.

'That's possible, April. Remember that my mother was considerably older than your father, very nearly twice his age. Perhaps she felt maternal towards him, since her husband's job was to guide him.'

She didn't want to come right out and say, 'I'm not your father's bastard,' but she needed to set their minds at rest. For a fleeting moment she thought of her father's eyes on her from his hospital bed. In some ways it would have been a relief to be David Culrose's love-child, but it wasn't feasible when you considered the age difference between David and her mother.

'What else did your aunt say?' It was Robert Eden this time, changing the subject, wary-eyed, as though warning her to watch her words. Emma began to bridle, and then let it go. She *would* have to watch her words: no point in telling two orphaned teenagers that their father had, in her aunt's opinion, been a swaggering ne'er-do-well.

She gave them a censored version of all her aunt and uncle had told her. 'I'm seeing them again tomorrow, so there may be a bit more. I haven't told them what I'm doing here yet. If we ... when we sort it out and Robert has fixed the will, there's no need for anyone else to know I was mentioned in it.'

'You'll have to have what Dad left you,' Stephen said stubbornly. He looked shaken but the set of his chin was still determined. 'We've never argued with that. It was his to leave and it's yours because he cared about your mother so much, and probably your father too ... I hope you'll sell us your share, but you must take it in the first place.'

'I can't and I won't,' Emma said decisively. 'And if you and April have any sense, you'll sell out and use the money to do something with your lives.'

'We are doing what we want,' Stephen said, without a glance at April. 'And what Dad wanted. We're carrying on the Culrose family business. There isn't any better future than that, not that I can imagine, not for Pud and me.'

'Have you asked April what she wants to do?' Emma said heatedly, but April had run away from the argument and when Emma followed her to the big kitchen with its ceramic tiled floor and spacious work surfaces, she found April preoccupied with the soup pan and unwilling or unable to discuss anything else.

As they ate they made a conscious effort to talk about inconsequential things. Emma told them something of SyStems and Robert Eden told tales of some of his more eccentric clients. They discussed the eclipse of the moon that was due during the night, and Robert Eden did a pretty good impersonation of Patrick Moore, reducing them all to giggles. 'We are all trying not to think about things,' Emma thought, looking from one to another. 'Perhaps because we're frightened to face facts.'

'This soup is good,' she said truthfully. 'Did you make it?'

April nodded. 'Mrs Hacker made the sarnies, but I made the soup.' Her eyes gleamed behind her glasses as Robert, too, praised her culinary flair.

'She ought to have contact lenses,' Emma thought, 'and a week at a health farm followed by years of tender, loving care.' Instead she would probably spend the next five years doting on Stephen, and the next fifty running after his wife and children. There were still put-upon maiden aunts, especially among the middle classes.

While April cleared away they went on with their search, looking at birth and death and marriage certificates, all in order; at occasional letters kept for some reason now unknown; at diaries full until February, and then tailing away. 'We're not going to find anything else,' Emma said at last. And then, turning to Robert: 'Can you do what I ask? If you can't wipe out the bequest, then I'll take it and deed it back to these two. One or the other . . . there must be something I can do? We know now that there was once something between their father and my mother but that doesn't entitle me to anything.' It was out in the open now and there was an almost tangible easing of tension.

She felt faintly virtuous refusing money for the second time that day but Robert's eyes, when they met hers, were not admiring. 'I'll look into it,' he said. 'There's sure to be something.'

'We won't take your third,' Stephen said, his jaw squared. 'You can do what you like, but you can't make us.'

'Well, let's leave it for the moment,' Robert said equably. 'Emma's had a trying day, and I think she should get some sleep. What about a nightcap, Stephen? Your father usually had a bottle of Drambuie in that bottom drawer for the end of a hard day.'

The liqueur was warm and fiery and came in generous measure, causing April to splutter and gasp for breath.

'Meet me for lunch, tomorrow?' Emma suggested. 'Better still, I'll pick you up at twelve, and you can choose somewhere nice. We'll talk without any men to shout us down.'

'Some chance,' Stephen said so gloomily that they all laughed.

After that it was time to say good-night and go. Emma drove into the road, aware of the Volvo behind her. Soon, if she remembered correctly, he would turn to the right. But the Volvo's lights stayed behind her all the way to her hotel, and when she got out in the car-park he was drawing up beside her.

'Have dinner with me tomorrow night? I'll pick you up at eight. No, don't refuse, it's not a social invitation. I think we need another talk, and over a restaurant table is a civilized way to do it. Otherwise tempers might fray.'

'I can assure you mine won't. Your office will do quite well. Besides, I can't think what we have to say to one another. It's a simple enough thing I've asked of you. If you can't handle it, I'll find someone who can.'

Robert had opened his car door and now he stood over her. 'My God, you're a master at the art of self-deception. You talk of "giving it back" as though you were Jesus restoring Jairus's daughter. Give back what, for God's sake? That business is on the skids and you know it. You're not *giving* them anything, you're copping out, Miss Gaunt – and if you can't see that, I bloody well can!'

He turned back to his car. 'I'll be here at eight, and you'd better be ready.'

17

Thursday 17 August

Emma had tossed and turned all night, furious with Robert Eden because of his unjust accusation, uneasy in case there was a grain of truth in it. She had wanted to refuse the bequest from the beginning, before she had known it was a comparatively empty one, so how could she be 'copping out'? She knew what Robert Eden wanted: he wanted her to assume some sort of responsibility for Stephen and April, and the only reason he wanted that was to enable him to wriggle out from under, himself.

At two a.m. she abandoned bed, lured by mention on her bedside radio of the eclipse. The old, familiar moon was in place, luminous and unchanged. Emma went on watching until a tiny smudge appeared on top and to one side, then she looked at her bedside clock. It was two-twenty. For the next hour or so the dark shadow crept over the glowing circle of the moon, looking jaunty at first, like a skull-cap, then sinister as it devoured more and more, until only a tiny sliver of light was left. And then the light was gone, to be replaced by an eerie glow that hung in the sky like a second sun. It was at once beautiful and terrible, and it made Emma feel small, as watching the skies always did. Small and safe. The gods would not have their cruel eyes on her now; she was too insignificant to matter. She went back to bed and slept, rising at six to run a bath, eager now for whatever the day might bring.

By the time she had bathed the papers were waiting outside her door, full of murders or silly articles meant for morons, the only spark of comfort being talk of Solidarity forming the next Polish government. A few years . . . even months . . . ago, that would have seemed impossible. Now it was happening.

She ate two croissants and drank a pot of coffee, then idled the time away until she could decently ring Amy. Mustn't look as though she was checking up. On the other hand, the sooner she was out of here the better. There were things to be done.

Amy was in the office when eventually she phoned. 'Everything's fine. We've got the Transio account: they confirmed it yesterday. Keith is going there today. He says Ivor was brill with them.'

'It sounds as though I'm hardly needed.' Emma was laughing, but a little part of her ached to be missed.

'Oh, you're needed all right. We can tick over very nicely without you for a while, but only because you've organized us so well. Stay away too long and we'd run down, like a clock.'

'Is any part of you Irish?' Emma asked, trying not to sound too pleased.

'Only my hips,' Amy said. 'I've got a definite potato-eater's spread. Joking apart, though, how are you? How is Durham? I went there once on a school trip.'

'Durham's fine. I am . . .' She longed to confide in Amy, and she had told her about Stephen's first call, so where was the harm? If they had been face to face, she might have done, but as it was she finished: 'I'm enjoying myself. I'll tell you all about it when I see you.'

When she put down the phone she reflected that she really was Esther Gaunt's daughter – a lone wolf, as her mother had been all her life.

She left the hotel and drove into Sunderland. Mr Winston was behind his counter and his face lit up as she entered. 'I was hoping you'd come in. Not that I've got a lot of gen for you, but I did find the work record. It was Grandad's ... well, I knew that.' He reached under the counter and brought out a blue index card. 'Take a look at that while I get your brooch out of the safe.'

The card was headed B417 and dated 5 October 1957. Under 'Customer' was written: '*J. Gaunt Esq., 15, Dovedale Street, Fulwell, Sunderland*'. The 'Work to be executed' column read: '*One gold lady's brooch in shape of ewe-lamb, to be set with gems to customer's own specification. (Details later).*'

Emma looked down the card. There were no details of the gems and when she turned the card over it was blank. The rest of the face of the card was full of scribbled technical detail and at the bottom: '*Deposit paid £100*'. Followed by: '*Account settled 25 October 1957, £380*'. Emma looked at the scribbled detail above and saw where a sum had been worked out, amounting to £480.

The jeweller was back now, the box in his hand. He opened it and lifted out the brooch. 'It's gold, as I said, 9 carat. And the first stone *is* a lapis lazuli, no doubt about that. It's one of the most valuable semi-opaque ornamental materials, comes from Afghanistan and Chile in the main. They found it in some of the lime-stone ejected by Vesuvius.' He was waxing enthusiastic now.

'It can take a good polish ... a bit like jade for that. These whitish speckles take this one down a bit, but it's a good blue. The Romans used to call it *sapphirus* ... not like the modern sapphire, of course. As to value –

274

the same as jade or a good turquoise. This stone's small.'

Emma nodded and waited for him to continue. He had screwed in his eye-glass and was regarding the brooch fiercely. 'This next one's got me jiggered. It looks like an emerald – as you said, I believe – but it's not. It's a garnet. I've done its refractive indices and that sort of thing, and it's a garnet.'

'Garnets are red.'

'Not always, but this *is* a bit of an odd one. The next stone's a red spinel: looks like a ruby but a tenth of the price. This one is nice but it's not first quality. Brilliant red are the best, and this is a touch violety for top ranking. Burma and Afghanistan, you find them, mostly. And this beggar here, which you called a diamond, is a colourless topaz. Might have come out of Mother Russia. One of the lowest in value of the transparent gemstones.'

He put down the brooch and eye-glass and pursed his lips. 'Now, what has me intrigued is this. Even at 1957 prices this was an expensive item. Today, in a London sale, God knows what it would fetch. I couldn't sell it here because the beggar's ugly, but down south they go mad for anything out of the ordinary. I could only give you gold price, and even that would be a tidy amount. Down there, in a specialist sale, we'd be talking thousands, quite a few thousands. But, to get back to what I was saying – here's my grandfather, a stickler for good work and a craftsman, he makes a damn good job of a gold sheep and then he studs it with four of the lousiest ... pardon my expression ... minor stones you'd see in a twelve-month. He could've used anything, turquoise, coral, amethyst, that would have been no more expensive, but a damned sight more attractive ... and he puts in four stones that don't tone, don't match. It's got me foxed.'

'He did it to the customer's specification,' Emma said.

'That may be . . . but customers have to be guided, sometimes. A man'll come in and say his wife likes a certain stone and he wants it set in platinum – nothing but the best. Well, you point out that platinum will do nothing for that particular stone, you guide him to the right mount, and he goes away happy. But in this case . . .'

'Did I read somewhere that stones were set in rings to give messages?' Emma asked. 'You know, diamonds for constancy and so on. Could it be that?'

He cackled triumphantly. 'I'm way ahead of you. I looked that up. Stones do have meanings, but this lot don't mean anything important enough. They're four stones chosen at random. I even wondered if Grandad had set it with something better, and they'd been taken out and sold. Well, I've had that item under a microscope and if it's been tampered with I'm a monkey's uncle. If you ever find out why it was done like that, will you let me know? I hate mysteries . . . unless they're on the telly.'

Emma thanked Mr Winston for his help and was about to take her leave when she remembered the number on the back. 'Did you find out if that number has any significance?'

He shook his head. 'It means nothing to me.' He screwed in his glass again. 'It's numbers and letters. IISXI2–5IISXIII–11. Nothing to do with us. He was scribbling on scrap paper. 'There you are, in case you can puzzle it out. It could be a code of some sort.'

It was nine forty-five when Emma got back to the

car. She was picking up April at twelve. She drove to the town-centre car-park and made her way to the Library, an imposing building fronting a pleasant park. Sunderland was a nice town, her birthplace. She felt a little glow of pride as she mounted the steps and made for the Reference section.

She asked for a copy of the Yellow pages, and carried it to a quiet desk. Seventeen firms were listed under DIY, and eight under building supplies. She copied the names and addresses of all those in bold black type, the more expensive entries, and went back to the car, where she took her Sunderland A-Z out of the glove compartment.

She sat in the car and marked out an itinerary to take in the five firms she had listed. Two of them were in Sunderland itself, one in Durham, and one in Peterlee. The fifth one was too far out and she crossed it from her list before she set out to explore.

By the time she reached the Culrose house she had discovered that there were three thrusting businesses in competition with Stephen, and one on a par with the Culrose set-up for its apathetic work-force and too-wide range of stock. If Stephen had had only one real competitor he might have made it. With three he was doomed.

She made no mention of her reconnoitre when she picked up April. They drove to a Chinese restaurant in Durham city and munched happily on crispy seaweed. 'I've never had this,' April said, once she had been persuaded to try it. 'It's scrumptious.'

'Did you eat out much when your Dad was alive?'

'No. Sometimes on birthdays or bank holidays, for a special treat. But not usually. Do you?'

'Quite a bit. I have business lunches once or twice a week and then dinner with friends if I go up to London.

But I used to eat out a lot with my mother. She loved eating out . . . probably because she hated cooking.'

'What was she like?'

'My mother? Well, her name was Esther and she was very smart, very attractive, a good businesswoman.' April's gaze was rapt. 'She wasn't a kissy-cuddly sort of mother. I loved her, but I didn't really get to know her until I was grown up.'

Had she ever really got to know her mother? Or had there always been some secret place within Esther Gaunt where no one, not even her own daughter, was allowed to trespass?

April's face clouded. 'I don't remember much about my mother, except that she was very nice. She did cuddle me, quite a lot I think.'

Emma couldn't resist reaching out to cover the bitten fingers with her own. 'Are you OK . . . happy, I mean?'

'Sometimes. Mostly I just feel fed-up, but sometimes it's worse and I want to cry . . . or lash out at Stephen or something. I know I've got to accept Dad's death, and everything, and I do, in a way. It's just . . .'

'I know,' Emma said. 'You'll be happy again, one day. Perhaps you'll marry and have children of your own.'

April smiled. 'I don't think that'll happen.' The smile turned into a grin but it was a rueful one. 'I don't suppose anyone would have me.'

Emma wanted to comfort her but April was no fool. False tributes would be rejected out of hand. 'You don't look as good as you could.' She watched for signs of hurt but April looked decidedly interested so Emma continued: 'Everything about you is OK. You have nice hair, good skin if a bit spotty, you're tall and straight underneath that extra weight . . . you have positively lovely eyes behind fairly horrendous spectacles. And if you stopped biting your nails your hands would look 100 per cent better. That may sound like a catalogue of despair, but in reality I'm saying you have all the ingredients, you just haven't got the mix right. Your clothes don't help. They're good but they don't flatter you. We could go shopping together one day, if you'd like that?'

'I would,' April said. 'And I'd like some advice about my hair. I see pictures sometimes of the way I'd like it and I take them to the hairdresser's, but they just say it wouldn't work.'

'We'll have a day out together one day,' Emma promised. 'You could come up to Manchester and see my shop. There's a super lady there called Poppy, who was really my second mother when I was growing up. She's very good about clothes. We could get her to help you . . . and I'll take you to my hairdresser and we'll demand you have any style you choose.'

'Even a Mohican!' When April smiled the sun really came out.

'You have perfect teeth,' Emma said with absolute truth and the conviction in her tone widened April's smile. 'By the way,' Emma continued, 'I want to thank you all for being in the church yesterday. It meant a lot to me, having someone I knew there.'

'That's what Robert said. I was coming anyway . . . and then he said we all should.'

'Did he?' Emma said. 'You do surprise me.'

'You should stay with us,' April said, when they parted company. 'It's silly paying for an hotel when we have so much room.' Emma promised to think about it, and waved until April was gone from her rear-view mirror.

She paused at the florist's to buy tiny blue iris and pink carnations for her aunt.

'These are for you,' she said, handing them over. 'Just to say thank you for yesterday. Not for everything you've done over the years, that's incalculable.'

'I was glad to do it. John was my brother, after all.' Peggy handed the flowers to Eddy and went to a reproduction bureau in the corner. 'There,' she said, turning back. 'That was our John in the old days. I got it out for you specially.'

The face that stared up at Emma from the studio portrait was handsome, if a trifle austere. Dark curling hair, blue eyes above a handsome aquiline nose, a mouth curved in a shy smile. Impossible to equate the smiling young man with the bitter spectre in the hospital bed.

'He was handsome,' Emma said simply and handed it back. Outside it began to rain, beating ferociously against the window-panes. 'That's good,' Eddy said, appearing with a tray. 'The garden could do with a drink.'

There were some people, Emma reflected, whose every word or deed sweetened life. They won no medals and died unsung but they were worth a thousand stars or public figures. Unfortunately, they were in short supply, the Eddys of this world.

When the tea was drunk and tidied away, Emma again brought up the subject of the funeral bill. Her aunt was pondering. 'Well,' she said at last, 'I suppose it's only right in a way. John set that business up for your mother with the bit money from his house, so you could say some of it's his by rights. All right, when the bills come Eddy'll send them on to you. Unless we see you?' There was a plea in her last sentence.

'Oh, you'll see me, all right. Now that I've found you I've no intention of letting you go.' Emma longed to tell her aunt about the Culroses; she felt mean keeping it from her. But it was bound to re-open old wounds, and the day after a funeral was not the time. Nor did it make sense to tell Peggy that the money from the house had been spent on a gold brooch. Her mother must have had a fair amount of capital to start up a business in a main thoroughfare in a big city, to buy the property freehold and kit it out in style. It had been improved over the years, but even at the beginning it had been quite Ritzy. Where had the money come from?

'You said they lived in Dovedale Street?' she asked. 'Would I find their house if I looked?'

'Eddy'll show you,' Peggy Colman said, her face cracking suddenly into a grin. 'Look at his face light up at the thought of a jaunt. Get out both of you and go on a guided tour. I'm sick of the pair of you.'

Once in the car, Eddy gave directions until they reached the tiny terraced house that had been her mother and father's home. It had new windows and an oak front door that would have graced a stately home, and children were playing in the tiny front garden.

'It's changed,' Eddy said, and Emma had to believe him for she had no memory with which to compare it.

They drove home along a sea-front bordered by fine houses on one side and a wide promenade on the other. There was a broad sweep of bay and a pier with a lighthouse. 'It's lovely,' Emma said. Out on the water yachts were gliding – tiny coloured wisps on the blue-grey water.

'Aye, it's canny,' Eddy said complacently. 'This is what they never show you on the telly.'

*

It was six o'clock when Emma got back to the hotel. She laid out her clothes for the evening and stepped under the shower, turning the controls from 'Hot' to 'Warm' to 'Cold' and feeling the water invigorate her.

Afterwards, dressed in a towelling robe, she lay on the bed listening to the news and changing the contents of her handbag to the pouch she would use that night. Taking out the jeweller's box, she opened it, and inside was the piece of paper with the numbers on it: IISXI2–5IISXIII–11. Letters and numbers. A code? And what about the stones? What could they mean?

The jeweller had said they had not been chosen to complement one another, so why those particular ones? She looked at them again. Blue, green, red, white. The Victorians had made rings of stones with a message: she had read that somewhere. So, a cryptic message on the front, a coded one on the back? '*I love you. Please come back*': was that it? In any event, it had been a gift of some importance.

Mr Winston had said these stones had no covert meaning, but he might be mistaken. She put the sheep back in the box and hid it in the drawer of her bedside table beside the Gideon Bible. Tomorrow she would go back to the Library and look up the meaning of gem-stones for herself.

She took time with her make-up and dressed care-fully, but she was still ready far too soon. She started for the lift to the foyer, but changed her mind: it would do Robert Eden good to wait a while! She watched from her window until she saw his Volvo turn into the car-park, then she went to the loo, checked her make-up and counted to twenty-five before leaving her room.

'I thought we'd go to a country pub I know,' Robert

said when she was safely installed in his car. 'The food isn't startling, but at least you can hear yourself speak.'

In fact the home-made steak pie and seasonal vegetables were delicious, the long, low dining-room cool and peaceful, looking out on a field studded with sheep.

'I wanted to talk to you,' he said when the waitress had ceased to hover. Emma met his eyes but offered no other encouragement. 'You're quite entitled to refuse the legacy,' he continued, 'but I hope you won't.'

'Why do you say that?'

'Because Stephen and April need some help. I think you can supply it.'

'And you can't?'

'Not in the same way.' He lifted the bottle of Mâcon and offered to top up her glass.

'No, thank you,' she said and waited while he refilled his own glass.

'I can watch their backs, and I will! But I have neither the time nor the talent to pull a dying business up by the bootstraps. You, on the other hand, could do it.'

'How do you know that?'

'Because I had you checked out.' Emma's gasp of outrage was cut off by his triumphant follow-up: 'As I bet you had us checked out . . . Culrose's, that is.'

It was true – that was exactly what she had done. Outrage was still flooding through her but she couldn't find words to express it. Useless to deny: this bastard probably knew all about her call to Harry Wattis.

'It's OK,' Robert continued, 'I wasn't making a dig. You're a businesswoman, why shouldn't you check your facts? A lesser man might wonder if you'd've been so quick to repudiate a more valuable bequest, but *I* don't think that for a moment.'

It was too much. Emma wiped her mouth with her napkin and reached for her bag. She would have stood up but his hand was on her free arm, holding it down against the table.

'Don't flounce off. That would disappoint me.'

She let out her breath in a low slow moan of fury and subsided into her seat. 'Damn you,' she said evenly.

'I already am damned,' he said. 'Others have been before you on that score.' She thought he flinched then and when he spoke again his voice was more subdued.

'Look. I'm putting this very badly and I wanted to do it so well. I haven't known you long but I've formed quite a high ... a high opinion of your capabilities. You're clever, you're competent and you have a business training. Moreover, you already have a foot in the door: whether or not you know it, young Stephen has accepted you. He doesn't bluster about your being allowed into the business over his dead body any more. He may not realize it himself, but I think he wants you there – someone to share the load, someone he can accept as an equal because they're almost family. I don't know why David Culrose made you an equal partner, and I don't want to know. It's none of my business. But as you are there, why don't you pitch in and help? And don't answer just to give me my come-uppance. Surely you can rise above that?'

'OK.' Emma tried to control her emotions. 'I do appreciate your motive in this, although your manner of presentation leaves a lot to be desired. But even if I was prepared to take on a "dying business", as you call it, I wouldn't do it in this case because I wouldn't waste time and effort on a hopeless task. No, hear me out. I've checked the market around here. There are three businesses identical to the Culrose operation – only they

are tight ships, no over-stocking, no unnecessary diversi-
fication, a small and motivated work-force. Have you
seen the Culrose outfit?' She rolled her eyes to heaven.

Robert nodded. 'I know. There's a lot to be done.'

'Too much. Two years ago we'd have managed, perhaps. Now, there's almost no chance. The boy must sell
... as a going concern if possible, but if not, then for
site value and anything else he can get. There'll be a not
inconsiderable sum if it's properly handled and, whatever you may think, I want no part of it. There'll
certainly be enough to set Stephen up in something else
and let April pursue some sort of training.'

'He won't do it,' Robert Eden said flatly. 'Young
Stephen is engaged in a crusade to preserve the Culrose
name in this county. He'll carry on to the last red cent,
and neither you nor I will stop him.'

'I have no intention of trying to stop him. It's nothing
to do with me. I came here to sort something out ...'
Suddenly and agonizingly she thought of Keith, and her
voice faltered. She had sorted nothing. The problem
was there waiting for her when she went back.

She caught Robert Eden's eyes on her, speculating,
and her chin came up. 'I came here for one thing and
one thing only: when I find out what lies behind this
affair, I'm off. I have nothing to stay for.'

'Except two orphaned kids who are destined for Queer
Street if they don't get help?'

'You'd like that, wouldn't you? You'd like to see me
stuck here, up the Swanee, playing nanny to a dying
business and two retarded adolescents!' Why did he
always make her sound like a bitch?

'So that's how you see April – a retarded adolescent.
I didn't realize.'

'Oh God, you're unfair. I like April. OK, I'm drawn

to her and I intend to do something for her. But I can do that equally well ... probably better ... when I'm back on my own home ground. And if you want to help April, remember what I said about changing Stephen's attitude and giving her some freedom.'

He shrugged. 'Let's finish our food.'

His sudden capitulation took Emma by surprise. 'Why are you so interested in those two? I know they've had a raw deal, but your concern goes deeper than ordinary compassion.'

Robert shrugged again. 'Fellow-feeling, I suppose. Not that I had an unhappy childhood – I was lucky. But I have a son, and I worry about his future. I'm trying to do for Stephen and April what I hope someone would do for my kid, if he needed it.'

'What's your son's name?'

'Edward. He's five.' He grinned suddenly. 'I do happen to have a photo.'

Emma threw back her head and laughed. 'I knew it. There had to be a crack in you somewhere ... you're a doting father!'

'Mea culpa.' He pulled out his wallet and handed over a snap of a smiling five-year-old.

'Do you miss him? Sorry, silly question – of course you miss him. Do you see him ... as much as you'd like to, I mean?'

'I have access, so I'm luckier than some. But she has a new husband ... there are difficult areas.'

'I'm sorry. I do know how tricky it can be.'

'You don't have ...'

'No, I don't have children.' She had known from the moment he spoke what his words would spark. She fought the pain of nostalgia, the memory of the small, damp body in the bed, the urgent little mouth at the breast, the thin arms around her neck . . . Lesley's arms, but Lesley was not a child.

'Do you want a pudding?'

Emma collected herself and turned to the sweet trolley. They chose their topics of conversation more carefully than their dessert, and spoke hardly at all on the drive home, wrapped in their own thoughts.

'I'm going back to Manchester tomorrow,' Emma said when he handed her out at the door. 'You know where to find me there. I start work again on Monday, and there are things I must do in Manchester before then. But I'm coming back here soon, probably next weekend.'

She half-thought Robert might kiss her again, but he was careful to keep his distance, and she was glad of it. Life was complicated enough.

When she got to her room she threw down her bag and dialled Poppy's number.

'It's me.'

'Hallo, darling.' Poppy was making an effort, but her voice sounded flat.

'Are you OK?'

'Yeah, fine. What news have you?'

Emma began her long tale, telling of the funeral and the brooch, of her evening with Robert Eden and his impassioned request.

'You could do it, you know,' Poppy said.

'Do what?'

'Save those kids. It'd keep you out of mischief!'

'Get me into hot water, you mean. That's all I need on my CV, a nice, juicy liquidation. That business is doomed, Poppy, whoever they bring in. The only hope is for the boy and girl to capitalize on their assets: business, house, everything. Then he should be off to university and she ... well, I'm not quite sure what's best for her. I'm bringing her to you as soon as I have the time.'

When Emma put down the phone she resolved to give more time and attention to Poppy. She had sounded so down tonight, and she didn't deserve it. After bathing and putting on her nightdress, Emma opened the sliding window as far as she could and looked out on Durham, lights twinkling as a breeze stirred the tree tops and agitated the coloured bulbs strung between them. After a moment she shivered. It was more than a breeze, it was a wind. She turned on the TV but the choice was American cops and robbers or dreary arts. She lifted the jeweller's box from the bedside table and took out the ewe-lamb. Four stones: blue, green, red and white. Lapis lazuli, unknown, spinel and topaz. Tomorrow she would find out what, if any, significance they held.

She replaced the box and climbed into bed, using the remote control to track round the channels once more. There was nothing that took her fancy, so she switched off TV and lamp and composed herself for sleep, thinking all the while of Robert Eden so that she need not think of Keith or Lesley at all.

18

Friday 18 August

The morning was sunny but when Emma went out to the car the wind was whipping across the car-park, so that it was a relief to be safe inside the Capri. She tidied her hair in the rear-view mirror and then switched on the radio. More talk of Lech Walesa and Solidarity. She put the car into gear and moved out on to the road. Her bags were behind her in the boot, but the brooch was safe in her handbag. If it had been a last, loving message from her father to her mother, she wanted to know.

She drove into Sunderland and parked in the town centre.

In the Library she asked where the gemmology section was, and selected from it half a dozen books to carry to a nearby table. The first was a dictionary of precious stones. She looked up lapis lazuli in the index and found the jeweller's information confirmed. Lapis lazuli was a complicated alumino-silicate found in Afghanistan and Chile and in the eruption of Vesuvius. It could take a good polish like jade and the best quality was a strong, lively blue with no hint of a violet tinge. There was no mention of its having any romantic meaning.

Emma looked up spinel and colourless topaz and found what she knew already, but no mention of any hidden significance.

It was the fourth book that listed meanings. Garnet meant constancy, diamond purity, sapphire repentance, topaz friendship. Of spinel and lapis lazuli there was no mention. She checked her list: Lapis lazuli, Unknown, Spinel, Topaz. Blank, blank, blank, friendship. No message there, or if there was she could not receive it.

On an impulse, and to clear her brain, she went in search of the book she had seen in Robert Eden's house. She found several volumes of poetry by the same author and then the book she was seeking: *Collected Poems* by C. H. Sisson.

She carried it back to the table and leafed through it, reading lines of poetry here and there, trying to tie them in with Robert Eden. And then she remembered the much-read page: 92. It had been page 92. She turned to it and a short poem called 'The Reckoning' seemed to leap out at her.

> My life dates from the day of my father's death
> When I lay weeping and it was not for him.
> Now I am to continue the degenerescence
> Until I enter his dream.
>
> There is nothing a drink cannot settle at forty
> Or money at fifty. The cure of all is death.
> But all lovers can remember a moment
> When they were not alone.

She read it again and again, realizing what it must have meant to him because of what it meant to her. Even when she had closed the book the words echoed uncomfortably in her head. 'The day of my father's death'. Her father, John Gaunt.

She sat back in her chair, watching the browsers among the shelves. Something was niggling in a corner of her mind and it wasn't poetry. She looked down at her list again: Lapis lazuli, Unknown, Spinel, Topaz. L.U.S.T. It couldn't be! She felt a terrible agitation at the word until reason reasserted itself. She had spelled out that word only because the second gem was unknown. The jeweller had said it had the properties of a garnet: that would make the letters LGST. Her father couldn't have used an 'unknown' gem, for there was no such thing. And no gem which began with a U or if one did, she had never heard of it.

She reached for the gem dictionary and ran her finger down the index at the back. There was only one. 'Uvarovite – a form of garnet. Green in colour. Found in Unst and Fetlar in the Shetland Isles, along with amethyst and tourmaline, chalcedony and other forms of garnet.'

Lapis lazuli, uvarovite, spinel, topaz. LUST. That had been her father's message. A biblical word for a man accustomed to reading his Bible. She rested her elbows on the table and pondered. Could it be as simple as that, the message of the brooch, or was there something more?

Emma took the gem books back to the shelf and searched for a copy of the Bible. When she sat down again with it, she took out the scrap of paper on which the jeweller had copied the letters and numbers from the back of the brooch. IIS XI 2-5 IIS XII 1-11. If you substituted Arabic for Roman numerals that could stand for Two S Chapter 11 verses 2-5 and Chapter 12 verses 1-11.

There was only one book listed in the index which began with S, unless you counted the Song of Solomon. That was Samuel, and there were indeed two books. She turned to Second Samuel Chapter 11 verse 2, knowing, before she did so, what she would find.

And it came to pass in an eveningtide, that David arose from off his bed, and walked upon the roof of the king's house: and from the roof he saw a woman washing herself; and the woman was very beautiful to look upon. And David sent and inquired after the woman. And one said, is not this Bathsheba, the daughter of Eliam, the wife of Uriah the Hittite? And David sent messengers, and took her; and she came in unto him, and he lay with her; for she was purified from her uncleanness: and she returned unto her house. And the woman conceived, and sent and told David, and said, I am with child.

Emma knew now, why she had been in David Culrose's will and why Esther had taken her into exile. She didn't need the second part of the quotation but she read it just the same.

And the Lord sent Nathan unto David. And he came unto him, and said unto him, There were two men in one city; the one rich, and the other poor. The rich man had exceeding many flocks and herds: but the poor man had nothing, save one little ewe-lamb, which he had bought and nourished up: and it grew up together with him, and with his children; it did eat of his own meat, and drank of his own cup, and lay in his bosom, and was unto him as a daughter. And there came a traveller unto the rich man, and he spared to take of his own flock and of his own herd, to dress for the wayfaring man that was come unto him; but took the poor man's lamb, and dressed it for the man that was come to him.

And David's anger was greatly kindled against the man; and he said to Nathan, 'As the Lord liveth, the man that has done this thing shall surely die: and he shall restore the lamb fourfold, because he did this thing, and because he had no pity.' And Nathan said to David, 'Thou art the man. Thus saith the Lord God of Israel, I anointed thee King over Israel, and I delivered thee out of the hand of Saul; and I gave thee thy master's house, and thy master's wives unto thy bosom, and gave thee the house of Israel and Judah; and if that had been too little, I would moreover have given unto thee such and such things. Wherefore hast thou despised the commandment of the Lord, to do evil in his sight? Thou hast killed Uriah the Hittite with the sword, and hast taken his wife to be thy wife, and hast slain him with the sword of the children of Ammon. Now therefore the sword shall never depart from thy house; because thou hast despised me, and hast taken the wife of Uriah the Hittite to be thy wife. Thus saith the Lord, Behold I will raise up evil against thee out of thine own house . . .

Emma couldn't bear to read any more. She took back the Bible and walked out into the sunshine, letting the wind whip her hair into her eyes so that she would have an excuse for tears.

Emma could only think of one place to go, one person here in whom she could confide. She drove to Robert Eden's office and was shown straight in. He took one look at her face and came round the desk with that surprising agility. 'Coffee – or something stronger?'

'Coffee,' Emma said and the secretary withdrew.

'Something's happened,' Robert said, taking a bottle of brandy from a corner cupboard.

Emma nodded. 'I know now.'

He put a finger to his lips as the secretary's knock came at the door and she entered with a tray. He poured two cups of coffee then put a slug of brandy into the first cup.

'Not for me,' Emma said but he laced the second cup just the same.

'Drink it,' he said and she found herself obeying him. The coffee was surprisingly good and she took a second sip before replacing the cup. Then she took the jeweller's box from her bag and pushed it towards him, speaking as he opened it and lifted out the brooch.

'I found that among my mother's effects. It was ugly

and it intrigued me, but I didn't attach any significance to it. Then I found this.' She pushed the receipt across. 'It was in my father's wallet. He was an ordinary man, of limited means. Extremely religious, and extremely bitter at the break-up of his marriage.' Robert Eden's eyes were on her now, calm and oddly comforting. 'He wasn't the type to commission jewellery, so I checked it out. The stones spell out LUST. . .'

The solicitor frowned slightly and looked down at the artefact, and Emma felt suddenly impatient. 'Lapis lazuli, uvarovite, spinel, topaz.'

'Uvarovite?'

'Exactly. He must have gone to great lengths to research those gems, to produce what he intended to be a badge of shame. That's not all. There are numbers on the back, and it turns out they refer to a biblical quotation. Second Samuel, eleven and twelve. It tells of King David who saw the wife of a man who worked for him and seduced her.'

'Uriah the Hittite . . . and the woman was Bath-sheba?'

'Yes. Only in this case the woman was Esther Gaunt, my mother. And I am the child of David . . . King David Culrose, the all-powerful king of a business empire.'

Robert was nodding and Emma saw that he was not surprised. 'You *knew*?'

'When I drew up the will he would tell me nothing, except that you were to be included. That meant you were mistress or offspring. As soon as I knew you weren't the one, you had to be the other.' He looked down at the brooch. 'What a crazy set-up!'

'I read the quote in the Bible this morning. It said God was angry with David and the sword would never depart from his house, that it would be filled with evil. That's what my father wanted to tell them. I expect there was a letter too, but he sent the brooch because it couldn't be destroyed like paper.'

'So he was cursing them?'

Emma shook her head. 'No. They cursed themselves, all three of them.'

'How do you feel? I'm not prying, I just wonder if there's any way I can help.'

'Thanks ... but it's something I have to come to terms with on my own. I think I feel relief, in a way. I didn't feel any affinity with John Gaunt ... there wasn't time, and the circumstances were against it, but I don't think it would've happened anyway, even if everything had been ideal. Now, I don't have to even try to know David Culrose, so it's a relief.'

'You'd have liked him, I think. He had humour, a kind of merriment, I suppose, even in the blackest moments. But he was essentially sad, and I could never understand why. Now I'm beginning to see.'

'It's still only supposition,' Emma said, suddenly nervous at the finality in his voice. 'I still want to keep on probing.'

'What are you going to do?'

'I'll have to think. Do we tell the kids? Will it help them to know, or harm them?'

'They'll have to be told something. And they're more sensible than you might think. I think they can take it. They may even have guessed.'

'I don't want to tell them yet.' Emma felt a sense of panic at the very idea of owning kinship with Stephen and April. With anyone. 'I *am* like my mother,' she thought once more. 'I want to walk alone.' But did she? If she chose, she could walk away from everyone, from everything. And yet she wanted to stay and wrestle with the problem.

'I'll leave it to you,' she said to Robert. 'If it comes up while I'm away and you feel it's right, tell them. Meanwhile, I want to talk to Caroline Culrose. You said she lived in London?'

Robert pressed a button and spoke: 'Can I have the address of Mrs Caroline Exton? You'll find it in the Culrose file.' A moment later he scribbled something on a sheet of paper and held it out. 'Do you want me to contact her for you?'

'No, please, I don't want her forewarned. She might refuse to see me. Just let me handle it myself.'

Again the inclination of the head, as if he was giving her permission. Emma felt her hackles rise and then subside. She needed all the allies she could get, even overbearing ones.

Robert walked with her to her car, taking the keys from her hand and opening the door for her. 'I'll be in touch. Try not to worry too much. We'll sort something out. And drive carefully.'

It was meant to sting her and it did. 'Chauvinist!' she said and let out the clutch. In the rear-view mirror she could see him watching until she reached the traffic lights and his figure was lost to sight.

She went into a call-box when she reached the Durham outskirts and dialled Peggy Colman's number. 'Aunt Peggy? It's me, Emma.' How could she tell this woman that their relationship, so recently created, was built on sand? 'I have to go back to Manchester for a few days, because of things at work. But I'm coming back . . . No I won't lose touch. Not ever, again.' She would never tell them, Emma decided as she put down the phone. That was the least she could do for the Gaunts, who had given her their name.

She rang April then. 'I'm going back to Manchester, darling.' The endearment slipped out but it seemed in place. 'Will you explain to Stephen and say I'm coming back soon? Perhaps next weekend. I'm at the office again on Monday, so it will have to be a weekend. The thing is, I wanted you to know that I will be back. And I'm going to fix for you to come and see me . . .'

No matter what she said, though, April sounded morose. She doesn't believe I'll keep faith, Emma thought. And why the hell should she believe me, poor little devil? When she got back to the Capri she stood for a moment, trying to work out her feelings for April. Motherly? Sisterly? Female solidarity?

In the distance she could see Durham cathedral, grey against the sky. For centuries pilgrims had crossed this beautiful county, coming from north, south, east and west to seek succour and sanctuary. If she came back . . . when she came back . . . she would go there. Not to find God but perhaps to find some peace of mind. She got into her car and sent it speeding towards the A1.

When Durham had been left behind her, her thoughts still lingered on God, the God of vengeance. How much hate it had taken to create the Bathsheba brooch. How bizarre to conceive a reproach too valuable to consign to flame or ash-can. She winced, thinking of John Gaunt, engrossed in his search for gemstones, using the Bible as a sword to wreak his revenge. And dying alone and aloof, years before his time. His eyes had seemed to glow with hatred, even from his deathbed. He had never forgiven Esther for her betrayal, and if his eyes were to be believed neither could he forgive Emma for being born. If the golden lamb had been intended to exorcize his anger, it had failed. No doubt there had been a letter with his gift, setting out its meaning. That would have been easy to get rid of, but how to get rid of a golden lamb? Her mother had not been able to do it. She herself must find a way.

Emma drove into a service point near Wetherby and tried to choose a sensible meal. There was nothing she fancied, but she chomped manfully through chicken à la king and vegetables, and drank a cup of coffee. The cafeteria was crowded with holiday-makers, coming and going between north and south.

At the next table sat a young couple, a baby in a high chair, a toddler climbing energetically up and over the seats in between accepting mouthfuls of food from his harassed father. The mother sat serenely spooning baby dinner into her daughter's mouth: the baby's head was just a golden fuzz, but its dungarees were pink. Pink for a girl, blue for a boy.

Emma looked at her watch: three-fifteen. Lesley would be sitting now, bare feet curled under her on the settee, Tom on the floor crashing cars to his heart's content. She would take the baby in her arms, the pink baby in pink dungarees, and put it to her breast!

Across the aisle the mother reached for the baby, but only to wipe its mouth and sit it on her knee for the final spoonful. Emma concentrated on her cup, stirring, watching the cold coffee churn around. 'I am ready now for a child of my own. I want it,' she thought. She had known it for months, really – ever since she had taken Keith into her bed. Perhaps even before. All that remained was to make sensible arrangements and invent a cover story for people like Amy, who must never know the truth about the baby's father. Apart from that one complication, it would all be easy.

It was so beautifully simple when you put it like that, so simple to comprehend and accept. So different from the sordid tangle of deceit and bitterness that lay in her handbag, exemplified in gold. '*Uvarovite – a type of garnet . . . found in Unst and Fetlar along with amethyst and tourmaline and chalcedony.*'

Emma switched her thoughts deliberately, thinking about Monday morning and ordered calm. A week's mail, acknowledged by Amy, would be waiting for her attention, and a list of calls to be returned. '*It's you, Emma. Glad you're back. Now this is the problem . . .*' And then she'd be alone with her terminal, using it to straighten out the knottiest of problems, making the rough places plain. That was biblical – or something like it.

The little boy across the aisle was making swooping movements with a yellow racing car. Brmm, brmm. 'Tom?' She felt the name well up in her throat and choked it back. The pink baby began to cry and the mother handed it to the father, his large hand easily encompassing the pink backside. 'There now, lamby. Come to your dad. What's the matter then?' He bounced the baby on his denimed knee until the sobs gave way to hiccups and then to smiles. Across the table the woman's face softened, taking on a look of satisfaction, of contentment so total that it was sensual. She looked across and caught Emma's eyes. 'Six months old and she's a daddy's girl.'

Inside Emma something soured but she smiled. 'They all are, aren't they?' she said, then she picked up her bag and went back to the car.

*

She drove well for the next twenty miles, moving through the gears, going into overdrive, using her mirrors to whip through the traffic. 'I am good at this,' she thought. 'I am good at a lot of things.' She hit the rush-hour traffic at Leeds and endured it patiently until she was free of it, and then was turning into her own street.

Two messages waited on the answerphone. *'Hallo, Emma, this is Lesley. I just wanted to remind you, in case Keith forgets: Tom's birthday on Tuesday ... next Tuesday, the 22nd. It's timed for daddy coming home, so if you come from the office with Keith that'll be fine. I do hope you're coming. I'll need some moral support apart from ...'*

She was cut off by the guillotine, and then the second message was activated.

'Emma? I don't know when you're coming home.' There was a pause. *'This is just to say I love you. I want you. I need you. Your terms. Any way you want it to be. We'll talk. I love you.'* Keith sounded flat. Determined but not like a lover. Love should be joyful, joyous, joy-bringing, and all it seemed to generate was misery.

Emma went through to her mother's room, smelling the dust that was slowly overcoming the remembered scents. She put the Bathsheba brooch back where she had found it, and looked around. Did Esther Gaunt linger here? Did anything remain? Some people had faith, and she had seen it working in them, bringing peace. But she had none. She sat down in the chintz-covered armchair, absorbing the silence. There was no sound at all. The clock had long since wound down and the windows were locked tight against intruders, shutting out any breath of wind that might have caused a stir.

On the dressing-table the powder bowls and brushes

of a lady were laid out, as they always had been. Here her mother had sat and brushed her thick and heavy hair, long strokes up and down until it gleamed.

Some lines from a long-forgotten poem about Marie Antoinette came into her mind: '*Here sat she while her maidens tired and curled the most unhappy head in all the world.*' Her eyes filled, thinking of her mother sitting at her mirror. And all the while the ewe-lamb had been there, a few feet away. Had Esther thought about it every single day, or had she blocked out the misery she had left behind her? Had her mother been the serene and competent woman she had seemed, or the greatest actress of all time?

Suddenly Emma heard her own voice, loud in the silent room, croaking slightly as though from disuse: 'Whom did you love? Which of them? Did you ever care for the man you married, or only for David? My father, David – did you love him? For God's sake, I need to know!'

She was silent then, as though waiting for the room to speak, to let her know the truth. On the dressing-table the silver and glass gleamed, dust swam in a shaft of light, a withered leaf on the African violet gave up the ghost and fell soundlessly to the floor. But there was no answer, no message.

'I will never know,' Emma said aloud and walked past the triple mirrors, reflecting a dozen images, to set about preparing for her trip to London.

19

Saturday 19 August

The sun was shining when Emma woke. She was catching a train at nine-thirty, and by seven she had bathed and was drinking orange juice by the open window of the living-room. Hearing Poppy's tread on the floor above her, she went out into the hall. 'I'm back,' she called up the stairs.

Poppy's door opened on the landing. 'Come up. I've got mushrooms and eggs. Bring your own bacon if you want it.'

Emma settled for wholemeal toast and a boiled egg while Poppy had mushrooms on toast. 'I'm going to London.'

Poppy's eyes were round with curiosity. 'London? Lucky you. Need a chaperone?'

'You wouldn't come without your Charlie.' Did Poppy's face cloud momentarily, or was it her imagination? Emma tried a joke. 'Some chaperone you'd be. You'd be off with the first handsome guy you laid eyes on and I'd be left alone and defenceless. Anyway, I have to go in half an hour, and I have a book . . . *a book* to tell you.'

Poppy wiped her mouth and refilled her cup. She had on a flowered housecoat with a ruffled collar that framed her handsome, fleshy face. Her hair was newly set and she had tiny pearl studs in her ears. 'You look really nice today, Pops,' Emma said.

'I'd appreciate that remark more if you didn't sound so surprised,' Poppy said drily. 'Now get on with it.'

'Well,' Emma said, 'remember that brooch?' As she told the story of the jeweller and the biblical quotation, Poppy's eyes widened.

'My God.' She pushed her plate away from her. 'And Esther never breathed a word. I can't get over that, Em. We were close, your mother and I. We cried together occasionally. We fought sometimes. I told her every-thing ... everything in my life. I thought she'd done much the same, even if she was a bit tight-lipped. And now this.'

'What did Mother tell you about where she got the money to start the shop?'

'She said she'd had a settlement of some sort, when she parted from your ... when the marriage broke up. He's not your father, is he? Are you sure, beyond any doubt?'

'I'll never know, will I? But I'm fairly sure. I think David Culrose was my father, and that John Gaunt knew it, but never told anyone. His sister is quite convinced she's my aunt, and I want it to stay like that.'

'What about the kids, Stephen and what's-her-name?'

'April. I don't know. If I thought I could satisfy their curiosity without telling them the truth, I'd do it. I don't want to damage their image of their father. I like them, especially her; but it's too late for me to be a big sister. I'm a loner, Poppy, like my mother.'

'A cat who walks alone?'

'Something like that.'

'I don't think you are like Esther. You resemble her, but you're not like her. Don't brainwash yourself into believing you're made in her likeness because I don't think you are. Anyway, why are you going to London? Not with Don Juan, I hope?'

'If you mean Keith, the answer's no. I'm going to London to see David Culrose's sister. She's the one person who might know something definite. If they were close . . . and according to Robert Eden, they were very close . . . she might have been in his confidence. But remember, he *thought* I was his daughter but he might have been wrong. He was just a boy: eighteen years old. Younger than Stephen. It's hard to accept that, because Mother was thirty-five when I was born. Women didn't do things like that in those days.'

Poppy hooted. 'Don't you believe it! There is nothing new under the sun – nothing! The only difference now is that it's done openly.'

'Anyway,' Emma said, when she got up to go, 'what's your news? How is Charles?'

Again the little change of expression in Poppy that betokened unease. 'Oh, he's OK. I've hardly seen him this week. I'm expecting him tonight, though. It's his night on at the golf-club – you know the committee takes turns. So I'll probably be out when you come back. Push a note under the door if you have any news. God, it's better than Barbara Taylor Bradford, this lot.'

Emma caught the train with time to spare and settled into her first-class seat. There were few other passengers and no one with children. She took out the clutch of newspapers she had bought and browsed through them. Branagh and Thompson again, of course; and still indecision in Poland. She read the reviews, and was putting the papers on one side when she saw a familiar face. Harry Corbett, the Sooty man, was dead – had died, in fact, two days before but the news had been withheld. She closed her eyes as the train sped between fields yellow with grain and remembered childhood: Sooty and Sweep on TV, hugging your knees and holding your breath for the inevitable custard-pie routine at the end. How easy life had been then, how straight the way ahead.

She had not returned Lesley's call nor had she tried to contact Keith. If only she could wipe them out of her memory – but they were both there, lurking, ready to overwhelm her. She went to the buffet for coffee, queueing with people mad keen to buy large buns with a thin sliver of bacon and tomato in them. Two young men at the counter were purchasing six-packs of lager and huge packets of crisps. Lager and crisps at ten in the morning! And yet they looked fresh and healthy and far from debauched.

In the mirror behind the counter Emma's own face looked ghastly. She would have to check her appearance before she turned up at Landscale Mansions – first impressions were always important but if you wanted someone to part with family secrets they were doubly so.

She went along to the lavatory when she had finished her coffee and washed the newsprint from her hands. In the mirror she looked pale but quite respectable. She applied lipstick and ran a comb through her hair. As a rule she seldom needed blusher, and so didn't carry it in her bag. She took out her purse-spray of Opium and squirted liberally. Nothing like pong for lifting your spirits. When she went back to her seat she felt ready for her mission, even impatient, but she could not think beyond the next six hours. She would use the time on the homeward journey to work out what to do next.

At Euston she hurried to the taxi rank and gave the Landscale Mansions address. 'Just drop me off at the corner,' she said. 'I have a few minutes to spare.' The cab sped towards Kensington, turning eventually into a tree-lined street near to the Gardens.

She paid off the taxi and walked slowly towards No. 18, a tall red-brick house, well kept, with window-boxes spilling colour down the walls. The windows were shrouded in white net and there was no sign of life behind them. She looked at the solid brass step and the gleaming bell-push at the side and kept on walking. Knock or phone first, that was the question. At the corner of the street she saw a telephone box. It seemed like an omen and she hurried towards it, fishing in her purse for change as she went.

She dialled the number and stood, heart pounding, as it rang out.

A woman answered. 'Exton residence.'

'Could I speak to Mrs Caroline Exton.'

'I'm afraid she's not at home. May I take a message?'

Relief made Emma sag for a moment, the hand-set shaking against her cheek. 'When do you expect her back?' What if Caroline Exton was away . . . for a week, a month even?

'She's expected back at two. If you ring at two-thirty, you should find her here.'

Emma said thank you and put down the receiver. She was reprieved. For a moment she contemplated abandoning the whole thing and scuttling back to Manchester without seeing Caroline Exton. But this was not a time for running away. There had been enough of that in a previous generation.

She was looking for a cruising cab to take her to Harrods when she saw the church, small and opulent with jewelled windows and imposing doors. It was quiet inside, when she moved in out of the sunlight, and empty except for a woman pushing a vacuum cleaner backwards and forwards at the end of the centre aisle.

Emma moved into a rear pew and bowed her head because it was the proper thing to do. In front of her the ledge of the next pew was stacked with prayer books and hymn books and Bibles in tooled leather. She reached for a Bible, turning automatically to the second book of Samuel. But it was in the first book of Kings that she found what she was looking for – the fate of King David, and his last words to his son. *'I go the way of all the earth: be thou strong, therefore, and shew thyself a man.'* A message for Stephen? Perhaps, too, a message for her.

For a moment Emma wondered if it was improper to pray to a God in whom you did not believe. But here, in this quiet place, it seemed appropriate. She put down her head and prayed for those caught up in a tangle that was not of their making – April and Stephen and Peggy and Lesley. She could not claim innocence in her own situation with Keith, and she asked neither help nor absolution, simply a quiet mind.

In the street outside she raised her hand to a cab and asked to be taken to Harrods. It was soothing to move between the counters, smelling the heady perfumes, fingering the silk scarves and the soft leather bags, enjoying the glow of porcelain and gleam of silver. She bought a silk scarf in sludgy browns and mauves, and a bag in glove leather, small and pouched with a gold clasp and chain. She wanted to spend more but she had run out of requirements. So on an impulse she bought a bottle of Rive Gauche for Poppy and some hideously expensive milk bath for Amy, as a reward for holding the fort. She asked the assistant to include a basket of bath luxuries, boxed in lace with tiny sprigs of artificial lilac here and there. She wanted to give Lesley a gift, and this seemed the sort of thing she would not buy for herself.

Emma walked to the lift, scanning the indicator board for the toy department. Once there she went from stand to stand, picking and discarding, turning keys in clockwork, holding furry pandas to her cheek or twitching the skirts of bright-eyed dolls. She had always wanted a doll's house when she was a child; she had dreamed of it every Christmas and hinted for it as loudly as she could. Now she found her dream house, Edwardian, with tiny figures among the delicate furniture. She stood as long as she dared, rearranging and admiring. At last she closed the front and latched it, and got on with business.

She found a pink velvet elephant for Zoë and a bright red boxed car for Tom. According to the blurb, it rode on three wheels, flashed its lights, sounded its horn and ejected the driver, all at the touch of a remote control. Her eyes brightened as she thought of the frantic brmm-brmms it would produce. On an impulse she bought its fellow in blue. It was more fun if you had two, more scope if someone could play with you.

A sudden crazy impulse to buy up the whole department – dolls, animals, cars, musical tops – took hold of her. A clockwork clown on a counter started laughing, wound up by mischievous fingers: 'Ha, ha, ha. Ho, ho, ho.' She fled from the store, clutching her purchases, and stood on the pavement until a taxi disgorged three Muslim women, hidden in chadors, and she could take their place.

This time she mounted the steps of the house. It was three-fifteen. She was late. She heard the bell ringing inside the house and after a moment the sound of high heels on a marble floor.

'Hallo. I wonder if Mrs Exton is at home? Mrs Caroline Exton?'

The woman wore the black dress and white apron of a servant but her hair tumbled luxuriantly over her shoulders.

'Just step inside and I'll find out. Could I have your name, please?'

Should she lie? She wavered for a moment and then gave her own name, Emma Gaunt, in a firm voice. Except that she was no longer Emma Gaunt – nor was she Emma Culrose. She was Emma No-name, bastard daughter of Esther Gaunt.

The maid reappeared in a doorway. 'Would you come this way, please?' The room was pale green and white, full of ebonized furniture, with bowls of flowers on every available surface. Caroline Exton *née* Culrose was standing in front of the fireplace. She looked Emma up and down for a moment and then went across to a chair.

'Do sit down.'

Emma put down her parcels and lowered herself into the deep settee.

'Thank you for seeing me.'

Caroline Exton was small and dark, beautifully groomed, dressed casually in well cut linen trousers and a white cotton sweater.

'You say your name is Emma Gaunt. Is Esther Gaunt your mother?'

Emma nodded. 'She was. She died last year.'

Caroline Exton bit her lower lip for a moment, seeming to weigh matters. 'Do you know?' she said at last.

Again Emma inclined her head.

'I guessed you must. That's the only reason you would come here, isn't it? Did my brother ... did David mention you in his will?'

'Yes. That's how I found out.'

'I thought he might. He'd wanted ... to do something for you for such a long time, but your mother would never allow it. He was told of your birth and that you had been christened Emma in a letter which bore no address. After that there was nothing.'

'Nothing at all?' Emma asked.

'Not a single letter or even a phone call. Until last year, when I think your mother must have realized that time was running out, and sent him some photographs and news of your success. He derived great pleasure from knowing how well you had done.'

Caroline got up and crossed to a bureau. 'This was your father ... around about the time you were born.' David Culrose looked back at Emma, smiling as he squinted into the sun, a sweater thrown carelessly around his shoulders, the rigging of a small boat behind him. 'He loved the sea,' Caroline said, taking the photograph back.

There was pride in her voice and when she looked at the picture there was pride in her expression. Emma thought of Peggy Colman, equally proud of a handsome young man in an old photograph. Two sisters whose brothers had thrown away their lives.

'There's so much I need to know,' she said, when Caroline had resumed her seat. 'I'm confused. I think I know the truth ... I won't go into how I found out, it's too complicated ... but even now I can't be sure. Do you know, know for a *fact*, whose child I am?'

'You're David's child. Some people said it was a trick on your mother's part, a ruse to get money out of the family. But I knew better. You're a Culrose.' She smiled. 'You even bear the name. Emma was my mother's name, and her mother and grandmother before her. I'm called Caroline Emma, and you carry the name for your generation. David wouldn't allow April to be christened April Emma, although Laura, my sister-in-law, had assumed she would be. He said the tradition had gone on long enough, and though the rest of the family was shocked, Laura accepted it, as she accepted everything; Caroline sighed. 'I don't have a daughter. I don't have any children.'

She rang a bell by the fireplace and ordered some tea. 'I've just come up from my husband's constituency, today: I had to hold the fort for him last night. The House isn't sitting at the moment, and he's in Brussels. Ah, good!' The tea had appeared almost instantly, and she presided over the tray, pressing Emma to tiny biscuits and rising to put her cup on a side-table.

'I expect you want to know all about David and your mother?' She sipped for a moment and Emma realized she wanted to remember it for herself, too.

'David didn't want to go to university, and my father backed him. I did want to go, but I wasn't given the option: I was supposed to get married and rear children. I've done one, but not the other. Anyway, David came back from school in the summer of '56. He had good A-levels, and Daddy was very proud of him. He gave him a TR3. I was so jealous! He made him a director of the firm, and he made John Gaunt a sort of . . . well, today they'd call him a minder.'

She looked at Emma. 'You never knew John Gaunt?'

'No. I always thought he was my father, but I never saw him until last week.'

'He's still alive?'

'He died a week ago. We never spoke.' No need to tell of the silent vigil in the hospital; there was sadness enough here already.

'I see. I'm sorry. He was a very strange man – quite handsome, and unbelievably upright. My father thought David couldn't be in better hands. Unfortunately he had reckoned without your mother. She was a striking woman, not beautiful – she was too angular to be called that. But she wore clothes well, she could make cheap garments look special. I envied her that. One so longs to have style when one is an adolescent. She looked quite severe most of the time ... and then her face would soften suddenly, especially at the sight of David, and you just wanted to watch her. I suppose she had charisma – and of course she had maturity on her side. She had seldom, if ever, been out of the county, but to David she seemed like a woman of the world. I was very angry with her at the time, but since then, I've had time to consider and I don't think she was any more to blame than anyone else. It was natural to see her as a predator, since she was a mature woman, well into her thirties, and David was an eighteen-year-old. A green eighteen-year-old!'

Emma put down her cup, feeling uncomfortable but anxious to hear every word.

'Esther had had a cold marriage. John Gaunt was a good man but I doubt he ever made her laugh. She and David went quite mad for a while; they couldn't stay away from one another and there was almost an electricity between them. He took her everywhere, he showered gifts on her, he was her lover, her slave, her lord and master too. They were bedazzled with one another. My mother thought it was obscene, but mothers are always the last to accept their children's sexuality.'

Bedazzled: yes, that was the word to describe the victims of consuming passion, Emma thought. It robbed them of their proper sight. Aloud she said, 'I'm very grateful to you for telling me all this. I know it can't be easy.'

'I often look back,' Caroline said. 'You do as you get older. At least I do. We were brought up to think we were special: we were Culroses and that meant something. I let it go to my head, I think. David was more aware of the outside world, less egocentric, but he wasn't prepared for your mother. He could have handled it so much more cleverly, if he'd thought it through and kept it from everyone.'

'My . . . John Gaunt's sister knew nothing about it at all,' Emma said. But Caroline was obviously unaware of Peggy Colman's existence.

'She must have been the only one, then. All our circle knew. It was unavoidable – there they were, wherever we looked. I saw them once, in the theatre. It was *Salad Days*, I think. Anyway, the lights went up and there they were in the stalls, absolutely engrossed in one another. They didn't even know it was over until they heard "The Queen".'

'Could it have been *Brigadoon*?' Emma said.

Caroline frowned. 'I believe it was, now you mention it. So depressing, that show. Why do you ask if it was *Brigadoon*?'

'They kept the programme . . . one half each. I thought it might be significant. But go on.'

'Well, it fell to pieces after that, as it was bound to do. Your mother was pregnant. You can't imagine how times have changed, Emma – for better and worse, I sometimes think. Certainly, we were too narrow then. There would have been no place in the family for Esther even if David could have married her, and John Gaunt made it clear there would be no divorce. Esther became consumed with guilt, just as she had been consumed with passion.'

Emma let out her breath. Had that been the purpose of the brooch, to bring home to Esther a sense of shame?

'David tried,' Caroline went on. 'He wanted to throw everything up and go off with Esther, but she wouldn't hear of it. By then she was so overcome with guilt that she wanted nothing to do with him. It killed my father: that sounds dramatic, but it's true. I bear no grudges, I just know that's what it was. He died of the grief and stress. David got the business, which meant he had assets but not a lot of cash. I'd had a settlement under the will, and so had my mother. David sold the business to get money to make provision for your mother and the child she was carrying. Then he moved to Durham, away from the scene of so much unhappiness.'

'Why did my mother turn against him?' Emma asked. 'Or was she acting in what she thought were his best interests?'

Caroline Exton considered for a moment, her head on one side. 'I've thought about this a lot,' she said at last. 'Of course, I can't be sure: I was a girl at the time, a child almost. But I have a theory. Your mother had been unhappy for a long time, as I said before, but never even considered breaking free. And then along comes David, young, infatuated, ardent beyond belief. She is swept off her feet for a little while and when she comes to her senses there is no going back to the old, cold way of life.'

'Did she really love your brother?' Emma asked.

'I don't know. Perhaps. You simply can't be sure. I

think she cut herself off from him for his sake, so she must have cared to some extent. But he loved her totally and he went on loving her for the rest of his life. He married Laura eventually but the marriage was a sham. I wasn't close to Laura: we had nothing in common. But I sympathized with her. She had David's name but she never possessed his heart, and I think she knew it. Have you met his son and daughter?'

'Yes. I like them. They're young and uncertain but that's no crime. They're compassionate and courteous, and I think they're unbelievably well-behaved in what must be an impossible situation.'

'I like them, too, but it doesn't blind me to their shortcomings. Stephen is headstrong, and April ... well, equally immature. I don't know what is going to become of them now. The business is finished, it seems. My husband's taken advice on the subject, and the advice is to sell. But Stephen is adamantly opposed to it.' She frowned suddenly. 'What did David do for you?'

'He left me a share in the business.'

'Oh dear. Still, you look . . .' Caroline hesitated.

'I don't need anything from my ... father's estate.' It sounded strange to call him that. 'My mother built up quite a flourishing fashion business, which I have inherited, and I have a job which pays well. I don't intend to accept anything from them. But I wanted to know the truth. I'm grateful to you for being so frank.'

Caroline raised her hands in a gesture of defeat. 'What else would have served? My husband is a great believer in keeping the lid on things ... on almost everything. Lately, I've begun to wonder if there's any point in it.'

She smiled suddenly. 'Now, you can repay all my revelations. Tell me about yourself.'

It was easy to talk about SyStems, nice to sense Caroline's approval. Emma skirted over her private life, causing Caroline to question her. 'And is there a man in your life?'

'There is someone.'

'What's he called?' Caroline said encouragingly.

'Tom. He's very nice ... quite special. But I don't expect there'll be a future in it.'

When it was time to go, they walked together to the door. Caroline Exton was very correct but Emma could sense a yearning in her. They paused at the door and Emma held out her hand. 'Thank you.'

Caroline took her hand and smiled. 'I don't have children of my own, and I've come to terms with it. But I often wondered what you were like – whether I'd like you. I think I do. I hope you'll come again?' There was an echo of that other sister: '*You will come again*, won't you?' So many people making demands.

Aloud Emma said: 'Yes, if I may I'd like to come again.'

The older woman looked at her bags. 'You've been shopping?'

'Yes ... gifts for a friend's children. Lesley was at university with me. We keep in touch.'

It was so easy to lie, Emma thought, as she walked to the corner to hail a cab. And half the people in the world were at it, if her own experience was anything to go by.

She went straight to Euston and stepped on to a pullman, settling in the dining car and ordering dinner and half a bottle of dry white wine. She hadn't eaten all day but she could do no more than pick at the salmon

316

Mornay. When the wine was gone she ordered Benedictine and sipped it with her coffee, watching the countryside speed by. She wanted to think over what Caroline Exton had told her, but a line of verse kept intruding, a line from the book she had seen in Robert Eden's house and read in the library.

> But all lovers can remember a moment
> When they were not alone.

Was that what her mother had done, spent the rest of her life remembering? Or was Caroline Exton's theory true, that David had been Esther's excuse to escape an unhappy life? She thought of Peggy Colman's words the first time they had met: '*Esther said, "I've got to go . . . if I stay now I'll be trapped."*' Trapped into the old narrow way of life, but this time with a baby to share her purgatory? 'Perhaps she went for my sake?' Emma thought. 'She exiled herself to make sure I was free, and all she had then were memories.'

John Gaunt had taken a strange vengeance on his errant wife: a gold ewe-lamb to spell out her sin. What did you do now if you found your partner had betrayed you? Cut the buttons from his Armani suit? Decustomize her Porsche? Or just bad-mouth him or her in circles where it mattered? Was there anyone now who would know how to exact a biblical vengeance? And yet the words of the Bible had stuck in her head as no newsprint or prose from a novel could have done.

'*And David sent and inquired after the woman. And one said, Is not this Bathsheba, . . . the wife of Uriah the Hittite?*' Then afterwards, when David had taken the poor man's one ewe-lamb: '*Now therefore the sword shall never depart from thine house . . . I will raise up evil against thee out of thine own house.*'

There was no way Emma could believe in divine retribution, but the sword never had departed from the Culrose house and if Stephen could not be persuaded to sell up, it would not go even now. Not that the Gaunts had fared any better: bitterness had killed one 'father', remorse another. There was not a great deal of difference in the end.

When Emma reached home there was one message on her machine: Keith's voice: *'Where are you, Emma. Please.'* That was all. But the one word stayed in her mind while she got ready for bed and slipped under her light-weight duvet. *'Please.'* She curled into a ball, trying not to think about the day or the morning or the things she must do tomorrow.

Instead she thought about Poppy, hoping that all was going well with the lovers. She wished with all her heart that someone could be happy, and there was no one who deserved it more. She felt the tensions of the day ebb as she tried to empty her mind of anything other than happy thoughts, but one regret would not be banished: that there was no single area of her own life which could be included in that felicitous category.

20

Sunday 20 August

The sun was still shining, which made the news coming from the radio all the more obscene. A pleasure-boat had sunk on the Thames in the night, drowning a group of whizz-kids, bright, articulate, ambitious young people come together to celebrate a birthday and lost now in the swirling waters of the Thames. It had been called the *Marchioness* and hour by hour the tragic details were retold.

Emma had lain in bed since dawn, half-listening to the radio and reliving the experiences of the last few days. In little more than a week she had discovered a whole family – two families. She had a brother, a sister and an aunt, and ... if the charade was maintained ... another aunt and uncle and two cousins. She probed gently to see if she was pleased or vexed by this instant background, but her guard was up. She felt nothing, neither pleasure nor regret. Only caution.

At half-past seven she got up and pushed the windows wide. Sunday morning. In France and Italy now peasants would be flocking to church, but England slumbered on. Nothing disturbed the Sabbath peace except the occasional far-off motor-car and the drone of a bee in the lavender beneath her window.

She made coffee and toast and ate it while she decided what to do with her last day of freedom. Tomorrow she went back to work, back to routine – back to the sight of Keith on the other side of the glass, his voice in her ear, his proximity in the lift or when he leaned to whisper against her cheek. A week ago they would have travelled back together, if all had gone according to plan, separating at the airport, flushed with love and guilt, he to return home with alibi well prepared, she to while away a happy week until they were reunited at work. Where had it gone wrong? When she had gone for that damned tape, or when Stephen had rung her? Or was it all down to poor little Zoë who meant no harm to anyone?

Up above she heard water running, so Poppy was out of bed. It was a relief to stop analysing a painful subject and scamper upstairs for a chat. Last night she had not slipped a note under Poppy's door, as she'd promised. Now she was longing to tell Poppy everything that had happened in London.

'Isn't it awful about that boat?' Poppy said, when she opened the door. She looked tired this morning, with huge circles beneath her eyes and her hair uncombed.

'Night on the tiles?' Emma asked sympathetically, as they sat down at the kitchen table.

'I didn't go out,' Poppy said, dropping her eyes to her cup.

'I thought you were going out with Charlie?'

'So did I,' Poppy said. She set down her cup and met Emma's gaze. 'I waited but the gentleman didn't show, as they say. Anyway, don't let's talk about him: he'll turn up when he's ready. How did you get on?'

'I met her,' Emma said.

'Nice?'

'Smart. A bit brittle at first, to be honest. Very Gucci. But when she talked about her brother I really liked her: she sounded as though she cared about him. And I

don't think her own life is a bowl of cherries. She's . . .
quite sad, actually.'

'What did she say? God, it's like trying to draw teeth!
Get to the nitty-gritty.'

'Sorry, it's just that she more or less confirmed what
we already knew.'

'More or less? Are you her brother's child or are you
not?'

'Will we ever know the answer to that one? Could my
mother have lied, Poppy? She got the money for the
shop from David Culrose: that much I do know to be
the truth. All the money that John Gaunt had, almost
£500, he spent on the brooch. It was David who tipped
up.'

'Could she have lied to him to get the cash, you
mean?' Poppy bit the side of her cheek for a moment.
'I'm thinking seriously, Em, because I realize how much
you need the truth. And having thought seriously, my
answer is "no". She was tough, your mother: tough in
business, tough with you, tough with me, sometimes.
But in all the years we worked and lived side by side, I
never saw her cheat anyone. She'd beat them down for
a price, she was always one step ahead of the opposition
. . . you're like her in that respect. But she'd return the
odd ha'penny if it wasn't hers.'

'You say I'm like her, Poppy . . . one step ahead of
the opposition. But I am wallowing, Poppy, positively
wallowing – I mean, floundering – about everything.
This . . . Keith . . . I don't even know if I want to get
back to work on Monday and usually I'm raring to
go after two weeks off. At the moment I feel like
getting on a train and disappearing – somewhere, anywhere!'

'We could take off on the Orient Express – I've

always fancied that! Drink your way across Europe and then have a spot of nookie in a gondola. Bliss!'

'Be serious, Poppy. I'm not in the mood for jokes.'

'I know, darling, that's why I'm cracking them. I'm trying to change your mood.'

Poppy was smiling but Emma could see that it was an effort. She leaned over and squeezed the older woman's hand. 'I know, Poppy. You're brilliant. Now go and get yourself tarted up before Charlie comes. I'm going downstairs to do the same thing.'

There was a man at the outer door when Emma reached the hall but it wasn't Charlie. 'Keith!' He had on grey slacks and a banded T-shirt, and his hair was still damp from the shower.

'I came out to get the papers . . . and I couldn't resist coming across. Where have you been? No, I know you've been up and down to Durham. Is it all right?'

She felt again the same irrational impulse to keep her news from him. 'Oh, it's much the situation as before. Do you want a coffee?' It felt odd to be standing here in the hall like this.

'No, I've got to dash. But I want to see you, I want to be with you, Emma. We're back to work tomorrow, and you know it's impossible then. I can get away today after the kids' lunch: can we go off somewhere, out of the city? Just for a few hours?'

Impossible to say no. Emma smiled at him. 'OK. What time?'

'I'll pick you up at quarter to two.' He leaned to kiss her, smelling of soap and bright fresh aftershave. 'I love you.'

By twelve Emma had laid out her clothes for the morning, checked her briefcase and put a load through the washer. She packed a bag with food and a thermos,

322

in case Keith was hungry, and then she poured out two glasses of wine and carried them upstairs. Poppy looked fetching in a black and white linen dress, bright red orbs at her ears to match the sandals on her bare feet. Her toenails were scarlet to match her fingernails, making a brave show of her arthritic feet.

'You look ravishing. Drink this before your swain arrives!'

'You've perked up.' Poppy's eyes were shrewd.

'I'm going out for the day.' Emma tried not to sound defensive. After all, it was none of Poppy's business.

'With Keith?' Poppy's face had drooped again.

'With Keith. But I don't know why you worry about it: I know what I'm doing.'

'Don't say that. I can only bear it if I think you *don't* know what you're doing. And after all you've discovered this week! If that didn't make you think, what will?'

'This is different, Poppy. There's no comparison . . .'

But Poppy's brows remained down and Emma was forced to take her leave eventually with the argument unresolved.

'I'm not sitting in judgement on your morals,' was Poppy's parting shot, 'only on your common sense.'

Emma tried very hard not to think about her conversation with Poppy. She went from room to room, looking out from the window at a Manchester suburb in its mid-Sunday comatose state. From the garden next door came the tinkle of glasses and the murmur of conversation. Once she heard the word *Marchioness* quite clearly, and the voices dropped for a while. And then, drifting on the air, came the unmistakable odour of barbecued meat.

They were a young couple, her next-door neighbours, with a baby in a pram. Emma laid her cheek against the cool of the glass, suddenly not wanting to see Keith, feeling anticipation of a day of freedom drain from her. At home now Lesley would be padding about her house in bare feet, hair tucked behind her ears, secure enough not to need lipstick or mascara. She would laugh at Tom's antics, make herself coffee in a half-rinsed mug, snuggle the baby under her chin, take out her breast and feed her child, safe in her own home.

It was a cheap home, by most standards. They didn't have a single good piece, no decent china or linen. Keith was a high earner but a worthwhile home took years to build unless you had a head-start with family possessions. They had none.

Emma looked around at her own environment. A good carpet, decently faded; the gleam of mahogany, china and silver; comparative affluence. 'That isn't what I want,' she thought. 'I want what Lesley has. Everything she has is what I crave.'

She felt suddenly heavy and tired, her eyes were sore, and she felt a faint pang of indigestion. She fetched herself another glass of wine but even that seemed to have lost its power to please.

It was a relief when she saw Keith's car. She picked up her bag and the picnic basket and was about to leave the flat when the phone began to ring. With the door wide open, she put down the bags and lifted the receiver. 'Emma Gaunt?'

'Emma? It's me, Lesley. I was wondering if you got my message about Tom's party?'

If she didn't come out Keith might come inside to look for her, calling out her name. She eyed the distance to the door, wondering if she could reach to shut it. She couldn't. She lied easily: 'Can you just hang on, Lesley? I've got a pan on.' She shut the door quietly and came back to the phone. 'That's better. Yes, sorry I haven't got back to you, but of course I'm coming ...' What was she saying!

'Oh, that's lovely.' The voice faded as the caller turned away from the mouthpiece. 'Aunty Emma *is* coming, Tom. To your party. Isn't that nice?' And then louder. 'He's smiling all over his face ... wish you could see him.'

So Lesley too could lie, when speaking to her husband's boss. Tom would be too preoccupied with his toys to spare a smile for some vague figure on the other end of a telephone line. But he had liked her: they had bonded very quickly. He would want her at his party. She could soon grow close to the baby, too, Emma thought, as she put down the phone. She stood in the middle of the room, arms dangling, eyes closed, feeling the baby move in her arms, its face turning into her, nuzzling, searching ... suddenly she remembered Keith at the door and a wave of fury swept over her. Damn him, damn him, damn him.

But as she hurried down the steps, careful not to look back for fear of seeing Poppy's disapproving face, she couldn't work out quite why she wanted to condemn him to damnation. His sin now was no worse than it had been in the beginning, and she had not minded then.

'Where does Lesley think you are?' she said, when she was seated in the car.

He didn't answer until he had manoeuvred away from the kerb. 'Helping someone fix up a burglar alarm. I'm quite a dab hand at electronics, you know. You don't realize how multi-talented I am.'

'You're a good liar.'

'What do you mean?' Keith sounded uneasy.

'Exactly what I say. I've just had Lesley on the phone.'

'Is she all right?' He sounded alarmed.

'Of course she's all right. Very all right. She sounded supremely happy – not at all like someone whose husband is driving another woman into the country.'

'I'm not going to rise to the bait, Emma, so you might as well drop it. I know it's a shit, all of it – but what else can I do? I care about Lesley, I really care about her. But I'm in love with you . . . besotted. I don't stand at home weighing up the ethical pros and cons of what I'm doing, I stand there thinking how quickly I can get out of the house to get to you. I wish it wasn't like that – if you knew how many times I've wondered why I ever left Chambers, Fisher. But I did. We met. You might as well blame me for time and tide: I have as little choice in that as in this.'

Keith was silent then and Emma waited until they were out of the thick of the traffic before she spoke.

'I'm sorry, I was being stupid. It's just that it threw me, having her ring like that. She wants me to come to Tom's party . . .'

'And will you?'

'I don't see how I can stay away. What excuse would I give?'

'As far as I can make out it'll be an exercise in controlled frenzy. Just show up and smile, and then melt away. Lesley will understand – she knows kids are not your thing.'

'*Not my thing*?' It hurt, a shaft driven home.

'I didn't mean anything,' he said quickly. 'You were wonderful with Tom . . . everyone says so.'

They had talked about her – he and Lesley, his

mother, her mother no doubt, Uncle Tom Cobbleigh and all.

'I like children! I'd like some of my own one day.'

Keith glanced uneasily sideways, and Emma decided to labour the point. 'I've been thinking . . .'

'What about?'

'About time. About life ticking away. I'm thirty-two, Keith. Almost thirty-three.' Why was she doing this? Normally she shrank from reminding him of her age. Why didn't she tell him all about the Culroses, about her mother and father? He would understand then, and sympathize. He would draw into a lay-by and turn to take her in his arms.

'Don't, Emma. I think about it too, about what I'm doing to you, how little I can offer you. I daren't let myself think too far ahead, I just try to think about seeing you today and tomorrow – about things working out somehow, for you and me. Some way we can't see at the moment.'

He sounded weak, and it frightened Emma into lashing out. 'Like Lesley conveniently stepping under a bus? I've thought of that too.' It was true: she had had that little daydream before, but it had always included the children. A clean sweep. Now, though, she wanted the children. They had become an essential part of the picture.

'Why don't you answer?' she pressed.

'I can't answer something like that, Emma. It's too vicious.' She let out her breath in pain and he turned, contrite. 'Oh God, I'm sorry. You're confusing me, saying things like you just said. Lesley wouldn't harm a fly.'

'I know. I'm sorry. Let's not talk about it. Let's not talk about us at all. It's sad about that boat in the Thames, isn't it?'

'Tragic. Someone's boobed.'

They were silent, then, each with their own thoughts, until they turned into a wooded lane and on to a grassy bank.

'There,' Keith said. 'Bet you've never been here before.'

A stream swelled out into a small lake where ducks sailed and green willow fronds trailed the water.

'It's wonderful!' Suddenly Emma was glad she had come. As they strolled away from the car she felt her burdens slipping from her, and it seemed right to slip her hand into the crook of Keith's arm as they moved further into the trees. He turned at last, putting down the basket, taking her shoulder bag from her, gripping her arms at the elbow and moving her until they stood face to face. She let go and sagged against him but she was still not ready to meet his eye.

'Oh Emma, I really do love you.'

'I know. Don't think about it. We're here, that's all that matters.' She wanted him now, it was urgent within her, so that it was she who led the way into a space between two trees.

'I want you, Emma.'

'I know, I know.' They were pulling and tugging at each other's clothes, whimpering a little with the pain of waiting.

'Is it all right? Can we?'

'Yes. Yes.'

The grass was soft against her cheek, wet almost. She turned her face, seeking the damp earth, uncaring of the hard ground beneath her, his weight upon her, bearing down. This was the only way she could possess him completely. She hesitated, half of her wanting to delay it, to prolong the safety of feeling him within and over

328

her, the other half hurrying towards release. And then they were panting together, and she was beating his back with soft fists, beating a tattoo to keep out the images that lurked on the edge of her mind.

When it was over they lay together, he removing himself carefully so as not to crush the breasts he had fondled a moment before.

'Keith?'

'Yes.'

'When did you last make love to Lesley?'

'For God's sake, Emma!' He sat up suddenly, trying to put right his clothing. And she, too, felt suddenly naked as though the serpent had entered into Eden and shown them the error of their ways.

They tried very hard to retrieve the afternoon, but it was almost impossible. Emma wanted to go home and bath, make cocoa and get into bed in her dressing-gown as she had done as a teenager when life was cruel. Instead they sat on the grass, throwing her carefully prepared sandwiches to appreciative ducks, pointing out with gusto individual birds who went to great lengths for choice morsels.

'Work tomorrow,' Keith said at last.

'Yes.'

'Will you be glad to be back?'

'I suppose so. It takes your mind off things.'

'Was it bad up in Durham?'

'A bit.'

'Poor Emma.'

'Poor Emma,' she agreed. Why didn't she want to tell him all about it? Two weeks ago she had wanted to share everything with him. What had changed?

'Is your mother still here?'

'Yes. She stayed on to help with Tom until Zoë was

100 per cent, and then the birthday party was coming up ...'

'She gets on well with Lesley.' It was not a question and Keith did not give an answer.

They walked back to the car but this time they walked separately except when he turned to help her over a tree root or past a patch of brambles. At the car he turned and reached for her and she came to him, leaning her head against his chest, hearing his heart beat. Poor Keith.

'OK?'

'Yes, I'm OK.' She reached to touch his cheek, feel his jawbone, run her finger along the indentation of his lip. He caught her hand and carried the palm to his mouth.

'Don't go away again, Emma.'

'I might have to. There are still things to be settled.'

'Well, not yet and not for long. I could spare you later for a day or two, I suppose.'

When they were back in the car and on the road he glanced at her. 'You haven't said much about Durham. What's still to be settled?'

'Oh, this silly bequest. It turns out it's not all it seems: 20 per cent of nothing, that sort of thing.' A vision of April rose up in her mind. She was a legacy, too, in a way.

'Well, let me know if I can help. Two heads ...'

He let her out at her gate and waited until she had ascended the steps to the front door. She waved and went into the cool hall, feeling a sense of relief that at last she was home but longing to run back outside and call to him because she did not want to let him go.

They couldn't go on like this for much longer: she could feel the crunch coming. It was good business practice to act first, to tackle a crisis before it erupted. She let herself into her own flat and shut the door behind her. She could stop taking the pill – she could do that from tonight. That would precipitate an ending of some sort.

There were two messages on the machine. She pressed the 'Play' button, still thinking of what options were open to her, and heard April's voice, young and breathless: *'Emma, I just thought I'd ring . . .'*

She was listening to the girl's words, bending down to unfasten her trainers at the same time, when she heard the sobbing. It seemed to fill the hall, coming from left and right, above and below.

'. . . and Stephen says it's a good idea . . .' April was burbling away, but Emma was wrenching open the door and taking the stairs to Poppy's flat two at a time.

'Poppy, open the door! It's me, Emma. *Poppy?*'

The sobbing shuddered but it did not cease as the dragging footsteps approached the door.

'What on earth's the matter, Poppy? Let me get inside.'

An almost empty gin bottle stood on the coffee table, with an overflowing ashtray, crumpled tissues and, oddly, a discarded panty-girdle, pulled off for ease.

'What *is* it, Poppy? What on earth's the matter? Is it Charlie?'

Poppy was nodding.

'He's not . . .'

'He's married, Emma. He was married yesterday afternoon, church wedding, reception, the lot . . . She's forty-three, young enough to be my daughter. I'm a fat, sagging sixty-five-year-old. I have haemorrhoids and bunions, and I can't see my hand in front of my face . . .'

'Stop that, Poppy. You're just lashing yourself for no reason. If Charlie has married someone else, anyone else, he's a goddamned two-timing bastard ... and a bloody fool, into the bargain!'

How could men be such shits? Emma asked the question for Poppy, not for herself. No point in blaming Keith for her own situation: she was her own boss. If she chose to be part of a deception, it was a choice made voluntarily and she could blame no one else. But Poppy...

'Come on, Pops. We're going to get you cleaned up and then we're going to have coffee and then we're going to make plans.'

She sounded confident, more confident than she actually felt. On Poppy's cheeks mascara had run from fold to fold, leaving her eyes oddly white and naked. 'Please God, help her,' Emma prayed, thinking as she did so that there was no help from anyone. In this, as in every human situation, you were strictly on your own.

21

Monday 21 August

Emma let herself into Poppy's flat at seven-thirty. It was still in darkness when she tiptoed into the bedroom and found Poppy sitting upright in bed, her face drooping, her eyes dull with despair.

'I can't go in to the shop today, Emma. Not today.'

'I'm not expecting you to, darling. We'll ring Elaine after breakfast and tell her you're under the weather.'

Last night Poppy had cried again; 'I'm sixty-five, Emma. I'm sixty-five years old, and I'm frightened.'

It had been a shock to discover Poppy's age. Emma had always imagined her to be fifty-five, fifty-seven at a pinch. When she thought about it, however, she had been imagining the same thing for quite a few years now.

'I had my hey-day in the war, Emma. Seventeen! There's nothing after that but going downhill – pretending it's all still ahead of you, telling yourself there's still time. I've had it, Em. I've known it since Esther went, really. I'm finished.'

Emma had tut-tutted, then, and pooh-poohed, but there was a change in Poppy and only a fool would deny it. She put down the breakfast tray she was carrying.

'I can't face it, Em.' Poppy shifted her bulk in the bed, slipping down and over until her face was turned away from Emma's.

'Come on, darling, you've got to eat something. He isn't worth starving yourself to death for.'

'It's not that. I've lost my appetite, that's all.'

She consented to drink a cup of coffee, and then slid down below the covers again and closed her eyes. 'Off you go, I don't want to make you late. I'll be all right on my own.' Above her on the wall was her signed photograph of Anthony Quayle, squinting into sunlight in *Ice-cold in Alex*.

'Close your eyes and sleep for a while,' Emma said, trying not to sound despairing. 'I'll ring later on, and I'll get back this evening as soon as I can. I love you, Poppy, remember that.'

On the way into the city centre she damned Charlie and all his ilk fluently and comprehensively. Why hadn't he been honest with Poppy, set her free to look elsewhere? Instead he had propped up her house of cards until he was ready to see it all come tumbling down.

Music was playing as she went up in the lift, and she hummed along under her breath. The doors opened and she saw SyStems ahead, glass and chrome, hi-tech and IT: the world where she belonged.

'You're back!' Amy said, sounding pleased. 'Stacks of mail, thousands of queries, but get your breath first. Keith's done all the urgent stuff.'

He came in through the swing doors, looking clean and tanned and young, holding his briefcase against his chest. 'Good holiday?'

Emma nodded. 'A bit hectic. I wouldn't say I'd had a rest. I didn't get to Egypt ... but of course you know that.' The trouble with lying was that you couldn't remember who was supposed to know what. She was aware of Amy, shrewd, intelligent Amy, drinking in every word.

'How's Zoë now? I'll ring Lesley later today. When she rang me yesterday, though, she said both the children were fine.' Give the impression of intimacy with the wife – that was sure to divert suspicion.

They walked to their respective offices together, talking inconsequentially of anything but the real fabric of their lives.

'Can we meet tonight?' Keith murmured as they separated.

'I don't know. I've got Poppy on my hands. She's not well. Let's leave it for now . . .'

Safe in her office Emma closed the door and played with the things on her desk while she tried to compose herself for a working day.

'Coffee,' Amy said, appearing in the doorway with a steaming cup. 'Here's a list of calls you need to make today, and I've a number of things we need to confer on. But I won't bother you with them now.' Amy's freckled face was full of concern for her welfare, and Emma found it moving.

'Are you free for lunch? We could eat at Rino's and compare notes.' As soon as it was out Emma regretted it, but it was too late.

'Lovely,' Amy said. 'Twelve-thirty?'

As Amy left the office, Emma reached for her phone and dialled the first number on her list. In spite of her worries, it was good to be back, to feel in demand – above all, to know precisely and in detail what she had to do.

She was half-way down the list, fixing dates in her diary, answering queries, giving advice, when the phone rang, just as she was about to lift it and dial again.

'Emma?' It was Robert Eden. 'I wondered how you got on in London. You did go to see Caroline Exton?'

Emma told him about her visit. 'So it seems as

though it's true that David Culrose was my father, after all. She seemed very sure of what she was saying.'

'Do you feel better for knowing?'

'I think I do. At first I resented it: resented the overturning of everything I'd believed. It's strange when you find the pillars of your childhood tumbling around your ears. It makes you question everything, doubt every relationship. If your mother has lied to you, who can you trust?'

'I understand, but I hope you won't let it affect you permanently. She lied to protect you. I think she was foolish to think she could get away with it forever – and I think she probably regretted it in the end, but hadn't the courage to face you with the truth.'

'Why do you think she'd have had regrets?'

'According to you she was an intelligent woman. For years ... a quarter of a century or more ... she resolutely shuts out David Culrose. He tries and tries, but she denies him any contact. And then, last year, she relents: she sends him photographs and news of you, which is bound to arouse his interest. I'm not saying she consciously intended this outcome, but consciously or unconsciously she must have intended an outcome of some sort.'

That made sense, Emma thought. Aloud, she said: 'It opens up a whole new can of worms, doesn't it?'

'The kids?'

'Yes. Do they know yet?'

'I haven't told them, but I'm sure Stephen has worked it out for himself, and I don't think he minds nearly as much as I'd have expected him to mind.' There was a pause and when Robert spoke again he sounded wary. 'Have you thought over what I said ... about the firm, the family firm?'

Emma was ready for him. 'Yes, I have. I can only repeat what I said: Stephen should sell out as quickly as possible. But . . .' She could feel him getting ready to argue: '. . . if that is out of the question, I'm prepared to find him someone who might just be able to work a miracle. I emphasize the word "might".'

'Why can't you do it yourself?'

'Because, Robert, although this might be difficult for you to comprehend, I do have a life of my own here. Business ties, personal ties . . . I own a home here, for God's sake. You can't expect me to drop everything for a wild-goose chase.' Through the glass she could see Keith, smiling as he spoke on the phone.

Robert was nothing if not stubborn. 'It might not be a wild-goose chase if you put your back into it.'

'And it might be an almighty cock-up, have you thought about that? I'm not obsessed with career advancement, but neither am I thirsting to have a liquidation on my CV.'

'Very shrewd.' He made it sound like an insult.

'I've said I'll find Stephen someone else to advise him. I know people who'd be just as good . . . better than I.'

'And who are less sensitive about their curricula vitae?'

'That isn't fair!' Always, always he manoeuvred her into sounding like a first-class bitch. Emma bit her lip and tried to retrieve the situation.

'I'm putting this badly. It's not just that I shirk the idea, although I admit that's the case. I don't think that company *can* be saved, which is one excellent reason why I'm the wrong person for the job. But I have responsibilities here. I share my house with my partner who's – well, she's elderly and rather unhappy and not at all well at the moment. I can't just walk out on her.'

He let it go then, much to her relief, and they talked about other matters – the will and her next visit to Durham.

'I'll telephone April today . . . now. I do mean well by April, I promise you.'

Harry Wattis rang before Emma could dial April's number. 'You're back then. Good. Nice holiday?' He wanted to talk about his advertising budget, asking her advice on limits and allocations. When she put down the phone she felt better. It was good to be receiving compliments again after Robert Eden's condemnations.

She rang the Durham number but there was no answer: April must be out. She made a note on her pad to call again later. But before she came face to face with the Culrose pair, she must think carefully. They must never know how much their father had loved Esther Gaunt: that was something she must keep to herself, even if they had to know the bare facts. She owed it to their memory of their mother.

Emma walked with Amy through the warm noontide streets, seeking their favourite restaurant, threading through the tables to a booth at the back.

'Nice,' Amy said as they ordered spritzers and had them served, clinking with ice. 'Let's make a vow not to mention the *Marchioness*. I can't bear to think of all those young people, people like you and me.'

'No,' Emma said, 'it doesn't bear thinking about.'

'Tell me about your holiday,' Amy said. 'Work chat'll wait. The last I heard, you'd been holding the fort for Keith's wife. And then you went to Durham to see that boy you told me about . . .' There was curiosity in her voice but the brown eyes were friendly. To tell or not to tell? Emma had already mentioned the boy's call, when it had seemed not to matter, but now it was different.

'I had some family problems . . . old scores, you know the sort of thing.' It wasn't her secret to share, really. It was her mother's secret, better left untold for now.

'Yes,' Amy said, 'we all have them. Hopefully the world's changing, so there'll be fewer skeletons in family cupboards in the future.'

'Only because they'll be sitting beside us at the kitchen table,' Emma said drily. 'Nothing really changes, Amy. The generations pass, but the old urges are still there.'

'You're wrong,' Amy said stubbornly. 'The world *is* changing and we must change with it. It doesn't mean it's changing for the worse. Anyway, I don't make judgements.'

'She's trying to tell me something,' Emma thought.

'You don't? Don't we all? Isn't it human to think what people are doing is right or wrong, honourable or dishonourable?'

'No.' Amy's shake of the head was emphatic. 'I think people must do what they must do.'

'Even if it causes pain to innocent third parties?' Emma asked.

'Even if! It's wrong to cause pain for a whim, but that's not something you or I would do, is it?' Her eyes met and held Emma's gaze, honest and defiant.

'You know,' Emma said.

'If you mean about you and Keith, yes, I think I do know. At least, I know there's something special between you.' She licked her forefinger and held it aloft. 'I could feel it in the air in the office. Enough to melt

339

glass. But I haven't told anyone else, and I don't think anyone else has noticed.'

'Thank God.'

'Hey, don't get so uptight. It's like I said, times are changing. One man, one woman is fine in theory – but what one man can satisfy one woman for maybe forty years? Or vice versa? It was fine in the old days when you only lived fifteen years together, if you were lucky ... and then one of you popped your clogs. Now we have this extended life-span. You and I will live to eighty or ninety, maybe more. I hope I'll be monogamous but I'm not promising. Besides, you and Keith are very *simpatico*, you strike sparks off one another. I've seen it right from day one. That's rare, and so I don't blame you. As long as you do the best you can for Lesley and the kids ... It happens to heaps of people. If you handle it decently, it's OK by me.'

If only Emma could swallow this persuasive doctrine, take it in whole. 'Perhaps you're right,' she said. 'Now tell me what's been going on among the mice while the cat was away.'

They walked back to the office as slowly as they could, enjoying the sun on their upturned faces.

'Anyway,' Amy said, as they turned into the doorway, 'you know where I am if you need a shoulder to cry on. Just holler.'

Emma reached for Amy's arm and squeezed it. 'Thanks. It helps.'

Back in her office Emma rang Poppy. The voice at the other end was heavy and slow, unlike Poppy's normal tones. 'I'm all right. Just tired. No, I haven't felt like eating much. Don't worry.'

'I'll be home as soon as I can, and then we're going to eat and eat well. Buck up, Pops. You've had bad times before. This isn't like you!' Oh God, she sounded so sanctimonious! Keith's office was empty and she was glad there was no temptation to run to him for comfort.

She contented herself with another promise to be home soon, and rang off. She wanted to finish work on the treatment of the Cousins' account: if she could land that one she would be home and dry. With so much competition around, image was everything in the IT world, and having a prestigious client was good for the image. Very good.

Emma cooked lamb cutlets and broccoli when she got home and carried them upstairs on a tray. There was fruit yoghurt and a glass of Piesporter as well, and three asters in a glass to make the tray look pretty.

'There now, how are you?'

Poppy looked ancient, the lines of her face almost darkened as though they had been touched up with grease-paint. She hasn't washed today, Emma thought uneasily, and there was the odour of human sweat instead of the usual heady perfume. Poppy was waddling away from the door, shapeless inside a cotton caftan. Everything about her had sagged, swags of fat hung from her upper arms, her chins drooped, even her breasts, free from a brassière, bulged and billowed indeterminably. She had lost her shape, as though Charlie, in going, had pulled some hidden ripcord and destroyed her core.

'How much have you had to drink?' Emma said, seeing the hands, still scarlet-tipped, tremble as they handled knife and fork.

'A bit,' Poppy said vaguely, as if it didn't matter anyway. She was only toying with her food.

'Have you heard anything, today?' Emma asked. Poppy smiled wryly.

'I've had the odd phone call from here and there: "Fancy you keeping so quiet about Charlie, Poppy ... because of course you must've known, being as close as you two were!"'

'People are cruel,' Emma said.

'Not cruel,' Poppy said. 'Curious. They want to poke me to see if I hurt, if I'm finished ... if I care at all, come to that.'

'What've you said to them?'

'Oh, I've kept the flag up. You know old Poppy, gallant old bird. Not much to look at, needs a retread, but gallant for all that. I'm sure that's the word ... gallant.' Her face crumpled. 'But I'm not really, Emma. Or, if I was, I'm not now. I'm frightened of all the days and nights stretching ahead when there'll be no foot on the stair, no one to say, "How's things?" No one to get pissed with, no one in my bed ever again, Emma. Never again to reach out in the night and just thank God for some other living, breathing soul.' She pushed aside the tray. 'I can't manage any more, do you mind?'

When Emma had helped her to bed, turning on the TV at the foot and putting the remote control to Poppy's hand, she paused in the doorway. 'Bang on the floor if you need me. I'm only pottering, so don't hesitate. And cheer up. I do love you, Poppy, I really do.'

There was a smile from the piled pillows but that was all.

'If I ever see that man again I'll Charlie him,' Emma thought as she went downstairs. She put a tape of her favourite singles on and carried a glass of Piesporter to the window-seat.

The sun was setting now, turning the sky a magnificent purple, streaked with pink and white and grey. Behind her Sting breathed menace. *'Every breath you take, every vow you break . . . I'll be watching you. Oh, can't you see, you belong to me, how my poor heart aches, every step you take.'*

And then a female voice, another song. *'Tonight the light of love is in your eyes, but will you love me tomorrow?'* Did Keith love her now, or was he simply attracted to a figure of authority, as women had been for centuries? What would happen if she took him from Lesley? She could do it if she tried – but would he ever forgive her for it? Would their love eventually sour and turn to hatred? Was that the inevitable end of love? She tried to think of anyone she knew who was truly happy in a longstanding relationship, but she couldn't.

'Should I believe the magic in your touch, will you still love me tomorrow?'

It was more than Emma could bear. She got to her feet and turned it off, putting on instead a tape of Pat Metheny whose magic guitar-playing was guaranteed to soothe her. But not even Metheny could stop her thinking. Yesterday Poppy had said she should have learned from her mother's story but there was no comparison with it – no comparison at all.

Her mother had not particularly wanted a child: it was poor, embittered John Gaunt who had longed for one. Esther had loved the child once it was a fact of life, but her initial indifference had communicated itself to Emma, even in the earliest days. She herself, however, would love to bear Keith's child, would glory in it, even. 'I have a right to this,' she thought. 'Every woman has a right.'

She put her head down on her knees, wrapping her arms round her legs to assuage her wanting. She could never leave Poppy now, not after those pitiful fears Poppy had expressed. 'I will always be there for Poppy,' Emma thought. 'I am meant to stay here, and if I stay I can no more give up Keith than give up breathing.' Besides, a child would be good for Poppy, someone else for her to love.

It was a relief to acknowledge what she wanted, to know at last what must be done. She and Keith would go on as they were for a while, certainly while his children were so small, so dependent. Emma could wait. And then, in a while, a baby of her own, and ultimately a life shared with Keith. Everyone would be taken care of, prepared for the change. If you tried to behave decently to everyone, it could be arranged. They wouldn't have to worry about money: between them they had more than enough for everyone.

When she went to answer the doorbell she knew it would be Keith. She smiled and drew him in. 'I'm glad you came.' They drank wine while the Metheny tape played on and then, as it clicked to a stop, she leaned towards him and began to unbutton his shirt.

They undressed one another slowly, loving each button, each buckle, each delicious slide of fingers on skin. They stood naked for a while, neither of them fully roused, no frenzy in the meeting of limb with limb, belly with belly, her cheek against his shoulder, his mouth against her hair. 'Oh Emma,' he said and when she looked up at him he was smiling.

'Seductress,' he said.

'I prefer seducer: I'll admit to that.'

'Sorry, but I'm glad you acknowledge blame.'

Emma put up a hand and wound it in his fair hair,

making pretence of dragging him behind her as they moved towards the bedroom.

Outside, the sky still flamed purple and there was just enough light to see their limbs, moving together, turning. 'This is all that matters,' she thought as he entered her. How beautiful to make a child like this, together, and see it grow and flourish to prove your love.

Afterwards he came round to kneel beside the bed. 'I love you, Emma.' He sounded as though he was going to cry and she put up a hand to touch his cheek. 'I know,' she said.

He moved to the shower at last, and she pulled on a towelling robe and went back into the living-room. Their clothes lay where they had been discarded and she began to gather his, ready for his return. She put socks and underpants on the arm of the chair and lifted his trousers carefully, so that nothing should fall from the pockets. His shirt was inside out, and she put her hands in the sleeves to pull them right side out.

It was then that she saw the button, sewn on in turquoise cotton, sewn on hurriedly and inexpertly so that a long end of cotton was left. Lesley had done it: Emma knew that instinctively, could see her doing it while Keith fretted that he might be late. Emma had seen that turquoise cotton before, in Lesley's sewing hidden behind the cushion the day she had tidied the house.

Lesley would have sat cross-legged on the settee, in the skimpy little négligé, tucking her uncombed hair behind her ears with thin fingers, pushing the needle in and out of the holes, lifting it at last to bite off the cotton with her even little teeth. 'There now,' she would have said, like a child who has accomplished a difficult task. And he would have leaned to kiss her and the baby, and swung Tom up in the air. 'Be a good boy for Daddy.'

Emma stood in the middle of the room, hearing Keith singing in the shower, holding the shirt with its turquoise badge of ownership against her mouth, all the wonder of a few moments before turning to gall inside her.

22

Tuesday 22 August

There were letters on the mat when Emma went into the hall, or two circulars and one letter to be exact. She picked them up along with the *Independent* and carried them through to the kitchen, using them to fan herself to relieve the heat.

She could hear water running upstairs. Poppy was getting a bath, which was a good sign. Emma decided to give her space and propped the paper up so she could read through her coffee-and-toast breakfast.

The paper still told of the sinking of the *Marchioness*. Outside the sun was shining, sending beams on to the newsprint. When Esther had died so suddenly the vicar had told Emma that the tragedy was 'shot through with faith'. Somewhere, now, some other vicar might be making an equally meaningless remark to the parents of a youngster lost in the tragedy. Emma found she had abandoned her breakfast and was clutching her arms to her chest, as though to combat pain. She was sorry about the tragedy, but this was something more – a kind of fellow-feeling, as though she too knew what it was to lose a child.

She folded the paper and buttered another piece of toast, chewing it mechanically while she tried to think practical thoughts. She was sick of vague feelings, unanswerable questions, of being torn this way and that.

Today she was going to Tom's birthday party, which wouldn't be easy. Emma thought again of the crumpled shirt and its button sewn on with inappropriate thread. Strange how such a tiny thing could turn your mood from euphoria to despair. She had hardly been able to be civil to Keith the night before, so great had been her sudden desire to get him out of her house. That was last night, however: today she was going to the party, bearing gifts, and she was going to be the perfect employer-cum-friend. She would enjoy the children, mix with them, help with the food and the washing-up, and then come home with the comforting feeling of a job well done.

Having ordered her thoughts she reached for her mail. The circulars she glanced at and put aside to scrap. The letter bore an indecipherable post-mark. She opened it and drew out two closely written sheets. It was from Stephen.

I suppose I knew, really, from the moment I saw you in Manchester. April says she did too, but she *would* say that. Anyway, we both feel it's right what Dad did. So we'd like you to know you're welcome here, whenever you want to come back.

He went on to talk about the business, then, of her 'rights' and what he felt might come about with the firm's future expansion. 'Poor fool,' Emma thought. Her coffee had gone cold and she walked to the kitchen, carrying the letter, to make a fresh pot.

'Shit,' she said, as she read on: 'Robert says he has spoken to you and you might accept some kind of executive function in the firm. He thinks Dad meant you to use your expertise, to make the business great again.'

When she got hold of Robert Eden she would emasculate him, very slowly, with maximum effort and minimum pain relief. He was putting pressure on her by employing the kid: how low could you get? It wouldn't work, however. She saw her duty to Stephen and April very clearly now, and that was to ensure their financial future, not tie them to a business destined for oblivion.

The next paragraph was a blow.

I know it's going to be a struggle to get the business back on the right track. Dad wasn't well for quite a long time, and I was away at school so things went from bad to worse. But we have the Culrose name and that means a lot. I'm going to make the business what it used to be or die in the attempt, and April agrees with me that we owe it to Dad. Now that you're here too, it will be much easier.

Brave words! Brave last words probably. The boy had as much chance of building up that business as a snowball has in hell, and Emma was not going to get involved. While Stephen was still employing euphemisms like 'Dad wasn't well', he was refusing to face facts. If he had said, 'Dad's alcoholism had a bad effect on trade', she'd at least have known he had taken a grasp of things. Might even have considered going back for April's sake. As it was ... she put the letter back in its envelope and went to get ready.

When she was dressed she went through to her mother's room and took the jeweller's box from the drawer. The brooch gleamed up at her, winking its message: LUST. But the sunlight had robbed the gems of sparkle and somehow the word had lost its impact. She lifted out the brooch and wrapped it in tissue. There was a sheet of writing paper in her mother's desk and she tore off the printed heading before she began to write.

'This brooch is 9-carat gold. The gems are lapis lazuli, spinel, topaz and uvarovite.' She mixed the names

deliberately so as to obliterate the word. *'If sold in the north it will only fetch its gold value, or a little above. Sold in a specialist sale in London it should raise several thousand pounds. I hope you will use it to maximum effect in your good work.'*

She put brooch and note into an envelope and licked it shut, then she carried it through to her own room and put it in her handbag. Her mother's photograph caught her eye, and she lifted it up. Would Esther understand what she was doing, what she must do?

There was just time to see to Poppy before she left for the office. On the way in she would have to give some thought to how the dress shop was to be run until Poppy recovered. What would happen if Poppy did not recover, Emma could not bear to contemplate. But keeping the shop buoyant would be an essential part of restoring Poppy's morale, and something must be done about that today. It didn't take long for the absence or inattention of a manager to show.

Inevitably this reminded Emma of the Culrose issue, but she put that matter firmly to the back of her mind. One hurdle at a time! She let herself out of her flat and turned to mount the stairs.

The first thing she saw was a black feather boa drooping over the banister at the top of the flight and then she heard Poppy's voice, as she came down the stairs to the tune of 'The Stripper', pausing on every fourth step to give an emphatic shake of the hip.

'Dah-dah-dah . . . de dah dah dah . . .'

From the crown of her immaculate head to the gleam of her polished nails in her peep-toe shoes, she looked magnificent.

'My God,' Emma said, when Poppy reached the hall floor and flung the boa over her left shoulder on the final note. 'My God, you look stunning!' She couldn't hide her amazement. 'What happened?' Mad thoughts of Charlie running back from honeymoon to his true love were chasing through her head until she saw that Poppy's mascara-ed eyes were extra-bright. Too bright.

'I had a think, darling, that's what happened. I thought: Poppy, you survived the Blitz and the Yanks and a couple of dozen assorted sods along the way. Are you going down to a pipsqueak like Charlie Andrews? And the answer was "No." So this is my best dress ... polka-dotted silk in aquamarine and black. Note the fishtail back.' She did a twirl.

'My hair is courtesy of Grecian 2000 and the face achieved by Beresford Reconstruction Ltd and Max Factor. I have on a new bra and girdle which will undoubtedly result in proud flesh by tea-time, but we all have to suffer in a good cause. I won't be home at tea-time. I may not be home all night. I have ...' She patted her patent handbag ... 'my little black book. I shall ring round until I find a fellow-sufferer, male or female ... hopefully the former. If it *is* the former I shall sample the delights of Venus – or is it Adonis? Anyway, we shall screw. If it is the latter, I shall worship Bacchus and get beautifully and mortalliously drunk. In either event I shall be all right, so do not put a lamp in the window.'

She leaned towards Emma on a wave of perfumed air and kissed her cheek. 'Don't worry about me. I may bleed a little but I always survive. I've told you that before.'

Outside in the street a horn sounded. 'That is my cab,' Poppy said. 'Close your mouth, darling. Your uvula is showing and it's not your best feature. Ta, ta!'

When she had tottered through the door on

three-inch patent heels Emma sat down on the bottom step, laughing at first and then crying. It was funny and not funny. God help anyone who had to run through their little black book in their sixty-sixth year. In the end she blew her nose and called upon the relevant gods to watch over Poppy, then she got to her feet and went out into the sunlight to join the traffic into the city centre.

Emma got into her own office without interruption and began to plan her morning. If she worked hard through lunch she could probably get away at three and go home to change and collect the gifts she was taking to the party.

She was about to ask Amy to come in when there was a rap on her door and Keith was inside and shutting the door behind him.

Emma loved him in the mornings, looking crisp and well turned-out, his hair still darkened from his shower. Strange that he managed to step so immaculately from such a chaotic home. She closed her eyes before a picture of Lesley could intrude and he mistook the gesture for impatience.

'I won't keep you. I'm off to Ryder's anyway, to see the 1992 projections. I just wanted to say – because I won't have a chance at the party – that I love you very much.'

She looked up at him and saw that he meant it. She nodded because it was all she could think of to do.

'I know. Now off you go.'

When he had gone she switched on her modem and let figures flit meaninglessly back and forth until her equilibrium was restored and she could summon Amy to a conference.

'You're going to the kid's party today, aren't you?' Amy said when they had hammered out the daily schedule.

'Yes. I'm hoping to get away at three. Can you ask Tony to put me on the sandwich list? Prawn and mayonnaise, I think.'

'One pack or two?'

'One. And a yoghurt, rhubarb . . . no, black cherry.'

When Amy was gone Emma spent the morning checking through the preliminary figures for next year's budget and sending them out to be processed. She ate her sandwich while leafing through a trade journal and then signed the month's expense chits.

It was two-thirty when she switched off the terminal and got to her feet. If she hurried there would be time to get her hair done.

'Good luck,' Amy said as she passed her desk.

'You can get me at Luigi's in the next half-hour,' Emma said. 'After that at home until about four-thirty and then at Keith's place. But only if there's a crisis.'

'There'll be no crisis,' Amy said. 'This is an Emma Gaunt establishment. Crises are not allowed.'

'Thank you,' Emma said quietly, meaning much more than thanks for a compliment and knowing Amy would understand what she meant. And then she was in the elevator going down and there was an empty feeling in her midriff at the thought of the ordeal to come.

She parked behind Luigi's and walked on to the main street. In the Save the Children shop there were several customers and two women sitting together at the till. She walked up to them and handed over the envelope containing the Bathsheba brooch. 'This was my mother's,' she said. 'She wanted you to have it.'

353

Some day, someone might stumble on the message in the stones or look up the Biblical quote, but they would never be able to trace it back to Winston and Son or to Esther Gaunt. The secret would be safe.

Emma walked along the sunlit pavement, through the jostling crowds to the shop Esther Gaunt had established and which still bore her name. Inside Poppy was displaying a beautiful black satin evening-coat to a half-persuaded customer.

'OK?' Emma mouthed across the pale grey carpet. Poppy lifted a red-tipped thumb in reply and Emma went back into the street, satisfied.

In Luigi's she sank into the adjustable chair and felt the warm water running through her hair, the gentle fingers pushing and pressing, making indescribably soothing circular motions at the temples, lathering and rinsing, lathering and rinsing again. She opted to have her hair lamp-dried for only one reason, that it took longer. She had a sudden need to sit and do nothing for a while, clad in pink nylon, a cup of rapidly cooling coffee in her hands, all of it suffused with radiance from the lamps.

But she could not stop herself from thinking. How different things might have been if Esther had loved David as much as he had loved her, and if they had then been brave enough to declare their love and defy the world. That was what people did nowadays. They owned up to an attraction so powerful that it negated their marriage vows. They made sensible arrangements, honoured their responsibilities and went forward together to find happiness. But Esther's love had not been strong enough. Perhaps she had not been capable of sustaining a great love. It was David who had done that and wrecked his wife's life in the process. And in an odd way, John Gaunt had known enduring passion – but in his case it had eaten him away.

'Your hair's a bit dry,' the assistant said when the lamps had been taken away. 'You'll need a treatment next week. I'm seeing it all the time: we don't have the hair for hot weather like this.' She sounded genuinely put out at the effrontery of a summer that wrecked her clients' hair, and Emma felt her lips twitch. Oh, if everything could be as simple as a battle with the elements!

The flat was cool when she let herself in but she went through to the kitchen and took ice from the fridge to make herself a spritzer. She drank it wandering barefoot from room to room, thinking of nothing in particular, letting odd pictures swim up into her mind.

Her mother and Poppy together at Brighton, walking along the promenade behind her so that whenever she looked back for reassurance they were there. They had both seemed so happy, so well established. In truth, one had been hiding a secret past, the other eternally seeking the one thing she had never found, a lasting relationship.

A bird thudded against the window, suddenly blinded by the sun's reflection from the glass. Emma hurried to the sill, expecting to see it lying, stunned, on the concrete below. There was no sign of it. It must have recovered instantly from the impact and soared away. She went back to her bedroom and began the ritual of party dressing.

She wore a Swiss cotton dress, something that would withstand the onslaught of sticky fingers. It had a gold leather belt and she added gold sandals and her huge gold hoops at her ears. She was still brown from her last tanning session: all she needed was lipstick and

355

mascara and a liberal douche of Ysatis, and she was ready. She picked up the gift-wrapped parcels and went down to the car.

She heard the party noise before she reached the gate: music and happy voices and one child crying above the rest.

'Come in, Emma.' Lesley had a white blouse on above a floral skirt. It was quite a shock to see her dressed but she still had an odd aura of *déshabillé*. Her hair had been lifted at the sides and plaited back to fall to her shoulders. She would have looked like a thirteen-year-old if it had not been for the full breasts above the tiny waist.

She embraced Emma and showed genuine delight and astonishment to find there was a gift for her. 'Oh Emma, you shouldn't have. Bath things!' She squealed with pleasure. 'I always feel so guilty if I use the kids' foamy stuff. This will be heaven!'

She extricated Tom and made him lift his face to be kissed. But his eyes were on the two parcels and when he had disembowelled them he had to be forcibly restrained from opening Zoë's gift too.

'Nothing for me?' Keith's words were innocuous, his eyes meeting Emma's were not.

'Fathers don't get presents,' Lesley said, her hand on his arm by way of consolation. 'Take Emma into the kitchen and get her a drink. She'll need something before the fray.'

In the kitchen Emma accepted a gin and tonic and she and Keith made awkward conversation. On the other side of the open hatch the party seethed and bubbled. The kitchen was strangely immaculate, all the clutter put away and replaced by rows of baking, trifles in paper cups, rows and rows of wax tumblers filled with drinks in exotic colours, each one containing a bendy straw.

'Lesley's prepared for an invasion,' Emma said and saw the gleam of pride in Keith's eye as he nodded agreement.

'Dad, Dad!' Tom erupted into the kitchen, a clockwork toy in his hand. 'Broken, Dad. Broken!'

Keith crouched down, taking the toy from the child. Tom looked up at Emma. 'Daddy mend,' he said confidently.

She felt treacherous pincers at the bridge of her nose and knew she must not cry. 'Of course he will,' she said. 'Your Daddy's very clever.'

She moved out into the living-room then. The doors to the dining-room had been laid back so that the children had space to play. The room moved and bubbled, a cacophony of noise, a kaleidoscope of colour, of tiny shining heads in party hats, little girls with necklaces or bracelets on dimpled wrists, little boys with cropped heads belying their babyhood. And Lesley, cutting through the swirling mass, dispensing drinks, kissing bruised knees, separating warfarers, admonishing aggressors. 'She is good at this,' Emma thought.

In a corner she found a padded stool and took a little girl on to her knee. 'I don't like parties,' the child confided and snuggled close.

'Neither do I,' Emma said.

Across the room she saw Keith helping Lesley, the pair of them moving together as one, anticipating the other's actions, smiling occasionally at one another when something went wrong.

Beneath Emma the stool creaked. Cheap upholstery, like the shag pile carpet, the veneered furniture, the thick crockery, the flimsy kitchen units. The cost of one of Emma's ear-rings would have paid for Lesley's outfit five times over. 'I have everything,' Emma thought. 'I am King David. I have everything except her ewe-lamb. And I had the power to send him out, to a far country, so that I might possess him.'

She had refused to admit comparisons with her mother's life but they were there – except that there had been a revolution in the interim. She, a woman, was the one with power now. But the passion, the selfishness, were the same.

Lesley was clapping her hands for silence and Keith was marshalling the children to begin the feast. 'She is strong,' Emma thought. 'Whatever else I might think, I recognize her strength.' She put the child from her knee and took her hand. 'Come on, we'll go and get some tea.'

After that she was busy handing out sausage-rolls and tiny cakes with hundreds and thousands set in pink icing. She wiped chins and felt sticky fingers tug her skirt. 'OK?' Keith asked once as they passed in the mêlée.

'OK,' she said and smiled.

At last it was seven o'clock and the stream of parents began to arrive. 'Say thank you, Susan.'

'Harry, give Tom back his gun and say thank you for having me.'

'We can have a cup of tea now,' Lesley said at last. 'Mum will look after the rest.'

'I have something to tell you both,' Emma said as soon as the three of them were alone in the kitchen. If she didn't speak now it would be too late. 'I'm leaving SyStems.'

She saw shock flood Keith's face and grieved for him, but there was no other way to do it.

'*Leaving?*' Even Lesley looked stricken.

'I'm going north – it's a family business, that's in a bit of a mess. I'm needed there. And I'm going to back Keith to get my job at SyStems: he deserves it. I'll keep in touch. How could I desert my boy-friend? I'll be back for his fourth birthday, at least.'

Emma felt a strange sense of relief as they murmured their shocked response to her news, and asked hesitant questions. She answered automatically, her thoughts on the months and years ahead. If David had not walked on the ramparts, Bathsheba would have lived out a happy life with her Hittite. If Keith and Lesley were left alone, she knew they would survive. There would be no other hurricane in Keith's life – he was too clever not to learn from pain. And she suspected he did not yet know how much he loved his wife. She was giving him space to learn.

She took her leave of Lesley while Keith was tied up with his children. 'Tell him I'll see him tomorrow,' she said.

'I do hope it all works out for you,' Lesley said, kissing Emma on the cheek. 'But these things usually turn out for the best in the end, don't they?'

Back in the Capri Emma pondered Lesley's words. Did she guess? Had she suspected it all along? If so, she had played a clever game.

'I'll never know,' Emma thought and let out the clutch. The car moved on, but she could not see the road ahead for tears. Perhaps she had been a fool to end it so decisively. At least she could have had Keith's child – something to treasure, a policy against an old age like Poppy's.

But did she have a right to one? Amy would say she did, but whether or not she had such a right, Emma knew now she would not exercise it. A child must never be the ultimate accessory, something to possess when you had acquired everything else. She had longed for a father when she was a child. It had been a void in her life. If you had no father, who would mend your broken cars? She couldn't deliberately do that to a child of hers.

She abandoned driving and let herself cry. It was over. Tomorrow she would enlist Amy's help to make sure she was never alone with Keith again. Tonight and every night she would listen to his voice on the answering machine, his knock at her door, but she would not respond. And in a month or little more, she would be gone.

She tried to feel brave and good but it wouldn't come. Had she given him up for moral reasons, or because she was too ambitious to settle for a mere portion of the cake? That was another thing she would never know. But the pain would go, because it always did in the end, and she would have another life of some sort. Like Poppy, she would bleed a little but still survive.

Her tears began to dry up and she wiped her eyes, using the pads of her index fingers to clear away any stray mascara from around her lids. Ahead, under a lamp, she could see a post-box and a telephone kiosk. On an impulse she reached for her bag and looked up Robert Eden's number.

'OK, you win,' she said when she got through to him. 'But I want you to know your methods stink.'

'You heard from Stephen?'

'Yes, you bastard. That was a dirty trick.'

At the other end of the line he chuckled. 'Admittedly. And, Miss Gaunt, in the words of Al Jolson, you ain't seen nothin' yet.'

He was too smug. It was not to be borne.

'I'm sorry to detract from your victory, Robert, but you're not entirely responsible for my decision. There have been things in Manchester that made me decide I needed a break.'

'I'm sorry. You said there were complications.' His voice softened and Emma suddenly felt her throat ache.

'Don't sympathize. Don't dare sympathize, you sod! The only thing I want from you is a fair fight.'

'To the death?' He was smiling now, she could sense it.

'To the death!' He was chuckling again, and before she could speak he went on, 'OK, Emma Gaunt, it's a fight to the finish. No quarter. With a bit of luck, however, we may have an enjoyable scrap.'

She put down the phone and walked back to the car. In the west the sky was streaked with red. She got into the Capri and tried very hard not to think of anything but what lay ahead.

No point in thinking of David and Bathsheba, long since Judaean dust. Or David and Esther, who had brought one another only pain. Even less use to think of Keith and Emma, and what might have been. In time, perhaps, she might allow herself to remember the moment she had shared with Keith, the moment when she had not been alone. Now she must think only of the future.

What had Robert Eden promised? *An enjoyable scrap.'* Yes, that could be a beginning.

The Stars Burn On

To whet the appetite of Denise Robertson's many
devotees, Penguin Books is delighted to include in
this volume the Prologue and Chapter 1 of her
remarkable new novel, published by Constable &
Co. in February 1991.

New Year's Day
1980

They raced one another to the summit, stumbling over the tussocky grass in the darkness, laughing through teeth that chattered with cold, buoyed up by booze and youth and Auld Lang Syne.

And then they were on top of the hill, the wind plucking at them as they looked down on the brilliant night-face of Sunderland to the east, and turned to see the dark acres of Durham County to the west.

'There it is then. Our roots. You wanted to see it. I hope you're satisfied.'

'I will be when I get this cork out.' There was a pop and then red wine was passing from hand to hand.

'Here's to the new decade,' someone said. 'May the next ten years be good to us all.'

'I'm freezing,' a girl complained. 'Can't we get out of the wind? Whose idea was this, anyway?'

'Cuddle in.' One of the boys was opening his long serge coat to enfold her. 'Better?'

'Yeah. Ta.'

There were eight of them there, all friends. Now they moved down from the summit, into the lee of the wind, drawing closer for warmth, wiping the neck of the bottle in turn and swigging the wine.

'Where will we be next year? Not all together, that's for sure.'

A belch and a chuckle. 'Cheer up. This time next year most of us will be earning – cling to that.'

367

'There are eight of us,' said the voice of authority. 'Statistically . . .?' There was a groan but the voice was undeterred. 'Statistically, one of us will be dead, in a road accident, probably, three will be married . . .'

'Me,' someone said and squeezed the girl inside his coat until she gasped, her breath a small cloud on the night air.

'. . . and two of us will still be looking for jobs,' the voice went on. 'If you don't count the one who's already earning, that means only one of us has a chance of being even moderately rich. And that bugger inherited it.'

'God, you talk like a politician already,' a girl said. 'Who's got the bottle?'

'It's dead, I'm afraid.' This voice was less northern than the rest, and apologetic. 'I've got some sangria and some gin here, if that's any good.'

They passed the bottles round, all drinking sparingly, anxious to share, one girl abstaining as she had done all night because she was driving her father's car and had given her word.

It was time for another toast. 'To freedom,' a girl said. 'To the year we all escape!' Suddenly there was shared apprehension at the thought of possible failure.

'Cheer up,' said the bringer of gin and sangria, sensing a hush. 'You'll all do brilliantly and conquer the world and I shall bask in your glory, having none of my own.'

'Pass the bottle,' said another. He raised it until it could be seen against the night sky. 'This is a libation to placate the gods of the hill. May they pour blessings on us all . . . even the silly sod who had the misfortune to be born a member of the ruling classes. And may we all reach those positions of power and affluence for which our superior intellects have equipped us.' There was a crackling noise as the sangria fell on to the frosted grass, and somewhere in the darkness a bird began cheeping.

'Let's meet in ten years, then we can see what's happened to us all.'

'You won't get me up here again in mid-winter,' a girl said firmly.

'Make it midsummer then: the twenty-first of June 1989, at 8 p.m. On this very spot.'

No one spoke.

'OK?' the proposer demanded.

There was a murmur of agreement.

'Right, now shut up. There's a mystic light in the east, or there bloody well should be, and I want to commune with nature.'

'He thinks he's a Druid,' one of the girls said, but she too fell silent as the sky lightened to reveal tower-blocks and spires, and the birds began to sing as though their lives depended on their song.

BOOK ONE

1980

I

New Year's Day

They stayed on the hill while the lights of the town grew pale by comparison and the birds became frenzied. The houses were still sleeping but here and there a lighted Christmas tree glowed in an uncurtained window. 'The houses are stealing the hillside,' Jenny thought, remembering childhood and waist-high grass where now there were driveways and patios.

'No rosy-fingered Aurora,' Alan said ruefully. It was true: there was no obvious source of light, but everything was taking on an incandescence. They were all shivering, the excesses of the night before beginning to tell, but they went on standing there, as though in awe, until the birds accepted day as a fact and ceased their song.

'Come on,' Keir said. 'I'm frozen.' They moved back over the summit and down towards the cars, stamping their feet on the frozen grass to restore circulation, blowing into their hands, each boy turning occasionally to help the nearest girl over a particularly steep patch.

'What must it be like in Afghanistan?' Jed said, suddenly serious. It was a week since the Russians had seized Kabul airport and their reinforcements had rolled across Afghanistan's northern border.

'They'll fight in the hills,' Alan said. 'Remember, we never managed to beat the Afghans.'

'We used kid gloves,' Euan said. '*Noblesse oblige* and all that. I doubt whether the Red Army has the same scruples.'

373

'Who taught you history?' Keir asked drily. 'Rudyard Kipling, from the sound of it. We were bastards when we were a colonial power. Don't believe anything else.'

'Not on New Year's Day, please, gentlemen.' Kath was turning back to glare. 'We don't want to be patronized today, Keir, thanks a bunch. We're not up to it.'

Somewhere in the distance there was the banging of car doors and shouted farewells. 'Someone else has had enough,' Euan said, and then, as they neared the allotments, 'I'm famished. Let's forage for food.'

'What food?' Barbara said.

'I don't know. Turnips? Maybe there's a hot-house there with grapes?'

'Silly bugger,' Kath answered amiably. 'They're allotments.'

'I was only joking,' Euan said.

'Can we get a move on?' Elaine's face was pinched, her eyes blue-ringed beneath mascara-clogged lashes.

'She looks awful,' Jenny thought, 'and at the same time beautiful.'

'Who's with me, then?' Euan asked, jingling his car keys, but Jed had turned back to look at the hill.

'Christ,' he said, 'did we climb that?'

'It's only a little hill.' Barbara was unlocking the door of her father's Escort. 'Come on, let's get organized.'

Jed was drawing Elaine to him, folding her into his coat again, but his eyes were on Barbara, the old animosity there, the chin with its new day's shadow beginning to jut. 'You know your trouble, Babs?'

'Don't call me that! My name's Barbara.'

'You know your trouble?' Jed persisted. 'You are stinking sober. Utterly, horribly un-inebriated. Your judgement's gone, your reflexes are shot to pieces, you are seeped in citrus juice, and your liver ... God, your liver ...?'

'Shut up, pillock,' Alan said, opening the car door wider. 'If she's sober, it's because she's been driving all night. Be grateful.'

'So has Euan,' Jed said, 'and he's managed to get pissed.'

'Yes,' Alan said. 'Let's hope he gets home without being nicked. Now, who's for Barbara's car?'

Jenny felt a glow of approval. If her instincts were right, Alan didn't like Barbara but he was being fair. He would make a good barrister. Her eyes flicked to Keir and then quickly away, afraid to meet his gaze in case he saw her love for him writ large on her face.

They separated then – Alan, Jenny and Elaine into Barbara's Ford because, like her, they lived in town; Jed, Keir and Kath into Euan's Rover because he was driving them out to Belgate, their mining village.

The two cars bumped along the track to the road and then down towards the town, Euan leading the way.

'Look at that!' Barbara said suddenly, scandalized. The car ahead had a sun roof and through it Jed had emerged, naked to the waist except for his college scarf.

'What's he doing?' Alan chuckled from the front seat. Jed was bowing left and right to the still-sleeping houses, moving his right arm in a royal gesture.

'Making an exhibition of himself, as usual.' Barbara changed gear with a venomous jerk.

'He'll get the car stopped if he's not careful.' Alan was making signs through the windscreen that Jed should desist. There was movement in the other car, too, and then Jed was pulled struggling from sight.

'Thank goodness they turn off here,' Barbara said as they reached the roundabout. The Rover went right, towards the country and the Escort drove on towards the town centre.

'He's canny, Jed, isn't he?' Elaine said. Close to her in the back sat Jenny could see how thin Elaine was, how pallid was the perfect skin, but her mouth had curved with pleasure as it always did at the mention of Jed.

'Yes,' she said. 'He's a nut-case but he means well.'

They dropped Alan at the end of his road. 'Usual place tonight?' Barbara asked, as he made to shut the door.

Alan rolled his eyes. 'I'm not sure I'm up to it. I'll see.'

'Come if you can,' Barbara coaxed. 'You'll be coming out, won't you, Jenny?'

She was pointedly ignoring Elaine and Jenny prickled with embarrassment. 'I don't know,' she answered.

'Let's all sleep on it.' Alan was already closing the door. 'Thanks for the lift.'

'You don't have far to go, do you?' Barbara said firmly, knowing Elaine's flat was quite some distance away but stopping at the next junction anyway.

'Ta,' Elaine said as she tottered off on her spindly heels. 'I'm working tonight. Pop in if you can.' Suddenly she reached down and slipped off the flimsy court shoes, turning to grin at the watchers before she sped barefoot over the icy pavement.

'She's so common,' Barbara said as they turned back towards the hill.

'She's so pretty,' Jenny declared fervently. 'Beautiful, even.'

'I don't know why she hangs on to us, though.'

'Because the boys are gone on her,' Jenny said ruefully.

'Who is?' Barbara asked.

'Jed for one. *And* Euan. *And* Keir.'

'And we know why!' Barbara said.

Jenny closed her eyes in vexation. 'No we don't, Ba, so we shouldn't say it.'

'Well, anyway, she has her job in the café so she doesn't have to be a barmaid. She must like the life. It wouldn't do for me.'

'She does it for the money,' Jenny said. 'She doesn't have doting parents like you and me. She needs two jobs.'

There were cars on the road now and the odd pedestrian walking his dog. It was a relief to Jenny to see her own gate and escape into the cold, clean air. 'I don't know if I'll come out tonight, but you can ring,' she said and Barbara made a face.

'Come if you can, Jen.'

Jenny was beginning to doubt her capacity to carouse again. All she could think of was bed, sinking into smooth sheets, curling up for warmth and letting go. Still, Barbara had been her friend since Infants' school. 'I'll try,' she promised.

She went up the neat path, between savagely pruned rose-bushes, past the tiny ornamental pool with its shell ornaments. The garden was her father's pride and joy but it was too neat, especially in winter when black earth showed stark between the planted rows. He kept the garden as her mother kept the house, immaculate.

Inside the house she moved slowly, terrified lest she woke the dog and his barking alert her mother. She took her shoes off in the hall and avoided the creaking stair, but all in vain.

'Is that you, Jennifer?'

She leaned her head against her mother's bedroom door to whisper. 'Yes, it's me. Don't wake Dad.'

377

'Did you have a good time?'

'Yes. Lovely.'

'What time did you get back to Barbara's?' Here it was: the lie! Not too late to cause alarm, not too early to be believed.

'Half-past one. We just saw the New Year in and came away. But I couldn't sleep much. You know, strange bed. So I think I'll have an hour now.' An hour! She could sleep for a week.

'Don't you want some breakfast?'

'No, thanks.' The drinks of the night before sat uneasily on her stomach. 'Just some sleep.'

'All right, get to bed. Don't sleep on your electric blanket.'

'I won't. Happy New Year, mum.'

Jenny switched on the electric blanket while she shed her clothes but the bed was still icy when she stepped into it. She tried hard to stay awake to give the blanket time to work but it was useless. She put down a hand and turned it off, pulling up her knees and putting her toes against her calves for warmth. Gradually the chill left the sheets and she thought of Jed, rising from the Rover like Neptune from the sea. Dear, funny Jed!

But before she slept it was Keir's face that filled her thoughts – dark beneath the blond thatch, with straight thick brows above turquoise eyes. He had hardly looked at her tonight, except at midnight when he had kissed her as he kissed every other girl in the room. Still, there was time. When she came down from Liverpool there would be more opportunity. Somehow, some way, she would make him really look at her. 'This is my year,' she thought and, comforted, drifted into sleep.

*

May Denton was awake when her son Alan came into
the house. She heard him fill the kettle and let out the
cat, and then the soft plop as the gas ignited on the
back hotplate. She listened as he moved around, assem-
bling tea things on a tray; she heard tea being spooned
from the caddy, heard it scalded by boiling water and
then the grating noise of the two-pot lid as it was
slipped into its groove. She could hear everything that
happened in this house. It was her shell, the only place
in which her heartbeat was steady, her mind serene.

'Mother?' His voice from the other side of the door
was hushed in case she was asleep.

'Come in, Alan.'

He put down the tray and bent to kiss her cheek.
'Happy New Year.'

'Did you have a good time?'

'Yes.' He was reaching for her bed-jacket, holding it
for her arms. She shivered in spite of her long-sleeved
nightgown and he frowned.

'It's cold up here. Drink your tea.'

The china on the tray was Copeland and had belonged
to Alan's grandmother. It was patterned with blue
daisies, and May had embroidered the traycloth beneath
it in matching colours. She liked things nice.

'Do you want toast?' He grinned suddenly. 'I could
do you a fry-up, if you like? Start the New Year in
style.'

There were only two links of sausage in the refrigera-
tor and two rashers of bacon – enough for Alan today
and tomorrow. On Wednesday she would have her
widow's pension.

'No, thank you dear. I never eat breakfast, you know
that.'

He was hesitating, almost as though he wanted to sit

down on the edge of her bed and talk. May felt a sudden flutter of panic and raised her cup to her lips to cover it. 'Run along to bed, now, and get some sleep. I'll hold lunch back till one.'

Did he look relieved as he straightened and made for the door? If he did, he only mirrored her own emotion.

Kath waved as Euan's Rover swerved down the cobbled back street of Belgate. The yard doors were all shut and the windows eyeless and curtained – forty houses in the terrace, and not a sign of life.

She went up the yard and mounted the back steps. The door was unbolted, the kitchen a sea of unwashed glasses and dead bottles. One thing you could say for the Botcherby family, they always saw the New Year in in style. Two inert figures were slumped in the living-room armchairs, and another was on the settee.

Kath inspected them and recognized one as her brother and the others as his mates. She regarded them as they lay, lost to the world, mouths open, sleeping off the excesses of the night before. Drunken buggers! Still, they would be back in the pit tomorrow and not much rest after that. Let them at least enjoy the first day of a new decade.

She moved past them to the stairs that led up from the living-room and began to tiptoe to bed.

'Kath?' It was her mother on the landing. 'Happy New Year, pet. How many's down there?'

'Our Ted and his mates . . . Jim Skerry and Poulson's lad. Dead to the world.'

'I'd best get on, then. They'll be screaming for fried bread next. Don't disturb your Dad, he's sound.'

'Want a hand?'

Her mother was rolling up the sleeves of her cardigan as she began to descend.

'No, pet. I'll eat that lot, once I've got hot water. Please God the fire's not out. Get yersel' to bed and get some shut-eye. You've still got those essays to do, mind on. It can't be one long holiday.'

Kath put out a restraining hand. 'I'll do them, you know that. I'm going to pass and make you proud of me. Remember the mink I'm going to buy you?'

'Never mind the mink, lady. You get a qualification and get yourself out of Belgate, that'll be my mink. Now, stop slavering and let me get on.'

'OK. But give us a kiss for Christmas.'

'It's not Christmas, daft ha'porth,' her mother said, but she let herself be kissed just the same. Kath was her only daughter, born after four boys to fulfil a longing for a girl, a girl who could be dressed-up and reared without any thought of a future in the pit. She had longed for a pretty girl. That Kath had turned out to be clever too was an unexpected bonus, and one to be exploited.

Euan and Jed dropped Keir at his corner, and turned on to Colliery Road. 'What do we do now?' Euan asked.

'Go home, I suppose,' Jed said mournfully.

'Your place?' Euan's tone was hopeful and Jed grinned. Euan was not over-fond of his own imposing family seat just over the Northumberland border. Jed had walked through the echoing rooms and he understood why. It was comfortable enough, but more like a ritzy hotel than a home.

'Our place, if you like. There's sure to be a few cans left.'

'I was thinking more in terms of tea and toast.'

'Tea and toast.' Jed was mimicking Euan's precise speech. 'I think the mater can manage that. Tell you what, though, I know where there might still be some activity . . .'

'A party?'

'What passes for a party – music, booze, female companionship.'

'In Belgate?'

'In Belgate! Down there, left . . . no, right. Right, silly sod.' The Rover halted, trembled and swung right.

'It's eight o'clock, Jed. Surely they'll all be in bed?'

'Not colliery folk, my son. We've got stamina. No blue blood, you see. All solid red stuff, built on generations of brown ale and coal dust.'

'You're sure?' Euan's tone was doubtful.

'Bloody sure. We haven't even begun yet . . . hear that?' The throbbing music could be heard even inside the car as they drew up outside the terraced house and summoned up their second wind.

Keir let himself into the yard, hearing the soft cooing from the shuttered cree. So his father was still in bed. Usually at eight o'clock he could be found in the yard, stroking a favourite bird, culling a shirker, handing out corn from a hand the size of a shovel. 'They get all his tenderness,' Keir thought. 'At least, they get more than me.'

He knew what emotions he aroused in his father: pride, run a close second by ambition. Pride in a son who had escaped the pit for Oxford, ambition for a son to live out his own fantasy of Labour rule. That ambition had been there from the beginning, from the day they had named him Keir Hardie after a socialist idol and ensured he would be ridiculed at school.

He looked around the neat kitchen with its apple-green paint and mock-tile wallpaper. If he stretched out his arms he could touch both walls. How did they stand it, and not only stand it but think it was the height of bloody luxury?

Keir spooned tea into a mug and scalded it, skimming stray leaves from the top before adding milk. He was just about to drink when he heard his father's stockinged feet on the stairs.

'Aye, you're back then.'

'Happy New Year, Dad.'

'Not much chance of that with the Tories in. Still ... have you mashed tea?'

'No, just a mug. I'll make you some.'

'Go on, then. Had a good night?'

'Yes.' As Keir spooned tea into the pot he wondered how much to tell. 'We stayed in Sunderland ... friends' houses mostly ... it was OK.'

'How did you get back. Shanks's pony?'

Dangerous to say 'yes': he might have been seen alighting from the car. In any case, why should he lie?

'I got a lift from Euan Craxford.'

His father slurped his tea and then shook his head. 'You'll get nowt from that direction.'

'He's OK. There's no harm in him.'

'He's a bloody Tory, isn't he?'

'I neither know nor care, Dad. And we've had this out before. I have to mix with people, all sorts of people. I can't pick and choose by their politics.'

'Mix with them ... mix with them by all means ...

you have to *mix* with them but you don't have to like them. That's when you go soft. I saw it in the old days, when the Londonderrys ruled the bloody roost. "No harm in the old Marquis," they used to say. "Canny chap, the Marquis." They were still saying it when he took the bloody bread out of their mouths. They do it now with managers. "He's all right," they say. You know what I tell them? He's a bloody gaffer's man, I say, so he can't be all right.'

Keir switched on the radio, hoping for diversion, but there was only more news of Afghanistan and the impending steel strike.

'Mark that, lad! The first national steel strike since '26. She's been in eight months ... eight short months ... and already she's trying to pick off the unions.' His father's final words were lost on Keir as he mounted the stairs to bed.

When his son had passed from sight Steven Lockyer moved to the back door and gazed out on the winter sky. It had been a risk, letting the boy go to Oxford: you could get tainted in that kind of situation. Still, he had good socialist blood on both sides. And, like it or lump it, you needed an education if you were going to achieve things. That was the way of the world.

The pigeons, sensing his presence, became agitated behind the green louvres. He reached for his boots and walked gingerly over the frozen yard.

The first bird rose up into the air and hovered above his head for a moment, its wings a blur, so rapid was the movement. 'By God, you're bonny,' Steven told it, feeling emotion surge at the familiar sight. Not even Thatcher's lot could come between a man and his birds. He plunged chilly fingers into the seed and began to indulge his favourites, hunching his shoulders against the icy cold, feeling the muscles contract and swell. He could still hew with the best of them, fifty-seven or not.

But his satisfaction was short lived. When the Belgate pit closed he would have to take redundancy, the fatal handshake. It was that or be bussed to another colliery, and he wasn't having that. He was someone in Belgate, his name a byword: Compen. Secretary for twenty-three years and a union stalwart. He'd stood up to more managers in his time than he'd had hot dinners. He would be nothing in another pit, a stranger in an alien land, too old to start again. So he would take the redundancy money and sell his job when the time came, learning to despise himself in the process. Not that all was lost yet: they must fight the closure, fight hard. He was still arguing against it, in spite of greed in the eyes of men promised money for relinquishing the pit. Never to go down the hole again and have a pocketful of money – that was how *they* saw it. It would take all Steven's skill to swing them his way.

He held out corn to the old cock bird. It would have to go soon; its wind was gone and it was useless, like he would be when he packed in, neither use nor mak to anyone.

He was feeling despair until he remembered his son. Keir! Keir Hardie Lockyer, a name to be reckoned with. He had prayed for a son to any and every god he could put a name to. The sods had kept him waiting fifteen years, until he had thought Cissie barren. And then they had relented and given him a cracker.

Steven smiled, thinking of his son's achievements and of what was still to come, more glorious than anything that had gone before. It was a new decade, after all. Another chance for everyone.

FOR THE BEST IN PAPERBACKS, LOOK FOR THE 🐧

In every corner of the world, on every subject under the sun, Penguin represents quality and variety – the very best in publishing today.

For complete information about books available from Penguin – including Puffins, Penguin Classics and Arkana – and how to order them, write to us at the appropriate address below. Please note that for copyright reasons the selection of books varies from country to country.

In the United Kingdom: Please write to *Dept E.P., Penguin Books Ltd, Harmondsworth, Middlesex, UB7 0DA.*

If you have any difficulty in obtaining a title, please send your order with the correct money, plus ten per cent for postage and packaging, to *PO Box No 11, West Drayton, Middlesex*

In the United States: Please write to *Dept BA, Penguin, 299 Murray Hill Parkway, East Rutherford, New Jersey 07073*

In Canada: Please write to *Penguin Books Canada Ltd, 2801 John Street, Markham, Ontario L3R 1B4*

In Australia: Please write to the *Marketing Department, Penguin Books Australia Ltd, P.O. Box 257, Ringwood, Victoria 3134*

In New Zealand: Please write to the *Marketing Department, Penguin Books (NZ) Ltd, Private Bag, Takapuna, Auckland 9*

In India: Please write to *Penguin Overseas Ltd, 706 Eros Apartments, 56 Nehru Place, New Delhi, 110019*

In the Netherlands: Please write to *Penguin Books Netherlands B.V., Postbus 195, NL–1380AD Weesp*

In West Germany: Please write to *Penguin Books Ltd, Friedrichstrasse 10–12, D–6000 Frankfurt/Main 1*

In Spain: Please write to *Longman Penguin España, Calle San Nicolas 15, E–28013 Madrid*

In Italy: Please write to *Penguin Italia s.r.l., Via Como 4, I-20096 Pioltello (Milano)*

In France: Please write to *Penguin Books Ltd, 39 Rue de Montmorency, F-75003 Paris*

In Japan: Please write to *Longman Penguin Japan Co Ltd, Yamaguchi Building, 2–12–9 Kanda Jimbocho, Chiyoda-Ku, Tokyo 101*

Stars and Bars William Boyd

Well-dressed, quite handsome, unfailingly polite and charming, who would guess that Henderson Dores, the innocent Englishman abroad in wicked America, has a guilty secret? 'Without doubt his best book so far ... made me laugh out loud' – *The Times*

Difficulties With Girls Kingsley Amis

Last seen in *Take a Girl Like You*, Patrick Standish and Jenny, née Bunn, are now married and up-and-coming south of the Thames. Unfortunately, like his neighbours, Patrick continues to have difficulties with girls ... 'Very funny ... vintage Amis' – *Guardian*

The Balkan Trilogy and The Levant Trilogy Olivia Manning

'The finest fictional record of the war produced by a British writer. Her gallery of personages is huge, her scene painting superb, her pathos controlled, her humour quiet and civilized' – *Sunday Times*

A Sport of Nature Nadine Gordimer

'The mature achievement of a fiercely intelligent writer ... grand-scale, rich and demanding' – *The New York Times Book Review*. 'Vast as the veld and teeming as a township, *A Sport of Nature* expansively encompasses over forty years of South African experience' – *Independent*

The Vivisector Patrick White

In this prodigious novel about the life and death of a great painter, Patrick White, winner of the Nobel Prize for Literature, illuminates creative experience with unique truthfulness.

FOR THE BEST IN PAPERBACKS, LOOK FOR THE 🐧

A CHOICE OF PENGUIN FICTION

Moon Tiger Penelope Lively

Penelope Lively's Booker Prize-winning novel is her 'most ambitious book to date' – *The Times*. 'A complex tapestry of great subtlety ... Penelope Lively writes so well, savouring the words as she goes' – *Daily Telegraph*

The Levels Peter Benson

Set in the secret landscape of the Somerset Levels, this remarkable first novel is the story of a young boy whose first encounter with love both bruises and enlarges his vision of the world. 'It discovers things about life that we recognise with a gasp' – *The Times*. Winner of the Guardian Fiction Prize.

Small Changes Marge Piercy

In the sixties the world seemed to be making big changes – but for many women it was the small changes that were the hardest and the most profound. *Small Changes* is Marge Piercy's explosive novel about women fighting to make their way in a man's world.

Scandal A. N. Wilson

Sexual peccadilloes, treason and blackmail are all ingredients on the boil in A. N. Wilson's *cordon noir* comedy. 'Drily witty, deliciously nasty' – *Sunday Telegraph*

Maus Art Spiegelman

'I can't find superlatives adequate to describe it. It's the best cartoon book I've ever read ... Very direct, very powerful, very moving' – Steve Bell. 'Anyone moved by *When the Wind Blows* ... will appreciate Spiegelman's genius for dealing with a subject many would say cannot be dealt with at all' – *The Times*

A CHOICE OF PENGUIN FICTION

A Theft Saul Bellow

Subtle and tense, the tale of the passionate Clara Velde and her stolen ring. 'The warmth, the kindness, the tenderness of *A Theft* overpower criticism' – *Sunday Telegraph*

Incline Our Hearts A. N. Wilson

'An account of an eccentric childhood so moving, so private and personal, and so intensely funny that it bears inescapable comparison with that greatest of childhood novels, *David Copperfield*' – *Daily Telegraph*

Three Continents Ruth Prawer Jhabvala

Last-of-line scions of a prominent American family, spoilt, blindly idealistic and extremely rich, Harriet and her twin brother Michael seem set to prove perfect fodder for the charismatic Rawul of Dhoka and his sinister Sixth World Movement. 'A writer of world class' – *Sunday Times*

The New Confessions William Boyd

The outrageous, hilarious autobiography of John James Todd, a Scotsman born in 1899 and one of the great self-appointed (and failed) geniuses of the twentieth century. 'Brilliant ... a Citizen Kane of a novel' – *Daily Telegraph*

Maia Richard Adams

The heroic romance of love and war in an ancient empire from one of our greatest storytellers. 'Enormous and powerful' – *Sunday Times*

A CHOICE OF PENGUIN FICTION

The House of Stairs Barbara Vine

'A masterly and hypnotic synthesis of past, present and terrifying future ... both compelling and disturbing' – *Sunday Times*. 'Not only ... a quietly smouldering suspense novel but also ... an accurately atmospheric portrayal of London in the heady '60s. Literally unputdownable' – *Time Out*

Other Women Lisa Alther

From the bestselling author of *Kinflicks* comes this compelling novel of today's woman – and a heroine with whom millions of women will identify.

The Old Jest Jennifer Johnston

Late summer near Dublin, 1920. Even before she meets the mysterious fugitive on the beach, eighteen-year-old Nancy has begun to sense that the old charmed life of the Anglo-Irish ascendancy simply cannot go on forever ... 'Subtle, moving and distinguished' – *Observer*

Your Lover Just Called John Updike

Stories of Joan and Richard Maple – a couple multiplied by love and divided by lovers. Here is a portrait of a modern American marriage in all its mundane moments as only John Updike could draw it.

To Have and to Hold Deborah Moggach

Attractive, radical and fecund, Viv has been lucky with life. In return, she is generous with her time and with her love: she can afford to be. And now Viv is giving her sister Ann – sterile, less glamorous, apparently conventional – the best present she can think of: a baby.

The Land of Lost Content

Fran's happy marriage to David has always been the centre of her life in the close-knit mining village of Belgate in County Durham.

Suddenly, shockingly at thirty-two she finds herself a widow, without a man to rely on. It feels as if her whole world has fallen apart . . .

Denise Robertson tells the story of Fran's struggles to raise her small son, to find independence, new confidence and love, in a powerful story full of memorable characters, vitality and warmth.

The Second Wife

Ellie has gone missing. Why?

Ellie is deeply in love with Richard, but two things stand in the way of her happiness. She is haunted by thoughts of Julia, Richard's first wife, and by another spectre – this time from her own past.

In a desperate bid to find Ellie, Richard enlists the help of Paul, her psychiatrist, and Terri, her best friend.

For Paul, entangled in a domestic turmoil of his own, finding Ellie becomes imperative when he realizes there is more at stake than Ellie's mental health.

For Terri – a talented journalist and herself a second wife, although her predecessor is very much alive – finding Ellie becomes a crusade to discover the secret that threatens her friend's marriage – and perhaps her life.

None to Make You Cry

A woman's deepest love is for her children.

Helen, growing up in the North-east in the 1960s, knows that the new mood of permissiveness will not extend to her. So she gives up the baby she has had in secret, and makes a new life in London.

Lilian, her sister, bound by the demands of her children and her coal-miner husband, envies Helen's freedom, little guessing the real reason for her flight.

Long buried secrets surface again when the tragic death of Lilian's daughter draws Helen north for the funeral. It is then she realizes that she must become involved in the life of her son.

'What the reader needs is ... the detail of domestic life that so few authors can convincingly handle but which illuminates a novel when it is done with authority. Denise Robertson has this gift' – Philippa Gregory in the *Sunday Times*.